PRAISE FOR

T0228862

A Very Bad Thing

"Once again, J.T. Ellison hits it out of the park. *A Very Bad Thing* is twisting, juicy, suspenseful, and heartfelt—a single-sitting read. I couldn't put it down."

—Meg Gardiner, #1 *New York Times* bestselling author

"*A Very Bad Thing* is a wonderfully smart, twisty psychological thriller infused with dark secrets, high drama, and edgy tension. Wow, what a ride!"

—Jayne Ann Krentz, *New York Times* bestselling author of *The Night Island*

"J.T. Ellison delivers yet again. *A Very Bad Thing* sizzles from page one. Moving at breakneck speed, Ellison's latest explores the complex relationships between mothers and daughters and delivers twists and turns that make for an irresistible read."

—Lori Roy, Edgar Award–winning author of *Lake County*

"A world-famous author, a devoted daughter, a persistent journalist, and one shocking murder—master storyteller J.T. Ellison has penned another winner to keep us up at night. In *A Very Bad Thing*, Ellison delves into the complex nature of mother-daughter relationships, the price of fame, and the danger of long-held secrets in this addictive, impossible-to-put-down thriller. Loved it!"

—Heather Gudenkauf, *New York Times* bestselling author of *The Overnight Guest*

"J.T. Ellison once again crafts a deliciously suspenseful mystery with the pacing of a top-notch thriller. Just when you think Ellison can't top herself, she does, and *A Very Bad Thing* proves it. Compelling characters, a twisty mystery, and a propulsive story, I savored the book through the very last page."

—Allison Brennan, *New York Times* bestselling author of
You'll Never Find Me

It's One of Us

"A smart, taut, mind-blowing thriller full of heartbreak and betrayal that moves along at breakneck speed. *It's One of Us* is a force to be reckoned with. I've always been a fan, but Ellison has outdone herself with this one. Readers will be obsessed!"

—Mary Kubica, *New York Times* bestselling author of
Just the Nicest Couple

"Betrayal, obsession, and familial ties that bind create a tension-filled story with an intriguing theme. Readers will race through the pages to an end they didn't see coming."

—*Library Journal* (starred review)

"A heart-stoppingly tense thriller about the price of secrets and the layers behind every marriage."

—Ruth Ware, *New York Times* bestselling author of
The Woman in Cabin 10

"J.T. Ellison has done the impossible by crafting a riveting domestic thriller full of twists and turns, but also heart and emotion. You'll root for her heroine, Olivia Bender, every step of the way, as soon as a knock on the door brings shocking news that threatens her marriage and her world. You won't be able to put this novel down!"

—Lisa Scottoline, *New York Times* bestselling author of *Loyalty*

"Expertly explores the intensely complex emotions surrounding infertility, loss, and marriage. Throw in murder, a vivid cast of characters, and shocking secrets, Ellison masterfully mines the human heart in this treasure of a thriller that will keep readers turning the pages long into the night."

—Heather Gudenkauf, *New York Times* bestselling author of
The Overnight Guest

"J.T. Ellison is one of my favorite authors. I eagerly await everything she writes. And in *It's One of Us* she is at the very top of her formidable game. Don't miss this layered, emotional, and twisting thrill ride."

—Lisa Unger, *New York Times* bestselling author of
Secluded Cabin Sleeps Six

"Beautifully written and impossible to put down, master storyteller J.T. Ellison will have you spellbound with this deeply layered psychological thriller. Immersive and propulsive, *It's One of Us* keeps you turning pages with an ending you'll never see coming. I loved it!"

—Liv Constantine, bestselling author of
The Last Mrs. Parrish

"An extremely compelling thriller shot through with twists and turns, a strong emotional pulse, and heartfelt exploration of the pressures of marriage and starting a family. Impressive and gripping."

—Gilly Macmillan, internationally bestselling author of
The Long Weekend

"Brings all the twists, chills, and thrills I expect from the preternaturally gifted Ellison, and it's also an emotionally resonant read that I can't wait to recommend to my book club. The secrets snarled in the threads of an unraveling marriage and a heroine who wholly won me over put this one on my keeper shelf—you are going to love it!"

—Joshilyn Jackson, *New York Times* bestselling author of
With My Little Eye

"One of the most compelling psychological suspense stories I've read in years."

—Jacquelyn Mitchard, #1 *New York Times* bestselling author of
The Deep End of the Ocean

"This gripping, breathless thriller adds an incredibly unique premise and delivers a novel that's also a deeply poignant story about our deepest desire for love, family, and happiness."

—Hannah Mary McKinnon, internationally bestselling author of
Never Coming Home

"*It's One of Us* is an emotional and thrilling psychological journey through the shadows of the human heart. Just when you think you know what's coming, prepare to gasp with each new revelation. Through multiple fascinating points of view, layers of secrets, lies, love, and loss are revealed. I did not put this book down until the last unexpected and breathless page. Unpredictable, intense, and riveting, J.T. Ellison is at her heart-stopping best."

—Patti Callahan Henry, *New York Times* bestselling author of
Once Upon a Wardrobe

"The perfect mix of edge-of-your-seat tension, deep emotion, and impeccably developed characters, J.T. Ellison's latest is a master class in storytelling. Secrets and lies, love and loss mix flawlessly to create a novel that touches every single emotion. Fans of Lisa Jewell and Ruth Ware will flock to *It's One of Us*, and book clubs won't be able to stop talking about it. Five dazzling stars."

—Kristy Woodson Harvey, *New York Times* bestselling author of
The Wedding Veil

"An extraordinary, unpredictable, absolutely riveting thriller and a fiercely insightful, emotional journey, this is psychological suspense at its most enthralling and intense."

—Jayne Ann Krentz

"Secrets and lies abound, relationships are tested, and the twists keep coming. Ellison outdid herself, a master storyteller. This is a must read, especially the author's note at the end, which gutted me."

—Kerry Lonsdale, *Wall Street Journal*, *Washington Post*, and Amazon
Charts bestselling author

Her Dark Lies

"J.T. Ellison weaves the old and the new, art and history, mystery and love story into one stunning tapestry of a novel. Elegant, propulsive, and utterly unputdownable, *Her Dark Lies* is the work of one of our most talented thriller writers at the very top of her game."

—Lisa Unger, *New York Times* bestselling author of
Confessions on the 7:45

"I loved *Her Dark Lies*. A great modern gothic. Ellison outdid herself— what an ending!"

—Catherine Coulter, #1 *New York Times* bestselling author of *Vortex*

"Stunning. *Her Dark Lies* is a gorgeously atmospheric thriller, a brilliant contemporary twist on a beloved classic. Beautifully written, psychologically chilling, and gaspingly surprising, J.T. Ellison proves she's our new Daphne du Maurier."

—Hank Phillippi Ryan, *USA Today* bestselling author of
The First to Lie

"Mesmerizing . . . Fans of Daphne du Maurier's *Rebecca* will want to check out this compulsively readable tale."

—*Publishers Weekly* (starred review)

"A compulsive, twisty thriller that is so deftly crafted, you're left wondering who to trust. A highly addictive and deliciously tense read, *Her Dark Lies* is fast paced and full of suspense. This book is a stunner! Readers are going to love it. I'm a forever fan, and I want more."

—Kerry Lonsdale, *Wall Street Journal* and *Washington Post*
bestselling author

Good Girls Lie

"[A] high-tension thriller . . . Alternating points of view raise the suspense, blurring the lines between what's true and false."

—*Publishers Weekly* (starred review)

"Ellison has created a complex, convoluted plot that mystery fans will savor."

—*Library Journal*

"*Good Girls Lie* is an entertainingly twisted coming-of-age tale, pitting the desire for privacy against the corrosiveness of secrecy and taking an often harrowing look at how wealth and power can lull recipients into believing they're untouchable."

—*BookPage*

Tear Me Apart

"Outstanding . . . Ellison is at the top of her game."
— *Publishers Weekly* (starred review)

"A compelling story with a moving message."
— *Booklist*

"Well paced and creative . . . An inventive thriller with a horrifying reveal and a happy ending."
— *Kirkus Reviews*

Lie to Me

"Exceptional . . . Ellison's best work to date."
— *Publishers Weekly*

"Comparisons to *Gone Girl* due to the initial story structure are expected, but Ellison has crafted a much better story that will still echo long after the final page is turned."
— Associated Press

"Immensely readable . . . lush."
— *Booklist*

"Fans of Paula Hawkins, A. S. A. Harrison, Mary Kubica, and Karin Slaughter will want to add this to their reading list."
— *Library Journal*

"Wonderful . . . A one-more-chapter, don't-eat-dinner, stay-up-late sensation."
— Lee Child, #1 *New York Times* bestselling author

"Fans of *Gone Girl* will gobble up this thriller about a marriage from hell, which moves at a blazing-fast pace and smoothly negotiates more twists and turns than the back roads of Tennessee. J.T. Ellison will keep you guessing every step of the way to the surprise ending!"

—Lisa Scottoline, *New York Times* bestselling author of
One Perfect Lie

"A wickedly good thriller about a picture-perfect marriage that is anything but, *Lie to Me* has it all: murder, lies, and betrayal. J.T. Ellison will have readers hanging on to the edge of their seats with her latest cunning tale."

—Mary Kubica, *New York Times* bestselling author of *The Good Girl*

A

VERY

BAD

THING

ALSO BY J.T. ELLISON

Stand-Alone Novels

It's One of Us

Her Dark Lies

Good Girls Lie

Tear Me Apart

Lie to Me

No One Knows

Taylor Jackson Series

All the Pretty Girls

14

Judas Kiss

The Cold Room

The Immortals

So Close the Hand of Death

Where All the Dead Lie

Blood Sugar Baby (novella)

Field of Graves

Whiteout (novella)

The Wolves Come at Night

Samantha Owens Series

A Deeper Darkness

Edge of Black

When Shadows Fall

What Lies Behind

A Brit in the FBI Series

Coauthored with Catherine Coulter

The Final Cut

The Lost Key

The End Game

The Devil's Triangle

The Sixth Day

The Last Second

A

VERY

BAD

THING

J.T. ELLISON

THOMAS & MERCER

This is a work of fiction. Names, characters, organizations, places, events, and incidents are either products of the author's imagination or are used fictitiously. Otherwise, any resemblance to actual persons, living or dead, is purely coincidental.

Text copyright © 2024 by J.T. Ellison
All rights reserved.

No part of this book may be reproduced, or stored in a retrieval system, or transmitted in any form or by any means, electronic, mechanical, photocopying, recording, or otherwise, without express written permission of the publisher.

Published by Thomas & Mercer, Seattle

www.apub.com

Amazon, the Amazon logo, and Thomas & Mercer are trademarks of Amazon.com, Inc., or its affiliates.

ISBN-13: 9781662520334 (hardcover)
ISBN-13: 9781662520310 (paperback)
ISBN-13: 9781662520327 (digital)

Cover design by Ploy Siripant
Cover image: © Dana Hoff / Getty; © Nataliass, © rangizzz, © Polina Katritch / Shutterstock

Printed in the United States of America
First edition

For Jameson, who got me where I needed to be.
For Laura Blake Peterson, who shepherded me
the rest of the way.
And as always, for Randy, the wind in all our sails.

I'm interested only in expressing basic human emotions—
tragedy, ecstasy, doom, and so on.
—Mark Rothko,
in *Conversations with Artists*

PROLOGUE

My darling daughter,

I'm not going to hide this from you anymore.

Many, many years ago, I did a very bad thing.

And I paid for it. Oh, did I pay for it. As did everyone around me.

We're all faced with choices, moment by moment, as we embark on our lives. There's no way to know what a day will bring—Joy? Abundance? Fear? Chaos? Terror? Death? When darkness falls, when you lay down your head, you are a different person than the moment your eyes opened hours before. Your day is driven by inexorable forces seen and unseen, felt and unfelt. You choose. Eat that food. Take that drink. Do that exercise. Murder that person.

It doesn't matter that I struggled with the choice. That I was sick in body and heart for months while I decided what to do. That I stopped sleeping, forgot to eat. Cried all the time. Left my young family to fend for themselves more than once? Terrible of me.

There is no excusing what I've done.

So why am I even telling you this?

Absolution comes in many forms. If you're reading this, it's because my sins have caught up to me.

Death, in all his great and disturbing glory, has found me at last.

Am I being grieved for now? I don't know. Oh, there may be strangers who think they know me who are upset. The people I've made rich will certainly be sad. You might, too.

But there are too many people I've wronged, and when they find out the whole truth of what I've done? Not the little bits and pieces I've put into my work throughout the years, the breadcrumb trail of half-truths and outright deceptions, but the real me? The person behind the public mask?

We're all hiding something. Big or little, tragic or unseemly. We keep our deep secrets; we hold our truths close to the vest. We don't share our true minds with anyone. Not really. No matter the words that come from your mouth or your fingertips on the keyboard, they are filtered. If they weren't, you would have no one. You would travel this life in a lonely world, one of your own making. An outcast. An exile.

Maybe you have tried to be your true self, here and there. How did that work for you?

No, you're smart, like me. You've hidden your truth so deep inside that no one will ever know. You will pass into the great beyond a perfect enigma, a mystical creature of great worth and seething dishonesty, unknown by even those closest to you, those who love you unconditionally and would forgive you every thought, no matter how depraved.

Almost every thought.

Were I not to share this, no one would know. And I would sail away that perfect enigma.

Now that's not exactly true, either. Someone does know. There is one person still on this earth who has full knowledge of the truth of what I've done. And because you're reading this, because I am gone now, chances are, they have decided it's time to get their revenge, to reveal the worst parts of my being to the world.

I don't blame them. I've waited so long for this. It's a relief, in many ways, to shrive myself of this burden. To admit, at last, the whole truth. Carrying a lie so big has killed my soul. Robbed me of any joy I might have had in this life.

But this is my story. And it's only right that I tell it. No matter what they say, they will twist this with their own lens and you won't get the complete picture. You must hear this from me. From my heart and mind, and no other.

So listen. Feel free to judge me. To hate me. To shake your head and put this down and say no more! I will understand if you choose to walk away. I won't blame you at all.

There are only a few motivations to do bad things. Love. Money. Power. (Madness, but that doesn't apply here. I am as sane as you; I can't claim a biological anomaly for my sins. I am culpable. I admit that freely.) It was one of those. All of them, really.

I swear to tell the truth. The whole truth. And nothing but the truth.

And when you've heard it all, I ask only one thing. Please don't hate me forever.

I love you very much,
Mother

FRIDAY

CHAPTER ONE
RILEY

Denver. The last night of book tour. Columbia Jones takes the stage with a wave and a flourish, her silk cape swinging around her shoulders, settling in soft folds as she approaches the microphone, and the room goes wild. Not a lot of women on the cusp of fifty can get away with the style—black jeans, white poet's shirt, storm-gray silk cape, chunky gold necklace—but on Columbia, it looks bespoke. Couture. Of course it isn't; though designers clamor to dress her, she isn't the kind of woman who takes to strangers suggesting what she should do. Her jet-black hair is cut in a severe bob that swings sharply above her sculpted collarbones, and she's managed a red lip and winged eyeliner that puts her squarely in 1940s-movie-star status. All on her own.

She is gorgeous.

Riley Carrington has been struck by this realization several times over the past few weeks. Especially when Columbia is playing the role of a lifetime, Author Girl, like she's some sort of superhero, with the clothes and the makeup and the confidence oozing out of her pores that makes Riley feel like she's ten years old.

Self-talk. Riley. She chose you. You, above every other writer.

Columbia stands with one brow cocked, waiting. The theater quiets. It has to; Columbia has a low mellifluous voice that makes people lean forward to hear her better. They hang on every word. She is their god. Their rock star. Their favorite author of all time. Some have traveled hundreds of miles to see her tonight. Every night of the tour has been the same. Massive crowds of invested fans, readers who love Columbia's work so much they tattoo themselves with her phrases and create art about her characters. There are fandoms, and then there are fandoms. Columbia Jones owns this world.

They've been on the road for a month, a traveling band of merrymakers and manic-depressives, alcoholics and teetotalers. Publicists, editors, publishers, booksellers, media escorts, family, friends, and Riley Carrington. One lone reporter. The only reporter Columbia Jones has agreed to speak to for this tour. She's press-shy, much prefers to interact with her readers directly. She hasn't done any meaningful publicity in years, generally letting her daughter and publicist, Darian, handle things for her. But *Ivory Lady* is being made into a full-length feature film with two of Hollywood's most bankable stars in the lead, and the budget for it makes *Lord of the Rings* look like a lemonade stand. The option sold before the book was finished and the film will be out in a couple of months. They got the jump. And there needs to be publicity. Columbia agreed, with one caveat. She got to pick the reporter.

Enter Riley Carrington. She knows what they say: up-and-coming journalist, hungry, talented. A good match for a juggernaut author. Will do her duty to the circus and present them with exactly what they need.

Riley's read the book, and the script. Of course, she's read all Columbia's books; she had to for the feature, but this one was something special. It's magical. Just the historical setting alone—ancient Ireland—is enough of a hook, but the characters . . . it's like she channeled them from the past, gave them life and agency, and passed along their genes to an even brighter cast. The script is one of the most faithful adaptations Riley's ever seen. She loves the actors. It's going to be the kind of blockbuster one remembers for a generation. It's going to win all the awards and make Columbia an even more celebrated name. Not to mention a mint.

Columbia Jones is living a charmed life, that is for sure. How many artists become famous? A handful at best. That she has the personality of a saint and the fortitude of a bullfighter? Who could possibly be in the public eye constantly like this and make every person they come in contact with, from busboys to studio heads to housewives, feel like they are the most special person in the world?

Yeah. It's been a rather amazing month. They're all exhausted; it's been relentless, event after event, sometimes two in one day, then jetting to the next city to do it all over. Privately, Riley thinks Columbia might be too good to be true and keeps waiting for her to slip up and show her that she's human: to snap at someone, to be snarky, to make a cutting remark, but no. The woman has been awesome on a herculean scale.

The crowd is roaring with laughter now. Riley has tuned out the patter—Columbia gives the same speech every night, and the audiences always react enthusiastically—but based on the time, she's warming them up with the joke about the frog and the sock.

Riley is observing, as she usually does, standing in the back, with the SRO crowd. Columbia's daughter, Darian, sidles up to Riley. Darian is almost a carbon copy of her mother, without the glamorous edge. The hair is lighter, a dark blonde instead of stark black, and the features softened, the smoother skin still plump with youth, not fillers. The work Columbia's had done is excellent, discreet, and nearly invisible unless one is up close. Darian's the genuine version of her enhanced mother, comfortably housed in white sneakers and vintage wide-leg jeans.

"She's in rare form tonight."

"No kidding," Darian says, smiling.

A sallow-faced woman with lavender hair shoots daggers their way and shushes them. Darian gestures for Riley to follow, and they step away.

"You'd think after a month of this, she'd be exhausted like the rest of us," Riley says. "But she's more revved up than ever."

"I gave her a triple shot in her latte." Darian covers her mouth and giggles, and Riley smiles in return.

While similar to her mother physically, Darian is normally Columbia's opposite in temperament. The only time Riley has seen Columbia get even remotely off kilter was when Darian—who, let's not fool ourselves, has a lot of pressure on her shoulders, but still—lost her temper with the team after the Houston event. It was a packed day with two talks, and because the books were late arriving from the warehouse, the signing line stretched on for hours, and it was nearing midnight when she blew her top.

"That's very disappointing to me, Darian, precious," Columbia said in her posh London accent, her plump lips pursed. "I think you should go back to the hotel now."

It was impressively dismissive.

That's what drives Darian crazy, Riley thinks, that her mother won't engage with her bad behavior, just scolds and retreats. It would drive *Riley* crazy; she's always down for a good row with her own mother.

No, there's more to this story. Riley has only scratched the surface. And it's a surface that's being curated for her daily.

"Does she ever come down to earth and just land hard?" Riley asks. She's asked this before, only to be met with smirks and knowing winks, but tonight, Darian isn't in the mood to play coy. There are dark circles under her eyes, and her shoulders slump. Her nails are chewed down to nubs. She's not able to hide her weariness anymore. Managing Columbia Jones is a full-time job; touring her is double the work.

"It's the last night of tour. She's like Cinderella. At midnight, the carriage turns into a pumpkin." Darian looks out over the room. "Trust me, you don't want to see it. Go home, Riley. You've got your story. She will sign off on the piece, and you'll get the paycheck of the decade."

"I'm not doing this for the money," Riley replies automatically. They both know it's a lie. This fawning is a bizarre defense mechanism that's haunted Riley since she first agreed to the gig. When Columbia Jones herself calls your boss and says she wants you to do a profile and offers quadruple your normal rate, and you're in the kind of debt she is? You march smartly to the edge of the precipice while shouting "Yes, ma'am. Anything you want, ma'am!"

Riley has become so complacent at these events that it takes her a moment to realize that Columbia has stopped talking and is staring into the crowd. A man has risen to his feet, right in the middle of the room. There are five thousand seats in this theater, and each one is taken, everyone crowded in cheek by jowl, a happy, good-natured group. This man is in a loge box, front and center. One of the pricier seats. Riley can see the back of his head, registers dark curly hair and that he's tall. But nothing else.

Columbia is staring at him, hands clutching the microphone. The man leaves the box, disappearing into the bowels of the theater, and Columbia shakes her head like a deer shaking off a fly and resumes where she left off. She's into the meat of her talk now, how she developed the main character's backstory, how she mined her own upbringing on the outskirts of London—Bromley, to be precise—to bring her to life, and normally the audience is literally falling into the rows in front of them at this point, hoping against hope Columbia will reveal something, anything, about her past.

But something has changed. Her voice, normally smoky smooth, shakes a bit. Riley can hear the tremble, and so can Darian. She frowns, staring at her mother as if willing her to get her shit together already; there's a show to put on. The audience senses this change, too. They shift in their seats and look at their neighbors as if to say "What's happening?"

"Oh, no," Darian says, and Riley's attention snaps back to the stage. Columbia has stopped talking entirely now and is swaying, face pale as the moon.

"She's going to faint," Riley says, inanely, because before she can get all the words out, Columbia Jones goes down.

CHAPTER TWO
DARIAN

The theater manager has the presence of mind to close the curtain, cutting off Columbia from the crowd. A small knot of people surrounds her mother, who lies prone on the stage. She isn't moving.

Oh, God, is she breathing? Is she dead? Is she gone?

Darian fights back a wail and pushes through the people to her mother's side. The organizer, a small woman with a thick swinging gray bob and red glasses, is speaking into her phone. She clicks off and reaches out a hand for Darian to stop her from charging across the stage.

"She's come to, but I called your people," she says, calm and steady. "One of the bodyguards who has medical training is with her."

"Thank God. Thank you, Ruby." Darian takes a shaky breath and makes her way to her mother, prone in the middle of the stage. She kneels by Columbia's side. Mason Bader, six feet of muscle and brains, is on duty tonight. He's solid, in more ways than one. He's taking Columbia's pulse, a calm and steady presence that makes Darian take a deep breath and blow it out. If Mason isn't freaking out, things must be okay. She takes Columbia's free hand. It is clammy.

"Mom? Mommy?"

"Darian," Columbia whispers, eyes closed. "I'm all right, precious. Just feeling a bit swimmy."

"Can we get her off the stage?" Darian snaps.

Mason shakes his head. "The EMTs will be here in a moment. We're taking her to the hospital."

"No," Columbia says, but weakly. "I'll be fine."

"Sorry, ma'am, but we're going to override you on this one. You hit your head when you fell, you've got a nice bruise starting on your temple. Need to get you checked out."

The EMTs arrive then, and Darian is gently pushed to the side while Mason and her mother are questioned about what happened. They set up and take her vitals, speaking to her quietly. After a moment, they slap on an oxygen mask and a blood pressure cuff, and she is loaded onto a modified black-and-red stretcher. They whisk her offstage, remarkably efficient. Darian is left standing there, bereft, watching her mother's dark hair disappear.

"I'll drive you to the hospital, dear," Ruby says.

"She's going to be fine," Mason adds. "I'm going with her. I'll see you there, yeah?"

"Yeah. Mason? Is she really going to be okay? You can tell me."

"Don't worry. She's tough, your mom." He disappears, stage left. God, she's found herself in a play.

"Ready, dear?" Ruby asks. Darian nods. "Good. I'm just going to make a quick announcement and we're off."

The woman steps through the curtains, and the whispers from the darkened theater increase. Darian hears her pick up the mic and tap it. Ruby's calm and presence of mind tell Darian this is not the first time an author event has gone south on her. Introverts and crowds don't always mix. Though it's not usually the author who creates the fuss.

"Ladies and gentlemen, our deepest apologies. Columbia is well but being taken in for observation." Gasps, groans, cries from the crowd. "I know. The altitude gets to all of us sometimes. She relays her thanks for your patience and asks that you limit your online speculation. For those who haven't already received their purchased book, signed copies are available from the booksellers in the lobby. On behalf of the store, and Ms. Jones, we wish you a safe evening."

The murmur of the crowd sounds like the buzzing of bees. Their queen is damaged; they must protect her at all costs.

Ruby bustles back through the curtain and crooks a finger at Darian. "Let's go."

For a small woman, she walks incredibly fast. Darian appreciates the urgency, and her planting the suggestion to the audience that the incident was related to the thin mile-high air. That will keep the worst of the rumors at bay for now.

Her mother, lying so still on the stage.

"Did you see the man who stood up, Ruby? The one she saw, then fainted?"

"What?"

"A man in the loge box stood up and stared at her, then left. She fainted right after."

They burst out of the theater. The clear night air is brisk, and the parking lot is full of people milling about. Riley Carrington is standing at the curb, looking stylishly lost. Not Darian's problem; the woman is a grown-up. She can figure out her own next steps.

"I didn't see anyone, dear. I'm sorry."

"It's okay."

They are quiet on the way to the hospital, lost in their own concerns, and Ruby drops her at the emergency room door. "Let me know she's all right, will you?"

"Of course. Thank you for everything, Ruby. You've been a huge help. I'll talk to Mary, we'll see about a makeup date sometime soon, all right?"

"That would be lovely, Darian, thank you. If Mary will let your mom come back, we'd love to have her."

Mary Preston is the longtime head of the publishing house, a combo platter of editor, confidante, and literary guru who shepherds Columbia and her books through the system. Her hair is red as fire, which matches her vivacious personality. She is as vital to the success of Columbia's career as Darian. Maybe more. She will want Columbia and Darian to get back to work, will be especially protective after all this time on the road, and they both know it. But the niceties must be observed. The booksellers are their lifeblood; Columbia's sales keep several of the major stores in business. It is a mutually beneficial relationship.

The hospital lights are an overbright glare, and Darian follows the wall signage to the emergency room. She marches to the desk, where a harried-looking man in blue scrubs is typing on the computer.

"My mother was just brought in. She's—"

"Darian? Over here." Mason waves at her from the other side of the glass, and with a quick "Never mind, thank you," she hurries over. The military trained all panic out of him; he is calm, cool, steady. She feels his composure move through her, takes a deep, much-needed breath.

"They're taking her for a quick CT scan. Just to rule out anything sneaky."

"Like what?"

"You know, just making sure there isn't a bleed from hitting her head."

Darian's heart flutters. "You don't think she had a stroke or something?"

"No, I don't think so. Precautionary only." Mason runs a gentle hand up her arm. He is muscles and crew cut and safety. She's still a little in awe of his measured, competent response. "You're cold. She's fine. She's probably dehydrated. The altitude really does do a number on people. Why don't you grab some coffee, and by the time you're done with that cup she'll be out, and they'll have a report."

"Right. Okay. Want some?"

"Naw." His smile is slightly crooked, the right side of his lips quirking up higher than the other. Has she never noticed that before? "I'm pretty jazzed."

He lopes away, and Darian feels alone. So alone. She wanders the halls for a moment, finds a water fountain that doesn't work, doubles back to the emergency room. Surely the harried man at the desk can direct her to some coffee.

The rest of the team have arrived now—the whole cadre from the publishing house. Mary Preston is gently berating the desk attendant, who looks both entranced and miserable. Darian joins them.

"There's nothing yet. Y'all can head to the hotel, and I'll call if something happens."

Mary shakes her head. "Not until I know she's okay." She takes Darian's hand. "I know you're scared, honey. Don't worry. She's tough as nails, your mom."

"Mason said the same thing. How many sales did we lose?"

"Darian Jones, you need to get your mind out of the gutter right now." Mary grew up in the South and has a soft accent that comes on strong when she's drunk or stressed or infuriated. "We are not worried about that at all, you hear me? She presigned three thousand for the store anyway, and after her dramatic exit, people will buy a book, signed or not, just to say they were there. We'll sell double, and if we run out of the presigned we'll steal some of the tip-ins from the B&N special edition. Now, are *you* okay? You look rattled."

Is she?

"I'm okay. Just . . . it was scary, you know? Hey, did you see the guy who stood up?"

"I did, but only as he was leaving. Must have had an upset stomach or something. I can't imagine anyone willingly walking out on one of Columbia's talks. She's too charming to lose one."

"No, he stood up and stared her down. I was in the back with Riley, but off to the side. I saw him stand but didn't get a good look at him. Ruby didn't see him at all."

"Well, no harm, no foul, right? Oh, Mason's watching you. When are you ever going to kiss that man, Darian? He's been half in love with you for two years, you know."

"Mary!" Darian slaps her on the arm. If she only knew . . . "Stay focused. My mom might be, like, really sick. I can't be indulging in matters of the heart right now."

Mary laughs, and Darian feels a little tension leave her shoulders. "She's not the first author to take a header at an event. She's going to be just fine, hon. Watch. Now shoo. I'll corral everyone and get started on our return to New York. You just worry about Columbia. Come grab me when you know anything. I'll be right here."

Darian moves toward the glass door again. Out of the corner of her eye, she sees a man her age watching them. He's wearing dark-rimmed glasses and has floppy brown hair. He looks like a writer. He smiles briefly and looks back down at his magazine. Must have overheard their conversation; Mary wasn't exactly being quiet. They need to be more careful. There's no privacy anywhere anymore. At least he didn't have his phone out. A rarity these days.

"She's asking for you," Mason says with that adorable crooked smile. "They have her in a private room, right down the hall. CT scan was clear. Minor concussion. They'll monitor her for a while, get some fluids on board. Other than that, she's all good."

"Thank God. Are they going to let her go soon?"

"I think so. Soon-ish, at least. Go see her."

"Thanks, Mason," she says, impulsively giving him a quick hug, not caring who sees. He blushes, the charming flush running right to his ears. She takes that with her down the hall. Mason is a nice guy. They've had a lot of fun this past month, and if Mary's comment is anything to go by, they have done a decent job of hiding it. Which suits her; Darian inherited Columbia's penchant for privacy. A dalliance with a bodyguard would make press and take away from her mom's glory.

She knocks on her mother's door, then enters the room. Columbia looks pale, with shadows under her eyes, but much more with-it than at the theater. She holds out a hand.

"Darian, precious, I'm sorry to scare you. I'm fine. Just exhaustion, they say. Some fluids and I'll be right as rain."

"You scared me, Mama."

Columbia smiles, visibly softening. Darian doesn't often call her by anything other than Mom. Or Columbia. Sometimes *that woman* when she's particularly irked.

"I know. But I'm fine."

"Who was the man—"

Before she can finish, Mason sticks his head in. "Darian? Riley wants to talk to you."

"Now?" Darian grumbles, but Columbia placates her.

"Stop. She's just trying to do the job we asked her to do. Be kind, precious. She'll remember that kindness. And you never know, the two of you could become great friends one day."

"I'll go talk to her in a minute. Mom, the man who stood up. Do you know who that is?"

Columbia's face grows guarded, and her eyes cut away from her daughter's face. "What man?"

"In the loge box. You fainted right after you saw him."

Columbia shakes her head, utters a tiny *meep*, and frowns, putting her fingers to her forehead. "Ouch. No, precious, I didn't see anyone."

"You did. You stopped talking and stared at him like you'd seen a ghost. Then you went down."

Columbia tsks. "No, I remember nothing like that. I was talking, then I was lightheaded, and then I woke up with you asking me if I was okay. That's all I remember."

"All right. Not to upset you, but maybe it's our stalker?"

"Darian, I've told you a hundred times not to use that term. He's simply a fan who connects too closely with the material. That is not stalking. And Mary's people ran a background and said he was harmless. Darling, stop. I have a terrible headache, and I'd just like to rest. Can we please move on? Go speak to Riley. See what she needs."

Darian dutifully turns to go. Her mother can be so naive sometimes.

"And Darian?"

"Yes, Mom?"

"No more talking about the stalker. Understand?"

CHAPTER THREE
RILEY

The EMTs were already on site at the theater; they're on call for her events because, sometimes, readers in the signing lines are overcome—before and after meeting Columbia. She was bundled off the stage and into a waiting ambulance like a head of state. Riley's always thought the medical entourage was ridiculous overkill but tonight is grateful for them because Columbia was at the hospital ten minutes after she went down.

It's a little much for a faint, but this is Columbia damn Jones, American treasure, and they are not going to risk losing the Queen of the Written Word—as she was called by the *Denver Post* this very morning.

The next hours go by in a rush, and Riley finds herself stalking the halls of Swedish Medical Center in search of food. Not such an easy task—she has food allergies, and everything out in the world not prepared by her own hand has the possibility of making her very, very sick. Sometimes, even her own cooking is not safe. Traveling is especially fraught; she's been living on coffee, peanut M&M's, and the occasional plate of grilled fish and asparagus. Her jeans have never looked better on her, though.

Riley finds—thank God—a Starbucks that is closed but with an employee behind the counter, still cleaning up. They have safe options. She flashes a twenty.

"Please. I beg you."

The barista smiles. "I've broken everything down. Sorry."

She grabs a marshmallow rice treat and a bag of the premixed Via that's still out on display. "Almond milk?" she asks hopefully, giving the full-wattage grin she knows gets her things when she needs them. "Please? It's going to be a long, long night. *Epically* long. I might not recover without a dose of caffeine. I could just eat the powder, but it's not the tastiest."

With a friendly eye roll, he ducks down and yanks a box of oat milk from the refrigerator. "Best I can do," he says, shaking it at her, and she places her goodies on the counter and clasps her hands in front of her chest.

"You are a saint, and I owe you forever."

"Careful. I might take you up on that." He produces a Venti cup and proceeds to make her a huge iced coffee, which he drops onto the counter with a flourish.

"I'm off in ten?" he asks hopefully, the transactional little shit.

He's a lifetime younger than her, with fluffy lips, a quiff of hair falling in his eyes, and the smooth face of a child who's recently outgrown his teenage skin problems. He's adorable, he knows it, and he's leveraged those puppy dog eyes before. Riley is a seasoned, grown-ass woman, and knows how to handle this.

She drops the twenty on the counter, swipes the coffee and marshmallow treat, and waves her thanks as she walks away.

Good job, Riley. Disaster avoided.

She finds the crew in the ER waiting room, close together, whispering. Nurses and doctors cast glances at them as they pass. The whole ER is buzzing—a celebrity in their midst. Fingers crossed no photos leak to online gossip rags. Columbia wouldn't like that. For a public figure, the woman is fiercely private.

Security Mason stands to the side, tall and silent as an oak. Riley approaches him with a charming smile. He watches her coolly—he has eyes for Darian only. Not that he's ever been rude; Riley just gets the sense he doesn't like her.

"Heya. All's well?"

"Well as can be. Darian's in there with her now."

"I really need to speak with her. Would you mind pulling her out?"

He waits a beat, then nods and disappears down the hall. A few moments later, he returns with Darian by his side. They are leaning toward one another. Riley wonders if they've already done the deed and are being subtle in public, or if they're still pining away for each other. He's very into her.

"You found coffee," Darian says accusingly, and Riley offers her cup immediately.

"It's oat milk."

"Yuck." Darian shakes her head.

"She's okay?" Riley is genuinely concerned, and Darian must see that because she doesn't push her away.

"They are going to discharge her in a few, and we can go back to the hotel. The team is going to head home to New York, but we'll stay for a day or two, until she's feeling better. They think it was just altitude sickness combined with no food. Nothing serious."

Columbia never, ever eats before an event. She's superstitious that way. She has a sensitive stomach. She and Riley bonded over their gastric betrayals on their first meeting. Riley doesn't think skipping meals a bad practice in general, considering her own limitations, and she's not surprised Columbia fainted. The woman's been going hard for a month, a different city every night, staying until the last book is signed, sometimes in the store until midnight. Burning the candle at both ends. A warrior author. No wonder the fans—and the bookstores, the libraries, the festivals—love her. More than her words, more than her stories. They love *her*.

Riley has interviewed plenty of them at the events, trying to put their starry-eyed adoration into words, and there is a common theme to the answers. They don't just feel seen by Columbia's work; they feel like she's their best friend. Like she's read their diaries, knows their true hearts, their true selves, and is basing her characters on their lives. She says things aloud they've only dreamed of. Riley has to admit, for a woman who is a household name, she is remarkably friendly and approachable and insightful to the strangers who flock to see her. And they worship her for it.

"Do you have any idea who the guy was who stood up and left? She looked . . . surprised when she saw him," she asks.

Darian shakes her head but looks interested. "I don't, and no one else saw him. Mom says she didn't see him, either. But something about him feels familiar. Maybe he was at the Poisoned Pen event in Scottsdale? There was a curly-headed man talking to Barbara Peters right before we left."

"Several of the big fans have been at multiple events. He might be a groupie."

"Maybe," Darian says, voice light. "It was terribly rude of him, to stand up like that. It threw her off. Anyway, you can go back to New York with the team, and—"

No way, sister. I am Elmer's glue . . .

"Why don't I stay? This is the perfect opportunity for Columbia and me to wrap the rest of the interview. I have a lot of questions left, and if she's grounded and not flitting from city to city, I could knock them out in a day, I bet."

Darian purses her lips—she looks just like her mother when she does—and Riley senses she's about to say no. She plunges on.

"She'd want me to stay. We're not finished, and there's more she wants to tell me. She told me so in Houston, when she was getting ready to go onstage at the Murder by the Book event. We got interrupted, but she wanted to share something. Without all the buzz and people, we can get to the meat of the interview. She hasn't told me why she decided I was the person she wanted to write the story, and I get the sense there's a reason. I think it's important, though. She seemed . . . *upset* isn't the right word. Distracted, maybe. Please, Darian? Let me do my job. I think I can get this wrapped up with another day of interviews."

Darian worries the skin around her thumb. "I'll ask, okay? No promises."

"Thanks. Appreciate it."

"Share? I'm desperate enough to brave the oat milk." She reaches out a hand, and Riley gives her the coffee. It's half-gone, and she waves it away when Darian starts to hand it back. She doesn't need the caffeine anymore. She is naturally buzzed. Riley is going to get this story if it kills her.

"Will you ask now? If she says no, I'll need to hitch a ride back to NY with everyone else."

Darian is the master of the little annoyed sigh. "Fine. Stay here."

She disappears into Columbia's private room—of course, no pulled curtains or mass triage spaces for our queen—and Riley glances at her phone. Three texts from Oliver, wanting to know what time her flight lands. She'd been scheduled to return to New York with the rest of the crew tonight, the jet flying home from Denver, landing in Teterboro, the car services ferrying everyone back to their regular lives. The ball is over, the fantasy dissipating, leaving a bunch of bedraggled housemaids without their glass slippers.

If she plays this right, they'll go without her, and she'll have Columbia all to herself.

It's nearly midnight in Denver, two in the morning in New York. She decides to wait to text him back; she doesn't want to wake him. Sends an email instead: Staying on in Denver a few more days. Private audience with the queen. I'll call you in the morning and fill you in. Love.

Love. Such a weird word. Does she love Oliver? Of course she does. They've been together for two years, and he's been devoted to her. He's smart and kind and funny and cute, and she could do a lot worse. He's a lawyer, works the kind of egregious hours Riley does, likes to read and take walks and go to baseball games. Wants to move to the suburbs when they have kids, summer in the Hamptons, and take a trip to the Cotswolds every couple of years. A normal affluent guy, living a normal affluent life, in love with a woman he thinks is a normal girl.

Riley is very good at keeping secrets.

Darian appears in the door with a thumbs-up. "Tomorrow at eight a.m. in the suite. It's time to wrap the story. We have a lot of work to do. Mom feels it's time to transition to something new."

Ouch.

Riley pastes on her puppy-dog, so-freaking-grateful-for-this-opportunity grin and says, "Great! See you then." But Darian's already closed the door, dismissing her, disappearing into the private world that is offstage Columbia. It's almost like a force field vectoring out from the woman's very being.

Riley giggles a little at the thought of Columbia in a plastic bubble with laser rays emanating from its center, calls a car, and Theseuses her way out of the hospital labyrinth to the ER doors. She has eight hours to figure out everything she needs to wrap her interview. To crack the enigma that is Columbia Jones at last.

It's going to be a long night.

CHAPTER FOUR

The Brown Palace Hotel is an elegant, old-school five-star spot. Lots of dark wood and brass rails, oil paintings, an interior that feels like Grand Central. Unsurprisingly, Columbia has a two-bedroom suite on the top floor. Riley was in there yesterday for a moment before the event, gearing up, as the team calls it. It's huge, paneled in dark wood, and there are fake elephant tusks—at least she hopes they're fake—arranged as an odd sculpture on either side of the door leading into the main bedroom. It's a lovely room, befitting their CJ.

This hotel's bar is Riley's favorite of the whole tour. It screams old old old money. Gold rush money. It's like being thrust back in time. She swings through, pulsing with the caffeine, hoping against hope she can still get a scotch to take to her room, and finds the bartender alone, polishing a crystal lowball, sleeves turned back to show a mass of intricate tattoos. He sees her and lights up, as if he's been waiting for her. They talked for five minutes last night after everyone had rolled off to their respective rooms, and he'd made it pretty clear he'd like to talk some more. He is cute, and willing, but she is taken.

Riley doesn't know what sort of weird vibe she gives off to strangers. She is not a beauty. She is too tall, too round in the wrong places, too loud, too much everything. She wears large glasses, and her wardrobe is uniform by necessity, not choice. She looks strange in anything but black jeans and a black turtleneck. Her hair is thick, long, and naturally blonde, her best asset by far, hanging in shining waves down her back.

She uses it as an accessory. Black clothes, blonde hair. Maybe a pop of color with her sneakers.

Definitely not a girly girl. She is not the kind of girl men want to protect, to cherish, to behave gallantly toward. To take home to Mom. To marry.

They are, though, always interested in a good old-fashioned flirt. And if she goes along, and things get out of hand, all the better.

Now, in her late twenties, she's grown out of that childish stage, that desperate need for affirmation from strangers. Mostly. She is picky about what her future looks like, and that's where Oliver comes in. They've been working well together, to her everlasting surprise. Riley thought this tour would be a good test of the depth of her feelings toward him. She was right. She's been too busy, too involved, to worry about flirting with anyone else. To be honest, she's having a love affair with the focus of her piece.

Being on the road with Columbia has healed a lot of broken places in her. The author does that for people. She's been kind, she's been forthcoming, she's given advice and gentle support.

Seeing someone beloved for their creativity makes Riley wildly jealous, naturally, but also hopeful. This might be her path one day. A woman in control of her destiny, of her business, of her creativity. The real deal. Columbia takes her work seriously, levels up her craft with each book, and seems to genuinely connect with her readers. Her books are well researched, perennial bestsellers, discussed by every book club, not only because they're thought provoking and inspiring but also because they're enjoyable reads. For many authors, that would be more than enough. But Columbia takes it a step further, makes the readers feel like they're part of her life. And for that, she is adored.

Riley asked her once if being so giving of herself was hard, trying to put into words the panic she felt at the idea of being in the limelight in a curated world. She'd stumbled around and finally blurted, "Do you ever feel like they take too much from you? The fans?"

"You don't have to give them everything," Columbia replied. "There are parts of me that I keep private. Things in my life that are for me alone, or for Darian, or Mary. So long as you keep enough of your true self back, you'll be fine."

Riley takes a seat at the bar. A thick handsome eyebrow is raised in invitation. She responds in kind, a small smile lingering on her lips. "Dalmore 18. Neat. In a glass I can take upstairs."

A pause as he registers she's there for the whisky, not him, then tosses her a rueful smile and pours. The stream of liquid purls in the glass, the color of rain-wet soil, smelling of sherry and mushrooms and vanilla and honey and chocolate, making her mouth water. One other really nice thing about this gig—the per diem is off the charts. This whisky is thirty-eight dollars a finger. And worth every penny.

"Charge it to the room," she says and saunters off, holding the glass, knowing he's watching her go, and enjoying the appreciation. There is real power in allowing herself to be admired and not acting on the impulses that admiration brings. She wishes she'd figured that out earlier in life.

Upstairs. Her room is not a suite, but it's also on the top floor just down the hall from Columbia's, with a lovely view over the city. It is comfortable, and the bathroom is marble and spotless. She takes a hot shower, then settles in front of her laptop with wet hair, the whisky waiting patiently. She gives it a taste, moans a little in delight, pours ten peanut M&M's from a wadded-up shareable bag onto the desk, eats three, then checks her email. Nothing of note outside a nudge from her editor, Nate. Just the kind of friendly, passive-aggressive reminder that used to make her palms sweat before she realized who was in control of things.

> Hey, kid, just checking on you. Tour's over tonight, right? Get home safe, let's have a drink next week and you can tell me all about it. Wink wink.

Yes, Riley used to date her boss. No, they are no longer intimate, not for lack of trying on his part. When Nate calls her *kid*, it makes her incandescently angry, and he knows it. It diminishes her as a reporter, as a writer, as a person, as a woman. He claims it's a term of endearment. It's an awkward situation.

But a lucrative one. He pays her 10 percent more per word than the high-end going rate so she won't use the former affair against him with HR. Riley would never do that, by the way. She's not an asshole, and it was a very consensual relationship. But he likes to cover his bases.

Back soon, she replies. Staying in Denver with CJ to nail down some last-minute clarifications. Draft to you by next Thursday, latest.

She doesn't respond to the request for drinks.

That sorted, she eats three more M&M's, opens the file with her interview notes, pulls out the notebook she always carries on her person, and opens a new page to start transcribing the day's observations, ideas, and queries. If she's going to have one last go at Columbia tomorrow, she needs to tighten this mess into a real set of questions. There's just so much left to ask. The questions she's been scared to chase off Columbia with. But it's time. Riley has to go there. She has to ask about Columbia's past. There's a gap in time, she's discovered, between Columbia leaving England and getting published. And she wants to know why.

And she really wants to know what Columbia was about to tell her in Houston.

Riley is just settling in when she hears arguing in the hall.

She glances at her watch. It's nearly two in the morning. Her stomach growls reflexively. The whisky in her glass is almost gone. The candy has disappeared. She gets up and steps to the door, pressing an ear against it. The voices sound familiar.

She cracks the door to see Darian and Columbia. They are having a fight, in the hallway of the Brown Palace, furious whispers, but loud enough for everyone to hear.

"Stay out of it, Mother."

"I will not. You ungrateful little brat. How dare you?"

To say Riley is shocked to hear Columbia Jones snarling at her daughter like this is an understatement. Delicate, lovely, compassionate Columbia Jones is gone—this woman is a furious stranger. Riley should do something to interrupt them, to let them know she's listening, that they are being indiscreet. Instead, she thumbs open her phone and carefully starts the video in her camera app.

Darian's face is contorted in anger. "I said I would deal with it, and I will. You have to trust me. He's been catfishing the socials for months, posing as all sorts of people. Now he's pretending to be a woman who's just gotten married and is pregnant. He's impersonating a person who you might be more inclined to interact with. That's stalking."

"Trust *you*? After what you've done? Affect *you*? You have no idea how this will affect *me*! Everything I've built, all of it, is going to come crumbling down because you couldn't leave well enough alone. My God, Darian. You *wrote* to him? That's why he came to the event tonight!"

Oh. The strange man. Columbia *does* know him. And apparently, so does Darian.

Perhaps the queen wasn't suffering from altitude sickness and low blood sugar after all.

"Mom, he's been all over your social media accounts. He's been posing as a fan. He is not who he claims to be. That's why I had Liam reach out to him. How was I supposed to know you actually know him? You didn't tell me."

"You don't get access to every little detail of my life, Darian. Not yet anyway."

Darian finally gets the key card to work, and the door unlocks with a clack. She enters, not waiting for her mother to follow. As Riley watches, Columbia reaches up to her scalp, grabs a handful of that shiny ebony hair, and yanks. Riley's initial cringey *ouch* is replaced by shock as the perfect black bob disappears and a spill of lush blonde hair falls down Columbia's back. Then she's inside the suite, the door is closed, and the moment is over.

Riley stands for a few moments in shock, then steps back inside her room and closes the door as quietly as she can. She turns off the video, gets her headphones and jams them in her ears, makes sure they connect to the phone, and hits play.

She got it. She got it all.

SATURDAY

CHAPTER FIVE
RILEY

After replaying the video several times, trying, and failing, to wrap her head around what she's heard and seen, then reworking the remaining interview questions to fit into this newfound but confusing knowledge, Riley somehow manages to get a few hours of sleep. Her alarm goes off dutifully at seven, and, unlike most mornings when she's tempted to hit snooze again and again, she practically leaps from the sheets and into her jeans and turtleneck. She piles her hair on top of her head and secures the resulting mess with an elastic and doesn't even bother with a cup of coffee—there will be plenty in Columbia's suite, the good stuff delivered from the local coffee shop, not the crap from the hotel room's automatic dispenser. A lone banana that she grabbed from the airport yesterday morning sits, unloved and quite bruised, on the counter. She cracks it open from the bottom and manages to eat half, a moue of distaste on her face at its mushy texture. She drops the other half in the trash can. That will do for now.

She grabs her leather bag, her recorder, her phone. Double-checks the battery, adds an extra charger and cord, shoves them all inside the bag, and nearly skips down the hall to Columbia's suite. She's had this feeling once or twice before—when she knows something more than her interview subject, and she's prepared six ways to Sunday to . . . not surprise them, exactly, but catch them off guard, shake them free from their preplanned answers, get something more candid, which lets her get a richer story. Riley doesn't have any idea who the dark stranger is, but armed with the video of the argument and the shock of seeing Columbia's real hair, not the curated image the world has of her, and the knowledge that this man is from her past, she's sure she will be able to get to the truth. Leverage is everything.

The door is propped open on the latch—not entirely unusual when they are expecting her, though she is a bit early. She knocks anyway, calling out a cheery "Good morning!"

No answer. Riley listens for a moment, waiting to be beckoned in. She doesn't like to just appear in people's private spaces. It's very quiet inside. Maybe Columbia is still asleep, or in the shower, or doing her morning meditation. She debates for a moment; she can come back, she is very early—but no, she needs to get this interview going, and Columbia is known for waking with the sun, regardless of how late she was out the night before, and working, getting her words down.

Riley knocks a little harder, then pushes open the door.

The stillness of the room is surprising, and she feels a spark of pride for Columbia, managing to find a moment of quietude. The woman is very good at managing her stress, knowing her needs, respecting her body's boundaries. She takes such good care of both her physical and mental well-being. Even on the road, in demand, under the duress of constant travel and nightly events with thousands of people clamoring for her attention, she's stayed grounded. Centered. She's been an excellent guide for Riley this past month. Riley's found herself putting up a few walls toward her own more difficult situations and feels better as a result.

She should step out; shouldn't disturb her. There has been very little stillness on this tour. It is always in motion—bustling, moving, packing, screeching from one room to another—a rollicking, happy dance.

But something stops her from leaving. There's quiet, and then there's too quiet.

"Columbia? Darian?"

Nothing. Did they check out? Have they abandoned ship and gone back to New York after all? Maybe Darian forgot to say anything. Maybe she was too distracted after the fight. It's not like her: Darian is as driven and focused as her mother in many ways. But that argument was a whopper.

But no. There are personal items strewn around the living room. They're still here.

The door to the bedroom is closed, though. Something feels . . . wrong.

Riley knocks on the door; there is no answer. She turns the handle softly, in case Columbia is meditating, or even still asleep.

Confusion.

Her brain can't comprehend what it's seeing.

Blood.

She shakes her head, heartbeat crashing in her ears.

Dead.

Columbia is in bed, unmoving; Riley sees the unfamiliar spill of blonde hair.

The bedding around her is soaked in red, sheets white as snow except where they wedge against her body. If she were a crime writer, this would be the ultimate crime scene; as it is, Columbia is lost in a sea of white, a small crimson boat floating in the liquid clouds of pale sheets.

Riley searches the room quickly but there is no one. She is alone.

She creeps toward the bed. She must check if Columbia is breathing, though she already knows she's not. Death has its hallmarks—cloudy eyes staring at nothing, limp joints, laxity of the flesh, the graying of the skin. Blood either leaves the body through an exit wound, an orifice, or pools inside, waiting to be sucked out and replaced with a fluid that will mummify from within. A soul departs and the machine is left behind.

And then there's the smell. As she draws closer it hits her: fresh blood, meaty and raw; lavender, sharp and astringent; the tang of urine.

Columbia's mouth is twisted and open; thick coagulates of blood have run from her lips and nose into this glorious, new, beautiful hair, soaking the pillow beneath.

Why would she hide her hair from the world? What else is—was—Columbia hiding?

Riley presses her fingers to the writer's neck—anyone would—and her skin is cold. Sorrow spills through her. She brushes a few strands of that alien hair away from Columbia's mouth, where they've gotten stuck against her cracking red lips. She tucks them behind the dead woman's perfect, small ear.

"I'm sorry," she whispers. "I am so sorry."

"Mom?" The call makes Riley jump away from the bed, and she turns to see Darian standing in the bedroom door holding two cups of coffee, face blank, then, as she takes in the scene, contorting. Riley watches her transform: her eyes go wild; she begins to scream. Bloodcurdling screams, full of panic and horror. The coffee falls to the floor, forgotten, and Darian knocks Riley aside in her haste to get to her mother's side. Riley hits the edge of the side table as she spins and goes down. Her hip will have a bruise. She lands hard on her wrist.

That's going to make typing really uncomfortable today.

Riley, you're compartmentalizing again. Focus.

It takes her a minute to realize Darian is screaming words at her. "One!"

"What?"

"Call 9-1-1!"

"She's dead," Riley says, but Darian is wailing now, sobbing and crying in a show of emotion she didn't know the woman had in her. Riley pulls out her phone and dials 9-1-1, as Darian's told her to do, as she should have done the second she stepped into this nightmare. Riley doesn't know why she didn't think of it, outside of the fact that she was admiring the pulchritude of Columbia's death and knew she was beyond whatever mortal help paramedics and doctors could provide.

The familiar words "9-1-1, what is your emergency?" finally bring her back into her body.

"I'm at the Brown Palace Hotel, and we need an ambulance. A woman has died."

The operator starts the litany of questions, which Riley can barely hear over Darian's cries. She answers as best she can. "No, she isn't breathing. She has no pulse. Her skin is cold to the touch. Yes, I'm sure she's dead. There's blood—"

"Tell them she's a celebrity! Tell them they have to be discreet! No cameras!"

Darian is shouting between her wails, and Riley must admit, she's impressed that even in this moment of extreme duress, Darian is able to think of her mother's privacy.

"Darian, I think we need—"

She turns on Riley, teeth bared, as if seeing her for the first time.

"You! You did this! You murdered my mother!"

Riley holds up both hands to stop the verbal onslaught as if Darian is throwing punches. "I didn't. I just found her a few minutes ago."

"A few minutes? A few *minutes*? Why didn't you call for help right away? What sort of freak are you? In here, playing with my dead mother's hair? Get out. Get out get out get out!" She's shoving Riley back now, and Riley realizes Darian's hands are wet with her mother's blood, leaving smeary red palm prints across her white T-shirt. She hears another voice yelling, realizes it's the 9-1-1 operator, who is trying to manage the scene.

"Ma'am? Ma'am? Can you hear me? Are you okay?"

Oh, God, this is all being taped. Riley hits the end button in a panic and runs from the suite to her room. Her hands are shaking; her key card won't work. She slaps it against the round black lock, over and over. The elevator dings, and the door slides open to reveal a man in khakis and a blue shirt. Hotel employee, her mind helpfully provides. He is staring at her, his mouth is a perfect round O of surprise, and she glances down to see what he's reacting to. She is covered in blood.

Columbia's blood.

The hallway is besieged with mayhem. Darian is screaming "Stop her, stop her, she murdered my mother" while the hotel employee stands, shocked, unmoving. Then it clicks for him, and he rushes Riley like an enraged bull. Before she can take a breath and explain, she is tackled to the carpet. She lands hard, her face shoved into the short pile, where all the people who've walked past these rooms have dragged in the bacteria and microbes and latent dog shit from outside. She gags, but he doesn't let up. He has a knee in her back and is pulling her arms as if he's going to handcuff her, but what sort of hotel employee has handcuffs? When the sharp metal bites into her skin, she realizes the stupidity of that question: the ones who are undercover as employees but are really Columbia's private security, that's who.

"What have you done?" he growls in her ear. "Why did you kill her?"

Riley's mouth is full of carpet, so she can't answer. She tries to shake her head, but it won't move; he has a hand on her neck. She's starting to see spots; he's cutting off her air. She's bucking now to get him off, and he must realize he's killing her because he lets up, just enough for her to grind out, "Not. Me. Found. Her."

"Bullshit. You're a bloody mess."

He's let her up enough that she can see into the living room. The door is propped open with a chair, and Darian, having warned this guy of Riley's supposed transgression, is now on the floor in a heap, sobbing.

"So is she," Riley points out, being pretty damn reasonable, considering. He lets up some more, then yanks her to her knees. Her arms feel like they're going to dislocate from their sockets. "Ow! Be careful, you idiot."

"Why'd you kill her?" he demands again, not a question; an accusation.

"I told you, I didn't. I had no reason to hurt her. I came to do my last day of interviewing and found her like this."

Whoever this security guy is, she hasn't met him before. He is coarsely handsome, with broad shoulders and dark hair, a three-day stubble, and she spies the sharply inked edge of a tattoo on his forearm where the sleeve of his uniform has slid up. He has green eyes, a bright, light green, like dried sage.

He looks tired. Sad. Disturbed.

Another ding, the blasted elevator again, and this time the hall is filled with uniformed first responders and a man in a very expensive suit whom Riley *does* recognize from when they arrived—the hotel's manager. They scurry toward Columbia's room, and she is ignored, kneeling awkwardly five doors away, hands cuffed behind her back, until the manager, looking around shiftily to see who might be exiting their rooms to witness this wild scene, notices her.

"Over here," he yells, and an EMT detaches herself from the scrum in the suite and barrels Riley's way. There are a few minutes of confusion as she tries to explain that *no, this isn't my blood,* and *no, I'm not hurt,* and *no, I didn't kill Columbia.* She looks for the tired man who tackled her, handcuffed her, but he has disappeared. Probably inside the suite in order to manage the scene. There are so many people milling around now that there isn't a chance this is going to stay quiet.

"Where are you hurt?" the EMT asks again. She has kind eyes and a steady manner that allows Riley to take a breath and think, finally.

"I'm not. This isn't my blood. Could you get these off me, please?"

"Who handcuffed you?" she asks.

"I don't know. Part of the security team. I don't see him, he's probably in there. The guy with pale-green eyes." She gestures with her head toward the door to Columbia's suite.

"Who's in there?" the EMT asks. "They have us on hold."

Riley bites her lip and doesn't say a word. She will not be the one who lets this story break. It's hers. This part, the month she's been on the road, the things she knows, the things she suspects . . . they're hers.

The EMT's eyes narrow when she doesn't respond, and the woman gets to her feet. "Hang on, okay?" She disappears into the suite, returns with the hotel manager.

"Who are you?" he demands.

"Sir, I'm Riley Carrington, I'm traveling with . . . them. You met me yesterday when we checked in. Could you please ask her to uncuff me?"

"Don't do it," he says to the EMT. "The daughter claims she's the murderer."

Despite her protestations, Riley is taken from the hotel by the Denver Police. She is properly worried at this point. Will she rot in a prison cell for the rest of her days until she is slid feet first into the ground, where she will join the other graveyard spirits in the dirt?

She proclaims her innocence several times, for what it's worth. She thinks the police officer who escorts her knows she didn't kill Columbia, but Darian was so blindly hysterical in her adamance that it was almost easier to give in, at least for the moment. A lawyer will tell her she's done exactly the wrong thing by speaking to them, agreeing to be moved to a third location, and otherwise being compliant. Still, she must believe in the fact that there will be cameras to prove that someone else was in that hotel room before her.

There have to be.

CHAPTER SIX
DARIAN

It began on a Sunday, at the bottom of the steps leading into St. John's Cathedral, when a girl stepped wrongly and twisted her ankle, and a boy stopped to help her up.

In another world, another lifetime, another moment, she stepped down without incident and walked into the parking lot, following her parents to their car, the world spinning as usual on its axis. But in this world, this lifetime, this moment, she slipped and fell, and the strong hand that grabbed her left an imprint that would last forever.

She smiled, shyly, and said, "Thank you. I'm so clumsy."

He smiled, winningly, and said, "So happy I was here to catch you."

They smiled together, eyes locked in, until she tried to put weight on her ankle and lurched into him, his strong, rangy teenage baseball body as hard as oak against her shoulder.

He swept her into his arms and carried her to her parents' car as if she weighed no more than a feather. Deposited her gently in the back seat. And said, "When you're feeling better, why don't you let me take you to the movies."

She agreed, and she went on their first date, on crutches, to see The Princess Bride, *which was terribly romantic, and after that, they were inseparable. They dated, graduated, and married, and a baby was born shortly after the wedding. A local scandal, nipped in the bud by the legitimacy of the child's birth.*

And then he died.

The handsome, do the right thing, always there in a pinch, probably going to be a pro baseballer father was murdered during a home invasion, leaving the mother and child alone.

She couldn't stand living without him, with memories on every corner. So she packed her infant, and a small bag of clothes, and her broken heart, and moved to New York to attend night college, and left the world of romance and happily ever afters behind forever.

That is the story the mother told the child.

Mothers tell many stories. Some are true. Some are false. Some are so brutal you can't imagine they're real.

The night my mother died, she told me one of these stories. She shared her truth.

She was a storyteller by trade, a much-beloved author who cultivated a persona that married danger with seduction. Her romances broke hearts and influenced millions.

No one really knew her. The night she died, I found out I didn't know her either. Not at all.

All the stories she told me were lies.

And now she's gone. I will never know the truth.

Darian closes the laptop on the story. It is a solid opening, the start of a new Columbia Jones blockbuster. Will it still say *Columbia Jones* on the cover, especially now that Darian will have to finish it?

She is in shock. It's the only explanation for why she can think these things, why she hasn't melted in a puddle on the shag carpet. Her hands, her fingers, her face—everything feels numb, like she's been out in the cold for too long without gloves and jacket.

It's not that she hasn't grieved. She has. She's cried. She's sobbed. She's accused. Finally, sensing how inconsolable she really was, Mason brought her a small white pill, which she gobbled down gratefully—anything not to feel this wretched tearing inside her. She cannot imagine this world without her mother in it. All she has now are photos, videos, and memories. And her words, immortalized on the page. Columbia leaves more than DNA behind. She leaves a legacy unlike any other. So long as her works are in print, she will never truly die.

A spike of heat burns through Darian, and she shoves the laptop across the table. No. *No.* It's too soon to even think about these things, about the magnitude of loss. Business will help. Work will help. She needs a distraction.

She yanks her dark-blonde hair back from her face, pins it in a loose topknot. Takes a lap around the room, sits at the table, pulls the machine toward her. Opens the laptop again, reads the words.

She doesn't know how Mary and the house will react if Darian tells them she has a few unseen manuscripts in various stages of completion, that the legacy doesn't have to end right away. They *should* be thrilled. Authors die and their estates continue publishing their work all the time, be it from completed novels found on computers, ghostwriters brought in to flesh out partially completed work, or even new names attached to the original brand to create something unique. No need for them to think this is anything other than good luck, that they will be able to kick the dead-author can down the road for a few more books, a few more years, and the press will still be fawning because the books were written prior to Columbia's death.

Columbia Jones might be dead, but there's no reason for her name to die with her.

Still . . . this plot feels terribly prescient now, almost as if Darian has conjured this situation into being simply by letting it play out in her imagination, and she'll probably have to abandon it. How is she supposed to write on about dead mothers and life-altering secrets when hers has just died? It's too much. Too big a loss. This can't be next. There are others. Darian has been very busy drafting stories based on Columbia's outlines.

What is wrong with her, thinking like this? She is definitely in shock. The only thing that matters right now is the fact that her mother is dead. Columbia Jones, writer extraordinaire, adored literary queen, is dead. And Darian, beast that she is, is contemplating the business of her mother's legacy.

Time for all this. She needs to be thinking of the more pressing issue. A funeral.

A shudder passes through her, and she feels ill. She runs to the bathroom, positive she will be sick, but the moment passes. She uses the bathroom, does a few yoga lunges, takes some deep, cleansing breaths. She wanders back to the living room. The hotel has moved Darian into another very nice suite on a lower floor, one almost nicer than the one they had before. The view is better, and the carpet is newer, that's for sure. Her hair is still damp, and the air kicks on, giving her a chill. She took a shower the moment she got to the room, washed herself clean of her mother's blood, but she can still feel it on her skin, cloying and sticky.

She will never feel clean again.

So much blood.

This makes her think of her mother's body upstairs, cooling in the bloody sheets. Or maybe they've moved her by now. She doesn't know. How can she not think of Columbia every second of this horrid day? She is a terrible daughter. It doesn't matter that she's just trying to process what's happened; she needs to do better.

My mother has been murdered.

Too passive. She runs the words over in her head, her publicist brain scrubbing them clean and giving them a sparkle.

My mother was murdered.

On the tour of a lifetime, my mother was murdered.

After a triumphant tour to celebrate the release of her new novel, my mother . . .

No.

After a triumphant tour to celebrate the release of her new novel, a tie-in to the movie releasing in the fall, Columbia Jones was murdered.

Shit.

Nothing can prepare you for a parent's death. Not the knowledge that it's inevitable, not even if they're sick. Especially not if they're healthy and hale and were screaming at you mere hours before.

And nothing prepares you for having to put together the press statement that announces what the world is already speculating is true. Her mother doesn't trust the house's PR for personal posts; she would definitely not want them doing this.

After a triumphant tour to celebrate the release of her new novel, a tie-in to the movie releasing in the fall, Columbia Jones was murdered Saturday night in Denver, Colorado.

Darian reaches a trembling hand toward her coffee and knocks it over. It drips off the table and splashes on the thick white carpet, leaving a brown stain. Who puts a white carpet under a dining table?

I am an orphan.

The enormity of this hits her, and she chokes back a sob. She has no one anymore. Her dad died years ago when she was just a baby. She never knew him. Her mom has been gone for a grand total of six hours, and she already feels her absence. There were so many things left to say. So many apologies to make.

She opens her mother's social media accounts, one by one. The outpouring of *best wishes condolences so very sorry you're in my heart my thoughts my prayers* is too much. She freezes, shuts down. She can't like them. She can't engage. The tidal wave of grief threatens to overcome her again. Compassion has always been difficult for her to process; too much emotion feels dangerous. This, the genuine tenderness, because the sentiments of the fans are real, is beyond her.

Maybe in a few days she'll be able to sort through them, say thank you, acknowledge the kindness of strangers trying to help her grieve. But for now, she doesn't respond. What is there to say other than what she is composing right now? None of it matters. No one else matters. Darian is alone and will be forevermore.

After a triumphant tour to celebrate the release of her new novel, Ivory Lady, *a tie-in to the movie based on the novel releasing this fall, Columbia*

Jones was murdered Saturday night in Denver, Colorado. The family asks for privacy during this difficult time.

Close . . .

After a triumphant tour to celebrate the release of her new novel, Ivory Lady, *a tie-in to the blockbuster movie based on the novel releasing this fall, Columbia Jones was murdered Saturday night in Denver, Colorado. The family asks for privacy during this difficult time and will share details as they become available.*

There. Got the name of the book, the news about the movie, the fact that she's been touring. Score one for the rational brain. Her mother would be proud. *"Business before emotion, precious."*

Darian opens the laptop again, posts the statement across the platforms, sends it in email form to Liam, their IT guru, to post on the website, and immediately logs out. Columbia's death is already trending. Her mother has been reduced to a hashtag.

Perhaps *reduced to* is a bit hasty. She is being immortalized in the only way this so-called modern society understands, one hundred forty characters and prayer hand emoji and platitudes at a time. Today, they mourn. Tomorrow, it will be another injustice, perceived or real. The tragic death of Columbia Jones—writer, mother, person—will fade in a week.

Well, depending on how quickly the police catch her killer. Columbia being murdered is the best thing to happen to the brand since Spielberg grabbed the rights to *Ivory Lady*.

A voice in her subconscious, one she knows she will never hear aloud again, not the real version anyway, flat British vowels and arrogant disdain: *True. But Jesus, Darian.*

Sorry, Mom.

A heavy-fisted knock sounds from the door, and she jumps, startled from the morbid thoughts. She swipes her knuckles under her eyes and swallows, hard, then goes to the door. A quick peep through the door's fishbowl shows a cop with his badge already out. He is compact and handsome, with sky-blue eyes. She glances guiltily at the spilled coffee. She hasn't even thought to clean it up.

This conversation is inevitable. It's not like she can avoid it. She opens the door.

"Darian Jones?"

"Yes. Come in." She glances at the coffee stain and sighs. He follows her gaze and deftly steps around the stain, then puts out a hand.

"I'm Detective Sutcliffe, Denver Police. I'm investigating your mother's death. Can we talk?"

She sits and points to the chair opposite hers.

"Thank you. I'm very sorry for your loss."

"Have you arrested her yet?" He cocks a brow, and Darian fills in the blank. "The reporter. Riley Carrington."

"Well, no."

"Why not? I caught her in the act."

He leans forward. His cologne smells of cedar. A woodsy scent to match his outdoorsy eyes.

"Did you? Catch her in the act?"

"When I came in, she was leaning over my mother, tucking a hair behind her ear, with blood all over her hands and shirt. Do you need more than that?"

"Miss Carrington says she was checking for a pulse."

"Miss Carrington is obsessed with my mother. I'm sure you'll find her fingerprints all over this. Literally."

"Obsessed? I understand she's writing a piece on your mother's career. Did she pursue the job?"

"No. But the moment my mother hired her, she's been like a ghost, shadowing her everywhere. And my mother . . ." She doesn't want to say it aloud; it sounds silly and petty. *My mother ate it up. She preened under the attention. She sought out a stranger for company instead of me.*

"I promise we are looking at every angle. Have you considered the possibility that your mother wasn't murdered?"

Darian shakes her head, sudden fury animating her. "How can you possibly think that? Did you see her body? She was covered in blood. I'm sure there was a knife or something."

Sutcliffe nods calmly. "It's a natural reaction to assume harm when you see blood. I understand your mother fell ill last night and was seen at Swedish Medical Center?"

"She fainted. She's been going hard. The doctor felt it was altitude sickness, and a minor concussion from where she hit her head. Nothing to do with her *murder*."

The cop's eyes flash in annoyance. "Miss Jones, I need to discourage you from using that term. Right now, we don't know *how* your mother died. There are no visible external wounds to her body. No stab wounds. No gunshots. No marks of strangulation, or petechial hemorrhaging, either, for that matter. Nothing that would indicate she was purpose-fully, or even accidentally, killed. We're certainly not categorizing it as a murder at this time, and I think you should refrain from that thinking as well."

Darian stares at him. She knows what she saw. "That can't be right. There's no way she wasn't killed by someone. Where else did all that blood come from?"

He doesn't answer, just shifts slightly and crosses his legs like he's got all the time in the world. "Where were you last night?"

This isn't happening this isn't happening. "I was here."

"Can anyone corroborate that?"

"No. Only my mother. We returned to the hotel around two, and both went to bed."

"Hmm. And this morning?"

"I left for a quick run and to grab some coffee at six thirty. When I got back, Riley was in the room. The tapes will show her coming in, show what time she did it."

"And this is your usual routine? A run and some coffee?"

"If we aren't heading to the next city immediately, yes. Look at the cameras. You'll see I'm telling the truth."

"Interesting that you bring up the cameras," he says, and that methodical, knowing voice makes her want to scream. "There are three—one in the elevator, one in the stairwell, and one that looks down the hallways and clearly shows the door to the suite. Not a single one was online last night."

A shiver of dread spills through her. "What?"

"Yes, it's quite strange. None of the cameras on this floor were working last night. As a matter of fact, not a single camera in the hotel was, either. They all shut down around noon yesterday, though security didn't realize because a loop tape was fed into the system. Everything looked completely normal. That is, until this morning, when we looked to see who might have been on the floor and realized they'd been spoofed."

The cop no longer looks relaxed, but predatory, leaning forward with an intensity that makes her want to run from his sight.

"So I'll ask you this, and I want you to be completely honest with me. Is there any reason why you might want to kill your mother?"

CHAPTER SEVEN

Careful, Darian. This is real. He isn't to be trifled with.

She looks at her hands, clenched right in her lap. "No. Of course not. And I can't imagine anyone else wanting to, either. Everyone loved my mother. She is an amazing woman."

He pounces. "Ah. Then why would you think Riley Carrington murdered her?"

"I don't know why, okay? She's just been hanging on to us like we're the only people in her world that matter. It's weird. She was super pushy last night about staying and doing the rest of the interview today. I slipped out for coffee this morning and returned to find her stroking my dead mother's hair, covered in her blood. You do the math."

Keep him on your side, Darian.

She blows out a breath. "I'm sorry. I'm heartsick right now. Riley is the only one who makes sense."

"Speaking of hair . . . How to put this delicately? I thought your mother's hair was dark. All the photos I've seen . . ."

Darian nods. "She's curated a specific look for the public. Being an author, one that's at her level, it's like being an actor. The readers expect a certain . . . branding. The black bob has been her signature look forever. For her to change would be a big deal. I can't remember her without the black hair. Obviously, having it done regularly became untenable during the pandemic, so she switched to wigs. Saves so much time on upkeep."

He accepts this answer and moves on. "Outside of Riley, is there anything new and unusual in your mother's life?"

"I mean . . . there's this stalker."

"A stalker? Why didn't you say something right away?"

Darian doesn't like the cop's tone. "Listen, that's your job."

"I'm glad you recognize my value here."

She lets that one slide. "Our IT guy already checked him out. He's harmless."

"You let me be the judge of that."

She gives him the basics—the name they checked out, that he's been posing as new people, working like a hydra-bot account that just makes ten new accounts every time one is blocked. Sutcliffe takes notes.

"With the hotel cameras being offline . . . Surely you do think she was murdered, yes?"

He leans back in the chair, and she takes it as a concession. "Possibly. It could be a coincidence. A decent defense lawyer would tear it to shreds. I need more to go on. A lot more. Was anything missing from the room? Jewelry, laptops, anything?"

"Not that I've noticed."

"And you were here all night, with her? No one came to visit, no one called or asked to drop by?"

"No, not that I heard, but I was sleeping."

"All right. Until we have more to determine cause of death, we're not going to declare this a murder."

Darian thinks briefly of the tweet she sent. "I may have shared online that she was murdered. I thought it was clear there was foul play."

The detective's face shows no shock or concern. "I'd suggest, then, that you clarify. Until our medical examiner has a chance to autopsy your mother—"

Her reaction is visceral and immediate. "No. I don't want an autopsy."

The detective sighs. She can tell he's heard all of it before. "In this, Miss Jones, you don't have a choice. Especially because you think your mother was murdered. An unattended death of this nature requires oversight by the OME. That's the—"

"Office of the Medical Examiner. I know. I also know I'm within my rights to request a minimally invasive autopsy."

He inclines his head. "Is this a religious requirement?"

"No." Darian looks down at the stain on the carpet, trying to force the parade of images the conversation is creating from her mind. "It's just . . . I've seen autopsies done. I do research for my mother's books. I don't know that I can spend the rest of my life envisioning her going through that."

The detective's face and tone soften. "I understand. We'll do our best, okay? But you're right about the blood. There's a lot of it, and there could be an underlying condition that caused this. We need to know exactly what killed her. Especially because *you* think she was murdered." He repeats this last with a raised brow, and she wants to slap the skepticism off his face.

"She was," Darian insists stubbornly. "I know it. The doctors last night wouldn't have released her if there was something, like, organically wrong."

"Did they run tests? Do a blood workup?"

"They did a CT scan, and I'm sure they did blood work. You'll have to check with them."

"All right. Did she take any medications? Blood pressure, anxiety?"

Darian shakes her head. "Nothing of note. She's very healthy. She dislikes taking anything stronger than Advil. She uses melatonin and CBD drops when we're on the road if she can't sleep. She's very anti-medication. Was. Jesus."

"Did she drink?"

"Not much alcohol. Coffee by the metric ton. It's her one real vice. She likes the good stuff. Liked."

She heaves in a breath. Talking of her mother in the past tense is surreal. A tiny jagged chunk of glass in her heart that rubs whenever she thinks of her. Drawing blood.

The cop doesn't seem to notice how uncomfortable she is. He just keeps talking. Probing.

"What about the rest of your family? Was she married? In a relationship?"

"No. My dad died when I was little, and she never remarried. She's had some relationships over the years but nothing serious lately."

"No jilted lovers, then?"

"Not hardly. Her last boyfriend was a pro hockey player—they broke up because he was on the road all the time and she was in her office writing all the time. In truth, she hated hockey but liked him. It was destined for failure. That was a couple of years ago."

"Grandparents, aunts, uncles?"

"Why, you think someone in our family killed her?"

"I have to look at every possible angle."

"I thought you said she wasn't murdered."

He huffs out an annoyed sigh. "You're the one who put out the public accusation, Miss Jones. It's not like we can all pretend otherwise."

"Touché." That gets a small smile. "My grandmother is still alive, she lives in England. We aren't close. Her name is Yvonne Maxwell-Dodd, she lives in Bromley." At his confused look, she adds, "She remarried. That's why she's no longer Jones."

"Ah. I see. Let's return to Miss Carrington. Your mother requested that she join the tour to write a profile for *East Fifth Magazine*?"

"Yes." Darian crosses her arms. This isn't going how she expected. Sutcliffe has an air about him, one of nonchalance, like he knows something she doesn't, and that makes her very uncomfortable. "I think she was spying on us last night when we came back. She was in the hall with her phone out, recording us. She's probably already sold that footage." Her voice drips with disdain. Unearned media is so tacky.

This makes the detective lean forward. "You saw her recording a video? You're sure?"

"Pretty sure."

"Why?"

"We were fighting."

"And what was the fight about?"

Darian leans back in her chair. "Nothing related to this. It was . . . personal."

The detective sits back, mirroring her position. He's even crossed his arms, like she has. "Again, Miss Jones, I'll remind you, I'll judge what's relevant and what isn't. What was the fight about?"

Darian sighs. She doesn't want to do this, and she will be damned if she lets a cop into the situation. But he isn't going to go away.

"Fine. It was about the stalker. I think he was there last night. In person. I tried to talk to him, but he left before I could find him. It upset Mom, and we argued about it. We blocked him from accessing her online, thinking that would be enough. It wasn't. He just opens new accounts and pretends to be someone else."

"And how do you know it's the same person?"

"Because he says the same thing every time, from every account. '*Do You Remember?*'" She uses little air quotes and a deep voice. "It's ridiculous. He's been a nuisance for months now."

"And he was at the event last night?"

"Yes. At least, I think it was him. He stood up midway through Mom's talk, just stared her down, then walked out. She got sick right after that. And then things were nutty. And now . . ."

"You didn't think this relevant?"

"Listen, the guy is just a wacko. He's not dangerous. Like I said, we've had him checked out before. I'm not stupid. He's just one of those jerks who gets off intimidating women."

"So there's no chance he laid in wait for your mother, murdered her in her bed, and fled the scene? No chance whatsoever?"

Darian is starting to feel like an idiot. "Of course there's a chance. But it was Riley. I *saw* her."

"Is there anything else you've held back about this stalker, Miss Jones?"

"I'm telling you, that's a dead end. He was online last night after the gig, and his IP address registered from Kansas. He even posted a photo from a rest stop at three in the morning. He wasn't in Denver when she was killed. Died. Not that I'm defending the asshole, he's made my life miserable with his weirdo antics, but the man who was in the theater last night was nowhere near Mom's hotel room when she was murdered."

"You're stalking the stalker?"

"I'm taking precautions because that's my job. That's what we fought about. But it's irrelevant. I failed to protect my mother from the very person who stands to gain from her death."

"Who?"

"I told you. Riley Carrington."

"Who else might want her dead?"

"No one!" Darian is close to tears. "This is not fair of you, to question me like I'm some sort of suspect. My mother just died. I knew we shouldn't have come here," she mutters. "Adding a date at the last minute was a terrible idea." She is on the verge of tears, and the detective makes a noise of consolation.

"I understand. And I'm very sorry for your loss. I'm just trying to get the whole picture here. You say there was a stalker, but you think the reporter killed her. But there were also fans staying in the hotel, isn't that correct?"

She takes a shuddery breath, pulling herself together again. "Yes. The VIP experience. Five of them got to meet her, have an official photo made, and have a signed book dedicated to them. Six, last night. There was a last-minute addition. A special one-on-one."

Sutcliffe leans forward. "Is that typical?"

"It happens sometimes. Usually it's a friend of the bookstore, a personal favor. There's also a voucher for a meal and room here at the hotel. We do it in every city that timing allows, so this was the eighth time this month."

"People pay for this?"

"Oh, yeah. They do. Everyone wants a piece of her. Wanted. Shit."

She can't sit here any longer. She moves to the window. The mountains are solid in the distance. They haven't changed. She has. She will never be the same again.

"You said Denver was added to the tour?"

"Mom wanted to come here. She insisted. Said she wanted to do a makeup date for the area since she had to cancel tour during the pandemic. And now she's dead. If we'd gone home from Arizona like we were supposed to, she'd be alive right now."

"I need the list," Sutcliffe says, and she appreciates that there's a new urgency in his tone. "Everyone she had VIP meets with last night, as well as during the tour. And all of the stalker's info. And since you're so on top of this, I assume you have more than one disgruntled fan?"

"You know how it is. When you're loved, you're also hated. We have a file. I'll get all this for you."

"Thank you. One more quick question. Your mother has professional security, correct? Why wasn't someone watching her room?"

"They're for the events, and travel coordination. Crowd control, keep strangers from approaching, limit too-enthusiastic fans, help us navigate the cities. Once we're settled back in the hotel, we don't need them. At least, I didn't think we did."

He nods. "I think that does it for me. I'll leave you my card. If you can email the info this afternoon, I'd appreciate it. The sooner I get it, the sooner I can start the investigation."

"Detective?" She turns from the window. "My mother . . . What's happening right now? Where is she?"

His voice is softer. "She's been transported to the medical examiner's office. Her personal belongings are being collected for testing. We'll do the autopsy in the morning. I'll relay your concerns to the ME, she's a good one. I've known her for a decade. She's very gentle. She'll do a good job."

Darian nods, swallowing back the tears that are threatening. Sutcliffe looks like he's going to say something more but tucks his notebook back in his pocket and sees himself out. She hears him talking to Mason in the hall, is comforted knowing the ginger-haired guard is nearby.

This isn't happening.

Columbia, dead. Autopsies. Murder. Detectives. It's like they've become a subplot in one of her mother's novels.

Darian sits at the table and opens the laptop again. The words swim, the tears finally dropping.

How is she going to manage this?

With Liam's help. He will have everything she needs. She wipes her eyes and sends him a quick text, only wondering briefly why he didn't respond to her earlier email.

Hey. I don't even know where to start. My mom's dead. I sent you wording for the website. And the police need the stalker file. Can you send?

He writes back almost immediately.

What? What happened? OMG Darian. Are you okay?

Not really. Found her dead this AM. Riley was with her. Lots of blood but the police aren't convinced it was murder. I don't know. It feels weird.

I will send everything right now. I am so sorry. Can I help?

We'll need to update the website and everything, but for now . . . No. I'll be in touch again when I have more details. Just do me a favor and track our friend, would you? You said he was in Kansas last night—still heading east?

Hold please . . . Yes. He's in Pennsylvania right now.

Thanks, Liam. Keep me posted. Please update the website as soon as possible.

OK. God, I am sorry.

She sets down her phone, the glass clinking on the table. *So am I. So am I.*

CHAPTER EIGHT
KIRA

Kira Hutchinson wakes to sirens. She groans and rolls over, pulling a pillow over her ears. This hotel is surprisingly noisy. Granted, being in the city overnight meant there would be noise, but she had no idea just how disturbing it could be. How long has it been since they'd come into Denver for an overnight date? Four years? No, almost five—the one-night babymoon when she was six months along with Hudson, when Luke ate the oysters that gave him food poisoning, so the moment he could be trusted not to barf all over the car, she'd taken him home. She is far enough removed from "the incident," as they call it—he had red wine with dinner, and the hotel's bathroom looked like a crime scene; he was so ill she thought she was going to have to call an ambulance—to be able to laugh ruefully.

They don't get a lot of breaks. The bakery takes up so much of her time these days, and what little time and energy that's left over goes to the kids. Luke runs their ranch; he's a farmer at heart. Not that she minds. Kira had always wanted a quiet life, one of meaning and depth, plugged into her community, her family, and her passions. She's present. She isn't on social media, though the bakery has a business feed run by her assistant, who doubles as the front-of-house manager. It isn't difficult to market themselves—take pretty pictures of the goods, post them, announce upcoming specials. Easy.

The sirens are getting louder, closer. She tiptoes out of the bed—like their three boys, Luke can sleep through a nuclear blast—and pulls back an edge of the curtain. The sun is barely up, and she can see the rotating flashes of light. They've come to the hotel.

Oh, how horrible. Someone must have gotten ill.

"Babe?" Luke's sleepy voice never fails to make her stomach clench. They met on the first day of high school, and she's been lost in those denim-blue eyes ever since. "You okay?"

"Yes." She lets the curtain drop and goes back to the bed. Crawls in. Lets him snuggle her into his arms. "Something must have happened to a guest at the hotel. There's an ambulance and fire trucks outside."

"That's a shame," he murmurs into her hair, drifting back to sleep. "Hope they didn't eat any oysters."

When she wakes again, the hotel has come to life around them. She has to admit, she wishes this could be their morning all the time—the cloud of a bed, the lack of urgency to rise, to tend to the needs of her people. She loves her babies, loves them dearly, and wouldn't trade them for the world. But she is looking forward to the day when they can make their own breakfasts a few times a week.

"Where'd you go?" Luke asks, running a hand down her leg.

"Where do you think?" she answers with a little laugh.

"They're fine. Your mom is the best babysitter in the world."

"I know. We just haven't been away from them in so long."

"Exactly." He sits up, grins, eyes mischievous. "Wanna order room service?"

She grins back. "Already did. I couldn't sleep last night so I filled out the card and put it on the door. You didn't budge. You were tired." This last is a bit softer, and she runs a thumb under his right eye. There are shadows there, something new lately. Luke is aging like a proper Colorado cowboy, settling into his bones, laugh lines grooving into his cheeks, sunbursts around the corners of his eyes from squinting into the sun too much, and radiant streaks of silver starting at his temples. He is glorious.

Kira is aging like a proper baker who's birthed three children, getting soft around the edges, a little fuller here and there. A mummy tummy. Nothing to worry about, nothing that can't be fixed with a little more exercise and a little less tasting of the goods, but she should get a handle on it before she moves into her thirties because she's heard that once you're past thirty-five it's hard as hell to get the weight to shift around. Then again, it's a pointless endeavor for right now.

Luke captures her hand and kisses the tips of her fingers. "I've been tired for weeks, babe. The expansion is taking a lot of energy. But it's worth it. You're worth it."

"I love you, Luke."

"I know." The kiss is warm and soft, and things are getting real when there is a knock at the door.

Kira jumps, guilty as a teen caught by her dad, which makes Luke laugh. "I'll get it. You stay here. It's called breakfast in bed for a reason."

She yanks the sheets to her neck when the young server rolls in the table. She notices incongruously thick jet-black eyebrows, a haggard grayness to his skin, as if he rarely gets outside, something rare in the healthy, outdoorsy Coloradans she's used to. He also crackles with excitement. The sirens: something has happened.

"Big morning?" she asks, trying not to be too awkward: here she is, naked as the day she was born, in bed, in front of a stranger. "I heard sirens."

The boy—he can't be more than eighteen; this must be his first job—looks over his shoulder, then, conspiratorially, whispers, "A guest was killed."

"What?" Luke's playfulness is gone. "What did you say?"

"A guest was killed. Murdered. An A-list, too. I heard they arrested the murderer." He raises his bushy brows. "I'm not supposed to talk about it."

"You've already talked," Luke says sharply. "Who was it?"

"That I can't say, sir." He hands over the receipt, which Luke barely glances at before putting a ten in the boy's hand. Then another.

"It was that famous author," he whispers, looking over his shoulder. "Columbia Jones."

Kira gasps. "No!"

"Yes, ma'am." He's imparted his news, gotten his reward, and is scurrying toward the door before she can register it fully. The reason they've come to town, the reason they are in this very hotel, was because Kira wanted to attend Columbia Jones's book signing, and Luke had gone above and beyond and turned it into a present for her, buying the VIP experience—a small block of discounted rooms in the hotel, a meet and greet before the event, a signed, personalized copy of the new book, and a photograph with the author. Last night had been sublime, an absolute dream come true, until Columbia collapsed onstage. And now she is dead? Murdered? Here in the hotel?

Her favorite author, the woman she felt closest to outside of her own mother, the one who seemed to peer into her very soul and pull out all her darkest, deepest secrets, her most precious emotions, is dead.

Kira starts to cry. Luke is by her side immediately. "It's so unfair," she snuffles into his broad chest. "Who would do such a thing?"

"I don't know, honey. I'm so sorry. This is incredibly horrible."

Luke might not understand the depth of Kira's love for Columbia Jones's books, might tease her for her obsession, but he loves his wife, and in this moment, she feels his sorrow, almost as deep as her own, is very, very real. It makes the truth harder to bear, and she cries a little harder.

Luke holds her until the tears slow. He hands her a tissue, then pours a cup of coffee from the carafe. "Do you want to eat something?"

"I don't think I can. You go ahead. It's too nice to waste."

The service is lovely, fine china and silver, the food cooling but beautifully appointed. She feels her gorge rise and is in the bathroom a moment later. Her stomach is empty, blessedly; she hates throwing up. She retches for a moment, then straightens and uses the mouthwash.

Luke is standing in the door to the bathroom—marble, heated floors, a soaker tub, so exquisite—with a brow cocked.

"You sure you're okay?" She can hear the question in his tone. He knows already.

She nods, glancing in the mirror. She's still a bit green. She hasn't been sure until this moment, hasn't taken a test or anything. And now's not the time; she wanted to wait until after breakfast, when they were full and happy, to tell him she suspects they are expecting again. But she's borne him three children already; he knows all the signs. She gets sick early. She's barely five weeks along right now, only a week late on her period, and already feeling the first flushes of pregnancy. It's always like this. The test will confirm it; they'll grab one from Walgreens on the way home.

"We may need to buy that Tahoe after all," she says anyway, a hand on her belly protectively, and Luke's handsome face blossoms into a smile so wide she almost forgets her pain at losing her hero. Almost. He grabs her in a huge hug.

"Oh, honey," he manages.

"I know it's unexpected—"

"Are you kidding? We haven't exactly been careful lately." He laughs, and his joy chases away another little bit of her sadness.

"I wanted to surprise you."

"I'm surprised," he reassures her. "Thrilled. The more the merrier. Maybe it's twins and we'll have that basketball team I've always wanted."

She groans but smiles. "Don't wish twins on me. At my age, I'll never get my figure back."

The main character in Columbia's latest novel has Irish twins, little girls born only ten months apart. The joy of sharing this life event with her husband is tempered again.

"We should check out. Get back home."

"You sure?"

"I am." She nods. "I can't stay here anymore, knowing she's died. She might still be here, they keep bodies at crime scenes forever, and it's so early . . . My God. Her poor family. Darian must be devastated."

"That's her daughter, right?"

"Yes. Daughter, publicist, business manager. I met her last night. Tough cookie, watched over Columbia like a hawk. Oh, Luke. Murdered? Let's go. I have to get out of here. This is freaking me out."

CHAPTER NINE
RILEY

They leave Riley alone in a bland room with a table bolted to the wall and four metal chairs that have seen better days. She is still cuffed; the officer who escorted her has her buckled into a chain that's attached to the front of the table, as if she's a dangerous criminal. There are no windows, which is a shame, because she enjoyed the brief views of the mountains on the walk from the car to the station. Last night on the way to the theater, the sun fell pink behind the snowcapped peaks, and she thought Denver was lovely, someplace she'd like to visit again, under better circumstances. Now, she wants to leave this place and never return. The initial meeting she had with Columbia seems years away right now; the excitement of this gig has turned to horror. She should have said no. She shouldn't have gotten so greedy. Look where it got her.

The door finally opens, and a wiry bald man enters the room. He's carrying a file folder, a cup of coffee, and a sweating Diet Coke, the last of which he sets in front of Riley. He glances at the file.

"Riley Carrington?" As if she could be anyone else.

"That's me."

"I'm Detective Sutcliffe."

He looks her over. Riley knows she's a mess. The blood has dried on her shirt; it makes little crackling noises every time she shifts. She must smell horrendous, but she's gotten used to the stench.

"Did you do it?"

She narrows her eyes. "No."

A smile flits across his lips, and he sits down.

"Do you know who did?"

"No."

"Do you—"

"Could you please get these off me?" She rattles the cuffs. "I'm willing to talk to you, without a lawyer present, and I'll drink from your stupid can of soda so you can have fingerprints and DNA, which you can have anyway if you ask nicely, but I would really appreciate some consideration here."

Another smirk. He's that kind of guy, has mastered the lip half up. Probably works wonders when he's picking someone up at a bar. He waits. She waits. They stare at one another, unspeaking. Finally, she shifts and sits back, head down. Defeated.

"I take them off, you'll talk to me?"

She raises her head. "A full statement. Official. On the record."

"Done."

He fishes out a key and unlocks her. Riley's wrists are so swollen that there are grooves in the flesh. She rubs at them surreptitiously.

"Deal's a deal," he says, glancing over his shoulder. The cameras have been on this whole time, naturally.

"I'm a staff writer for *East Fifth Magazine*." At his blank look, she adds, "It's like the *New Yorker*, the *Atlantic*, long-form journalism, a family-owned business, based on the Upper East Side off Fifth Avenue in New York."

"Ah. Upper East Side, Fifth Avenue. *East Fifth*. Clever."

"I don't know if it's clever, but it's been in circulation for over fifty years and has a paid subscriber base of over a million. I'm doing a story on Columbia Jones. I've been on the road with her for a month as she's crisscrossed the country on book tour. Last night was the last gig. She fainted onstage, had to go to the hospital. They diagnosed altitude sickness and sent her home. When she got in, she had a knockdown fight with her daughter in the hallway. I have it on tape. I spent the rest of the night prepping for what was supposed to be my last day of access to her, and I shaped the interview around the argument I saw. This morning, I showed up at our scheduled time and found Columbia dead. I felt for a pulse, even though that was clearly a fruitless endeavor, then her daughter came in and flipped out. I called 9-1-1, got tackled and cuffed by one of Columbia's security guys, and now I'm here. End of story."

She cracks the lid on the soda and takes a long drink.

"That's quite a story."

"It's not a story if it's the truth. And it is. I have no idea who killed her."

"Assuming she was murdered—"

"Wasn't she? I mean, there was a lot of blood." She punctuates this fact by pulling her shirt from her body.

He narrows his eyes, the corners crinkling, and she can envision him standing on top of a mountain, having just taken off his sunglasses, squinting against a cold blue sky.

"Until we get an autopsy, there will be no declarations on the manner of death."

Riley sits back in the chair. So much blood—it never occurred to her that this was anything but foul play.

"Wow. Okay."

"You have this fight on tape?"

"Yes."

"Why didn't you break it up?"

"Not my place. It was clearly a family thing."

"Meaning?"

"It was a pretty intense mother-daughter argument about some fan who'd come to the event last night. It got heated."

"Well, with all the accusations flying . . . If she has been killed, do you think her kid did her in?"

Riley sits with that for a moment. Darian, murdering Columbia? Her mother, her boss, her meal ticket. They got along, considering Darian is the Sherpa, in charge of dealing with everything that's not been thought of and whatever goes wrong, in addition to her official titles, and sometimes Columbia seemed to forget that.

"Maybe? I truly have no idea. You know everything I do."

"Oh, I doubt that," he says. Smirk, smirk, smirk.

He's right. She does know more. But this is all he needs from her. Nothing else she can openly share will have any bearing on Columbia's murder. Death. Whatever. At least, she doesn't think so.

Finally, he shifts in his chair. The staring contest is over. "That's it? That's your statement?"

"Yes, sir."

"Show me the video."

"You have my phone."

"No, I don't. It didn't come in with you."

A flicker of unease. "Maybe it's back at the hotel?"

A tiny crease starts between his brows. He shuffles the file and plops a yellow pad and pen onto the table.

"Write it up. Put all your personal details, too. Then you're free to go."

She tries not to jerk in surprise, relief flooding through her. "You don't think I did it."

"Let's just say someone put in a good word."

"Who?"

"Mason Bader."

"The bodyguard?"

"He was coming back from the gym and saw you enter the suite, then saw Miss Jones enter on your heels. That particular timing doesn't line up for you to have done it."

She releases a breath. "Too bad he didn't see the real killer."

"That would have been convenient, yes. Still, I'll need to see that video, Miss Carrington."

"Happy to share as soon as I have my phone." She leans over the table; puts down her name, phone number, email, and address; adds her editor's name and phone number; and starts to scribble her statement. Anything to get out of here, anything to get away from the censorious looks of this man who—let's be honest—has her life in his hands. Too many people have been in this position over the years, in control of her destiny. It's hard for her not to run screaming, but she's learned how to master her emotions.

She writes. Reads. Scratches out one word and replaces it, then pushes the pad across toward him. He nods, and they both stand as if this was a first date gone awry.

"I can't call a car without my phone."

That smirk again. "Oh, I'll give you a ride back to the hotel. The video, remember?"

CHAPTER TEN
COLUMBIA

Two Months Before the End

The dulcet chime of the doorbell pulls Columbia from the paragraph she is pretending to belabor. She's been distracted all morning, and the words aren't very good. Instead of writing, she spent three-quarters of the morning staring out into the courtyard, watching the robins flitter about. Thinking. Mired in her past and dreaming about the future. Certainly not her normal workday; by now, she's usually written at least a few pages. But with the upcoming tour and the visitor she is about to receive, her mind is—understandably—elsewhere.

No matter; there is always tomorrow. Novel writing is a marathon, not a sprint.

Voices now, bleeding up the stairs as the visitor approaches her lair on the fourth floor of the town house. When she bought the brownstone in the midnineties, she'd immediately converted two bedrooms on the fourth floor into an open, airy space with floor-to-ceiling shelves on both sides, installed a thick blue carpet, outfitted a sitting area perfect for reading in front of the fire on one side, and placed her desk on the other side with a view out to the courtyard. A private bath with a marble shower completes the space, for those long nights when she doesn't want to be alone in her room and works through the night. A shower always helps her think.

It is comfortable, very private, apart from the rest of the household, and generally, not open to visitors. But today is special and Columbia wants to open the doors, literally and figuratively. It's time.

She stands, breathes in deeply, smooths the invisible wrinkles from her wide-leg trousers, and slips the bouclé Chanel jacket from the back of the chair and onto her slim shoulders. She realizes she's genuinely nervous. This is a momentous occasion. One that can—might—change everything.

"Riley Carrington, ma'am," Karstan, her house manager, announces in his crisp London accent, and a young woman enters Columbia's office.

The first impression is a shock. She's only seen pictures. Riley Carrington in person occupies more space than Columbia ever expected. She takes in the totality of the girl. She's statuesque, blonde, broad shouldered, with long, trim legs encased in denim and a bosom women pay good money for hiding beneath a black turtleneck. Despite the casual uniform, it is clear she has a lovely hourglass figure. Her thick blonde hair is in a ponytail. She has a clear brow, green eyes, and a respectful, excited smile on her face.

She is breathtaking.

Riley puts out a hand. "So nice to meet you."

Columbia realizes she's staring and smiles, grasping it warmly, wrapping her left over their clasped hands like a benediction.

"And you. Riley. An Irish name."

"Irish Catholic, yes."

"Thank you, Karstan. I'll take it from here," Columbia says in dismissal. He politely nods and disappears down the hallway.

"Please, have a seat."

Riley arranges herself on the sofa, looking around the office with a happy smile on her face. "These bookshelves are amazing. Are these first editions?"

"Some. Most are in the cellar in a climate-controlled room so they don't disintegrate. Wouldn't do to have them disappear on us, would it? Can you imagine what Lewis Carroll would think if I sent his Alice down the nonproverbial rabbit hole to the dump?" She laughs, charming, and Riley laughs with her, obligingly. Columbia is not the best at icebreakers or small talk; she doesn't like strangers. But Riley is no typical stranger. If all goes according to plan, she is about to become a part of Columbia's life in a very big way.

Before they can go further, Karstan clears his throat and enters again with a tray—tea, scones, clotted cream.

"Light snack," Columbia says, noting the alarm that crosses Riley's face. "Oh, don't worry. These are all completely gluten-free. I know you have celiac. I have a very delicate system, too, actually, so I have a very strict diet. This is a recipe from the University Arms Hotel in Cambridge. I had a boyfriend who rowed for Queens' College, and he used to take me for tea after the races. Such fun."

To illustrate, she plucks a scone from the plate, tops it with the clotted cream, and takes a large bite. "Mmm. See? Safe as houses."

Riley takes a scone and tops it with cream as well, then sets it on her plate to reach for her notebook. Columbia doesn't push. The girl needs to eat; as voluptuous as she is, she still seems malnourished. She has dark circles under her pretty eyes, and her skin is pale as skim milk. There is no reason for her to trust this stranger who has summoned her, especially with something as delicate as food.

"Can I ask . . . I don't mean to be rude, but I saw the Rothko downstairs. Is that . . . real?"

Columbia nods. "Very real."

"I like Rothko."

The smile on her face is genuine. "How lovely. So do I. I haunted Sotheby's until one came up for auction that was in my budget. That was many years ago, but it's a wonderful piece, I think. Now, you must be wondering why you're here," Columbia says.

"I am, if I'm being honest. It's been my understanding that you don't give interviews."

Straight to the point. Those guileless green eyes are like lasers and filled with curiosity.

"I normally don't. And I don't exactly have an interview in mind. I'd like something a bit more . . . intimate."

Riley has a notebook out, and a pen with blue ink. Columbia feels a little thrill—she loves blue ink, too, won't use anything else.

"Do you mind if I . . . ?"

"No, no. Of course. Take all the notes you want. But for the moment, let's talk, you and I."

Riley shuts the notebook, a finger holding the page.

"I'd like you to accompany me on tour for *Ivory Lady*. We'll be on the road for a month, with thirty-plus stops. And while we do it, you'll write a piece for *East Fifth Magazine*. A very long piece. The definitive Columbia Jones. With the release of the book and the movie so close together, the first truly intimate portrait of my life and creative process should gain you quite a bit of attention. Not to mention money. It will be . . . lucrative."

Riley Carrington is surprisingly hard to read. She has an excellent poker face, manages to contain what Columbia expects must be overwhelming emotion. This is the opportunity of a lifetime, and they both know it.

"Will you have editorial control?"

Columbia edges back in her seat. "I'd like to think I won't need to. I think once we get to know one another better, we'll be able to trust each other. Yes?"

Riley takes a sip of tea. Despite the assurances, she hasn't touched the scone. Columbia follows suit, annoyed to realize her damn hand is shaking. Riley has noticed, too; her eyes dart away. Columbia's nerves are shot. She should have taken an Ativan before this meeting, but the medicine dulls her creativity and she wanted to work this morning.

She puts the teacup into the saucer with a tiny chink. She has nothing to lose by being honest here.

"Forgive me. I'm nervous. This is an unusual request for me. I don't often invite people into my life."

"So why now? And why me? I mean, no offense, I'm honored that you want me to do this. But . . ." As a show of faith more than anything, she thinks, Riley takes a nibble of the scone. Columbia relaxes a little. Trust is the only way they're going to get through this. She can dole out the information bit by bit, but she needs to control the when, the where, and the how of this story.

"You're an excellent writer, you're unmarried with no encumbrances, and I think you're still hungry enough to want a shot at making a name for yourself. This will make your career."

Riley has a bad habit of tapping her pinkie nail against her front tooth, and Columbia stops herself from saying "Don't do that!" It is a habit that will need curbing. She had to ride Darian for years not to bite her nails, not that it works. Nagging Riley is no way to start their relationship.

Columbia isn't stupid—she might be one of the most successful authors in the world, but she needs this to go well, and being a harpy will not get them off to a good start.

Instead, she debrides the edge of the scone and waits for a reply.

"No encumbrances. You mean, I don't have children?"

"You don't. I've done a little research myself, of course."

"I would expect nothing less. I do have a few encumbrances—family stuff. I don't know that I can be away for a whole month."

"Yes, I know how difficult that can be. Did I mention I'm paying ten dollars a word? And I assume you'll do no less than ten thousand, preferably fifteen. Or twenty. However much it takes to get the story just right. I spoke with your boss, Nathanial. He assured me you would find that more than satisfactory. Plus all expenses, of course."

"Oh."

Riley Carrington is being offered a full house, aces over kings, and she knows it. She froze at the mention of the money. Columbia knows the girl has debt, and while it is unfair to play that card, she will if she needs to.

She doesn't. Riley gathers her composure and nods. "Assuming I can make the timing work, yes, I'd be honored, Mrs. Jones."

Columbia smiles conspiratorially. "Here's our first secret together, then. There is no Mr. Jones. So please, call me Columbia. Would you like some time to think about it?"

Those assessing green eyes. "I assume Nate already cleared the decks for me to say yes?"

"He did. He strikes me as a smart man."

"That he is. So tell me what it is you'd like me to cover, exactly?"

The notebook is out again. The girl is all business. Hungry. Reckless, probably, for Columbia to be playing with fire like this, inviting a reporter into her life, but it feels like time.

"My career. My process. My life," Columbia finishes lightly.

"This sounds more like a biography than an article."

Columbia lets a smile play on her lips. Riley's eyes go huge.

"You want me to be your biographer?"

"First, we walk. Then we run," Columbia says. "And I'm thinking something experimental, a cross between a memoir and an autobiography. Have you ever ghostwritten before?"

The girl's face falls. "No."

"Your name would be on the cover, of course."

"Oh, sure, great. It's not that. It's just not something I've ever done. I know a few who do, though. If you want someone more experienced, I can give you some names."

Columbia smiles gently, knowing how much that gracious offer cost the girl. "I want *you*, Riley. I feel we have a connection, and I want to help you."

Riley brightens again. She is like a sunflower turning her face to the sun when she's excited. Columbia finds it utterly charming.

"Then I will learn how to ghost, if that's what you want."

"Good. This is a test drive. After a month, we will know each other a little better, and we can discuss whether we want to continue going or not. The focus of this article will obviously be *Ivory Lady*. It's meant to be a PR tool, so naturally the studio offered their own person, their own avenues. But I wanted someone I'd read, someone I'd enjoyed. Someone I thought I'd like to spend time with. You have an insouciance to your work that I find quite refreshing. Joan Didion meets Rachel Syme. You're smart but you don't take yourself too seriously. Rather like me."

"First off, keep comparing me to Joan Didion, and I'll never leave. Thank you. That's an unbelievable compliment and I am—" She breaks off, grinning. "Shit. Didion?"

Columbia laughs and, for the first time in weeks, relaxes. "Yes. Shit. Didion."

They've finished the scones and are talking about Riley's time in journalism school when Darian steps into the room.

Columbia forces a wide smile; she hates interruptions, and Darian knows it.

"Yes, precious?"

"Mary is on the phone for you. She wants to know how—" Darian waves in Riley's direction.

"Tell her all is well, and I'll call her back."

"But she—"

Columbia turns to her daughter. "Darian, we're still visiting. Tell Mary I'll call her back. And then come meet Riley properly."

Admonished, Darian shoots Riley a look, then slinks away. Columbia apologizes for the interruption, but Riley is already putting away her notebook.

"Oh, you needn't leave. Mary is my publisher, she can wait. This is more important."

"I appreciate that, and the tea. But I have a meeting this afternoon downtown, I'm going to be late if I don't shove off now. I'm very excited by your offer, Columbia. Thank you for thinking of me."

"Does that mean you'll do it?"

Riley hoists her bag over one shoulder and puts a hand on her hip. A frisson sweeps through Columbia's body. She has no idea.

"We both know I'm going to say yes. But I need to talk to Nate, and to my boyfriend, Oliver. Just formalities. Cool?"

"Of course. Cool." The word sounds ridiculous in her mouth, but Riley smiles and offers her hand again. Columbia shakes it and walks her to the door of her office. Karstan appears, gesturing toward the stairs. Within moments, Riley Carrington is gone.

"Jesus," Columbia says, shoulders dropping.

"She said yes, I take it?"

Darian appears on the stairs, coming down from her own office.

"Yes. She'll accompany us on tour and write a piece about *Ivory Lady*."

"Mary won't be pleased. She wanted you to go with the girl from *Vanity Fair*."

Columbia bestows her only daughter with a brilliant smile.

"Fuck what Mary wants. *I* want Riley. She's the only one for the job. Now, I need to work. Toddle off and I'll see you at dinner."

She sweeps back inside her office, pleased as hell with herself, ignoring the glare Darian shoots at her. No, Darian won't be pleased by Riley's presence. But she doesn't get to make this choice.

If Columbia is going to be forced to tell her story, she will choose her partner in crime.

CHAPTER ELEVEN
RILEY

Now

Riley is relieved when the detective is quiet on the ride back. She needs time to think, to regroup. She's in shock, and no wonder. She hasn't had a second to process what's happened.

The hotel is buzzing when they pull up. There's a scrum of paparazzi spreading like a fast-growing fungus across the street from the hotel. The fire trucks and police are still here, accompanied by a van from the medical examiner's office. This was not handled with the subtlety the Jones family would have preferred, for sure. Riley can only imagine how badly Darian is losing her mind. A stickler for details, Riley has only ever seen Columbia's daughter manage situations large and small with efficiency, almost always with tact and professionalism. Losing her mother like this could break that stony facade.

Hopefully, Darian won't try to hold Riley responsible any longer, but she has a feeling she's going to be the recipient of a lot of vitriol over the next few weeks. Columbia's fans will not like that no one's been found responsible yet.

If *she was murdered,* she reminds herself.

The cop follows her into the lobby and says something to her as they enter. She can't hear him over the din, turns to ask him to repeat himself, and, when she does, bumps shoulders with a woman scurrying across the room toward the door. She has a purse slung across her body, is wearing jeans and boots, her floss-blonde hair bouncing around her shoulders. Her expression is pained, and her eyes are red. Riley is a New Yorker, she's used to people smacking into her without apology, but this woman makes her stop and follow her progress out of the building. There is something about her that feels familiar. Like she's seen her before. Met her, maybe.

Riley dismisses it almost immediately; she has a terrible tendency to see the familiar in strangers. She didn't realize quite how much she does it until the past month, out on the road with Columbia. She seeks comfort in these strange faces, searching, searching, for the one who looks like home. It's a function of being adopted, of not knowing her birth parents, having something to grow toward, to compare features. Photos don't work—Riley has no photos of her real mother. She can only imagine that she shares the cupid's bow of her lips, the arrogant arch of her brows, the lush bust line. People pay good money for the features Riley has been gifted by a ghost.

Recognition hits. The woman who bumped into her was at the VIP event last night, that's why she feels familiar, but there is still something else. Riley thumbs through her mental filing cabinet, a talent she has, being able to reinsert herself into a certain situation and run a video of the event through her mind's eye. The woman who's just run out of the hotel took a picture with Columbia, Riley is sure of it, because she remembers thinking they looked alike. Not exactly; though Columbia's hair was dark and this woman's light, they shared features. Everyone has a doppelgänger, right? Riley recalls thinking of course Columbia would not be immune from such a thing.

Satisfied that the reason she recognized the woman was because of the event, she refocuses on the cop, who is waving a hand in front of her face to get her attention.

"Hey. Miss Carrington. Hello?"

"What did you say?" Riley shakes herself back to reality. "Sorry. Yes?"

"Follow me," Detective Sutcliffe commands, and she does, weaving through the lookie-loo guests and the hotel staff, all milling around. You'd think they'd clear the scene, get as many people out of the hotel as possible, but what does she know? The sum of Riley's experience with modern police investigations is what she sees on true crime documentaries and follows on social media hashtags. And why is there a police investigation at all, if Columbia wasn't murdered? This is all too weird.

Then again, she is getting a front-row seat as a "suspect," so maybe she'll write this up, turn it into a true crime podcast, script a few shows, and sell it for a hefty sum. Get contracted to write the companion book. Make all her troubles disappear.

The elevator is expectantly empty, and the doors slide closed with a whisper.

"You don't really think I had anything to do with her murder, do you?" she blurts.

Sutcliffe's eyes are the color of the clear Colorado sky. They train on Riley, and his right eyebrow lifts, just a touch. He is relatively handsome. She allows herself a moment of appreciation. It is beyond awkward.

"You don't," she says, more confidently than she feels. "You wouldn't be bringing me back here if you did."

"Let's just say I'm intrigued by your argument." His tone is clear. He might as well have said *Let's get a drink after*.

They arrive. The doors hitch for a second before opening. The hall is still chaotic, but there is an orderliness to it that feels more controlled. Riley relaxes a hair. A table has been set up, manned by a young woman in uniform. It contains a clipboard, which Sutcliffe promptly signs and times; boxes of gloves and booties, from which he takes two pairs each, handing one set to Riley. Once they're sanitized for their protection and have successfully passed the checkpoint, he points down the hall.

"Who's in charge of evidence?"

"Debries," the cop says. "He's set up in a room down the hall from the crime scene."

"Thanks." And to Riley: "Let's get your things. Head that way."

He trails her down the hallway. People look up, eyes shuffling over her with mild curiosity before landing on Sutcliffe, and let them pass.

There's a uniformed officer standing guard in front of the room next to Riley's—they're connecting, she remembers, wondering if they've opened the doors between them. Sutcliffe badges him and demands to be let in. The cop hesitates.

"We need her phone. It's most likely been taken into evidence. Ms. Carrington's computer bag would have been in the suite. Her phone is in it."

Another cop approaches. He's built like a squirrel, long and twitchy. The silver nameplate over his pocket says *H. Debries*. She wonders what the *H* stands for. Harry? Hercules? Hermit?

"What news, Horatio?"

No.

"That never gets old, Sutcliffe. What's happening?"

"Ms. Carrington's bag should be in evidence. It looks like—" He breaks off and gestures to Riley.

"Brown leather tote. Laptop, three Clairefontaine notebooks, a package of pens, my cell phone, chargers, batteries—"

"Yeah, yeah, I get it. Hold on."

He swipes the key card, and the door opens. The room is full of brown paper bags, neatly stacked and labeled. "I bagged and tagged it, left it over here . . ."

He stops, looks around. Grabs a notebook off the table. As he flips the pages, she realizes it's an inventory of all the bags in the room. "Weird. It's labeled number twenty-one, and it was right here."

He points at a space on the bed, flustered. Bag 20, and bag 22. No 21. Which is strange, admittedly, as clearly the man is a paragon of efficiency.

"I'm sure it's here somewhere," Sutcliffe says, and they start looking, two old bloodhounds on a foxhunt. Five minutes later, the room has been thoroughly searched, and they've come up empty. The evidence bag with Riley's things inside is gone.

"It has to be someone who had access to this room," Sutcliffe says between gritted teeth.

Debries shakes his head. "I've had someone stationed at the door the whole time."

"Did you check the adjoining door?" Riley asks.

Debries levels a glare her way that would make someone younger—or guiltier—quail. "Of course. We made sure the door was locked." To prove his point, he strides to the door in question and yanks the knob. The door opens. The connecting door to Riley's room stands accusingly ajar.

"Um."

With a muffled curse, Sutcliffe scrambles through. Riley tries to follow, but Debries jostles her out of the way to get through first.

Riley's room looks just how she left it—the bed is a mess from her tossing and turning, the chair is pulled away from the desk, it smells of overripe bananas. The only difference is the key card, on the carpet, in the middle of the floor in the small foyer to the hall door. It doesn't take a genius to realize what happened. Someone opened the door, went into the evidence room, took her bag—just hers—and bolted.

"Ah, hell," Debries says. "I gotta find out what's going on. Don't leave." He barrels back into the evidence room.

Sutcliffe glances at Riley sharply. He's been keeping up. "Who knew you were doing the profile on the deceased?"

"For God's sake, she has a name. Columbia. It wasn't a secret. Her team, her family, my team, my . . . boyfriend. All the people we've met on tour."

"Social media? Have you been sharing your progress with your followers?"

"Not really. I'm superstitious like that. You never know when a story might fall apart or get bumped. I don't usually mention it until it's in print or online."

Sutcliffe crosses his formidable arms. "Then who would know where you were staying, that you were on tour with Columbia Jones, and come to steal your work?"

"Gotta be an inside job, pal," she says, trying to keep 1940s mob moll out of her expression. She fails, because he narrows his eyes and shakes his head.

"This isn't a joke, Miss Carrington. The subject of your exposé is dead, and you've been accused of taking her life. You might think about taking this seriously."

Riley has had just about enough lecturing from the detective. "I *am* taking it seriously. That's a two-thousand-dollar laptop, and my life is on it. Not to mention the bag has my phone, my wallet, my passport . . . How am I supposed to go home without an ID? I'm screwed, and we both know it. But you really should drop me as a suspect. I didn't kill her. Obviously. I couldn't have stolen my own bag out of evidence. Is someone trying to frame me?"

"We shall see."

Her mind is churning furiously. What can they access? Can they get into her computer? It's password protected, so it won't be easy. Her phone has Face ID, and a passcode, so that's relatively secure. She's diligent about passwords and two-factor authentications, plus the company does security training with the staff monthly to hammer home how fragile their bubbles of security online really are. As a result, like the rest of her generation, she stores things in the cloud.

Shit. Her watch. That doesn't have a passcode because it's always on her wrist. But this morning it was in her bag in anticipation of several hours with Columbia, the only time she takes it off outside a quick charge, because she likes to be as focused on her subjects as possible when she's interviewing them.

From her watch, a stranger can get to pretty much everything.

"What is it?" Sutcliffe asks.

"My watch isn't passcode protected. And it was in the bag."

"Okay. Tell me you're one of the smart ones who has your stuff hooked into the parent company's ecosystem?"

"I do."

"Excellent." He actually rubs his hands together. "There's a store nearby. Let's go have them access your account, and we'll see where your things are."

CHAPTER TWELVE

The drive to the store is brief, as promised. The downtown Denver streets are teeming; it's lunchtime, and the office drones and construction workers and homeless mingle with the tourists and mountain bikers: some wandering, some moving with purpose. In this way, it feels a bit like New York, but the sky is so very different here. Even surrounded by the tall buildings, glimpses of blue skies and snowcapped peaks appear every few steps, making sure you know you're in the West. It's easy to imagine what the place would look like without the many buildings; in New York, that's impossible. The infrastructure is the setting there; here, the setting is built to enhance the natural infrastructure.

Riley stays silent beside Detective Sutcliffe, mind spinning. Someone stealing her bag means only one thing. She has captured something significant that could lead to a resolution of how, why, Columbia Jones is lying dead in a pool of her own blood. Right? What else could it mean?

Sutcliffe holds the large glass door for her, and inside they are quickly intercepted by an associate in a powder blue shirt—it matches the sky, and the detective's eyes. Colorado is big on blue.

"Welcome in. I'm Harris. How can we help you today?"

Sutcliffe has his badge out, and Harris's eyes go round. "We need to track a stolen device."

"Of course. Um, do you have a warrant?"

"It's my device," Riley adds. "Or, I should say, devices. My laptop, watch, and phone. Someone took my bag. The detective is helping me find it."

Sutcliffe shoots Riley a raised brow, but Harris huffs out a relieved sigh. "Oh, man, that's a bummer. Let's see what we can do. What's the email address on the account?"

It takes less than three minutes to narrow down the location of Riley's phone. It's near the Brown Palace Hotel, not moving. Riley is overcome with relief. Sutcliffe calls Debries and tells him to send an officer to check the alley behind the hotel, the dumpsters, everything in the small area that the target has zeroed in on.

"Can you check the cloud for a video?" Sutcliffe asks.

"Sure. If the phone backed up after the video was taken, it will be in there."

"It should," Riley says. "I watched it last night, there should have been plenty of time for it to feed through the system."

She's already logged in to her account, surfs over to the Photos app. Sutcliffe watches over her shoulder and she wants to tell him to look away, not because of the video, but there are other photos on her phone, photos she would prefer no one see. But to say so would indicate she has something to hide, so she hopes for the best.

There is nothing uploaded from overnight. No video. But no photos, either. "That's strange."

Sutcliffe looks dubious.

"I was on a VPN and didn't have the hotel Wi-Fi activated," Riley says. "It's not entirely secure, even with the VPN."

Harris, somehow sensing she needs saving, chimes in. "If the file was big, or if your phone is set to only upload on Wi-Fi, it's probably still local. But you haven't been uploading to the cloud for at least a month. Must have that setting unsynced."

Riley shoots the woman a smile and shrugs. "Guess we need the phone itself, Detective."

"Guess so."

"You know you've got some pretty nasty viruses lurking in this system, don't you? You need to be careful what you download. I've cleaned it up for you. But that might explain why you're not uploading."

"That's unbelievably kind, thank you. And a good point. I've been on the road for a month and hooked into a bunch of different Wi-Fi. Who knows what I've picked up."

"I'd switch VPN providers, if it were me. That one you're using is a magnet for hacks."

They thank young Harris and hurry back toward downtown.

"It's a huge relief that we found my bag," Riley offers. Sutcliffe is still weirdly quiet, and it's making her nervous.

"Yeah."

"I'm sure the video just hasn't uploaded."

"Probably."

"You know, Columbia will be very missed. She was amazing."

"I'm gathering that."

Man. He is like a boulder. "Do you have a lot of murders here? In Denver, I mean."

"More than usual since the pandemic. We're working on it."

"Most large cities are having the same issue," she offers, sympathetically. "New York has seen a big uptick in violent crime in the past few years. I live and work in a pretty safe area, but even there we've had a serious increase in assaults and burglaries. It's just part of the landscape of a modern city."

No response.

She's a reporter, she can't help asking a few more questions, chattering nervously. Sutcliffe won't engage, so she finally falls silent and takes comfort from the fact that she was the one peppering him with inquiries and banalities, rather than the other way around. She admires the blue outline of the mountains until they slide behind the downtown skyscrapers.

When they arrive at the hotel, Debries is standing in the lobby, holding Riley's bag. She sighs in relief when she sees it.

"It was dumped behind the kitchen entrance," he says. "Under some cardboard. You're damn lucky none of the homeless ended up with it. Want to look through and see what, if anything, is missing? Try not to touch the items, we need to print them."

Sutcliffe gives her a pair of purple nitrile gloves. "Put these on."

She tries not to be grabby, puts out her hand as if she doesn't have a care in the world. The leather strap is so worn it almost folds in her hand. She judges the weight. It all *feels* right . . . She takes a seat on a banquette near the door and opens the flap.

Laptop. Notebooks. Watch. Tape recorder. Tapes. Batteries. Even her phone, nestled into the side pocket where it always resides.

"Everything is here," Riley says with a huge sigh of relief. "It's like whoever took it grabbed the bag and dumped it without even opening it. Can I pull out my phone?"

"If it's all there, let us dust for prints first. I don't want to take any chances."

"Have at it," Riley says. "I'd love to know who lifted my bag."

It takes thirty minutes for their tech to print everything, and she cringes watching her pristine white-papered Clairefontaines get dust along the edges, but finally, Sutcliffe says, "Okay. Run them. And let's open the phone and see this video."

He's hovering now, anxious, and Riley is happy to acquiesce. She really wants to get out of here. These cops, this situation, are making her nervous.

She's never been more thankful for the Face ID; she doesn't have to touch the screen to unlock it. The gloves make it cumbersome, but she manages to get her photo app open. She touches the video folder.

"Damn it," she murmurs, looking up at Sutcliffe. "The video is gone."

"I'm shocked," Sutcliffe says. He's already dismissing her as a decent lead. He doesn't believe her about the video, she can tell. But he has nothing to hold her with.

"Hey. That's not fair. I did take the video. Someone had my bag, and someone must have deleted it. Whose prints are on all of this?"

"Yours," the tech says. "They're all you. The phone screen is smeary, so I can't get anything decent, but I have a big thumbprint on the back, and it matches you."

"That doesn't mean someone didn't erase the video using gloves."

"You also might not have hit the record button," the tech inserts helpfully, though Sutcliffe shoots him a nasty look. "Sorry," the kid mutters, and packages up his kit.

"This proves nothing, and you know it." Riley huffs out a breath. This is frustrating and scary, and she's exhausted suddenly. "Listen. I know what I saw. But apparently I can't prove it. So I guess that means unless you're going to charge me and hold me, I can go home?" She can't help the hopeful pleading in her tone. She wants to get out of here. Get back to New York. Re-create what she can, get the story together, get it put to bed. Her subject dying will make it even more enticing to read, and Riley needs to find a way to make it as tasty a treat as she can. The police will sort out the evidence and figure out how Columbia died. Riley has her own job to do.

Sutcliffe nods once, curt. "Get your suitcase and get out of here. But be available. I will have more questions."

She is more than happy to comply.

SUNDAY

CHAPTER THIRTEEN
DARIAN

They say there is no such thing as bad press.

Whether that's true or not, whether it was P. T. Barnum or Oscar Wilde who said it first, and the world of media glommed on and used it for good or ill, Darian thinks no one could have possibly envisioned the modern landscape of the internet and how quickly a spark of conspiracy can morph into a full-blown forest fire.

Darian doesn't have her own social accounts, but she monitors her mother's, and they have turned into a free-for-all. She's already muted the comments on all the platforms because her phone overheated from the string of constant notifications. It's utterly astounding how quickly the news of Columbia's death has spread. One tweet from Darian and her mother's gone viral, like a particularly virulent flu bug.

Her laptop is open on the table, and the coffee stain disappeared when the housekeeper made up the room. She sits there now, looking at the open tabs one by one. Indulging her deep anger by reading some of the visceral reactions her mother's death has caused. The majority have been consoling and kind, but there are plenty of horrific comments to wind her up. As she scrolls, the nasty comments just keep on coming, a tsunami of cruelty. How can someone be loved and so reviled at the same time? Has Darian just missed the negativity because she's been too busy with the reality? It tarnishes something as incredible and meaningful as *Ivory Lady*. She can only take comfort from the fact that the positive far outweighs the negative. Hurrah for the incorruptible book lovers out there. She took a peek at the numbers, and her mother's death has caused a massive spike in sales. More than any book she's published before.

Darian knows how many units of each title sell because Darian is the one who manages the royalty statements. She manages the bank accounts. She manages everything. As the only child, the sole beneficiary, the trust was set up specifically for her control. And as the literary executor, too, she will have her hands full getting everything through probate and aligned again. Even without new material, the publishers will find a thousand ways to exploit what rights they still have, and the management of the licensing rights with the movie, the tie-in, and the next book that's already in the can—her prolific mother has of course already turned in her follow-up. There will be backlist repackaging and movie tie-ins, long-held options executed. Columbia Jones might be dead, but she is going to live on in the hearts and minds of the people she left behind.

She deserved to die. You know it.

Darian sighs, a deep, shuddery breath. Disgusted by the outpouring of hate, she slaps down the top of her laptop and walks the suite, alternately staring at the mountains, the sun drifting down, turning the sky magenta, and taking in the vast emptiness of the room around her. She has to check out in the morning and go home. She has to leave her mother behind. The thought makes her sick.

Worse, there will be a funeral. And then a memorial service for the masses. Her mother's wishes are spelled out in the will—cremation, being scattered in the ocean—but she didn't plan her funeral. Said that would be morbid, picking out music, photos, a venue. Like a wedding in reverse. Then she wrote a short story about it, a wicked satire of a preplanned funeral. They had a laugh, the two of them. Not realizing that only a year later, Darian would be faced with making the very decisions they giggled about. It doesn't seem funny now, not in the least. She wishes she knew what her mother wanted. That there was someone she could ask.

Oh, God. She's forgotten entirely to call her grandmother.

They always call her nana together; Darian doesn't even have the number in her phone. She is so unprepared for this. Columbia wasn't supposed to go now. It's too soon.

Darian hasn't seen her grandmother in person in years. She lives in Bromley, England, thirteen short miles from London, but Columbia always refused to go back there to visit. She would never tell Darian why, only said it brought up bad memories. Once, when she was little, Nana came to New York. They walked around Central Park, and when Darian wanted to stop and feed the pigeons, Nana gave her a disapproving glare and said "No, they're filthy rats" with such vehemence Darian shied away from the birds forever.

Darian will never forget the sneer. Then, it scared her, so she was thrilled not meeting in person again. As she grew older, she longed for the familial connections, though she didn't act upon it. Columbia was totally fine with little to no contact with her past. She didn't seem to care what that did to Darian. Darian had Columbia. The moon and the sun and the stars in the sky. What more could she possibly need?

The police have Columbia's phone, so she sends a text to the detective.

> I need some contact information from my mother's phone. The entry will be under Yvonne Maxwell-Dodd.

She doesn't have a grandfather on her mom's side; he passed when she was tiny. Her father's parents died soon after he did. She's been alone with her mom since pretty much the beginning, and now it's just Darian and a woman called Nana who Darian doesn't know outside of her hatred of pigeons and the few calls they've had over the years.

Which means she's pretty much alone in the world.

That is unutterably sad, but she's not going to dwell on it.

Her phone dings with a contact card.

Should she call? FaceTime?

Better to call; she can't promise to govern her face, which she can feel is a puffy, blotchy mess.

She replies to the cop with a folded-hands prayer emoji, opens the contact card, and taps on the number.

A few clicks, then that odd two-tone ring. It used to excite her so. It was like they were calling another planet. Columbia always made such a huge deal out of calls to Nana. A production. They only did it now on Darian's birthday. Which is sad, but they are always so busy, and it's not like Nana is calling them every Sunday . . .

A smoky, snarly voice answers. "Whaddaya want?"

"Nana? It's Darian."

"Who?"

"Darian. Darian Jones. Your granddaughter?" she adds, frowning.

She can hear distant murmuring, then silence, as if someone has put their hand over the phone. A moment later, her nana gets on the phone. She must have guests over, and someone picked up her phone by mistake.

"Darian! Hullo. How are you?"

"I'm fine. Who was that, Nana?"

"Who was whom?"

"The person who answered?"

"Oh, that's no one. Why are you calling, precious? Didn't recognize the number." And to the murmuring in the background, "Shhh!"

It grows quiet, then Darian hears sounds she recognizes, a door closing, the chirping of birds, and the idyllic English country garden that has always been the backdrop for their calls comes to the fore. Darian's shoulders drop a notch.

"I'm so sorry to have to be the one to tell you this, Nana. But Mom—" She chokes on a sob, swallows it down, hard. "Mom died this morning. We're not sure exactly what happened. The police are investigating. We're on tour, in Denver."

Silence.

She can hear nothing but the birds chirping, and the heavy breath of a woman starting to grieve.

Finally, her grandmother speaks. "And the will. Do you know when it will be read?"

"The . . . will?"

"Yes. Your mother's will. When will it be read?"

Darian is filled with horror and rage. "I'm telling you your daughter died, and you want to know when you're going to get your cut? What is wrong with you?"

A short, guttural laugh, and the uncultured voice that answered comes back.

"Darian, you're a fool."

"Okay, this isn't funny. Put my nana on the phone, right now."

"If Columbia Jones is dead, I am no longer your nana," the stranger's voice says. "And I expect my promised share, so don't even try to screw me out of it, do you understand?"

"What are you talking about? Who the hell are you? I want my nana."

A wail is starting, the river of grief flowing through her bubbling to the surface, a geyser about to erupt from every pore.

"Like I said, if Columbia is dead, then so is your nana. Be sure I get that check." And she clicks off.

Darian is so surprised the tears don't come. She stares at her phone, then dials the number again. Surely she just connected with the wrong person. Surely this is all a huge misunderstanding.

The two-toned ring, then the snarly voice is back. "Don't call me again unless you've got the check in hand."

Click.

That's it. This day is unbelievable.

Darian collapses onto the floor, weeping.

CHAPTER FOURTEEN
RILEY

Riley buys a ticket on the red-eye and pays the exorbitant nonadvance fees to fly herself home—in the chaos after Columbia's death, the team hadn't really been concerned with her travel. It's a miracle the credit card went through on the fare, which was nearly the same amount as her first—and only—car. Riley is a New Yorker now, and who needs a private vehicle in the city, anyway? Most everyone manages on the subway, with walking, rideshares, and the occasional car service. She is more than happy to join them.

She boards the red-eye gratefully, half expecting Detective Sutcliffe to pop up in line next to her with that stupid smirk—"Just a few more questions, if you don't mind." But he doesn't, and she shuffles aboard, takes a window seat near the front of the plane, slips in her earbuds, and stares out the glass to the tarmac lights.

It is not until the plane guns it down the runway and flings itself improbably into the night sky that Riley is able to take an unimpeded breath. She will be home in four hours. She will lie in Oliver's arms and listen to his heart thump reassuringly under her ear, and tomorrow, she will tackle the revision of the Columbia story.

She hasn't allowed herself the grief, and now, looking out the window at the disappearing ground, it hits her, hard.

She liked Columbia Jones. Quite a lot. She was fun. Funny. Dedicated. Intense at times, for sure. But silly and gracious and so devoted to her fans and her work. Her legacy. That was something Columbia had said at least eight times over the course of this tour. She'd been *destined* to be a storyteller, had seized the opportunity when it presented itself, and never looked back. The legacy she was leaving behind was the realization of her destiny.

For a girl who grew up poor on the outskirts of London, Columbia really made something of herself. Everyone loves a rags-to-riches tale, especially if the subject is a woman.

The altitude indicator dings, and the flight attendants relay their sanctified permission for the captive rats inside this particular tube to pull out their full-size electronic devices. There is a general shuffling through the cabin, and Riley joins in, saying another tiny prayer of thanks that her bag is intact. So freaking weird that it was taken and dumped, and that the video from last night was erased. Who did it? The only one who might have known there was footage was Darian herself. Her vehement insistence that Riley was somehow responsible for Columbia's death—was she possibly trying to deflect attention away from her own involvement?

She has a banana and five M&M's—she forgot to buy another bag and she needs it to last four hours—no way is she eating anything else with this long flight ahead. She's a little lightheaded from lack of sleep and food, too much caffeine, and a hefty dose of worry, but it's only a few hours. Laptop open, she takes out her notebook and pulls on the ribbon bookmark, which flips her to the last page of her notes. The interview that never was. Maybe that's the lede for the story? Not like she'll have any control over the headline—that's above her pay grade—but it's a thought.

Unfamiliar handwriting stands out on the page, a dark hasty scrawl.

Your devices are compromised. Call me on a burner, and make sure you're alone. I need to keep you safe.
896-555-0988.

Adrenaline shoots through her, her heart thudding so hard she's sure her seatmates can hear it. She has to close her eyes and focus on her breathing so she doesn't have a full-blown panic attack.

When she feels more in control, she flips the remaining pages of the notebook but sees nothing else unusual.

She pulls in a breath and casually stretches, looking behind her, around the cabin. No one is obviously watching her; everyone aboard seems glued to their screens and books. Air travel has become so ubiquitous no one seems to marvel at it anymore. No one looks out the windows but children, and even for them, it's just more time to plug in to the matrix.

She looks at the words again. If there was any question that Columbia has been murdered, there is none anymore.

Her first instinct is to look up the number, but if this stranger is right, then that would undo the first commandment of this note. Whoever wrote it was clearly at the hotel, and logically was the person who stole her bag. To leave her this note? Probably. And to delete the video from her phone, too.

Why, though? What was it about that video—the argument between Columbia and Darian—that was so important?

The details of it are already fading; Riley lazily relied on the video to give her the details in regular replays. She hadn't done a transcription. Sloppy, sloppy, sloppy.

They were arguing about someone from Columbia's past. A past that Riley, too, has been trying to crack, to shine a light in its corners.

Shaking off the creepy, awful feeling of violation, she looks at the note again. *I need to keep you safe* sounds very personal and is possibly the most insidious part of the whole thing. Keep her safe from what? From whom? Whoever killed Columbia Jones?

"Shit," she says aloud, causing the woman in the center seat to glare at her. "Sorry."

She tilts the edge of the laptop and angles herself away from the woman, who is now paying too much attention to her.

Riley is not a true crime aficionado; she is too easily spooked by the horrors of reality. But there is one thing she knows every crime has in common.

Motive.

So who had motive for killing Columbia? And why in the world would Riley be a target? Is Darian in danger, too? She should call the detective as soon as she lands. Tell him someone's reached out. That he needs to take this seriously, that there's no way Columbia's death is anything but a murder.

And then?

Find out the rest of the things you don't know about her, Riley. Dig into this woman's past and examine every last inch of her world. You already know something's not right about her. You can do this. She's private for a reason. Find the why, you'll find the truth.

Just don't get yourself killed along the way.

Columbia has a single bio online that she's been using for years, just updating a few key details when a new book comes out.

With over two hundred million copies of her books sold, Columbia Jones was born and raised near London and wrote her first novel when she was sixteen. After a move to New York City when she was twenty-two, Columbia sold that novel to Doubleday and has written multiple subsequent worldwide bestsellers since. Ivory Lady (coming in April) tells the story of a woman destined for greatness who is waylaid by war and fate and is her most autobiographical novel to date. The feature film of the same name is being filmed now.

That's it. That is all she has been working with. The interviews she'd done with Columbia rarely filled in the random little details. She wasn't like Riley's other subjects, who sprinkle the conversation with anecdotes and humblebrags. Eschewing memories—stories about her schooling, her childhood friends, her parents—Columbia always preferred instead to talk about the various books she'd written over the years. How the stories came to her, how she built the fragments of people into beloved characters, her few indulgences—art, mostly. Her writing process, how much she enjoys the annual interaction with her fans on tour. Riley realizes now that every time she got more than superficially personal, favorite foods and notebooks and pen and vacation spots, silly things like that, Columbia gently steered her back to the books. She loved her characters as much as her fans and is—was—wildly animated when discussing some of her favorites. But talking about herself? Not so much. Just the basics, really.

Was she hiding something? Or were those early days just a time no one would be interested in, simply a young Columbia with notebook and pencil, absorbing the world around her and distilling it onto the page in clumsy, awkward prose, working at becoming the writer she dreamed of being? She'd grown up on a council estate, an only child with parents who by all accounts supported her dreams but didn't have the means to get her there. If that were Riley's upbringing, she might gloss over the finer details, too.

Riley has a long list of items that both she and the magazine's copy department need to fact-check, and she pulls this out now. Might as well start at the beginning. Nate is going to want a detailed report on where she stands. This piece has just turned into a ticking time bomb. It will make or break her career, there's no question about it. To have been present at the scene where Columbia died gives her an angle no one has ever had. To be temporarily arrested for her murder? God, he won't pull her off and give it to someone else . . . No. Surely he won't. Then again, when she shows him the note in her notebook—because she will be damned if she plays the go-it-alone route here; a woman has died, and Riley doesn't want to join her—he might decide things have gotten too dicey. Nate is overprotective of his journalists; it's what makes him both a great and infuriating boss.

Focus, Riley. Stop borrowing trouble.

She's taken pages upon pages of notes, talked to fifty different people, read every book, every article, every mention of Columbia Jones since her career began. She's transcribed the interviews she's done with Columbia during the tour. She was set to wrap this up, just wanted to ask a few more questions about her childhood in England. She hasn't been able to nail down anyone from Bromley yet. And she's been waiting until the end to ask about the cryptic dedication of *Ivory Lady* again. Columbia had refused to answer when asked throughout the tour, saying dedications were always only for the author and the dedicatee. With the tour finished, Riley was certain she could get the true answer.

For JC. It's all because of you.

Who was JC? Jesus Christ? Juicy Couture? No, it's someone in Columbia's life, and Riley has no one in her notes with the initials *JC.* One more thread to pull.

Riley spends the rest of the flight pulling together a list of items to show Nate, see what he thinks is important, worth exploring, and what she can jettison for now so they can be first to press with this bombshell postmortem interview.

MONDAY

CHAPTER FIFTEEN
DETECTIVE SUTCLIFFE

No one enjoys an autopsy, but Sutcliffe particularly despises them. It is enough a part of the job that he is desensitized to the horrors of it, though he still isn't a fan. But he is far too curious about the death of Columbia Jones not to attend.

An unexplained death that certainly feels like a murder is one thing. Add in that it was a celebrity; that naturally ramped it up for him. A frantic daughter accuses the reporter shadowing her mother: interesting. And though he wasn't up on the board to catch the next case, the manager of the Brown Palace Hotel asked for the most senior detective, so despite his full deck and being out of the rotation, his LT called him in from a day off to deal with the request.

And he's grateful. Because now he's in it. He couldn't hand it off if he wanted to.

There is the usual traffic congestion on I-25—road construction by the Tech Center, as always—so he times it rather awfully, or rather well, depending on the perspective, and walks in just as the lead medical examiner, Dr. Vanessa Duran, is finishing up.

"I think it's safe to say she OD'd," Duran says when she sees him in the doorway. "Well, don't just stand there. Come in."

"Good morning to you, too."

Columbia Jones looks smaller than he remembers, especially with the skin of her face peeled down and her cranium cracked open with the skull key to expose her brain. At least he's missed the head saw. He averts his eyes from the massive Y incision still splitting her open, thinking about his promise to Darian Jones. He hadn't lied; Duran is the best. But this process, no matter how gently performed, isn't exactly noninvasive.

The place is bustling with technicians and more bodies in various stages of interpretation. An orchestra playing a danse macabre, a ballet of precision and timing: that's what the autopsy suite always reminds him of. Duran labels a sample and sets it on the tray, then almost lovingly replaces the skull, and the skin rolls back into place. Columbia Jones's face appears, and Sutcliffe can't decide which was worse, being able to readily identify her, or looking into the cavity that previously housed her genius. He decides on the former. At least when the brain examination is happening, every body becomes anonymous.

"Overdose, huh? On what?"

She nudges her glasses up onto her forehead with the back of her hand. "That's the ten-thousand-dollar question. The full tox screen will take at least four weeks."

"All right. Without external trauma, and assuming this is some sort of OD . . . we have the exciting question, Did she take her own life, or did she OD on accident?"

"Well, that's the fun part. I did find some external trauma. Because of the lividity, it wasn't readily apparent on the first exam at the scene, but once we got her cleaned up . . ."

She gestures to her tech, who helps her roll Columbia's body onto its side.

"We have a wound, five inches deep, between the fourth and fifth ribs. Punctured her lung, which helped with the froth, and nicked the aorta. Much easier to see the damage when I got her open. I think it's an injection site."

"So she was stabbed in the back? *And* ingested something."

"Well, a needle in the back, but yes. And whatever she either ingested or was injected with, I can't help but feel like this is going to show up as poison."

He knew it. She *was* murdered. "Now you have my undivided attention. What sort of poison?"

Duran uses her left biceps to push back a piece of hair that's fallen in her face, sparing herself from changing out her gloves. "There aren't a lot of things that someone would take willingly—for fun or to alleviate an issue—that causes this kind of foam cone. Do you remember a few months back when we had that rash of deaths from spiked delta-8?"

"The synthetic pot? Yeah. Rat poison, right? No bueno."

"It was laced with brodifacoum, to be exact. This looks similar enough that I asked for a special rapid test on a separate blood sample from the regular extended tox screen. I'll know in a few days. Called in a favor. Another jurisdiction in Alabama is having a spike in tainted Spice, so the labs are on high alert."

"You're magnificent."

She sketches a curtsy, scalpel in her right hand like a conductor in front of a particularly gruesome orchestra.

"So which killed her? The ingestion or the injection?"

"Undetermined at this time. And I don't like using gut instinct to prove a theory, but since she's so high profile, I figure you're going to be in the hot seat until there's an unassailable answer. We're testing all the bottles of drugs found in the suite, too. Nothing exciting, just melatonin, CBD, ibuprofen. You know, it's always easier to declare an OD if there's an open bottle of pills on the night table and an empty glass nearby. Whoever did this wanted to be sure she was dead."

"Okay. Okay. Since no one at the scene is aware of the injection wound, let's hold that back, don't announce it. Cool? I need to find the damn thing, too, there were no needles at the scene. She wasn't diabetic or anything."

"I'm happy to hold it back. Just for clarity, this would have been the kind of needle that they do joint injections with. Big long fuckers. For a moment I wondered if an EMT accidentally stabbed her during the emergency call, which is entirely possible, but I think this was intentional. As far as the drugs, I can't promise answers quickly, but I'm working on it. Crime scene pulled some alien DNA off the vic's body, too, a hair. Short, dark, could be from anyone, but we're running it."

"She was wearing a black wig."

"No, this had a tag attached. It was a real hair from a live follicle."

"She was at the hospital that night, and all the EMTs . . . We have to run everyone. Let's see if it matches anyone in the system first, then I will go person by person and collect samples to rule out the staff."

"Sounds good. I got four more this morning, so if you don't need anything else?"

"No, that will do for now. I'll see you later," he says, and turns to go.

"Sutcliffe?"

"Yeah?"

Her lovely face is arranged in a calm but concerned visage. "Be careful. I have a bad feeling about this."

He frowns. "Yeah. Me too."

CHAPTER SIXTEEN
RILEY

Despite the dawn arrival, Oliver meets Riley at the airport. They haven't done that . . . well . . . ever, if she stops to think about it. She can't help but think of the old joke about couples and airports, memorialized on the screen when Harry explains to Sally the stages of a relationship based on the airport trips. It's real: taking someone to the airport in New York is a freaking pain in the ass. But Riley guesses her reports of the drama in Denver were enough to get him into an Uber and out to LaGuardia. Riley would normally be touched by this romantic gesture, but Oliver looks worried, waiting on the other side of security with a frown on his face. He takes her carry-on automatically when she reaches him. Ever gallant, her knight. He starts walking, barely looking at her.

"My dad talked to Joe Heavenly in the criminal division, and he's on board. If they try to charge you, he's ready to mount a defense."

"Hello to you, too."

He stops, gives her a chaste, quick kiss, and says, "Sorry. Hi." He looks her up and down. "You're so skinny. Did you eat anything while you were gone?"

She glances at her legs. She has lost weight, but the way he says it, like it's something bad . . . "It's been a month of M&M's, the tour food was difficult. And I won't need a lawyer, but thank you."

"You don't know that, Riley. You don't know what they're going to uncover. These things can go sideways in a heartbeat, especially if someone else doesn't turn up as a viable suspect. The police will circle back to you."

They've reached the street and started the hike up the road to the checkpoint where they allow the rideshares to pick up before he says anything else.

They stop, and she sighs, heavily. She can't help it. She was excited to see him; this hasn't started on the right foot. It all feels wrong.

"You okay?" he asks softly, as if finally realizing she might actually be a little torn up about all this. She can't help it; she rubs the spot where the ghost of the handcuffs lingers on her wrist.

"I'm okay."

"Have you ever been arrested before?"

"No! I mean, yes, but that was beach week right after graduation, and they just rounded us all up and gave us a lecture for having open beer on the beach. That doesn't count, it's not like it's on my permanent record or anything."

Her attempt at a joke falls flat. Damn. He really is worried.

"Seriously, Ollie. They wouldn't have let me fly home if they thought I killed her."

A tourist with a suitcase bigger than she is stops, head turning, mouth open in shock. Riley gives her a simpering smile and keeps going. A light rain begins to patter down, and Oliver, ever prepared, hands her an umbrella he's stashed in his jeans pocket. She attaches herself to his side. It's not big enough for them both, shelters only one-half of him. He doesn't even notice. Something is bothering him. Something major.

"Listen," she starts, but he shakes his head.

"Not here."

"Okay, now you're freaking me out. What is wrong? Are you dumping me because I got briefly arrested for murder?"

He's silent for a moment, and her heart starts to pound merci-lessly, shaking her chest enough she puts a hand to her breast to quell the movement. The adrenaline pours through her, and she drops the umbrella, not caring that rain soaks her almost immediately. She's been worried about this, that he's been seeing someone behind her back. There have been some missed check-ins, some rushed and banal catch-ups. Their conversations in the beginning were filled with sultry innu-endo; in the end, it was all logistics. She's only been gone a month, but it feels like a lifetime. It feels like she's lost him.

"Oliver? What the hell?"

He looks down at her, quickly getting drenched, and pushes the umbrella back up so their heads are within its shelter. "Don't be daft, Riley. I'm not dumping you. But I have a conflict of interest here. I think it's best for me to move out of the flat for a few weeks, and we won't be able to talk until all this is resolved."

The "flat." Oliver did an overseas semester at the University of Reading and came home a total Anglophile. He says *whilst* and drinks tea and is addicted to the *Guardian* and the BBC, is obsessed with anything to do with the royal family. It's normally adorable, something she teases him about, but at the moment, the affectation makes her want to scream. It reminds her of Columbia, her crisp words, as if she's just come from tea with the King, of the sea of white and red, of the questions, of the note.

Call me.

Their Uber arrives, a new Tesla, and after providing the appropriate PIN to the driver, they climb in the back. The driver looks at them drip-ping all over his lovely back seat and sighs. Riley assumes there's been worse. He pulls from the curb, and she twists in the seat to face Oliver.

"What's the conflict of interest?"

"What do you think?" He pushes the vintage Oliver Peoples horn-rims that he found in a shop on Shaftesbury Avenue (of course he did) up his nose and raises a brow expectantly.

Oliver is an estate lawyer, so this piece of relationship shorthand only takes her a second to interpret. Riley's voice rises in incredulity by the last word.

"You represent her *estate*? Why didn't you tell me?"

"At home, Riley," he says with a finality that shuts her up. For a nice guy, Oliver can be forceful when needed. It's actually sort of a turn-on.

They spend the rest of the ride in silence. Her brain is going a thousand miles an hour anyway. And she's not proud of what it's thinking.

How does she get Oliver to show her Columbia Jones's will?

Because then maybe she can figure out what's going on.

Their "flat" is a cool industrial with remarkably large rooms, tall black-framed windows, hardwood floors, vaulted ceilings, exposed brick, two bathrooms, and a rooftop deck. It is also spotless. And belongs to Oliver's dad. Actually, it belongs to the umbrella company that holds all the assets the Mathers family has accumulated over the years. Oliver is ridiculously generationally wealthy. Riley, on the other hand, is ridiculously in debt, still, from her college loans and other family issues she's been faced with over the years. She refuses to let him pay her bills, and it drives him mad. He thinks she shouldn't be stressing to make the minimums; she thinks taking his money would be admitting defeat and would ruin her self-image as an up-and-coming hardscrabble reporter.

Riley is a lot like Columbia that way. She, too, came up hard and found her vocation young. Hers made her money in her sleep, though, while Riley's is barely enough to cover the bills. Getting paid by the word is freeing in many ways but also means you're on a constant loop of submission and rejection. This gig—covering Columbia Jones on tour, at her request—is more money than Riley has seen at once in her whole career. Hell, her whole life.

Will I still get paid? her venal brain wonders. *Now that she's dead? Will the estate hold up the bargain?*

Oliver would laugh and tell her not to worry. Of course, he could burn hundreds and not make a dent. The world is a weird place.

Thinking about Columbia's tour takes Riley right back to the hotel room again, to that still blue-gray body juxtaposed against the snowy white sheets and the crimson puddle of blood. So much blood. Why is she obsessing about this? She must make a little noise, because Oliver takes her hand.

"It's going to be all right. We'll figure it out."

"I don't understand why you have to leave the flat. I mean, yes, I'm doing a piece on her and you rep the estate, but surely we can keep those separate."

"It's not that."

Then what?

He looks pained.

"It's a huge conflict of interest, Riley. I don't make the rules. Dad said—"

"Oh, '*Dad said*.' You're going to take his side over mine?"

Oliver flushes, a frown of hurt crossing his face. "Don't. Please. Just . . . hold on a second, okay?"

She starts to fight back, to snap at him again, but he hurries out of the room. She can hear him rustling around in the office, the guest bedroom they set aside for the two of them, with the facing desks, so they could work at home during the pandemic. They enjoyed the setup enough to leave it in place.

He comes back with a priority-mail envelope. He hands it to her.

"This is for you."

The envelope is thick, heavy. The prepaid label has her name and address on it. The return is Oliver's law office.

"What is this?" she asks.

"I don't know."

Riley sighs. "Oliver. I have had a shit few days. Would you please stop being so cryptic?"

"Just open it, Riley."

She stares at him for a long moment, then pulls the long tab. A manila envelope is inside, and paper-clipped to it is a note, with spiky handwriting Riley recognizes. It is Columbia's. And the note takes Riley's breath away.

In case of my death, please send this to Riley Carrington at East Fifth Magazine.

CHAPTER SEVENTEEN

Riley tries to keep her shock from showing. She sits down hard at the counter on the stool with the leg that wobbles just the slightest. It fits how off kilter she's feeling. She puts a hand on the envelope possessively. She wants to examine the contents immediately, spill everything onto the marble, but she needs to be cool here. Needs to keep some altitude. She is a reporter; she works with facts; she is about to get some sort of major scoop. She is going to be professional. She is going to keep an emotional distance from this.

"There's more," Oliver says.

"More?"

"Why I need to recuse myself for the time being. You're mentioned in the will."

"I'm *what?*" Her voice ends on a shriek, and Oliver cringes. No more playing it cool. "You tell me what's going on this instant, Oliver Mathers. You can't drop a bombshell like that on me and not show me. Or at least tell me."

"You know I can't do that." Oliver looks miserable, pushes his glasses up his nose. "Here. Their letter is in the package."

She pulls out the creamy paper, the very paper she's seen Oliver run through the printer in their office a hundred times before. Did he print this letter himself?

Dear Ms. Carrington,

This letter is to inform you that the last will and testament of Columbia Jones was recently filed for probate with the Manhattan Surrogate's Court of New York. Because of the private nature of this endeavor, there will be an in-person reading of the will on May 15, 1 p.m. ET at my office. All beneficiaries are required to attend.

If you have any questions about the will or the probate process, please do not hesitate to contact me.

With my condolences, I remain, sincerely,

Preston J. Mathers, Esq.
Preston J. Mathers, Esquire.
Senior Partner, Mathers and Mathers

She slides the letter back into the envelope.

"What is this, Ollie. What's happening? Why am *I* in Columbia Jones's will?"

"You know I can't say."

"Am I a beneficiary? She's not just giving direction for what she wants done with the article?"

"Yes."

She slides off the stool. "That makes exactly zero sense. I've known the woman for a month. Did she update the will *after* she met me?"

Oliver shakes his head. "I can't say any more, Riley. I'm sorry, I should have handled this better. I'm just tired. I've been so worried about you." He moves forward as if to embrace her, but Riley leans back. Her heart is kettledrumming, and she feels faint. She does not want to be touched or soothed. She wants answers.

"Oliver. Stop. Seriously. This is me. My life. *Our* life. You have to tell me."

"I'm sorry, Riley, I can't. Not until the will is read."

"You're serious?"

"As a heart attack."

"You're doing an actual reading of the will like we're in some sort of gothic novel? You have to assemble all the beneficiaries in a crumbling old mansion and shock the hell out of them and then they all die one by one?"

Oliver frowns. He's cute when he frowns, but right now, she's too jacked up to care.

"I'm being serious, Riley. And yes. Columbia wanted her beneficiaries gathered and a formal reading to take place. No copies of the will are to be disseminated before that, either. She was quite specific."

"But no one does that anymore. They just email the relevant parts of the will. Can't you just tell me why I'm in it?"

"No. I can't. And I don't know why there's a date on the letter, that must be a mistake. Dad said the will won't be read until after the article is released. There are stipulations built in that are unbreakable. Article first, then the reading. It's what she wanted."

"I don't understand. How would that timing be coordinated before-hand? You're making it sound like she knew she was going to die."

Did she? Did Columbia somehow plan all this?

Oliver is looking paler and more upset by the moment. "I can't speak to that. Riley, please. Don't ask me again. Go file the article. The sooner it's finished, the sooner we can have the will read. Okay?"

"Why did you even tell me?"

"Because I didn't want you to lose steam on the piece. How close are you to being done?"

"Close enough."

Close enough only counts in horseshoes and hand grenades. She has five thousand words, almost half the piece, polished and ready, but . . . she doesn't have answers. How can she publish before she knows how, why, Columbia died? And now this? Riley is in the woman's will?

"Nate won't go for it. It's too diffuse now. He's going to want to wait for the will to be read."

At the mention of Nate, Oliver closes up. He always does. His voice grows distant.

"You'll have to forgive me, Riley. I need to pack a bag."

He disappears into the bedroom, leaving her reeling.

She simply can't wrap her head around it all. Yes, when her boss had come to her and said Columbia asked for her specifically, Riley was over the moon and more than a little flattered. When she first met Columbia, they got along well. Every interaction since was fun, exciting, illuminating. Spending time with a number one internationally bestselling author was fascinating. A glimpse behind the curtain. They developed a real affinity for one another based on mutual respect. And they had weird things in common. Their food issues, for starters.

She of course wondered why Columbia chose *her* in the first place, but it wasn't a *huge* leap. Other authors' teams have requested Riley before. She is a damn good journalist, has been doing these in-depth profiles on pseudo and real celebrities for years.

Columbia hinted more than once about Riley doing her memoir/biography. A full-length work, not just the article. Compared her to Didion, for Christ's sake. Could that be why she's being summoned for the reading?

All right. That makes more sense. It's going to be specifics on how Columbia's life story is to be written, maybe even journals or digital files for her to work from.

But something feels sinister about the request. The demand to have the article first, then the will . . .

Oliver emerges with his duffel, disappears into their office, and comes out with his briefcase. He stands ten feet away, hands full, awkwardly shifting his weight from foot to foot.

"Aren't you going to read the rest?" he asks.

Riley looks at her hand, resting now viciously on the envelope, nails clawed into the paper. She is torn. For some reason, this feels private. And since Oliver is keeping secrets, why shouldn't she?

"No."

"You're mad," he says.

"Damn right, I'm mad. I hate being manipulated."

"No one's manipulating you, Riley. I'm in a bad position here and trying to do the right thing by my client."

"Instead of by the woman you share your life with? Excellent to know that your clients take precedence. Thank you for that."

"Oh, come on, that's not fair."

Riley grabs her bag, throws the envelope in it, and storms out, sweeping past him so quickly he drops the duffel. She ignores his calls of protest.

Leaving first has always been her greatest gift.

The city is gray again, loud and bereft. Their neighbor with the nervous harlequin whippet is out for a walk and waves, smiling, approaching for a chat, but Riley doesn't stop. She is on a mission.

In the coffee shop two blocks over, she sets up shop and starts sorting through her files. If Oliver is right and the will won't be read until her piece is published, she needs to get it done.

But first.

She pulls the envelope from her bag as if it is a rattlesnake about to strike. There's no going back once she looks at the rest of the contents. Of course, there's no going back anyway.

She carefully undoes the top, then decants the interior. Out spills the letter from Oliver's dad, some typed pages, a flash drive, and a yellowed newspaper clipping.

The clipping is from a newspaper called the *Crossville Chronicle*, clearly something local she'll need to look up. The date is September 3, 1995. The headline screams, in thirty-point font:

MURDER!

There is a man's photograph beneath the lede. Broad shoulders. Curly hair. He feels familiar in a way that makes Riley completely uncomfortable. Like she should know him.

She reads the short article.

> Nashville native Knox Shepherd, 28, will spend the next twenty years in the Riverbend Maximum Security Institution after being convicted of murder in the second degree in the death of Benjamin Mears. It took a Cumberland County jury just four hours to return a notice of conviction. Judge Deaver proclaimed the sentence.
>
> The trial for Shepherd's accomplice, Devon Mears (19), is slated to begin in October. Mears will be tried for both murder and perjury and faces a life sentence if convicted. Mears's lawyers have argued for a delay on compassionate grounds to allow her to give birth before the trial begins, which has thus far been denied.

She sets the clipping aside and looks at the flash drive. It's a branded one from a writers' conference that happened in 2013 in San Diego. She pulls out her laptop and the special adapter that allows her to insert a USB into a USB-C slot and clicks it open.

It whirs for a moment, then pops up a plain gray screen with a white box in the center. Password protected.

She halfheartedly tries COLUMBIA then CJONES and stops. She doesn't want it to lock on her for too many tries. Maybe the paperwork has the password.

She ejects the flash drive, puts it and the adapter in her bag with her other electronics, and turns to the stapled pages. There's a title page, with the word LEGACY in the center. She immediately realizes this is a manuscript. It's old—it's been typed, the paper is thin, the font an original that modern word processing programs try to imitate with various typefaces.

She flips to the first page and starts to read.

Legacy Draft–
Prologue

When I wake, the body is cold.

I am assailed by confusing images, jagged fragments from the night before. Screams, scents, fear, deep and corrosive. Memories? Bright copper, metallic on my tongue—my blood? His? The remnants of dinner; what was it? Lasagna, garlic toast. It rises in my throat, and I swallow convulsively.

There was a fight. I have bruises on my arms. I touch a finger to my nose and wince. It is broken, the blood dried, crusting along my lip and into the creases of my neck. I can feel my hair crackling as I move my head.

How long have I lain here, next to his body?

Long enough for it to grow cold, for the blood to dry.

What have you done? What evil hath you—

"Riley? Riley Carrington? Is that you?"

Riley jumps, looking up, clutches the pages to her chest. A woman with blonde hair twisted up in an artful chignon, a long camel coat over winter-white trousers, black sunglasses in her left hand, and a wide smile is approaching her. For a moment, she thinks it's her mother, then realizes it's worse.

"Hi, Mrs. Alexander," she says.

"Oh, we're adults now. You should call me Barbara. Imagine, bumping into you here, of all places. The city is so busy! I've been overwhelmed since I got here. We came up for a shopping date—look, over there. Julia is getting us a latte. How are you, dear? Are you visiting the city?"

Shit, Julia, too?

Riley steels herself, pastes on a smile. "What a coincidence! I'm fine, just fine. I live here now. This is my neighborhood coffee shop."

"We know, that's why we chose it! Julia's seen it on your socials, dear. Oh, how exciting! We all talk about you moving to the big city and becoming such a celebrity. I see your byline all over the place! Some folks say . . . Well, never mind, you know how small towns are, the rumor mill just churns and churns. Have you been home recently? I saw Faith the other day, coming out of the library. I waved, but I don't think she saw me. She seemed preoccupied. And no wonder."

Unasked, but implied: How is your darling sister Maisie? Poor thing. Poor mostly dead thing.

"Mom and Maisie are fine," Riley answers, mentally crossing her fingers behind her back for the lie and steeling herself against the barrage of friendly but searching chatter. "No changes. I saw them last month. I've been on the road, working on a big project."

Julia takes this moment to appear, flustered, pretty, the roundness of her teenage body morphing into the lush, healthy curves of a former cheerleader who likes her desserts and a bit of wine.

"Riley!" Julia's slightly southern drawl gets the attention of the patrons to their left, who gawk as if she is a parade float drifting through their midst. "So good to see you!"

Julia hugs Riley awkwardly, an intimacy Riley was not expecting. They were friends in high school, but only just. They ran in different crowds. Riley was always a bit too wild for Julia's cadre. To be hugged by a practical stranger makes her feel like even more of an outsider. Riley has become the city—the impersonal, the rush, the detachment. It's why this is the perfect place for her. No more small towns.

"Good to see you, Julia. You look well."

"Oh, you're sweet. I don't, I've put on a thousand pounds. Baby weight just won't budge. You look incredible, though. What's your secret?"

No babies? I don't eat? I'm a New Yorker now?

In comparison to the Riley they knew, yes, she does look different. She's taller and thinner than in school, has an expensive haircut and nicer clothes. They have no idea how she roils inside. That she can't eat half the time, and the other half is spent violently ill, cursing herself for taking the chance on the very food she needs to sustain her own life.

"We have a matinee for *Hamilton* this afternoon," Julia says brightly. "But maybe we could get a drink later?"

"I'm not a big drinker," Riley says automatically. This is true; she will have the occasional scotch, a treat after a hard week, but the words are a knee-jerk reaction, especially with people from her past.

The Alexander women share a sympathetic glance. They know why she claims she doesn't drink. They know why Riley Carrington is a teetotaler.

Julia tries again. "Dinner, then?"

"I'm sorry, it's just not a good night for me. I'm on deadline. I'm afraid I won't be able to. But it's been lovely seeing you. Have a blast on your trip."

Before it can go any further, she shoves all her things into her bag and gets the hell out of there, leaving two women who were doing nothing but being nice to an old friend staring after her with identical looks of astonishment on their faces.

She just cannot handle her own past right now. She feels guilty enough about her present circumstances.

CHAPTER EIGHTEEN

At the corner near the coffee shop, Riley looks uptown. She could head to the office, but she wants to get her ducks in a row before she faces Nate, and damn it, she needs ten minutes to absorb all this news and read some more of this very raw manuscript.

The Museum of Modern Art—MoMA—is only a few blocks away. A perfect place for her to find a bench and read the short story, and then put her world in perspective. Art does that for her. Her gift is words; she can't draw a stick figure properly, but being in the presence of oils and watercolors and textiles and sculpture centers her.

She has an annual pass, a reasonable indulgence that's worth every penny because she spends a lot of time here. She jumps the long line of people queuing up to the left of the doors in front of the ticket kiosks and waves it at the priority entrance. Her friend David is manning the kiosk, and she stops to chat with him for a moment before entering the hushed space and taking the escalator to the fourth floor. She winds around the corners until she reaches Gallery 403, which houses the Rothkos she loves so much.

The room is full, but a guided tour of elementary students soon moves off to the next space, and she has the bench in front of the massive painting *No. 16 (Red, Brown, and Black)* to herself.

To her left hangs the vibrant orange, blue, and green *No. 3/No. 13*; to her right, the softer blue and yellow of *No. 10*, which looks to her like the Ukrainian flag, of fields of grain. The colors are almost Van Gogh–like, and she feels bolstered by the three diverse milieus.

She meditates for a moment, looking at the paintings, losing herself in them, until another group comes in and the chatter draws her out of herself again.

The short story is only fifty pages, and she crosses her legs and dives in.

She doesn't make it ten pages before she senses someone else has entered the room. Nothing unusual there; the museum is crowded day and night. He comes to the bench she's sitting on, takes the far end. He's not looking at the paintings. He's looking at her.

"Amazing work," he says. She glances over, sees a man in a red baseball cap.

"Yes," she replies, bending her head to her work again.

"I can see why you like him. Rothko, I mean."

She nods but tries not to engage further. *Go away,* she begs silently.

"You know he committed suicide, yes? Swallowed a bunch of pills and sliced open his arm. Wonder if anyone thought to use the blood for one last painting."

She shoots the man a look and finds him smiling.

"It would be worth a mint," he continues. "Can you imagine? All that blood, spreading on the floor, all the talent in it, wasted. Slap it up on the canvas, it would look a lot like this one." He gestures to the painting she's facing, and the image of the red block as dried blood is inescapable.

She tenses. What an awful thing to say. "Please leave me alone."

"I don't want to. *Riley.*"

At the utterance of her name, she bolts, shoving the papers into her bag and moving quickly toward the nearest guard. "That man is harassing me," she says, pointing, but he's gone. There are so many ways in and out of these rooms—this floor in particular is a labyrinth you can easily get lost within—but if you know your way, it's a seamless serpentine walk from one end of the building to the other. She knows her way. Does the stranger, too?

"Are you okay, ma'am?" The guard is clearly worried for her, but with no one to identify, there's nothing to be done.

"Um, yeah. Just a stranger who seemed to know my name, and I didn't know his," she says. "He's wearing a red ball cap."

"I'll keep a lookout. If you see him again, just come over to one of us. We'll keep you safe."

"Thank you."

No way is she sitting back down. Her peace is destroyed. She needs to find another place to read, and now she's jittery and uncomfortable. Might as well go home. At least she can control who sits down next to her.

She weaves her way back to the escalator, sees a flash of red by the elevator. He's waiting for her. Shit.

She winds back to the Rothkos. The guard is still there. He must be new; she's never seen him before. "Hey, that guy is out by the escalator. Can you let me in the service elevator?"

"Did he do something? Touch you?"

"No, just said something super creepy about Rothko's suicide."

"Oh. All right. How's this, I'll see you to the escalator. Make sure he's not hanging around."

She doesn't want to look weak, scared, so she agrees. God knows where the creeper is now. At the down escalator, the guard nods. "There you go. You're safe now."

"Thank you," she says, and starts down. There are too many people; she's crammed in, and can't push her way down the stairs, but figures the crowd will keep her safe, too. But just in case he is watching, waiting for her downstairs, she ducks off at the second floor and goes into the women's room. She counts off three minutes, then steps out, planning to head to her right and take the back stairs down into the museum's shop.

A flash of red to her left, and she sees him. He must have seen her on the escalator.

He winks.

Trying not to panic, she runs. She knows this place, and there are a ton of people here, so long as he doesn't have some sort of weapon . . .

People are shouting, pushing at her as she streaks past. She can hear him behind her, the thud of his soles as he draws closer. She hits the stairs and scrambles down, two at a time, praying she doesn't slip, doesn't turn an ankle. One flight. Two. When she hits the store level, she glances back over her shoulder.

A hundred strangers, and none wearing a red hat.

She's lost him.

She doesn't waste any time. She hurries across the floor to the exit, elbowing her way out, then turns right toward Times Square. She doesn't run, but walks quickly, peering over her shoulder at every light to make sure he's not right there.

Panting, heart thundering, she makes her way through the throngs streaming along the sidewalks back to her apartment. Once inside, she feels safer. They have a front desk that's manned twenty-four seven, and the security is tight.

The elevator has never taken so long before. She bursts out onto their floor and into the flat, slamming the door behind her.

"Ollie?" she calls hopefully but is met with silence. She pulls a chair in front of the door—like that's going to help keep someone out, but it makes her feel better—and heads into the kitchen for a glass of water. She guzzles it down, notices Oliver has left her a note.

I'll be at my folks'. Call me when you get back. I love you.

She leaves it pristine on the counter and goes to their joint office.

And stops in the doorway, mouth dropping.

It is a disaster. Chairs overturned. The filing cabinet on its side. Drawers pulled out.

Oliver tore the place apart looking for something and left the massive mess for her to clean up. What the hell?

It takes Riley a moment to realize there's no way on earth Oliver would do such a thing, and the next moment to catch her breath from her heart pounding in her ears.

Not Oliver.

A break-in.

Someone has broken into their flat and trashed their office.

CHAPTER NINETEEN

Riley freezes, listening carefully to see if the burglars are still inside. But there's nothing, just the disaster in front of her of paperwork and pulled-out drawers and overturned furniture.

What were they looking for?

Three guesses.

Riley's not stupid—she's been given an envelope by a dead woman who was most likely murdered. There must be something in it that is of value. But what? An old short story? An article? Doubtful. But there is the flash drive. She needs to get to a safe place, with an IT professional, and get it opened.

Without touching anything, she backs out of the room and calls Oliver. It goes to voicemail. Figures.

"Call me when you can. It's an emergency."

She hears herself, hears the edge in her voice, knows he will, too. She is furious with him. Absolutely furious.

Furious enough that she's starting to wonder what, exactly, has her so upset. Is it because some creepy stranger accosted her at MoMA? That their place was broken into? Or that she feels like he chose his job over her?

Or is it deeper? Is this the anger of a woman who thinks—knows—her relationship is on the rocks and the slightest provocation will shatter it apart? Admittedly, she's been gone for only a month, but even when he picked her up at the airport, things felt different between them. This realization makes her unbearably sad. She does love him. He loves her. But she doesn't think they love each other *enough*.

She throws a few things in her bag, moves the chair out of the way, and bolts the door behind her, noticing the scratches on the lock. Forced entry, no doubt about it.

She tries Oliver again as she hits the lobby. He answers, harried. "I'm in a meeting."

"Someone broke into the flat. They took apart our office."

"What? When? Did you call the police?"

"I'm fine, thank you for asking." *Check that tone, Riley.* "I'm downstairs and about to do it."

"Did they take anything?"

"I honestly don't know. But considering what's been happening the past couple of days, I assume they were looking for something related to Columbia."

"Bugger. I'm on my way. Do not go back up there alone."

"I won't."

Hell no, she won't. She calls 9-1-1, the second time in a week, and explains the situation. The dispatcher promises to send someone out. She hangs up and approaches the front desk.

"Rami, I have a problem. Someone broke into the apartment. Did you see any strangers? Specifically, a guy in a red baseball cap?"

Rami is appropriately horrified. This does not happen in their building. "No, I didn't. But Miss Carrington, are you all right?"

She smiles. "Thanks for asking, I'm fine. Shaken up but fine."

"Thank goodness. I just came on duty. But the cameras . . . Let me run back the security footage."

Riley sits on the bench by the desk and crosses her legs. This break-in, combined with the murder, and the guy at the museum, and having her bag stolen and found in Denver, is totally freaking her out.

She digs into her bag and gets her notebook, where she shoved Detective Sutcliffe's card. It's sticking half out of the notebook, its edges battered and frayed from banging around in the bag.

She dials the number and is relieved when he answers immediately.

"Miss Carrington? Everything okay?"

"Hi, Detective. No, actually, it's not. I'm back in New York, and someone broke into my house, among other things."

"Are *you* okay?" She can hear him perk up; his voice gets sharper.

"I'm pretty rocked, actually. Whoever it is tossed our office. My boyfriend is a lawyer, his firm actually represents Columbia's estate, as I've just found out."

Sutcliffe is quiet for a moment. "That's an . . . interesting coincidence. I assume you've contacted the local authorities? New York is obviously out of my jurisdiction."

"I have. I'm waiting on them now. Our desk security is running the footage to see if anyone out of place shows up. Someone approached me earlier today at the museum where I was . . . reading. I don't know if it's related to the break-in, or if any of this is related to Columbia's death, but I thought you should know."

"I appreciate you filling me in."

"One more thing. Apparently, I'm in Columbia Jones's will. She left me some papers, but there's going to be an actual reading, with everyone gathered."

"Old fashioned."

"Quite." Rami is headed her way. The light pouring through the glass door winks out as he approaches, then comes back in full force, almost blinding her. "Hold on a sec, will you?"

"Miss Carrington, the feeds are gone."

"Gone?"

"Deleted. There is nothing from midnight until now."

"Did you hear that?" she asks Sutcliffe, quieter now. She can't help but think about the warning in her notebook. Damn it. She is totally compromised, and now beginning to believe she is in real danger.

"I did. That's quite interesting. Same thing happened at the Brown Palace."

"What? Are you serious?"

"Yes. The video feeds from the night of Columbia's death were deleted. Someone hacked the system and wiped it."

"Okay, now I'm getting scared. Surely you can't still think she died of natural causes."

"I never said I thought that. I just have to prove it's murder on its face, and without the full toxicology screen, my hands are tied. Her autopsy was . . . inconclusive."

There's something in the hesitation that makes her sit up straighter. "Inconclusive?"

"We can't provide a manner of death yet, but it's probably an overdose of some kind, considering the foamy blood that was everywhere. Please keep that to yourself, Miss Carrington. Can we agree that was on background?"

"Agreed," she replies without hesitation.

"Thank you. I'm only telling you as a courtesy so you won't keep digging until I have concrete answers. And so you'll watch your back. Yes, to answer your question. This is starting to look very suspicious. And you are definitely a target."

You are definitely a target.

That's all Riley needs to hear. When they hang up, she writes a note and rips the page from her Clairefontaine, folds it in thirds, and waves Rami over. "Oliver will be here shortly. Please give him this message, all right?"

"You aren't going to wait for the police?"

"He can handle them. I have someplace I need to be."

Before he can say another word, she darts out of their building, hails a cab, and heads directly to the offices of *East Fifth Magazine*, reading frantically from the pages Columbia left to her as she goes.

Legacy Draft— Prologue

When I wake, the body is cold.

I am assailed by confusing images, jagged fragments from the night before. Screams, scents, fear, deep and corrosive. Memories? Bright copper, metallic on my tongue—my blood? His? The remnants of dinner; what was it? Lasagna, garlic toast. It rises in my throat, and I swallow convulsively.

There was a fight. I have bruises on my arms. I touch a finger to my nose and wince. It is broken, the blood dried, crusting along my lip and into the creases of my neck. I can feel my hair crackling as I move my head.

How long have I lain here, next to his body?

Long enough for it to grow cold, for the blood to dry.

What have you done? What evil hath you wrought?

The sun is climbing into the sky; the baby whimpers, I can hear her rustling. The dog whines in response, nails scratching. He's been locked in his crate this whole time.

I must rise from my grave and tend to the needs of my family. And then I must call the police.

I rehearse what I will say.

"My husband is dead."

"My husband has been murdered."

"Please hurry, I think he's dead."

"I woke to find him this way."

"I don't remember what happened."

That is not true; I do. So clearly. Too clearly.

I can't do this. I can't. We have a plan, but I can't go through with it. Those things done in darkness always feel wrong in the light of day. Murdering my husband is one of them.

I sit up gingerly, pulling myself from the blood-soaked floor. I don't look at his body. I don't want to see him like this, lifeless. Cold. Empty. It doesn't matter what we've been through. The good, the bad, the terror. I feel no joy in this. He was the love of my life. Until he wasn't.

The baby is crying now, full-throated shrieks. My breasts tingle, then leak, and I am up and moving. I whip open the crate and the dog shoots through the door into the back-yard without a second glance. I sprint the stairs to the nursery, trying, and failing, to ignore the pain. I hurt everywhere. The beating was thorough, I'll give him that.

My daughter, cherub face and Botticelli lips, stares accusingly. How long has she been crying? Calling for me, for him, for anyone? I lift her from the crib and shush her, tapping her little back as I fumble open my shirt and present her with my right nipple. She latches on, voracious, mindless, and I relax into her need, hunching my shoulders around her tiny body protectively.

Did he get away? Is he safe?

When I sit in the rocking chair, I feel the blood flake off. Little pieces fall on her head. I fight back the nausea, the horror, the terror I've felt for so long. A new fear takes its place.

How will I explain this to her?

How will I cope with what I've done?

It's my fault.

It is all my fault.

Legacy Draft— Chapter One

You never really know when you've met the man who's eventually going to murder you.

For me, it was a chance meeting. We bumped into each other at the grocery store. We were both reaching for a bunch of bananas, and he stumbled over a box left on the floor. Crashed right into me. Grabbed me with both hands, whether to steady himself or me, who knows.

His eyes were brown. His hair was unruly. He hadn't shaved in a few days. He looked like a model, a swimmer, too-broad shoulders, trim waist. He wore button-fly jeans and Chelsea boots, a light blue button-down with the sleeves rolled up showing wrists and forearms that spoke of great and gentle strength. I may have even thought to myself how interesting those long fingers were, wondered what they would feel like trailing over my skin.

"I'm so sorry. Are you all right?" Baritone. Reverb. His voice locked me in place. His eyes searched mine.

Finally, finally, I was able to speak. "Hello."

"Hello," he replied, smiling now. His teeth were straight and square. Not blindingly white, not the fake white of bleached teeth, but a normal color. He realized he was still holding on, released me, and I felt bereft. I wanted him to touch me again. I wanted him to do many things to me.

A stranger. Something I've always wanted to experience. That instant connection, sneaking off to a private spot, giving in to the temptation, then never seeing them again. The connection was there. He seemed to be interested, hadn't moved away. We could—

The baby kicked in my belly, dragging me out of my fantasy.

My hormones were on overdrive. Nearly thirty-seven weeks along with my first, my body had betrayed me in a million tiny ways. The early pregnancy fear and excitement had given way to claustrophobia. I loved my baby, but I couldn't escape from her. Soon, so soon, my sentence would end. The lustful thoughts would recede. The swelling in all the wrong places would go away. I would be a normal person again, not the object of attention wherever I went. A woman so very close to giving life is like a beacon to those around her. She is fascinating to behold.

"Go ahead," I managed, embarrassed. I could feel the flush running up my neck.

"You look like you're about to pop."

"It's not nice to comment on women's bodies. You never know if they're pregnant or carrying a little extra weight."

My girl took that moment to roll over, the flesh tight across my stomach rippling.

"Never knew anyone overweight to have independent muscle control. Besides, I'm a doctor. When are you due?"

"Anytime now," I said casually, placing a hand on my bulge.

"Then you should have a seat and let me finish your shopping."

"No, that's all right. The bananas are the last thing I need."

"Then at least let me carry the basket out for you."

Why did I say yes? What compelled me? His pretty eyes? Or was it something . . . more? Something electrical that passed between us when our hands touched? I'd felt it, that jarring sense of completeness, an arcing that I'd never felt with David. Don't get me wrong, I loved my husband. Very much. We've just been together for longer than I have memories, and there was never this moment, this utter intensity, the friction of someone new. I met David in kindergarten when he threw a rock at my head, and I'd tripped him in return, and we'd been inseparable since. Thirteen years together.

I'd gotten pregnant prom night, like an idiot, and we married after graduation, my belly just starting to show. My nineteenth birthday was yesterday.

I followed the stranger to the front of the store. Paid for the groceries. Waddled out to the car. All the while, he kept up a steady patter, chatting me up. Flirting. I may not have had a lot of experience with men, but he was definitely flirting.

"You know I'm married," I said after he set the brown bag gently in the passenger seat.

He looked at me then, really looked. Deep into my eyes. A smile bloomed on his lips.

"You know, I don't really care. Where have you been all my life?"

Legacy Draft— Chapter Two

His name was Patrick Connolly.

And from that moment forward, he was always around.

I never believed in love at first sight. I thought it was silly. A romantic fantasy someone like me couldn't afford.

But that night, across from David at the table, I saw my husband for the first time.

There was a fleck of bread at the corner of his mouth. Though we were the same age, his mousy hair was already thinning. And his red-rimmed eyes were narrowed at me.

"Where were you today? I called."

"Grocery shopping."

"Did you pick up beer?"

Uh-oh. "No. I forgot." I forgot because I was caught up in a conversation with a stranger who was weird enough to be flirting with a monstrously pregnant woman and

I didn't want to stop because his attention felt so good, so I neglected to bring you home your elixir. "Sorry."

His fist slammed down on the table, rattling the plates and glasses. "How hard is it to remember one little thing? Now I have to go out and get some. And I've had a long day. A hard day. I work, you know, while you're out gallivanting around town, showing off your stomach like a prize heifer. You really are worthless, you know that?"

David worked, yes. At his dad's law firm, as a pseudo-paralegal. He'd wanted to go to law school, follow his father's path to the firm. Instead, he had to make do with the scraps from his dad's table. We were all set to go to the University of Tennessee in the fall, then the lines turned pink and we had to get our deposits back to pay rent. Now he's stuck home with me in our little town starting a family. With the baby coming, we need the money more than he needs the education.

He blames me for getting pregnant and ruining our lives, though he was the one who decided we didn't need to use a condom. He never stopped to think that I, too, was giving up my dreams, because it had been preordained since elementary school that we would be together forever. We just got started earlier than we'd planned. And that was okay. I loved David. I really did. He used to love me, too.

"I'm sorry," I whispered again. The glint in his eye made me tense. This could go two ways. He could leave and go to the store and come back with his beer, drink it up while watching the Braves game, and I could slip into the bedroom and pretend to sleep. Or he could take it out on me.

I felt the punch coming before my mind registered the movement of his fist. He caught me on the side of the head, my neck snapping to the right. "I'm sorry!" I said again, arms up protectively, but even I could hear the edge in my voice, and that was all he needed. David had a talent for going from zero to sixty in a heartbeat. One minute he was annoyed, the next, enraged.

"Closet," he snarled.

"No. No, please. I'll go get you the beer."

But there was no stopping him now.

I disassociate sometimes when he's like this. It's the only way through. He dragged me down the hall, ignoring my screams and pleading, and threw me into the hall closet, locking the door behind me. He slammed out of the front door then, which meant I'd be stuck in the dark, cramped space for a while.

I dabbed at the blood coming from the corner of my mouth and settled uncomfortably onto the floor. It is always so desolate in the dark, but tonight, curled around my belly, praying he hadn't harmed my girl, I had the face of a stranger to keep me company.

CHAPTER TWENTY
DETECTIVE SUTCLIFFE

The twenty-minute drive down I-25 to Aspen Grove is scenic today, the piercing late-afternoon blue sky making the snowcapped peaks stand out in bas-relief to the west. Sutcliffe has gotten the call he's been waiting for—the warrant has been served and the theater's video is ready for him to look at, and more.

He's already talked to the majority of the VIPs from the event, and so far, nothing's stood out. He needs to go north to Boulder to talk to one more, but he probably doesn't have enough time to pull that off today. He'll head up first thing in the morning.

He finishes off a Coke Zero and a bag of raw almonds before he goes in. He's been training for an Ironman that will take place at the end of the summer, and the soda is a rare treat. Caramel-colored drinks are terrible for your kidneys and cause rampant inflammation, he knows this, but figures one every few weeks won't kill him.

He locks the car, and stops for a moment to admire the mountains, still enshrined in the late-spring snows. He smiles as he enters the building. Over twenty years in Denver, and the view never gets old. The Tattered Cover bookstore is just down the street: he will duck in after and grab something to read. He favors Daniel Silva and John Sandford; they both have new releases.

Inside, he takes the stairs two at a time, up three flights, noting his breathing doesn't change. He's in the best shape of his life, but the regimen is grueling. Training at high altitude means he's in even better shape.

He knocks on the door of Ruby Erickson, the woman who organized the event for Columbia. She's on the phone but quickly hangs up when she sees him. She bustles around the desk.

"Detective Sutcliffe?"

"Yes, ma'am. You're Mrs. Erickson?"

"Oh, Lord, call me Ruby. I'm just sick about all of this. Do you know what happened yet?"

"Nothing new, I'm afraid," Sutcliffe replies. "I heard you have the video for me?"

She nods and hands over a flash drive, abrupt and efficient. "I do. Sorry we couldn't release it without the warrant, but there were too many third parties to protect. It's just the two views of the theater and one of the doors to the lobby, I'm afraid, but I took a look and I think you're in luck." She pushes a printout his way. "You'll want this, too. The ticket was purchased the same day the tour was announced. The tour dates all sell out so quickly. Her fans know to watch for the announcements so they can grab the tickets early. These are well-coordinated events, actually, and while there's certainly no way everyone who wants a ticket can get one, we make sure that once the in-person tickets sell out, there are plenty of online available."

"So this guy bought his ticket the day they were announced?"

"I said the ticket was sold the first day. There's no way to know for sure the person who sat in the seat was the same one who purchased the ticket."

Sutcliffe fights back a smile. "Now you sound like a cop."

"Not a cop, Detective. A reader. We pay attention to the details." She flashes her dimples, bright teeth shining in the sunlight.

"You have the name of the ticket purchaser, and the video from that night. Anything else?"

"If I had more, I wouldn't be a reader. I'd be a cop." She grins again, and he laughs out loud.

"All right. You win. I'll be more specific. Is there anything else you'd like me to know?"

"No. You now know everything I do."

"Thank you, Ruby. I appreciate the help."

The teasing smile is gone now. "Catch him, Detective. Columbia deserves better than all of these rumors and innuendos. The community is certain she was murdered by a fan. Everyone is scared. I trust you'll have answers soon?"

"I sure hope so. Thanks for this," he says, and gets out of there before she manages to get herself deputized.

He has a laptop in his car, pops in the flash drive, makes sure it gets swept for bugs by the system before he opens it. While the video is downloading, he opens his computer to type the name of the ticket holder into the National Crime Information Center database.

Knox Shepherd.

Sutcliffe freezes. He knows this name.

NCIC spits out a match almost immediately: there's a Knox Emanuel Shepherd who has an arrest record. It's a unique enough name; doesn't mean it's the same person, though.

Sutcliffe digs a little deeper while the video loads. No active warrants, but a conviction on the record.

He switches databases, pulls up the department of corrections, and puts in his password. It doesn't take long to find a "Knox E. Shepherd" entry that belongs to a felon from Tennessee, released in 2010 after serving fifteen years of a twenty-year sentence for second-degree murder. And like that, it all clicks.

"I will be damned," Sutcliffe says.

The DOC booking appears, and Sutcliffe is thrust back in time. Knox Shepherd's booking photo captured the man perfectly. Dark hair, curly; square jaw; light-green eyes. Terrified: you can see it in the tension in his face, the wild look in his eye. A handsome guy—not exactly a kid, but young, so young.

He gets that tingle, that frisson, that tells him *something's here*. But dread, too. It all feels wrong. This is an awfully big coincidence, having something so elemental from his past show up now, all these years later, in the form of a high-profile case that he's been pulled into. The manager wanted the most senior detective. Was it truly the manager requesting Sutcliffe? Or is he being manipulated?

Don't jump to conclusions. Make sure.

The theater's video feeds pop onto his screen.

He scrolls through to the thirty-minute mark, when he knows Columbia passed out, and runs it back a few minutes until he gets to the moment the man stands. The video buffers, then starts to play. The first view is from behind the loge boxes to the stage; hard to see anything worthwhile, but the second camera angle is from the stage to the seats. The lights make it almost impossible to see the crowd, but there is a shadow in the middle of the screen that must be the man standing up. Sutcliffe tries to increase the size and loses clarity. There's a side angle, though, and when he switches to that he sees a profile of the man standing, walking toward the exit, through the door, to another camera angle, this one from the lobby, and . . . "Yes!"

A full-front face shot, and there is no doubt in his mind the man he's looking at on the video and the man in the booking photo are the same. Sutcliffe should know. It was the case that chased him out of Metro Nashville, the very reason why he's in Denver.

And now there's no denying it.

Knox Shepherd, convicted murderer, was at the event. When Columbia Jones saw him, she grew faint. And twelve hours later, she was dead.

What are the odds?

CHAPTER TWENTY-ONE
RILEY

The taxi makes good time but hits the usual traffic at the south end of Central Park so she's able to get the rest of the story read. She places the pages in her bag carefully, as if they are a bomb that might go off with the tiniest movement.

The writing isn't going to win any prizes, but it is so visceral, so intense. So sad. Riley realizes there are tears running down her face, wipes them away with a knuckle. This is definitely the bones of a Columbia Jones blockbuster; Riley recognizes the writing style. And though it's unpolished, raw, a beginner's work, not the powerful words that Columbia is now known for, the topic is incendiary; the story itself is propulsive.

But it is just a story. Why is she so unsettled? More importantly, the same question she's been asking herself since she realized what this is: Why has Columbia given it to her? And what is she supposed to do with it? She has no rights to Columbia's literary estate; obviously, Darian will have to be told about this story.

It is also worth a mint. An unpublished story, unknown to the canon of a beloved author who has recently died on tour, probably murdered? It is going to cause a stir, no matter what. She can already envision the social media eruption. #Legacy.

You never really know when you've met the man who's eventually going to murder you.

That's a haunting-enough phrase right there. Creepy as hell. The very idea that anyone on the street, any smile, any door opened, any date, might lead to murder is downright chilling.

This is all just way too weird.

Add in someone trashing her apartment and the guy at MoMA . . . Riley is beginning to think she's not the only one who knows about this story.

She realizes traffic ahead has ground to a stop, asks the cabbie to drop her at the corner. She is out and walking, making better time, head still spinning as she marches up Fifth Avenue, that *why, why, why* resonating with every step.

She crosses the street at Seventy-Fifth and halts at the red light, waiting, waiting. It's taking forever. She feels someone close by her and turns her head just as a strong hand lands in the middle of her back, and shoves. She stumbles out into the street to the shriek of brakes and the furious horn of an Escalade. It just misses her, swerving wildly into the middle lane.

Heart pounding, she whirls around, looking for a face, something familiar, and catches a flash of red. A laugh echoes, chilling her blood.

Then the light changes and the crowd surrounding her starts streaming past as if she hadn't almost been killed moments before. She is bumped and spun, and there's no way to see who might have pushed her.

Or if she even was pushed. This is New York, everyone is in a hurry, everyone has the right of way. There's no way to say for sure. If she'd been pushed, surely someone would have called out. Right? Maybe not. This is a mixed-use residential area, doctors' offices and art galleries and colorful flower gardens around the established trees, interspersed with brownstones and condo buildings. It's always—always—felt safe.

But she did not mistake that hand, square in the middle of her back, and the eyes on her. No. She isn't imagining it. Nor is she imagining the flash of red.

It was the man from the museum. She's sure of it.

Shit.

She starts walking again, moving fast, and keeping her head on a swivel. She sees nothing alarming or out of place. If anything, she's the one who looks wild and crazed.

No one seems to be following her. Half a block away lies her sanctuary, and she hurries toward the safety of the green awning and solid glass and brass doors, stepping adroitly around an upended Frappuccino growing sticky in the sun. At least, she hopes that's what it is.

Inside the megalithic old building that houses *East Fifth Magazine*, she relaxes a touch. The building's exterior has been recently renovated, a huge sparkling tower built upon the original historical base, and the interior is now much more modern. Riley steps through the metal detector, waving to the security guards. The guards are armed, and no one can get to the floors without electronic passes. Security is tight these days. She is safe. For now.

"Hey, I think someone was following me. If a guy in a red ball cap comes to the lobby, or anyone asks to see me, will you call up to Nate's office, please?"

"Name?"

"I don't know his name. Just trying to be safe."

"You got it, Miss Carrington."

She swipes her pass and ducks into the designated elevator, which whooshes upward without stopping, decanting her seconds later on the twenty-third floor.

She sweeps through the open, clattering room without acknowledging anyone. This place is her home, almost more than the flat. She loves the people she works with, loves that they challenge her to be a better writer, push her to take chances, honor her grit and determination. This is her dream job, and she worked like hell to be here, to be accepted, respected. But today, she wants only one person's attention.

In the corner office with a beautiful view of Central Park, Nathanial Jordan Walsh IV—Nate to his employees—is leaning back in his chair with his feet up on his desk, crossed at the ankle, eyes closed, a set of AirPods in. Riley knows he's thinking while listening to classical music; he's completely addicted. He grew up on the New York Philharmonic; his mother was a cellist. He plays, too, quite well. Especially for an audience of one. Don't ask her how she knows.

They were always destined to fail. He liked her too much; she liked her job too much. Not to mention, when they got together, he was still technically married, though very much in the throes of the divorce. To the younger, more naive Riley, that made him safe. Little did she know the chaos their affair would create.

Yes, Nate was a fun, albeit complicated, mistake.

Oliver is easier. Low pressure. Their lives never overlapped until now. She should call him after this meeting. Or maybe before. Maybe now. But no. The note should be explanation enough.

Someone's tracking me. I'm going underground. Be careful. I love you.

It might put him into hysterics, but this is too important. She needs a plan, and she needs it fast.

She needs to talk to Nate.

She starts to knock on the doorframe, but at that moment, Nate opens his heavily lashed hazel eyes as if he's sensed her near him. At the lazy grin that slides across his face, she realizes she and Oliver might be in serious trouble. She's not over Nate, not by a long shot, but she can usually keep a healthy distance between them. This is why she often works from home. The attraction between them is magnetic and hard to miss.

Now, she's chosen him to help her muddle through this insane situation, and damn if she isn't glad she did. As much as it pains her to admit, she always runs to Nate when she's in trouble, even when he calls her *kid* and makes her feel like she's ten years old. Nate is safe. That this is where she is right now speaks volumes. That her shoulders are dropping and she feels like she can breathe for the first time in days speaks volumes. That warmth pools in her stomach at the sight of him speaks volumes.

He is not hers, though, nor is she his. She must tread carefully.

"There's my superstar," Nate says, lighting up. He pulls out the AirPods. It's a nice gesture; some would simply tap and pause, waiting impatiently for the interruption to cease.

"At least you didn't call me your black hole. How are you, Nate?"

"I'm good. Putting together the pieces for next month's magazine." He gestures to his temple. He is the king of brainstorming, will show up to the daily meeting with a dizzying array of requests for his various departments without ever writing anything down in advance. "How're things? The Jones piece? Looks like you've stepped in it."

"That's why I'm here." Riley shuts the door and plops down on one of the bouclé-covered chairs in front of his desk. It's like perching on a fuzzy marshmallow; there's absolutely no way to look graceful sinking into the fluff of them. His ex did the office, and Riley swears she put in these little monstrosities as punishment. "These chairs, Nate."

"I know, I know. I'll get her to replace them. Have to wait for next season's inventory to arrive. Anyway, you okay?"

Riley bites her lip. "Okay. Here's the deal. The Jones piece is blowing up on me."

"I expect it is. Losing her like that. Have the police shared anything?"

"Mmmm."

"You don't have to reveal your sources . . ."

She thinks about the phone call with Detective Sutcliffe. If her devices are compromised, sharing this won't be news.

"On background, they deferred declaring a cause of death pending a toxicology report, and that could take weeks. They aren't saying it was natural causes, they aren't saying it was murder. But there's more. Is there someplace we could go that's private?"

The smile broadens into a naughty grin that makes her heart stutter, but she shakes her head. She puts a finger on her lips, then hands over the notebook, the note from the stranger marked with her finger.

He reads. His smile flees, and he stands. "Come with me."

"Wait. Will you put these somewhere safe?"

She unloads her bag—laptop, phone, watch—and after a second's confusion, Nate nods and puts them all in his safe. She keeps the notebook, stashed lonely inside her messenger bag, just in case.

As they leave the lobby, Riley notices one of the guards detach himself from the wall and follow. Nate's security. He's had a detail for a few years, ever since the piece they did on Sir Salman Rushdie, when the threats against Nate went up a notch. There were always threats, some more credible than others, the nature of the modern media beast, but what she's always wondered about—was someone really going to take a shot at Nate, of all people? Or does he keep the detail for show?—she is now grateful for. The silent man walks a few steps behind them. Close enough to react, far enough away to be inconspicuous.

East Fifth Magazine's offices are on Fifth Avenue and Seventy-Eighth by the Payne Whitney House, and it takes three minutes to cross the street, hurry down the cobblestones, and enter Central Park from Seventy-Sixth Street. They wind into the leafy world within a world and start south toward the model-boats lake. The weather is perfect, the paths hum with dog walkers and nannies and tourists. Someone has hooked up a speaker to a violin and is playing a mournful selection from Debussy's *Préludes*. She's half afraid this was a terrible idea, and half more settled than she has been in days.

"Are you okay?" Nate asks. "Seriously?"

"If I'm being honest . . . no, I'm not." She yanks hard on the bottom of her ponytail, a childhood habit that rears its head under pressure.

"I've seen my subject covered in blood and nonresponsive in her hotel room, been arrested for her murder, been given a warning note by a stranger who stole my bag, been given material evidence, and now someone's broken into my apartment. Oliver is there with the police, probably wigging out that I'm not answering my phone. Add in the weirdo who talked to me about Rothko's suicide at MoMA, who I'm pretty sure pushed me in traffic on my way here? No, I'm not okay. And no, I didn't kill her, if that's your next question."

He is more serious than she's ever heard him. "Don't be smart with me. Of course you didn't. But something is certainly going on. We need to get you a burner and call this source."

"You think that's the best move?"

"Yeah, I do. I'm going to do it with you, though. No chance in hell I'll let some stranger light you up without backup."

"Well, there's more. I'm in her will."

Nate pulls up, snaps "What?" A jogger passes them, looking curiously over his shoulder.

She yanks on his elbow. "Keep moving. I'm feeling really freaked out right now." When they are walking again, she tells him the rest. "I haven't mentioned this to anyone because it felt presumptuous, but the first day we met, Columbia mentioned that she was considering me to ghostwrite her memoir. I'm assuming that's why I'm in her will, she's left me her journals and notes on her life works so I can write it. A biography, now . . . Anyway, here's the crazy part. Oliver's firm is handling the estate."

"Your Oliver? Hmm."

Nate doesn't think much of Oliver Mathers and has never been shy about it. The feeling is mutual, she knows. In another life, were she not in the middle, the two might have been friends. They came from the same world, after all.

"When I got home, he had an envelope waiting for me that said 'In the event of my death give this to Riley Carrington.' Inside, there was a password-protected flash drive, a clipping from a newspaper about a murder in Tennessee, and an old, like really old, short story. Never been published, at least not that I can tell. I've read everything she's ever done."

"What's it about?"

"A young woman and her lover who murder her husband," she replies. "I'm wondering if it's tied to the article she left."

"It's in the office?"

"In your safe, yes."

"Okay. Good. Jesus, Riley."

"No kidding. And here's the third stunner. Oliver said they won't do the reading of the will until our piece is published, even though the letter says the reading is on the fifteenth. So we need to get this story wrapped and out, because that's the weirdest part of all of it. It's like she knew she was going to die and wants a specific narrative to be on the record."

Nate whistles, long and low.

"Where are you on the piece? It's slated for release Friday. Can we make it? Are you close?"

Riley nods. "I'm halfway there. Drafted the rest. Just a few somewhat important bits to fact-check."

"We'll put a rush on everything. You'll have to get me the draft tomorrow, though."

"I can do that. Assuming you can find me a quiet place to work where I don't get taken out in the meantime."

Unconsciously, Nate has put a hand on her shoulder and is rubbing lightly. Former house cat that she is, she lets him, trying not to arch into his touch.

"So now what?"

"There," Nate says, pointing to the park exit ahead. "We're going to have Tony from IT bring us a burner phone, and we're going to call this yahoo."

CHAPTER TWENTY-TWO

They buy a couple of coffees while they wait for Tony, who shows up ten minutes later, red faced and breathing hard. He hands over a phone like he's doing a CIA drop and disappears up the street. They go back into the park and find a bench by the lake. Nate's bodyguard sets up shop three benches down. He looks like a very tall and hefty Tom Cruise; people going by pay more attention to him than the two reporters furtively breaking open the plastic on a phone.

"I hope it has a charge."

"It will, enough for at least one call," Nate replies, finally cracking into the packaging and turning on the phone. "Tony could have opened the damn thing."

Riley flips the notebook to the page with the warning, and, with a deep breath, turns on the speaker and dials the number.

It rings three times before a voice answers. A voice that sounds familiar, but she's never heard it before.

"Are you safe?" the man demands.

"Yes. Who is this?"

"Oh, thank God, Riley. I've been worried sick. You need—"

Nate grabs the phone. "Whoa whoa whoa whoa whoa. We need some answers. Who are you, and what do you want with Riley?"

Silence. She tries again. "I was scared, and I went to someone safe. I swear to you, he will not say anything."

"Is that Nate Walsh?"

Nate's eyes widen. "It is. You want to do me the courtesy of sharing your name?"

"No. Put Riley back on the line."

"I'm right here," she says. "Will you give *me* your name?"

"Are you still on speaker? Turn it off."

Nate shakes his head, but Riley is intrigued. She takes back the phone and turns off the speaker. "All right. I'm listening."

The urgency in the stranger's voice gives her a chill. "You can't trust *anyone*. Not even Walsh. Do you understand? Not a single soul. Columbia Jones was murdered. You can't be next."

Not even Walsh.

Riley looks sharply at Nate, and almost imperceptibly, leans back: away, apart, from the only person she truly trusts.

"I have to trust someone," she says quietly, ignoring Nate's furrowed brows.

"No one is safe. Do you understand? No one. You need to drop the story. Stay the hell away."

She puts him back on speaker. "I can't stay away from this, sir. I'm a reporter. I've been hired to tell Columbia's story, and that's what I intend to do."

A muffled curse. "Just like her. You're too stubborn for your own good."

"How do you even know that? Are you stalking me?"

"No. I'm not. But he might be if you stir up too much dust."

"*He*? Do you mean the person who killed her?" Riley has her pen poised above the paper; she has reverted to Journalism 101. Ask questions. Get him to talk. "Who is he, sir? Do you have a name? A description? We can call the police and have him arrested. Detective Sutcliffe in Denver is a good guy. He's been on my side all along. That's the logical step here, you know. Subterfuge is not the best course of action."

"I don't know his name. And I don't know where he is now. But he was in Denver Friday night long enough to kill Columbia."

"How do you know all this?"

"Time's up. Get another burner, call me tomorrow. Be safe."

The line goes dead. She looks at Nate, who's frowning.

"He hung up."

"Shit," Nate says. "Okay. Back to the office, now."

He takes the phone from her, yanks out the battery and the SIM card, and throws both pieces into the lake.

"Littering," she says mildly.

"Stop. Riley. Come on. This is serious. We're going to get you all-new equipment that I can be sure isn't compromised and set you up in a hotel. Your choice about who stays with you—me, or Oliver. But one of us is going to be with you at all times from now on until we figure this out."

"I am a grown woman, and I—"

"Riley Carrington, I swear to God, shut up before I murder you myself."

She shuts up.

She isn't going to play games, not anymore. That voice, too. There's something in the growl of it, but she can't place what is bothering her about it. She appreciates she's in trouble; anyone with half a brain would. Warning her off Nate, though . . . that's unsettling, to say the least. She has to trust someone. And Nate has the means to help her the most. Not that she's using him, never that. But she needs him.

The sidewalks are packed, and she doesn't speak until they're back in the office.

"You," she says as they enter Nate's office. "I choose you. Only because we can work nonstop, understand? Oliver has a real conflict of interest, and until the piece is done and out, the will can't be read. So no funny business."

"He's not going to like it. Are you prepared for the fallout?"

Are you prepared to lose him over this? That's what he's really asking. *Are you prepared to throw in your lot with me, for real?*

"It's just work, Nate," she says. "I'll explain that it's life and death. He won't care if he knows it's a real threat. He'll want me safe."

"Good choice, kid."

She narrows her eyes at him, but he ignores her, bustling around his office, then sending a few emails. Five minutes later, Tony from IT shows up with a laptop and another cell phone, both still in their packaging.

"Can we pull her files and make sure they're clean?" Nate asks.

Tony is no more than twenty-three, with wavy hair and black glasses. She's always liked him; he's a good kid. Now she's even more grateful that she has good relations with the magazine's staff. They are going to be the ones to save her, in the end. They are her family.

Tony is clearly curious what's happening, but professional enough not to ask. "Only way to be completely safe is to print off everything and work on paper. I can't guarantee the files themselves. They're in the cloud with all the rest of our work. It's as secure as I can make it, but if she's been compromised . . ."

"Then someone's sent us a sophisticated Trojan horse. Okay. Do it," Nate says. "Riley, show him what you need. You have a password-protected flash drive, too? Tony, can you crack it?"

"Oh, yeah, easy. I'll hook it to a program I've written that will find a way in. What else do you need, Riley?"

"I just need access to my local documents, that's where I have some notes, and the office cloud account. By the way, the computer tech in Denver told me there was some malware on my uploaded files. She cleaned it up for me, but you might want to check my devices thoroughly. I assumed it was something I picked up on a hotel Wi-Fi somewhere, but now . . ."

"I will. Good idea."

"Get her files on a new laptop, but make sure they're clean," Nate says. "And then run a full system integrity check, make sure no one's knocking at our back door."

"Got it."

Riley marvels at the intense efficiency of this preppy, laid-back, I've-inherited-it-and-I-don't-really-care man who has turned into a journalistic bulldog over the course of an hour. She likes this side of Nate. She likes it a lot.

Tony, who clearly recognizes something major is happening, says, "Check your socials while you're here, too, because you won't be able to look at them again for a while. Best way to track your physical movements is through those accounts."

While Riley has accounts on all the major platforms, and a few of the more minor ones, too, she hasn't looked at them since she landed back in New York. Not surprisingly, Columbia's death is trending in several iterations, including #belovedauthor, #ColumbiaJonesMurder, and #authormurdered.

It doesn't seem to matter that her death hasn't been officially classified a murder—Darian Jones hasn't deleted that original tweet, hasn't even bothered to comment, and that's fueled the fires plenty. An accusation that's driving the gossip mill—a bell that can never be unrung.

Also not surprisingly, there are a slew of private messages for Riley, colleagues who knew she was traveling with Columbia's entourage, strangers who think she should look into the story. Messages of concern and support. And one that makes the hair on the back of her neck stand on end. She doesn't recognize the sender, though it has to be someone she follows in order for them to send direct messages.

You look pretty, it says, a link helpfully provided. The preview shows an article from the daily newspaper in Denver, with a photo of Riley being led from the hotel by Detective Sutcliffe. The story is vague, only hinting that Riley is a suspect. But it has her name, and that she works for *East Fifth Magazine*, plus the photo of her looking decidedly not pretty, but disheveled and scared.

This is the wrong kind of attention. Though the rules of PR are clear—any publicity is good—this isn't the kind she is willing to suffer.

There are freaks everywhere. She's fended off plenty over the years, and she instinctually knows she must be very careful not to set this one off. Yes, it could be someone just sliding into her DMs, but it feels wrong. It has that same sinister feel as the brief conversation with the guy in the red hat at MoMA.

Dread filling her, she clicks on the profile. It's a private account, the profile pic the back of a head staring out at a lake. Nothing to identify the sender, no pronouns, no website or description. She is unsure why she followed them in the first place. A source, perhaps, someone who commented on another's feed and seemed to have something legitimate to say. So many accounts have been purged recently, there's no telling who this is.

Or, just as possible, he is the nameless murderer a stranger has warned her about.

"Nate," she says, sliding the computer over to him. "Gotta block this yahoo. I don't recall following him. And I have no way to prove it, just a gut feeling, but I bet it's the same guy from MoMA."

He reads it and nods at the IT guy. "Don't block him yet. Tony, find this person for me, okay? I don't care how you have to do it. And check with MoMA, see if they have any video of the man who approached Riley."

"You got it, boss. Riley, where did you see him?"

"The Rothko room. Fourth floor. Again on the second floor. I was running through the area, so they can probably time-stamp it. He was wearing a red ball cap. Also"—she glances at Nate—"when I was coming up here, someone pushed me into the intersection at Fifth Avenue and Seventy-Fifth. I was coming to the office. It could have been anyone, but I thought I saw a flash of red. And just FYI, something super weird to be aware of. The video feeds at both Columbia's hotel and my apartment were tampered with. If MoMA's cameras were down, now we have a real pattern. Is that easy to do? Mess with cameras like that?"

Tony scratches his jaw, the scraping of his thumb against his beard loud in the space. "Well, I wouldn't say easy, though there are plenty of jammers that can render them useless. But the CCTV cameras for the city? Those would be hard to corrupt. If I can't find anything at MoMA, I can at least search the intersection and see what I can find."

"Do I want to know how you can do all of this?" Riley asks, a slight smile on her face.

"You don't," Nate replies for Tony. "If you find out who it is, send me an email that says this." He hands him a Post-it, and Riley can just make out the words—*Got you a reservation at Carbone tonight, 8 p.m.*

"Is this . . . code?" Tony asks.

"No, it's my fucking dinner plans. *Of course* it's code."

"Yeah. Sorry. Sure thing. Good luck." Tony disappears, ears red in embarrassment.

Nate watches him leave, a small smile quirking the edges of his lips. "I didn't mean to snap."

"Yes, you did." Riley starts to open the new laptop, but Nate shakes his head.

"Wait. We'll do it in a bit. Let's go."

"If someone's following me, what's to stop them from just tagging along behind us?"

"Chances are they're using your devices, right? It's too hard to track you physically, in person, in a city like this, unless you have a team of watchers. Or there's a tracker in your bag. You have cleaned out your bag, yes?"

She stares at him for a second, then walks to his conference table and dumps out her messenger bag. Notebook. Pens, tampons, granola bars, a bottle of water she got on the plane.

And a small white-and-silver disk.

"Fuck! I am an idiot. Why didn't I get a notification that there was a tracker? Remember that article we did? I thought they fixed that bug."

"You're not an idiot. And it's not an Apple tracker. I don't know what brand it is, but it's clearly geotagging you." He turns it over thoughtfully. "How long do you think—"

"Since the morning of the murder, I suppose. I didn't think to look for a tracker and—" Riley's heart is racing. "God, Nate, he's been following me this whole time. This stranger has seen every move I've made. That's how he knew where I was at MoMA, and that I was heading here to the office. He knew I wasn't home, too, and could break in."

Her voice breaks. Nate has his arms around her and her head tucked into his chest a heartbeat later, shushing her gently.

"Come on, Riley girl. Something big is at play here, and you can't blame yourself. Okay?"

She hears him, but it doesn't matter. She's fighting back the tears, frustration and fear and a horrid sense of violation working their way through her, and she's trying to ignore how much better she feels when Nate is touching her. *Let us stay like this for a while,* she silently pleads. *Don't let go.*

She is a traitor. An idiot and a traitor. This is impossible. She is with Oliver now, and she must—she must!—keep Nate at arm's length. She doesn't want to blow up her world.

Yes, you do.

She gently puts her hands on his chest and steps back a foot, putting some space between them. She can't breathe with him so close. He doesn't move but doesn't try to reach for her again.

"I'm sorry. I should have asked—"

"Stop," she says, not meeting his eyes. "It's fine. I appreciate the comfort. I apologize for losing it. Where are we going?"

"You'll see," he replies grimly. "Leaving everything here will confuse things long enough for us to get you someplace safe."

She leaves her bag behind, too, and together they head for the elevator. Inside, Nate leans back against the wall, crossing his feet at the ankles and folding his arms on his chest.

"I think we need this article out right away. I don't think it's safe to wait until Friday."

"I think you're right. I can pull an all-nighter if you can."

His smile is crooked and lights up his eyes. "You know I can."

CHAPTER TWENTY-THREE
COLUMBIA

One Year Before the End

Columbia Jones types *The End* with a sigh of relief. It always feels like a miracle, finishing. This one has been difficult: there's something not quite right with the story, and she's been fighting with it for weeks. Coming off her last one, a book that had written itself, this new, unnamed behemoth is more like a mammoth in its last days, wandering the steppes. It's the nature of the beast, forgive the cliché, that some books are easy, and some difficult. And some, it's like digging fossils from rocks with a toothpick. This has been the latter.

She rereads the last paragraph, feels the chill spread through her body. No, she's got it. This is right. From the moment she conceived this idea, she's been waiting to type these words. She's superstitious; even when she knows exactly how a story ends, she resists typing the final lines until she is actually at the end.

She blows out a huge, relieved breath.

"Pizza!" she shouts, her voice carrying through the house. Moments later, Darian clatters down the stairs, a wide smile on her face.

"You did it? You're finished?"

"I'm finished." Columbia leans back in her chair, puts her feet on the desk, and laces her fingers behind her head. "This one was a bitch, but I tamed her in the end."

"Congratulations, Mom. Proud of you."

"Thank you. You did a nice job with the setup," Columbia says. Darian's getting quite good at helping her draft the stories. They brainstorm for days, outlining the high points at length, and on this book, Columbia let Darian write the first draft. That's probably why there was something not quite right from the get-go, but it's good training. Soon enough, Darian will be coming up with her own stories, and she needs these skills. So far she's claimed not to want to write under her own name, but they both know she's lying. Of course she will, and with the years Columbia's put in, meticulously training her in craft and dedication to storytelling, she'll be a raging success.

Tell her that, her subconscious says, but Darian's already turned to her phone to order dinner, and the moment passes.

"What's the title going to be? Have you decided?"

Columbia shakes her head. "Maybe after I get a glass of champagne in me to celebrate, the right title will appear. If not, Mary will help. She's always been good at titles."

"I'd go with *The Lonely Shore* if I were you. It fits perfectly."

"It does, I agree, but it's too melancholic. And done to death. We need something the algorithms won't compete with. *Ivory Lady* fits that bill, but I don't know. We'll see. The movie people will want a say, too." The option for this book sold months ago, and they put together the entire package and started shooting before she was even done writing, planning to have the film out within a few months of the book's release. It was a risk, but she's Columbia Jones, and at this point, they're paying enough that she can afford a gamble here and there. She's been furiously moving toward the end; they will be thrilled to know they can finalize the scripts now. They know the basic shape of it, but she's kept the details to herself.

They just need the right title.

Darian flashes a smile. "Don't worry, Mom. You could call it *The Iliad* and, with your name on it, you would win the algorithm. I'll go get the plates. Shall we eat by the fire?"

"Thank you, precious. Yes. Let's." She watches Darian's head disappear down the stairs, feeling a warm glow. Her daughter doesn't usually offer up platitudes or compliments, but that was nice.

She opens the computer, logs in to her socials, planning to share a quick note with her fans that she's finished the book, at last. She has a private group, and they've been cheering her on while she fought her way through the recalcitrant story. They deserve to hear the good news.

She starts a new post with the single word, code that they will understand as well as Darian had: *PIZZA!* They know how she celebrates the finale of a book. Every author has their traditions: hers are pizza and champagne. She probably got the idea from watching *Romancing the Stone* when she was a kid, seeing Joan Wilder bawling happily over the last lines of her latest romance, typing *The End*, then celebrating with an airplane bottle of Grand Marnier and a can of tuna for the cat.

That movie made her want to be a writer. To affect people. She wanted her name in lights, for people from all over the world to recognize her words. It was a foolish, childish dream, but one she's somehow managed to make come true.

Joan Wilder was so lonely in that scene, though. At least she has Darian. And the fans.

She presses Post and, reliable as always, the hearts and comments start almost immediately. These are her people. She communicates with them often and honestly, and they are thrilled to hear she's got another book for them to read. She will never truly be alone so long as her fans love her.

Her message notification goes red, and she is so high on the joy of finishing and the dopamine rush coming from the accolades that she clicks on it without thinking, even though she doesn't recognize the avatar. The message is startling, and she has to read it twice to fathom the words properly.

I know what you did. I know who you are. It's over. Or have you forgotten where you come from?

Tell them. Or I will bury you.

Before she can even register who sent this, what account it's from, the message disappears. Deleted, unsent, she has no idea which, but it's gone.

A terrifying chill spreads through her body, visceral and intense. She shakes, once, as if she's been dunked in cold water. Then the fury starts, burning through her. Sickening rage, violation, horror. She can't catch her breath.

"Mom?"

Columbia starts and slams the laptop closed just as Darian's head peeks above the stairs. "Do you want the Perrier-Jouët rosé? Or Dom?"

She can't speak, can't find her voice. She holds up two fingers, and Darian says "Dom it is" and disappears again.

Columbia reopens the laptop, staring at the now empty spot where the message appeared, then disappeared. How is that possible? And worse, who sent it?

There's no way. She has been so careful. So very careful. Her heart is thudding so hard she can hear it pounding in her ears, and she has to take three deep breaths to slow it down.

She stares at the screen until Darian comes clinking into her office with the chilled bottle of Dom Perignon and two flutes.

"You can tinker with it tomorrow. There's plenty of time. Now, we need to celebrate." She pops the cork and pours, hands over a glass. Columbia closes the laptop again and takes it, hand shaking.

"You okay?" Darian asks. "You're pale."

Columbia nods, and finally finds her voice. "I'm fine, precious. Right as rain." She taps her glass to her daughter's. "Here's to another one in the can. Chin-chin."

CHAPTER TWENTY-FOUR
DARIAN

Now

In the Upper East Side brownstone she's lived in most of her life, the one her mother bought with the ridiculous advance on her first book, Darian descends the stairwell from her room and her mother's office, marveling. Seeing this place with fresh eyes, open eyes, for the first time in years.

It's so easy to take your life for granted. So simple to ignore the rumblings of reality, to become complacent, to think things will never change. Of course, they do, and almost always when you least expect it.

This place, it is all so very Columbia. The Tabriz silk rug, the Regency side tables, and the George II mirror, all brought from her family home in Bromley. When her grandparents fell on bad times and had to sell everything else, these were the only things they kept. The Wedgwood and the English King flatware, stored neatly away. The library of first editions she's collected over the years—Austen, Hemingway, Woolfe. The closet full of St. John knits. The cashmere throws and cracked Chesterfield sofa. Understated, all. Everything is luxurious and expensive, but not showy. Classics. Elegant and sophisticated and timeless.

Columbia was a woman of good taste. Her success, the wealth she gained from her work, never went to her head. She had a real sense of humility, which was part of the reason her fans loved her. Yes, she liked nice things, but she didn't throw it in people's faces. (Except for the Rothko—an untitled blue-and-green color-field painting that was her pride and joy. She delighted in showing it off; the canvas hung in a place of honor, the only piece on the entire living room wall.) She recognized her place in the world, where she came from. Everything to nothing to everything. Cinderella.

Cinderella wasn't murdered at the ball, though.

Cinderella had an evil stepmother and two horrible stepsisters who made her life a sheer hell until she was swept off her feet by a hot dude who proceeded to turn her into a broodmare and made her wear uncomfortable shoes.

Maybe this isn't the best analogy.

Darian steps off the curved staircase into the living room, a space so familiar as to be alien today. Even the Rothko's blocks of blues and greens look unfamiliar. It all comes to her. Every inch of the estate, from the house and its handsome furnishings to the literary legacy, is now in her command.

As is stipulated in the will.

Darian got it out of the safe the moment she arrived home. Signed, sealed, witnessed, with Darian as the sole beneficiary. There is nothing in it about a woman in England by the name of Yvonne.

Darian hasn't called her grandmother back, but she did give her name to Liam to see what he could find. He's one hell of a bloodhound. And what he's found—or hasn't—is worrisome, to say the least.

Liam swears the woman doesn't exist. There is no one in Bromley by the name Yvonne Maxwell-Dodd—not in Bromley, not in London, not in all of England. The phone number that she has does go to a woman named Vonda West, though.

Vonda West has a long history of crimes, according to the filched copy of her arrest records Liam was able to provide from the UK's Police National Computer. Petty shit, namely identity theft.

What's worse, the photograph of the woman named Vonda West matches the mental image of the pigeon-hating woman Darian met all those years ago.

Darian has no idea what this means, and diligent searches through her mother's files have turned up nothing. Nothing.

Sunlight shivers into the living room. Darian swooshes open the drapes, then thoughtfully picks up a small white marble statue from the sofa table. Two lovers intertwined—a Rodin knockoff they'd bought from the museum the first time they were in Paris. The piece makes her blink back tears.

Though Darian's had several days to wrap her head around the fact that her mother is gone, forever, now the anger has set in. So many stages of grief for her to tackle. In the meantime, she must work. The meetings this week alone—lawyers, publishers, publicity, police—she's already drowning, and she hasn't even had a cup of coffee. Not to mention she needs to plan the memorial service. According to the will, her mother wanted to be cremated, that much Darian knew. That horrifying event is still in limbo until the Denver medical examiner finalizes the autopsy. Which is hopefully happening this morning.

So by next week, her mother will be dust.

Darian will fly back to Colorado for the cremation and bring the ashes home. And then, the process of allowing the people who loved Columbia to say a proper goodbye will begin.

But will it? Is there ever a way to say goodbye?

As if he knows she's thinking of him, her phone rings, and Detective Sutcliffe's name pops up on the screen. She stabs at the green button as if it is a glass of water in a very large desert.

"Detective? What did you find?"

"Hi, Miss Jones. Your mother's autopsy is complete."

"And?"

"Well, we don't have a conclusive cause of death. We have to wait for the toxicology screen to come back, and that's a multiweek process, as I've explained. But Dr. Duran has fast-tracked a separate screening for a few individual toxins. We'll know more conclusively in forty-eight hours."

"Two days? Can you tell me what she fast-tracked?"

"Not yet."

"Can you tell me if she was murdered?"

"Not definitively, no. I will say this, it's entirely possible she overdosed on something."

"*Overdosed?* Like on drugs? My mother doesn't do drugs."

"You've said that repeatedly."

"Then it's possible someone gave her something. Forced her to take it. Oh. Wow." Darian feels faint. Someone actually has killed her mother, and now there's proof. Sort of. More than a hunch. "Were you able to get Riley's fingerprints off—"

"I feel rather confident that Riley Carrington is not a suspect."

"So you're suggesting a stranger got into my mother's room and forced a toxic drug into her?"

"There's nothing that points to your mother being forced to do anything, Darian."

His voice is soft, and she feels the rage surge inside her.

"Are you saying she killed herself?"

"No, I'm not. And I'm not saying she was forced, and I'm not saying she was murdered. I am saying it looks like she ingested something that might have caused her death. Other than that, I'm keeping all of my avenues open, and so should you. This investigation is early days. This isn't a television show. The real world takes time."

"Yet you had a suspect in handcuffs, and you let her go."

He huffs an annoyed sigh. "I think your acrimony toward Miss Carrington is misplaced. Someone stole her bag while she was in custody, and that doesn't sit right. It's not like she could have taken it. I'm almost certain she's being targeted, too."

"Too? Am I being targeted as well?"

"I don't know. But you should be careful, regardless. Now, I hate to rush off, but you will be able to retrieve your mother's body for the cremation as soon as the paperwork is finished. I'll be in touch. And Miss Jones, please. No speculation online. You're making my job that much harder."

And he's gone.

Damn it, it infuriates her when he dismisses her like that. Plus, she'd wanted to mention Vonda West. She debates calling him back, but she's so annoyed right now, it might be best to cool off.

An overdose? That makes exactly zero sense. Darian wasn't kidding; her mother did not use drugs. She never took anything stronger than melatonin or a drop of CBD oil to help her sleep, and only then if it was dire. The police took the bottles she carried with her for emergencies with them for testing, along with all the rest of her things. Which would take six to eight weeks. It didn't matter that Columbia was a celebrity; these things take time.

But that was it. She didn't even like to take an Advil if she had a headache.

This apparently didn't matter to the police. Sutcliffe's theory: between the knockdown, drag-out fight about the stalker that ended almost as soon as the door closed because Darian, hurt and frustrated and so damn tired of being the target of her mother's ire all the time, had stormed off into her own room, and around 7:00 a.m., Columbia had managed to find and partake in a drug that killed her?

Absurd. Not to ding her mother—Columbia was a fantastic writer, but not so great at life. She was too distractible for the minutiae. That's what Darian did. Food. Clothes. Appointments. She managed her mother's day-to-day existence, she managed her business, she managed her moods and her fears and her insecurities and her grandiosity. She outlined and sometimes drafted her books and often pretended to be her on social media, and she made sure she slept and ate and showered. She ran herself ragged so her mother could shine.

To think that Columbia could, in a strange city, in the middle of the night, somehow leave the hotel and find her own agent of death . . . no. Darian isn't buying it. She clings firmly to her own facts: someone murdered her mother.

She brings the small Rodin statue with her, puts it on the mantel above the fireplace—ignoring that voice, the one belonging to a ghost, shouting "Put that back!"—and moves into the kitchen. The terra-cotta floors are warm under her bare feet, and she starts the ritual of making coffee.

Life goes on. It somehow marches in tune with the second hand on the clock on the wall—tick-tick-ticking its way forward. Like a heart, beating, again and again and again. Until it doesn't, until it stops, and there is no more . . . and now she's back in tears, damn it. She has to stop thinking. Thinking is her enemy.

The water is ready, the French press set. She waits a few minutes for the timer to beep.

Finally, the nectar she's been dying for.

Shit.

The entire lexicon of life is all about death.

She brushes it off, grabs a granola bar and banana, and weaves up the staircases two floors to her own office. It is one floor up from her mother's writing office—Columbia loved squirreling herself away on her "floor," two bedrooms merged into a full-blown workspace with floor-to-ceiling bookshelves, with an antique French rosewood desk and a rose marble fireplace. Elegant and inspiring, it is also everything Darian is not. Darian's office looks more like a bomb has gone off. Papers, books, boxes, galleys, three computers lined up edge to edge. It is a lair instead of an office, and the only place downstairs she feels like herself. The only place she can be herself.

She settles herself in front of the computer and opens her email. Two hundred unread. Since yesterday. A quick glance through shows she can safely delete most of them—subscriptions and newsletters and ads. The rest are filled with condolences, which have been coming in for days. She can't even imagine what her mother's website's contact email is going to look like. She hasn't opened it; she doesn't want to deal with the outpouring of loss from the fanbase.

How sad is her life? A twenty-nine-year-old woman living at home, answering her mother's email? Darian hasn't had time for her own life since . . . well, ever. No time for serious boyfriends, or close friends. The only people she knows well are those who circle her mother's world—when she does go out, most of the time it's with an editor or publicist from the house, and they always talk about Columbia. Even with her uncle Vic, not an uncle by blood, but by longevity, it's all about her mom. There's been no time to cultivate her own friendships, much less an actual relationship. Plus, people who aren't in the book world confuse her. She needs people who speak the same language, who understand the lingo, the stresses, the responsibilities. Books matter. She can't understand people who don't feel that intrinsically, feel it in their marrow.

Yes, it's been a little lonely. Lucrative, but lonely. And now it's all going to be on her. She won't have the excuse of having to be at her mother's beck and call. She is faced with a choice for the first time in her adult years. Get a life? Or stay in the shadows.

And now there's Mason. She can feel things shifting between them, and in her world. For the first time in years, Darian is in control of her destiny.

The doorbell rings, and she waits for Karstan to text her. The house is six stories, and they have a comfortable, convenient shorthand so neither is trudging up and down the stairs constantly. Then she remembers she gave Karstan a few days off to grieve and grabs her phone to tell whoever it is to leave whatever they've brought on the stoop.

"Sorry, ma'am, I have to get a signature from Darian Jones."

Grr.

"I'll be there in a minute."

She shoots the coffee a longing glance and hurries down the stairs.

There's a messenger wearing a bike helmet and Ray-Bans, shifting from foot to foot impatiently. He's holding a clipboard and an envelope.

"Sign here, please."

"What is this?"

"Dunno, lady. They just pay me to deliver them."

She prints her name, and he hands her the envelope and sprints off to his bike. He's gone before she closes the door.

She looks at the return address on the envelope in confusion. *Mathers and Mathers, Attorneys at Law.* The address is in Midtown. What the hell?

She rips open the envelope and spills out the contents.

> Dear Ms. Jones,
>
> This letter is to inform you that the last will and testament of Columbia Jones was recently filed for probate with the Manhattan Surrogate's Court of New York. Because of the private nature of this endeavor, there will be an in-person reading of the will on May 15, 1 p.m. ET, at my office. All beneficiaries are required to attend.
>
> If you have any questions about the will or the probate process, please do not hesitate to contact me.
>
> With my condolences, I remain, sincerely,
>
> *Preston J. Mathers, Esq.*
> Preston J. Mathers, Esquire.
> Senior Partner, Mathers and Mathers

What the actual hell is this? All beneficiaries? And who the heck is Preston Mathers? This is not one of her mother's lawyers.

This must be a mistake. A ridiculous, stupid, dreadful mistake.

CHAPTER TWENTY-FIVE

Frustrated and confused, Darian pulls every piece of legal paper from the safe in Columbia's closet and sets it all on the dining room table. This situation is straight out of one of her mother's novels. She half thinks it's some sort of joke, her wishful brain expecting her mother to pop out from behind the curtains with that chortling laugh—"Ha, precious, got you!"—like she used to when Darian was a child and they played hide-and-seek. Darian was forever hiding in places she thought were completely obscured from the world, and Columbia always, always, knew where she was.

"I love you so much I have radar when it comes to you," she'd say, scooping Darian into a hug and carrying her, giggling and squirming, to the kitchen for ice cream.

Don't do it, Darian's mind warns. *Stay mad at her. If you start remembering the good stuff, you will fall apart.*

The paperwork is as familiar and morbid as it was when Darian saw it last. She flips through the holdings until she finds the will itself. Dated and witnessed in 2020; when the COVID pandemic swept through the world, Columbia updated everything, just in case. She left the whole estate to Darian, who was horrified to be having the conversation over the table as if they were scheduling a book tour, replete with the exquisite bottle of Château Latour Bordeaux her mother broke out for the occasion. It was a gift from her editor Mary the first time they hit number one for fifty-two weeks straight. Columbia rarely drank, only on special occasions. They both caught COVID in the first wave, and they both luckily recovered relatively unscathed. But after that scare, Columbia got serious and updated everything, commenting relentlessly about how impermanent life is and you never know what might happen. When all was signed and witnessed, she broke open a bottle of the good stuff to toast their fortune and to tell her only daughter she was going to be set for three lifetimes and then some, not to mention the bevy of literary and animal charities who were going to benefit once Darian started writing them checks. They'd split the whole bottle, and neither could work the next day, dragging around the house, headachy and grumpily craving carbs.

It was a weirdly good night.

Now, she is grateful her mother was such a nut about it all. This Mathers and Mathers letter is a mistake.

She picks up the letter they've sent. The phrase *all the beneficiaries* leaps out again.

She calls Victor Guul, her mother's primary attorney and friend, who prepared the will she's holding in her hand. He answers right away, his warm-uncle-who-isn't-related-to-her-but-loves-her-to-pieces tone a small comfort.

"Darian, my dear. I am so happy to hear from you. We are all gutted—gutted!—by the news. Do you know what happened yet?"

"Thank you, Vic. Me too. We—I—don't know anything new. It's pretty clear she was killed, though the Denver Police are dragging their feet on saying that. There was blood everywhere. It was horrible."

She can almost hear him shudder. "I can't imagine. I am so, so sorry."

"Me too. We obviously have quite a bit to talk about, but I have a question before we do. Did Mom update her will recently?"

"The last time was in 2020, right after the two of you recovered from the plague."

"That's what I thought. I'm really confused. I have a letter from another firm, Mathers and Mathers, saying they have a current will and are summoning 'all the beneficiaries' to a reading. As you know, I'm the sole beneficiary, that's what she said she always wanted."

"Yes, she did," he agrees. "This is quite irregular, Darian. Mathers and Mathers, you say? I know the name. Father-and-son shop, relatively bluenosed, old school. You need to have a house in the Hamptons to get on their radar. Preston Mathers is a Yalie, by all accounts a decent guy. I don't know why in the world they would have any sort of connection with your mother, though. She's been with me exclusively her whole career."

"That's what's so weird about this, Victor. I'm going to call them and see if I can get to the bottom of this."

"I'm happy to make the call, Darian. Keep you out of the trenches."

"Sure. That would be great."

"Let me try right now. I'll call you back in a few."

Grateful as always for Victor's no-nonsense attitude, she hangs up and makes herself a cup of mint tea. Her nerves are jangling, and more caffeine will send her right over the edge into an anxiety spiral.

She paces, staring at the letter. *All* the beneficiaries.

She pounces on her phone when it trills to life. "Victor? What did they say?"

His voice sounds strangled now.

"You aren't going to like it. I don't like it, it smells to high heaven. Apparently, they have a new will, dated in January of this year. If they've done it right, it supersedes the one she did with me in 2020."

"What? When . . . how . . . oh my God, Victor. What the hell? When would she have even had time? I keep her appointments and I've never seen this name before."

"I understand completely, and I will continue trying to find out what's going on, all right? Don't panic. Any judge with half a brain will understand that the extended relationship—"

"A judge? Am I going to have to contest this?"

Victor blows out a small breath, through the phone. Darian can almost smell the coffee-and-mint-Nicorette-tinged breath that is his signature. "I suppose it depends on what she's done with her holdings, Darian, and whether you've been cut out in some way. Let's not get too far ahead of ourselves."

"Cut out? Of my mother's estate? The hell?"

"All right, take a breath. I misspoke. Of course, you haven't been cut out, not if you've received a beneficiary letter. But clearly, something is happening, because it's highly irregular for your mother to have dealings with another firm. Highly irregular. I've known Columbia since you came to New York, Darian. Almost your whole life. She wouldn't do this without good reason, and until we know what this new will says, we can't jump to conclusions, okay?"

Darian has immediately jumped to a million conclusions—anyone would—but she doesn't tell him that. "Okay."

"I would suggest you go through her things closely. Datebooks, schedules, anything that might give us an idea of why she might decide to do an end around and change things up. January . . . What was going on then?"

She thinks back. It feels like time should be measured in decades, not months. "Nothing. We were finishing up the last round of edits on *Ivory Lady*. Spielberg was finished casting, Mary and the team were doing their thing to set up the tour. She invited that reporter along, remember? Riley Carrington. That was a bit out of character, but she wanted to have a big splashy piece that was the 'definitive Columbia Jones.'" She uses air quotes even though Victor can't see her.

"And this Riley character, what sort of access did she have to your mother?"

"They just talked a lot, you know? Riley asked a lot of questions, and Mom answered them. She was actually pretty good natured about it, considering, but she was the one who wanted the piece done, so I supposed she went with honey instead of vinegar, you know?"

"I'm going to do a background check on Riley Carrington immediately, make sure she didn't exercise some undue influence over your mother. We can't be sure there's not something untoward happening."

"My God, this is a nightmare. I want to talk to Preston Mathers directly, before the reading. Can you make that happen?"

"He might not agree to that, but feel free to try. In the meantime, I'm going to get digging. Hang in there, okay? Let me know if you find anything else. I'd give your mother's papers a closer look if it were me. Maybe she's written something down that you missed."

"I will. But I still want to call the lawyer myself."

"I understand. Talk soon, dear."

She snatches up the letter from the strange lawyer and dials the number. When the receptionist answers, she doesn't bother to greet her.

"My name is Darian Jones, and I need to speak to Mr. Mathers immediately. He's sent me a letter concerning my mother's will and I have questions."

The reply is so automatic Darian knows it's a lie.

"I'm sorry, ma'am. Mr. Mathers is not available. He's working on a case out of the city. I'm happy to leave a message. Could I get your information, please?"

"Darian Jones. 212-555-6787. Tell him I have a beneficiary letter here. My mother has just passed, and I know for a fact we didn't use your firm for her estate. Did you get that?"

"Yes, ma'am."

She slams the phone down onto the table, takes a few deep breaths. She's feeling rather unhinged. Stalked. Screwed. Confused. Clearly, her mother has gone behind her back and done something. The question is, Why?

She looks at the paperwork on the table with new eyes. Skeptical eyes.

"What the hell were you up to, Mom?"

Darian starts at her mother's desk again, going through every piece of paper she can find.

The coffee goes cold, a skim starting on the surface. The light shifts, morning glow to afternoon shafts, catching tiny dust motes happily escaped from the staff's relentless cleaning.

There is nothing that mentions Mathers and Mathers, but after an exhaustive search through desk, office, closets, safe, and drawers, through online files and manila folders, she realizes there is something missing.

Her mother's journals are nowhere to be found.

An enthusiastic but not religious diarist, Columbia loved a specific brand of leather-bound journals that she ordered in bulk from France. Thick, lovely paper, perfect for a fountain pen, and all dated sequentially. It took Columbia about a year to fill one; if there were pages left over, she nonetheless started a fresh one every January first. When finished, they were stacked out of the way in the back of her office closet. Darian respects her mother's privacy and has never tried to read them. Even now, the thought of diving into her mother's mind without permission feels like a betrayal.

But the journals are not in their place.

Before she has a chance to go any further, her phone dings. It's Liam.

Hey—what's up?

Darian, are you at home?

I am.

OK. Our friend is in town. He pinged at Fifth and Seventy-Eighth. You need to be careful, all right? 😬

What the hell, Liam? Can you track him closer than that?

No. He only pops up every once in a while. I think he knows we're watching, and he's taking some precautions.

She blows out a breath.

This is freaking me out. We still think he's harmless, yes?

Yesssss . . . But hey, if you're not comfortable being alone, I can always come hang.

She feels an absurd spark of pleasure. Liam is cute. But not really her type.

I'm okay for now but thank you for the offer. I might reach out to some of the security guys who were on the road with us. They offered, too. I need to do some work with them anyway.

Right. No problem. Just shout if you change your mind. I'm an A train away.

You're awesome, Liam. Thank you.

Darian scrolls to Facebook. Sure enough, the stalker is there, disguised as another new member of the street team. How he gets in, she will never know, because she stopped allowing new members ages ago in an attempt to stop him, but on the post announcing Columbia's passing there is the photo of a smiling blonde woman with shiny teeth and a deep tan, and the simple comment *Do You Remember?*

Someone has been playing a very cruel game, and she is done with it.

She snatches up the phone again and hits a favorited number. Mason comes on the line moments later.

"Hey, Darian. I've been meaning to reach out. You okay?"

"No, I'm not. Are you back in New York by chance? Or are you on another job?"

His voice ticks up a notch. "I'm here."

"Can you come over?"

She hears the whisper of fabric as he stands and feels faint with relief at the warmth in his voice.

"I'm on my way."

Legacy Draft— Chapter Three

I woke in labor. The pain was beyond anything David had ever inflicted on me, physical or psychological. My pants were drenched in fecund liquid, and I screamed for David to help, to come let me out of the closet, but he refused. Maybe he was drunk, passed out. Maybe he hadn't come home, seeking refuge from his temper in a bar. Maybe he was just punishing me.

It went on forever, rolling waves of pain. The closet was just big enough for me to prop my legs on the opposite wall, a strange sort of stirrup presentation, and when I felt like I was going to split apart, the urge to push overtook me.

My darling girl was born on the floor of a coat closet, her mother bleeding, bruised, and terrified. It was dark in there—David had long since removed the lightbulb—but cracks of light stole beneath the door as if even the sun wanted to meet my girl.

David found us the next day. I was lucky; the bleeding had stopped, and my little girl was latched onto my breast. The mess we were in was rather disgusting, but we were safe, and she seemed healthy.

He was sorry. He always was. When he opened the door and saw the mess, he apologized, yanked me to my feet, and trundled us off to the hospital, watching me to see if I'd say anything.

I wasn't stupid. What was I going to do? Say? I had nowhere to go. He had control over everything. We lived in a small town, with people in each other's business. Everyone knew about his temper, but they turned a blind eye. This town, this small town with its good old boy mentality, they let David be the hero, the captain of the football team, the prom king, the son of the wealthiest man in town, the son of the man who knew everyone's secrets. What was I going to do? I had no one. My parents had passed when I was fourteen, and I'd lived with a girlfriend's family until we married. I'd told her, once, how David liked to use me, and her eyes got big. I never heard from her again.

Some friend.

The doctors brought me my girl after they'd finished checking her out, patted David on the back as if he'd done the hard work. I'm sure they could smell the stale alcohol on his breath and see the redness in his eyes, but they said nothing. Why would they? Someone here saw him out last night, I'm sure. They aren't dumb. They know he's a drunk. They know he's a bully. They don't know why I put up with it.

Neither do I.

Legacy Draft— Chapter Four

My stranger found me in the park two weeks after my girl was born, taking a break after walking the dog, using my foot to rock her stroller.

The bruises had healed. They always do. My heart, on the other hand, was torn. Something happened that night in the darkness. Being forced to give birth in a dank closet, bruised and battered and alone, had broken me. I wasn't able to look at David without a new hatred. A hatred that meant leaving, one way or another. The future was over for us. He'd killed it dead with his bitterness, with his fury, with the resentment he disguised as love.

Getting away, though, was going to be difficult. He would follow me. He would track me down and kill me. I needed a plan.

I needed an ally.

So when the handsome doctor stepped into my sunlight and smiled, at first, all I saw was opportunity. Not love. Not joy. Not peace.

A way out.

I didn't tell him that, of course. I didn't want him tainted. Patrick was an opportunity, yes, but after that? A future. A life. Love without conditions.

"How are you feeling?" Patrick asked, taking a seat next to me on the bench. It was warm today; I was wearing a tank top and my nursing bra was chafing the tender skin of my breasts.

"I'm all right."

"The baby is gorgeous. What's her name?"

"Saria."

"That's cute."

"Where are you from?" I blurted. "I mean . . . this is a small town, and you didn't grow up here like everyone else."

He didn't seem at all offended, just stretched his long legs out in front of him, relaxed as could be. "No, I didn't. I'm from Nashville. Did my final rotation at Vanderbilt, had a couple of offers in town, but I wanted something less complicated. So I moved here, and took a job at the hospital. I like it. The scenery is nice."

He wasn't talking about the trees and the grass. I blushed.

"I'm coming on too strong. I apologize."

"You're a bit much." He knew I was teasing; the sidelong glance he gave me was anything but annoyed.

"I'll go away if you tell me to."

He started to rise and I put a hand on his leg. "No. Please don't."

It was the boldest move I've made in my short life. I knew exactly what would happen if I stopped him from leaving. I was right.

It wasn't too hard to find moments together. Since he worked at the hospital, and I needed to take my baby in for checkups, I was able to legitimately visit his place of work weekly. The dog was always happy for a walk, which was a good excuse to visit the park. We walked the paths by the river, meandering with the stroller. It was so easy to pretend that he was the father of my baby. That he was my partner.

I never truly believed in love at first sight, but Patrick did. It wasn't a huge surprise when he started making noises about us being together for real.

"People get divorced all the time," he said.

"People have affairs all the time, too," I replied.

"I don't want to have an affair with you. An affair means things are temporary. I want you. All of you. Forever."

"I want you forever, too."

"Then let's go see a lawyer and start the proceedings. I'll go with you to talk to David—"

"No!"

The panic flowing through me made me stop in my tracks. The day had been so pretty, but just the thought of us showing up together for this major conversation made the skies above me darken and rain start to fall. That's how powerful our emotions were, we could change the weather on a dime.

We ran for the shelter of the trees. Once I made sure Saria was okay, I noticed Patrick was watching me, a small divot in the flesh between his eyebrows. I reached up and smoothed it away.

"I don't know how he's going to react, other than badly. I need to ease him into this. He's not happy, and I think he'll go for it, but I'm going to have to frame this just right so he thinks it's his idea."

"When?"

"You have to trust me. I'll figure it out."

His hand drifted to mine, his thumb caressing my palm. A lover's kiss.

"I don't want to wait."

"We have to."

I didn't want to wait either. I wanted him, so badly. Saria cried then, breaking the spell, and I left for home, leaving my future on the tree-lined path behind me.

CHAPTER TWENTY-SIX
RILEY

Nate checks them into the most anonymous hotel he can find for a last-minute reservation, the Sheraton in Times Square. It is full of convention goers and tourists, and the crowds hide them well. He scores a suite on the fortieth floor, two bedrooms and a cramped living space. It's not going to win any awards, but it's clean. Riley is grateful that the temptation of sharing a bed is eliminated, and the room is surprisingly quiet considering its proximity to the hustle and bustle. There are still sirens and horns, ubiquitous to the city, but they're muted behind the thick glass.

She doesn't want to know what it must cost. She isn't a stranger to the disposable income of the people in her life but can't help but have a mild panic attack at the thought of a month's rent for a single night in a hotel.

Nate gets a call, talks for a second, then hangs up. "Oliver is trying to reach you. He called the office."

She nods. "I need to call him. At least let him know I'm okay." Nate tosses her another of the burners, and she dials Oliver's number.

He is, to put it mildly, furious. After she says hello and he starts yelling, she actually pulls the phone from her ear and lets him go to town, waiting until she doesn't hear shouting anymore to respond.

"Are you through?"

"Where. Are. You?" His teeth are gritted; she can envision that angled jaw clenched, the muscle jumping. Oliver is usually pretty mild mannered, but when he gets mad and they fight, it's one for the ages.

"I'm safe. All of my devices were compromised. I had to get to the office and try to salvage the story. I'm sorry I scared you."

"You're sorry? Come home, right this minute. We will talk when you get here."

"Um. No."

Silence. "You're with *him*, aren't you?"

"Ollie, stop. We're trying to get the article finished. This is the safest place for me right now. We've discovered some—"

"Riley Carrington, if you love me at all, you will pour your ass in a cab now."

As if she's drunk, out on the town with her friends, and not caught up in some sort of crazy life-and-death situation not of her own making. She sees red but understands his frustration. He's scared for her. She can hear that. She tries to be reasonable.

"Don't bully me, Oliver. I know you're upset, and I apologize for scaring you. But I have to see this article through."

There's a pause. "Then I'm coming to you. Where are you?"

Nate, who must have turned off the music on his phone and is eavesdropping on the conversation, looks up and shakes his head vehemently. "Let me talk to him."

Reluctantly, she hands over the phone, and Nate hits speaker.

"Oliver, pal. Relax. She's in good hands. I won't let anything happen to her. But we have to get this piece done, and the cop from Denver wants her protected. I have security here. She's safe with me."

"You smug bastard. You probably arranged all this to get your hands on her."

"Don't be ridiculous. I would *never* put Riley in danger."

A string of very un-Oliver-like invectives pour through the speaker.

She snatches the phone back. Nate's tone isn't going to defuse the situation. If she can hear the proprietary longing, so can Oliver.

"Ollie, calm down, and talk to me like a grown-up. What's happened with the break-in? What have the police said?"

"They haven't said anything. They took the report, said there was no sign of forced entry, and I couldn't see that anything was missing, so nothing." His voice shifts. "I need you here, Riley. Please. Come home."

The pleading tone is also unlike him, and she's tempted to just give in. Oliver means safety, certitude, comfort. She should go to him; she should be with him. But she can't. She's going to choose her work over their future, and they both know it.

"I can't. You told me I had to finish the article, so I'm doing it as quickly as possible."

"You can do that here."

"What, in the flat? By myself? Without resources? While I'm being stalked by some creep and accused of murder, and someone's already broken in?"

"I'm here. I can help you. Like when we went to Cabo that time, and I helped you research the article on the drug cartels. You can decipher what's on the flash drive, we can figure out the password together. I'm sure it's in the paperwork somewhere. Unless you've already figured it out?"

"I haven't. And I thought you had a conflict with this because you're Columbia's lawyer?"

"Yes, I do. I did. I've recused myself. Now that I'm involved—"

And . . . that's it. Riley's temper flares to life.

"You were *involved* before, Oliver," she snaps. "With me. With us. *Our* life wasn't important enough for you to step away, but your precious flat gets burgled and suddenly you're all willing to get involved? To hell with that. I'll be in touch."

"Riley, wait—"

She ends the call and tosses the phone to Nate, who says nothing, just raises a brow.

"I hate it when he gets bossy," she says.

"Are you okay? You look like you might burst into flames at any moment."

"I just might." Riley pulls off her glasses, shakes her hair out of its bun. "Let's just get to work."

She ignores the nagging feeling that she's missed something talking to Oliver. She ignores that voice that says *Call him back, make it up to him. You were cruel. And you're going to lose him.* She ignores the voice that says Oliver sounded weird. She needs to work. She needs to figure this out. She can go back to Oliver later, when she's cooled off and the draft is done. He will understand when she can explain what's at stake.

They spread out through the living room, and Riley breaks open the new laptop. The online cloud service *East Fifth Magazine* uses should be secure; Tony hasn't rung any warning bells that they're compromised. Just in case, she resets her password and gets the authentication code through Nate's phone. Up and running, she pulls her files onto the new computer and opens the piece on Columbia, then reaches into her bag and pulls out the short story.

"You might want to read this. See if you can figure out why she sent it to me, and the article."

"All right. Before you settle in, when did you last eat?" Nate asks.

Her stomach traitorously growls in response. She thinks back. "I don't know. Maybe the coffee shop earlier today?"

"You need fuel. What can I get you?"

She leans back on the sofa. "Honestly? This is too important to stop if I get sick. I don't think I can risk it."

"You can't crash out a piece without food."

"Just get me some peanut M&M's and a banana and set up the coffee maker to run hot water for tea. That will do."

"I can have anything in the city delivered. What's your current favorite?"

"Peanut M&M's and a banana. Seriously, Nate, I can't chance it. Maybe add a Coke Zero for extra caffeine."

"There has to be some sort of celiac study you can get into," he grumbles, leaving her to it.

Five minutes later, the requested sustenance arrives. She tips the banana toward him.

"Thank you. Now I'm going to disappear for a bit." She pulls her headphones from her bag in illustration. "But hey, I'm feeling bad about how I left things with Oliver. He was only trying to help. The last thing we need is some investigator from Mathers and Mathers searching for us and blowing it all. Maybe you can reach out to him? Explain the stakes? But don't tell him where we are, or he'll be banging on the door."

Nate frowns but nods. "Will do. Anything else?"

Hold me again. Tell me I'm safe. "No. Thank you."

"You're welcome. You work. I'm going to find out who this Knox Shepherd guy is," Nate says, and she nods absently, already running through what she has, what she doesn't, and what she actually needs to confirm before they run the piece. Her opening line needs to be adjusted.

Columbia Jones is arguably the world's most successful author.

Well, that won't do. Not now. She chews on a nail and starts over.

The author of your favorite book has died.

And she's off.

CHAPTER TWENTY-SEVEN
OLIVER

Oliver hangs up the phone and looks over at the man who's sitting at the counter on the wobbly stool—the last place he saw Riley before she burst out of the flat like a quail flushed from the brush—and shakes his head.

"She's not coming."

"Tsk," the man says, sighing. He's Oliver's age but looks like he's had a much rougher life. His skin seems almost leathery, as if he's spent his whole life outdoors getting sunburns and the skin peeled off again and again, damaging it like a burn. Maybe he was burned as a child. That was possible. The skin shimmers in certain lights, at certain angles, like he's put on a great deal of moisturizer. Maybe he's just sweating.

"So now what?" Oliver asks, keeping up the bravado. The gun pointed at him is enough to make him want to scream, but he needs to stay calm, to keep his head. When the police left after taking his report, he wasn't surprised to hear a knock on the door, assumed one of them was back to ask another intrusive question or fingerprint him again—as if he'd break into his own flat. "Exclusionary, sir," the tech said, but Oliver felt the eyes on the back of his neck. The police never took a statement at face value; it just wasn't in their nature.

He had answered the door only to find himself staring at the long barrel of a suppressed gun, and a man behind it in a red ball cap who was inside a heartbeat later, Oliver backpedaling into the living room so fast he tripped over the ottoman of the broken-in Herman Miller lounge chair he spends evenings in, reading.

Sprawled on the floor, he saw the stranger close and lock the door, then advance, the gun pointed directly at Oliver's forehead. The stranger's eyes were flat and black, like a snake's, and Oliver knew at that moment he was about to die.

"Where's Riley?" the man demanded.

"I don't know."

A gun to the temple hurts, badly. The blow knocked off his glasses, and then the world was a blur. Maybe that was better. He didn't want to see into the depth of this man's soul any more than he already had. It was a wasteland.

"You're going to call her and ask her to come home."

"I can't. I've been trying to call, and her phone's turned off. It just goes straight to voicemail."

"Then call her office. But get the girl back here. You understand me? Do that, or you and I aren't going to get along very well."

Oliver called Riley's office, and of course, the front desk said she was unavailable. He said it was an emergency and was still denied access. "Please tell her to call me as soon as she can. It's life or death."

"Now we wait," the man said amiably. "Got any food? I'm famished."

Fifteen minutes and a turkey-and-provolone sandwich and beer later, Riley called. Oliver had never been so relieved, but he also knew he had to keep her safe. If she got mad at him, she wouldn't come home, maybe ever, and that was the risk he needed to take. He also needed to warn her. But the stranger hit speaker, so he heard every word out of Riley's mouth. *Be clever, Oliver.*

So he did what he had to, acted the jealous boyfriend, insulted her, insulted Nate, cursed and fumed. The stranger watched with a hiked brow, as if he knew of Oliver's meager attempt to save Riley's life. He slowly shook his head and racked the slide of the pistol. Oliver changed tack. He begged. And that should have warned her off, too. Oliver Mathers did not beg.

"I need you here, Riley. Please. Come home." He heard the crack in his voice; she must have as well, because her tone softened.

"I can't. As you pointed out, I have to finish this article."

"You can do that here."

"What, in the flat? By myself? Without resources? While I'm being stalked by some creep and accused of murder, and someone's already broken in?"

The creep in question smiled nastily, and Oliver's blood chilled. *Do something!*

"I'm here. I can help you. Like when we went to Cabo that time, and I helped you research the article on the drug cartels. You can decipher what's on the flash drive, we can figure out the password together. I'm sure it's in the paperwork somewhere. Unless you've already figured it out?"

"I haven't. And I thought you had a conflict with this because you're Columbia's lawyer?"

"Yes, I do. I did. I've recused myself. Now that I'm involved—"

"You were *involved* before, Oliver," she growled at him, thoroughly pissed, and he did a silent little dance of joy, because there was no way in hell she was coming home now. "With me. With us. *Our* life wasn't important enough for you to step away, but your precious flat gets burgled and suddenly you're all willing to get involved? To hell with that. I'll be in touch."

"Riley, wait—"

But she's gone.

"I love you," he says quietly to dead air, peace stealing into his roiling heart. She's safe. He's saved her. And hopefully, she's going to figure out sooner rather than later that he was saying things under duress. Might take her a few to come back down and analyze the conversation—he got her riled up. But she'll get there.

Forgive me, Riley. I really do love you.

"Dang, buddy. You don't have control of your woman, do you? Such a shame. It would have been easier on all of us if she'd agreed to play along. Now, be a good boy and give me your phone."

"Why?"

"So I can find out where she is and go pay her a visit myself." He pulls something the size of a stack of ten credit cards from his pocket, snatches the phone from Oliver's grasp, and plugs it into the device. "See, she got smart and ditched the tracker I put on her. And she's shut down her phone, and her laptop, so the software I planted isn't doing us any good, now is it. But since she kindly cooperated by calling, now I can pinpoint her location again."

"What do you want with Riley? She's innocent."

"Ah, but is she?" The man's leathery skin is disquieting; it seems to shimmer as he talks, but he's staring at the screen in his hand, not at Oliver anymore.

"Of course she is. I don't know what you think she did."

"Oh, she did plenty. But she has something I need. And I intend to get it."

"That's why you broke in here, isn't it? And you killed Columbia Jones, too, didn't you?"

The man laughs. "Now there's a bitch who deserved every bad thing that happened to her. Ah, here we go. Seventh and Fifty-Second." He pauses, consults his own phone. "They're either at the Sheraton, or the Manhattan, but either way, your girlfriend and her boss are shacking up. That must piss you off, man."

Oliver looks down. Yes, it pisses him off. He's always known Riley was still attached to Nate. He thought they were going to make it past that until she leaped at the chance to go on the road with Columbia Jones, to disappear into that world for a month, and he knew he had lost her, even if she didn't know it herself. But at the moment, he doesn't care. In fact, he's grateful for her attachment to Nate because that means she's safe. He wants to get his hands on his phone, call her back, warn her. Hopefully she'll pick up on what he said, realize he was sending her a message. Even if she doesn't, even if this jerk finds her at the hotel, Nate's security will protect her.

The leathery man smiles, putting his phone back in his pocket and unplugging the device attached to Oliver's phone. He's set the gun down. Maybe if Oliver moves fast, he can grab it. The man wipes the phone off carefully, sets it on the table, and Oliver starts to move. But the stranger snags the gun, a move so fast, so fluid, Oliver recognizes the weapon is almost a part of this man. A limb. He feels a chill go down his spine. Men who are so well versed with weapons aren't going to be deterred. He's not wrong.

"No, no, no. I don't think so. Sit back and relax, Oliver. This won't hurt a bit."

"Come on. We can settle this like gentlemen. Do you need money? I can help there. I can get you as much as you need."

"No, thanks. This isn't about money. Thanks for your help, pal. See you in hell."

"Wait—"

The last thing Oliver Mathers hears is the *pffft* pop of the silenced pistol.

TUESDAY

CHAPTER TWENTY-EIGHT
KIRA

It is half past six on a sunny Colorado morning, and Kira Hutchinson is covered in flour—her happy place. She pops a batch of Lindt tarts into the oven and heads to the sink to wash. That's everything for the morning bake in the ovens. Now she can pull a decaf espresso and catch her breath. She's tired. These early weeks of pregnancy are rough.

She collapses onto a stool gratefully and doesn't even look up when the door chimes. It will be Alex or Lisa, both of whom are running late, it seems.

"Ma'am?" A stranger's voice. She glances at the door and is faced with a bald man taking off his sunglasses. He has sky blue eyes and a compact mountain biker's frame.

She smiles. "We're not quite open, but if you'd like to wait for five minutes, I could make you a coffee and drag a second-day croissant out from the back . . . Today's are still in the oven."

"Are you Kira Hutchinson?"

The tone freezes her. She is a wife; she is a mother. No one uses that questioning tone when things are going well. "Yes. Is everything okay? Has something happened?"

Out comes a black leather case with a silver badge inside. "Detective Sutcliffe. Denver Police. Major Crimes Unit. Do you have a few?"

She shoots to her feet, heart in her throat. "Is it Luke? Is he hurt? The boys?"

"No, ma'am. Sorry to alarm you. I'm here to talk about Columbia Jones. You were at the theater that night. I'm talking to the VIPs."

She is overwhelmed with relief and feels a spike of guilt for that. "Oh. Okay. You scared me. It's such a shame. I can't believe she's dead. Have you figured out what happened yet? The paper said there were conflicting reports about how she died."

"Don't believe everything you read," Sutcliffe says lightly. "I'll take that coffee, if you don't mind. Espresso is great."

"It's decaf. Not a robust blend," she warns.

"No worries. Preferable."

She gets him a cup—branded with the bakery's name and logo— and pulls a second espresso. "Anything in it?"

"Black's fine. Thanks."

He takes it from her and shoots it down like a proper Italian. When she raises a brow, he smiles. He has a nice smile. Very unthreatening for a cop.

"I studied art history in Florence for a semester. Got used to it this way." He sets the cup in the small saucer. "So you purchased a special VIP experience with Columbia Jones the night she died, is that correct?"

"My husband got it for me as a birthday present. The gesture blew me away. I've been a fan for a long time. It was a very special night, we got to talk for fifteen minutes or so. I just can't believe she's gone."

"Since you are such a fan . . . Was there anything unusual, anything she did or said that felt out of place? How did she seem? Relaxed, on edge?"

"Tired. She seemed tired. She covered it well, but she seemed to lack the spark I've seen from some of her events. They broadcast them all, so people who can't make it can tune in for the talks. They charge, of course, you have to buy a book and the receipt has the code to watch. I buy all her books, but until last week, I've only ever seen her digitally. Even on a screen, she was a vibrant soul. Friday—meeting her in person, talking to her, it was incredible. She was very kind and surprisingly open."

"Open how?"

"Oh, just even friendlier than I imagined. Asked me about my kids—when we apply for the VIP, there's a questionnaire, I suppose to give her a leg up on us. I bet they do research into us to make sure we're not nuts or something. I would if I was her."

Her sous-chef chooses this moment to breeze through the door. He's smiling with some sort of plausible excuse for why he's late until he sees Kira's face, and immediately ducks his head and puts on his apron. She hears the oven doors opening and returns her attention to the cop. Alex can handle getting the store open for her.

"Everyone's running late today," she says. "So we were talking about the VIP event. I didn't see anyone there out of place. We were all super excited, and she was really sweet to everyone. It was very exciting to mix and mingle with our favorite author. After she left we all just sat there, starstruck."

"So nothing else stood out, other than she seemed tired? No tension?"

"No. Darian—that's her daughter—manages her pretty tightly. They'd been on the road for a month, touring. I just assumed Columbia was exhausted from all the glad-handing. She's very *on* when she's touring. It can be hard for an introvert, and she was definitely an introvert."

"How do you know that?"

"Oh, she talks about it all the time. You'll see it on her social media. She's always been open about her need to recharge after doing an event."

"Right."

"I will say, I wondered when she fainted if there was something more going on. If she was sick or something. Not like altitude sick, but ill."

She's reaching, and the cop deflects.

"I'm sure that will all come out sooner or later. Did you see the man who stood up during her event?"

She thinks back. "Sure. I was in the loge box next to him. All the VIPs had the best seats. I assumed he was with us, but I hadn't seen him before then. He wasn't at the party before the event."

"Can you describe him?"

"Tall. Curly brown hair. Square jaw. Seemed intense. He was scowling when he stood. Why? Do you think he had something to do with this?"

"If I showed you a photo, think you could identify him for me?"

"Yeah, definitely."

He hands her his tablet, which has a grid with six men's faces on it.

"Him," she says, pointing to the first man on the bottom row. "Did he do something wrong?"

"I'm just trying to put the pieces together. Figure out how she got dead."

"So she *was* murdered?" Kira asks, alarmed by the idea of a suspect. "And this man is responsible?" A heartbeat. "Do you know who he is? Where he is? Am I in danger?"

"No, no. Slow down. You're not in any danger. I do know who he is, I was just confirming that we have the right man. And again, I'm just looking at all the angles. They pay me to ask questions." That soft smile again. "Did you meet the reporter who was along for the ride?"

"I did. Riley Carrington. Are you familiar with her work? She's truly an impressive woman. I'm not at all surprised she's going to do a biography of Columbia."

"A biography? I thought she was just writing a piece for *East Fifth Magazine*."

"She is. But Columbia mentioned to me that Riley was going to do her memoir. I can't imagine anyone better—I mean, Darian would be good, she's an accomplished writer, but Riley has a magical touch. She's very readable and, at the same time, relatable."

"I'll be sure to look up her work. Was this memoir common knowledge?"

"No. She actually told me not to tell anyone. Guess I've slipped up, huh? I heard . . . I mean, there have been a lot of rumors floating around on the internet, and in the private fan groups. I heard Riley was arrested. I suppose I assumed you'd already talked to her?"

"I spoke with her just like I'm speaking with you. And I think I have what I need for now. Please reach out if you think of anything, all right?" He taps the photograph. "Thanks for the chat, and the coffee. It was delicious. This place has a great reputation. Best bakery in Boulder."

Kira recovers herself long enough to go into chief-chef marketing mode. "Well, you need to take a bag of treats with you. No doughnuts, ha ha, but we do have fresh raspberry tarts and almond croissants and lavender cupcakes."

She gets Alex to put together a sampler, hands it to the cop with a smile. She's feeling nauseated and just wants the detective to leave. This whole situation is heartbreaking—Columbia being dead only the beginning. The papers and social media have been almost gleeful in their coverage of her death. Respectful, but the was-she-or-wasn't-she-murdered angle is juicy, and the world is bored. Soon enough there will be another splashy tragedy and they'll move on.

Kira won't. Forevermore, she is one of the last people on earth to see Columbia Jones alive, and her death will be tied to the small life growing within her.

It's not something that goes away easily.

The door swings closed, and she shuts her eyes, taking a deep breath. Whoever the curly-haired man is, she assumes he is in big trouble.

It is strange because he feels so familiar, like she's seen him before. She thought that at the event as well. Maybe he's come into the bakery. That makes sense. If she weren't so tired, maybe she could think it through, but for now . . . she has a big day ahead. She's feeling off but needs to get back to work.

The detective's visit has stirred up all her emotions again. She spent the whole weekend in tears. She still can't believe Columbia is dead. The loss is a hole in her heart, an ache so deep it's almost like she's lost a family member. Columbia Jones has been a part of her life since she was a girl and read *Pretty Baby* and insisted immediately on cutting her long blonde still-baby-fine hair into a pixie because the main character's daughter gets lice and has to do the same. She was convinced, *convinced*, it would happen to her. That was the power of Columbia's worlds, they became more real than reality.

Kira assumes all the fans are feeling this desolation, this dislocation. They are all in mourning. It is such a shame to lose someone so amazing, who affected so many lives.

She touches her stomach. Maybe there's a way she can pay tribute after all. Columbia is a pretty name.

Smiling at the thought that maybe, possibly, they've finally created a girl, she hustles back to the kitchen.

CHAPTER TWENTY-NINE
DARIAN

Darian wakes slowly, blinking hard, eyes watering against the sunlight streaming through a tiny crack in the drapes. She starts to roll over but senses a presence in the bed. She closes one eye to focus—she realizes now she has a horrid headache, she had whiskey before bed and that always does it to her—and sees red hair against the white satin pillowcase.

Additional perusal confirms her first impression. The owner of said hair is shirtless, showing off a broad chest and thick shoulders, both covered in a dense webbing of freckles. She smiles to herself, remembering when she first saw Mason remove his shirt. They were in Miami, sneaking around, and the room was dark enough that she hadn't noticed the freckles. She hadn't been paying attention to much, actually, except the solid feel of him in her arms, the sense of safety and arousal that combined to a desire she hadn't known she was harboring until the third glass of wine loosened her morals and her legs.

There was nothing wrong with having a tour fling with one of her mother's bodyguards. Nothing at all. They were very discreet, sneaking around like teenagers, having fun. Letting off steam.

Now, though, back in the real world, it feels different. Like they're going to have to talk about it. Put a label on it, maybe.

Did you sleep with him so he'd stay over, and you'd be safe? Precious. I expect better.

"No!" she answers her mother's scolding ghost, aloud, and this disrupts the sleeping giant next to her. He opens a blue eye, raises a brow, reaches out an arm and pulls her to him, snuggling her deeper into his body. She sighs, lets her eyes close, and relaxes bonelessly into him. Her head throbs in time to her heart, and she soon realizes he's not fully asleep, either. She deliberately pushes her bottom backward, and he laughs, a low rumble in his chest.

"I feel dreadful," she whispers.

"So do I." A steady series of beeps sounds from the nightstand. He groans. "Someone's texting you."

"So I hear." She doesn't want to move. She's quite comfortable, thank you very much. But when the phone rings, she rolls over with an "Oof."

"Shit. It's the cop in Denver."

Mason leans up on one elbow. "Better get it then."

"Hello?" She sits up, the sheet spilling to her waist. Mason traces a finger along her ribs, making her shiver. She bats his hand aside with a smile.

"Hey, Darian. Detective Sutcliffe here. I sent you a couple of texts. Could you do me a favor and take a quick look at a six-pack for me?"

Resisting the quip—*Already looking at one, sir,* which she is; Mason's cut like a freaking model—she puts him on speaker and swipes over to her texts.

"You'll see an array of men, and I'd like to know if any look familiar."

She enlarges the photo. Six men. She looks at them carefully. Only one seems familiar, and she says that.

"Which one?"

"Bottom middle."

"Where have you seen him before?"

"At the theater? I think it was him, the guy who stood up."

"Does the name Knox Shepherd mean anything to you?"

"No. Good character name, though. My mom would love it."

That searing pang of loss bolts through her, and she gasps. It's too soon to think of Columbia in this way. Mason reaches for her hand, squeezing it tightly.

"You okay?" Sutcliffe asks.

"Yeah. Sorry," she says. "No, I don't recognize him. Who is he?"

"A convicted felon who was released from jail over a decade ago. The real question is, Who was he to Columbia?"

"You have a suspect," Darian breathes.

"We need to have a conversation with Mr. Shepherd, that's all. He was at the theater, but without video from the hotel to confirm, we can't place him there. I'm doing a canvass this morning of the hotel's staff to see if anyone's seen him."

"So Riley really wasn't involved."

Sutcliffe is silent.

"Fine. I guess I owe her an apology. What do you need me to do? Should I put his photo up on social media?"

"God, no. You don't do *anything*. We don't know if this man is simply a fan of your mother's work or if something more sinister is at play."

She curls her legs under her body and leans back against the headboard. "I have to tell you something. Mom's stalker is in New York. His cell phone pinged last night. Our IT guy, Liam, has been tracking him for me, and called to warn me. Do you think this is the same guy?"

"I don't know, Darian. But you need to be careful."

"I have resources," she says, and the corners of Mason's mouth rise.

"Good. Stay aware of your surroundings. I'm going to reach out to your precinct and tell them what I know. And I need your IT contact. It's time for him to share his access points and my team to take this over."

"I don't know how much he'll like that, but I understand what you're saying. His name is Liam Reeves, and he works for a firm called 49 Spiders."

"Got it. Thank you. Keep aware of your surroundings, all right?"

"Thanks, Detective. Hey, you said Shepherd is a felon. What was his conviction?"

A pause. Sutcliffe clears his throat. "Second-degree murder. He killed a man in Tennessee."

They make breakfast, and it's over the orange juice and scrambled eggs that Mason jars her back to reality.

"I told the detective about us."

"What? When?"

"In Denver. After you talked to him the first time. I didn't want him treating you like a suspect anymore."

She's not sure how she feels about this but smiles at his protectiveness.

"Giving me an alibi?"

He nods, suddenly serious. "I didn't want what happened to Riley to happen to you, too."

"Do you think Riley did it?"

He shakes his head. "I don't. What would she have to gain by killing Columbia? Do I love the chick? No. But I can't imagine she has murder in her."

"You do think my mom was murdered, though, right?"

"Absolutely. Sutcliffe does, too. He just doesn't want to get hung out to dry. You're going back to Colorado?"

"Yes." Darian sits hard on a stool at the marble counter. "I want to be there when she's cremated, and bring back her ashes. I've been trying to wrap my head around a funeral. It's impossible."

"I can help you, if you want."

"Really?"

"Sure. I assume you'll do something private to start, then a public memorial service down the road?"

A bloom of relief sparks in her chest. She's been dreading this so much. Not having to do it alone?

"Yes. That's what I was thinking exactly. The publishers will want to do something, too. She and Mary were close. She's been with them since the beginning of her career. I haven't ever done anything like this. And with the lawyers, and all the weirdness . . ."

She trails off.

"What weirdness?"

She pours some juice and takes two Advil, offering him the bottle. He shakes his head.

"Mom has a second will that I wasn't aware of. I'm the sole beneficiary of the one I'm familiar with, but she has a secret one that our lawyer says will supersede it. Multiple beneficiaries. I don't know what to think."

"That is incredibly strange. For her to make a new will, then be murdered? I mean, come on. No wonder you're so stressed. Can I see the six-pack the detective sent you?"

She hands over her phone, and he takes it and enlarges the photo. He stares for so long that she nudges his foot with hers. "Your eggs are getting cold."

He smiles, hands the phone back. "Have you thought about talking to Riley?"

"No!" She hears herself, the petulant child, and is embarrassed. "I mean, I wasn't exactly on my best behavior when we last talked."

He takes a sip of orange juice, the muscles in his throat rippling. She feels lightheaded.

"Sure, I hear you. You probably do owe her an apology, getting her arrested in the first place. But she's spent the past month with your mom, locked up in hotel rooms and cars and planes, talking. Maybe she knows something about this new will. About the Yvonne woman. Maybe Columbia said something to her."

Darian taps her fork against her plate. She knows she should reach out, but she isn't ready to swallow her pride just yet.

"I want to wait until Vic tells me if he finds anything in the background check. He was really upset. Let's see it through. Anyway, who is this Knox Shepherd guy?" she asks. "I bet Liam can check him out for me."

"Well, I looked him up while you were making the eggs." He pushes his phone toward her. "There's not a lot online, the case predates social media. But with his record? Serving fifteen years for murder isn't something to take lightly. Obviously, he's a viable suspect."

"You know . . ." She looks at the picture again, a chill shivering through her. "I think he was there that morning . . . in the hotel. He came in the room." She shuts her eyes, tries to re-create the scene. "Yes, I'm sure it was him. God, Mason. Did he follow us from city to city until he had the perfect opportunity?"

"That's freaking creepy. Maybe? I never saw him, but now that we have a picture, I'm sure Sutcliffe will share it with the rest of the team. Maybe one of them will know something."

"Why do you think he'd want to kill my mother?"

"I don't know," Mason says grimly. "But you can rest assured I'm not leaving your side until he's arrested." He reaches across the table, touches the top of her hand with a finger, tracing it up her arm. "I can't lose you, too."

She is in his strong arms moments later. Grateful, so grateful, to feel protected and cherished. To have something good come from this horrid situation.

When she can catch her breath again, she smiles shyly. "The eggs are ruined."

Mason laughs, and she feels love in the music of his voice. "We can make more."

With Mason in the house, Darian feels less scattered. Together, they sketch the plan for the next few weeks—setting a date for the private funeral according to the will Darian is familiar with, sending the invitation to the small group of people Columbia wanted to attend, and then tackling the public memorial with the PR team at the house, and Spielberg's people to coordinate their plans going forward, getting everyone on the same page. She's been at a loss since she came back from

Denver, and now is in control again. There will be time to discuss the creative soon enough.

In response, a note comes from one of Spielberg's people, and she reads it aloud to Mason.

"'Sorry again, Darian. This sucks. Forgot to ask, your mom was going to tape a video for us, her reaction to the casting. Any chance you know where it is? We'd love to use it in the director's cuts.' Huh. I don't remember doing this with her."

"You handled all the media, didn't you?"

"Yeah."

"Have you checked her computer? Maybe it's on there. Might be worth a look."

Darian frowns. "I guess. But I'd keep something like this in my files. Her computer isn't even connected to the internet. Well, that's not entirely true, she has two. A writing laptop and a desktop for business. She writes on the desktop sometimes when we're home, but she liked to keep the two parts of the job separate. But the police still have her laptop."

"But what about her actual files? Do you have access to them?"

"Yes. I mean, it's all in a shared account."

"When's the last time you took a look? Maybe there's something new. Maybe she left you a message."

She smiles despite herself. "Now you're thinking like a mystery author, that there's some sort of coded message explaining everything in her work."

He grins back. "Well, I do read. It's not entirely out of the question."

She stands, wobbling just a touch until he grabs her arm to steady her. "All right, why not? Let's go take a look."

CHAPTER THIRTY

Just sitting at her mother's desk feels like a betrayal.

Darian touches the space bar on the keyboard gingerly, as if it might cause the computer to explode, and the desktop whirs to life, the display a series of green and blue boxes that look like computer-generated stained glass, a generic default that came with the computer fresh out of the box. Columbia never saw the point of deviating; it wasn't like she spent a lot of time staring at the images.

She enters the password, and the interior of the system appears.

Columbia had always been organized to a fault on her computers. She resisted replacing them until they were no longer usable. And when she did get a new one, she always had Darian set them up the same way, with the track pad set opposite of its default settings, the dock magnified, and from right to left, her internet browser, her email, her journaling app, her writing software, Zoom, and the weather. That's it. Clean, simple.

All the files are also organized in a system Darian devised that shows the number of the book, the title, and what year it will be published. The folders then contain everything broken down by the various steps: Art, Editorial, Marketing & PR, Media Kit. They also tie directly to Darian's computer in a shared cloud account. Columbia may have liked Darian to handle things, but she also wanted everything to do with a title at her fingertips.

Darian pulls up *Ivory Lady* and looks in the Marketing & PR sub-folder, scrolling through the multitudes of interviews, essays, podcasts. Columbia has always been generous with her time around a launch. She blocks off the month before tour to dedicate to the PR, and the month of release for the physical tour itself. Two months away from writing, though she always sneaks in a little. Then they take a two-week vacation somewhere fabulous, and she gets back to work. They were meant to be in Saint-Tropez right now. Darian hated canceling the hotel and flights. It made this so real.

Darian scrolls through, hitting video after video, all things she shot or that were provided by the interviewers. *Good Morning America* had featured *Ivory Lady* for its monthly book club, and had come to the house to do a shoot. Darian smiles ruefully, remembering the chaos from that morning—Columbia had lost one of the earrings she wanted to wear, and everyone in the household was looking for it. At least she can look back on it and laugh; that morning, Columbia had called her some pretty choice names before the doorbell rang and the film crew arrived, then flipped the switch and became God's gift to literature.

Her mother wasn't abusive. She was just abrasive.

A wave of grief overwhelms her, and tears prick the corners of her eyes. The last words she shared with the one person on the planet who was supposed to love her unconditionally were in anger. Fury, really. Darian will never be able to undo the fact that the last thing she said to her mother before she died was "I hate you." It is only made worse that her mother had said it back.

"You okay?" Mason asks softly.

She clears her throat and winds up her still-damp hair. "Yeah. I'm not seeing anything that matches the casting reaction. Maybe it's in another file."

She searches around for a while but sees nothing that isn't readily available on her own machine. On impulse, she types *Vonda West* into the search. Nothing pops, but she notices there are files living in the

Documents folder on the hard drive. She clicks on this and is met with a gray box asking for a password.

She types in the shared password they use for the account. The box shivers but doesn't open. "What the hell?"

"What's wrong?"

"She's somehow managed to turn on password protection to the local documents drive. I swear. This woman shouldn't be allowed anywhere near technology."

"Unless she did it on purpose."

Darian shoots him a look. "Mason. You know my mom."

"I do. And don't take this the wrong way, but she was pretty sharp. It was probably a thousand times easier to let you manage everything, but in a pinch . . ."

She ignores the tiny spike of annoyance because he's right. Columbia could do many of these things, she just chose not to. And the technology changed so quickly that she didn't want to feel left behind, so she made Darian show her how to manage when something new happened. "In case you're off gallivanting and I need something immediately, precious."

She looks at the blank space for the password. When she typed in Vonda, this appeared. Worth a shot. She starts to type.

"What are you trying?"

"V-O-N-D-A."

Nothing.

"What about the whole name?"

"Okay. V-O-N-D-A-W-E-S-T."

And, like magic, the file opens, and a series of documents appears. Darian tries, and fails, to make sense of what she's seeing.

There are manuscripts. Lots of manuscripts. She opens a few; they are stories she doesn't recognize. The dates are in the early 2000s. Judging by the file sizes, there are at least twenty novel-length manuscripts and a series of short stories.

"More novels?" Darian says, breathless. "Holy shit. It's going to take me ages to go through all of it."

"Why would she have it password protected?"

"I don't know. But since the password is the name of this woman who's tied to my grandmother, chances are it's something she didn't want me to see. Though I have no idea why. God, this is frustrating."

"What's that?"

Mason is pointing to a file titled "Daughter." Curious, Devon opens it, and a letter follows.

> My darling daughter,
> I'm not going to hide this from you anymore.
> Many, many years ago, I did a very bad thing.

Darian reads the letter once, twice, trying, and failing, to wrap her head around the words. Finally, she points at the screen. "Do you think it's the beginning of a story?"

Mason is shaking his head. "That feels awfully personal to me. Like it's meant for you. *My darling daughter* . . . Who else could it be addressed to?"

"It has to be a story fragment."

"Maybe. What else is in there?"

She scrolls through the files, all titles and names she doesn't recognize. "I don't know what these are." She makes a decision, and gently, deliberately, presses the red X that closes the folder, then puts the machine to sleep. It's all too much. She can't do this with Mason here. She needs privacy, because she truly doesn't know what else she's going to find, and the dots are starting to link together that her mother was hiding something from her. Something big.

"I don't know what's going on, but before I do anything else, I want to talk to Vic. I want him to sit down across from me and explain what the hell my mother was up to. He's been her closest friend for nearly thirty years. Clearly, there are things she didn't trust me with. I know she was killed, and I know the logical thing to do is sit here and read everything I can, but—damn, somebody is blowing me up!"

Darian's phone has been vibrating in her pocket for the past few minutes, and she finally pulls it out to see a list of notifications. "Mary's trying to reach me."

Mason touches her on the chin and gives her a tiny kiss. "I'll give you a minute. Come get me when you're finished."

When he's on the stairs, she calls Mary, who sounds harried. Her southern accent is pronounced.

"I didn't think you were ever going to call me back. Don't you believe a word of this, you hear me? Your mother was a saint, this is just the usual nastiness that starts oozing out of the cracks when something newsworthy happens. Just ignore them. They'll go away."

Her stomach sinks. "Believe a word of what?"

Mary goes quiet for a second. "You haven't been online?"

"No. I've been up to my ears planning the funeral and talking to the Denver Police." And screwing Mason, and digging through her mom's weird hard drive, but she doesn't feel the need to share that.

"Well, you'll see it soon enough. We've already filed a complaint and asked for the original feed responsible to be shut down, and we've brought in the crisis management folks, they're on top of it. There will be an injunction in place shortly, I guarantee, and—"

"Mary, what the hell is online?"

"It started with a tweet that said 'Columbia Jones is a fraud.' It blew up from there. People are saying all sorts of terrible, untrue things. That she's a murderer, that she's some sort of criminal. There are some videos—that's why the injunction is necessary, someone made some *vile* deepfake with her face planted on some porn star's body, and somehow, her feed retweeted it and then started tweeting some absolutely insane accusations. Those went haywire, and basically, the entire internet is being overwhelmed with this horrible stuff, threats against us, against her books, against you—"

"Stop. I need to look."

Darian puts Mary on speaker and opens her mother's social media apps one by one, heart in her throat. It's like every post from every person online has some variation of her mother's name, face, or book cover in it, interspersed with the cheery, tone-deaf, preprogrammed feeds of people who haven't picked up on the gleeful chaos that is undoing a celebrated career. Canceling a human takes absolutely nothing anymore. Piling on is too much fun.

The sympathy and compassion surrounding Columbia Jones's death has been supplanted by the horror of false statements, fake feeds, and the outrage of the general public.

"Thank you for doing what you can, Mary," Darian says. She feels surprisingly calm, considering. "I'm going to get with Liam and have him shut down the accounts entirely. If there's nothing to link to, this will die down. My mother isn't a fraud, she isn't a murderer, and her real fans will understand this is a hacking situation, just a smear campaign, I'm sure of it."

"Oh, yes, absolutely, that's a good idea. I hate for her to lose followers, but we have the newsletter, and those people don't care what happens on the socials anyway. We'll rebuild everything once these jokers are caught. I just know nothing that's being said is true . . ."

The way her voice trails off, there is the tiniest question in her tone that makes Darian think that perhaps Mary is wondering if there *is* any truth to what's being said, but Darian isn't about to share that something completely nuts is going on here, too. "I'm going to let you go. Stay in touch."

She hangs up and screams a very nasty word into the ether, then dials Liam, who answers immediately, completely frantic.

"I've seen, I'm doing everything I can to stop it, but someone's in the system and they keep multiplying, it's like some sort of hydra program. Every time I delete a post it's replaced with three more. It's everywhere, across every social media outlet. God, I am so sorry, Darian, I don't know what happened—"

"Kill the accounts. Delete them entirely."

"Wait, are you sure? I won't be able to re-create them."

"I don't care. Yes. Do it now, before this gets any worse."

"Okay. Okay. Hold on."

Darian goes to the profile, scrolls quickly past videos of her mother, on all fours wearing a spiked collar with a headless man behind her and other tasteless shots, to the beginning of the chaos.

Columbia Jones is a fraud.

She looks at the computer and thinks about the letter.

Many, many years ago, I did a very bad thing.

"What the hell did you do, Mom?"

Liam finally confirms he's deleted the accounts, and with that part of the chaos contained, Darian slips upstairs to find Mason sound asleep, face down, stretched across her bed like he fell there. She climbs in next to him, trailing an arm along his shoulders. He wakes, and she is thrilled to see how he lights up when he realizes it's her. "Man, I passed out. What time is it? Are you okay?"

She is not okay. She will never be okay again.

"Shh . . ." She kisses him, and he is more than happy to comply. This is all she can handle right now. Whatever chaos her mother's past is going to show, whatever she did that apparently got her murdered, Darian just can't deal with it anymore. Answers are coming. She doesn't think she's going to like them.

CHAPTER THIRTY-ONE
KIRA

Luke calls her at lunchtime to check in, and she tells him about the detective's visit. "Can you imagine my reaction when a cop walks through the door? I about fainted. He was really interested in the VIP meet and greet. I told him you got it for me as a surprise."

Luke makes a noise of assent. "You know, there's a story behind that. I never told you because it didn't matter in the end, but I got denied when I first applied. They said it had already sold out. I was bummed, so I sent the contact page on her website a note, said you were a lifelong fan, that I was trying to surprise you. I never got an answer, and then out of the blue, I got an email with the tickets. I wasn't about to question it, I knew how thrilled you'd be. In retrospect, it does feel off."

"Maybe. But I don't care. I got to spend fifteen minutes with my favorite author before she died, and that's all thanks to you, babe."

"You're worth it. You'll be off in time to grab the boys?"

"Yes. I'm almost wrapped. We'll see you later. Don't work too hard. Love you."

"Love you." She hangs up and finishes invoicing for supplies, and is just about to shut down her computer when her dad calls. She sits back at the desk, feet propped on an unopened box of new industrial sheet pans.

"Hey, Dad. How was your golf weekend?"

"Good. Good. One of these days I'm going to shoot my age. Hey, listen, there's a package here for you. I'm not sure why it came to our address instead of yours, but it's registered mail. I signed for it. Want me to drop it by the bakery?"

She looks at her watch. Nearly one. "Actually, I can swing by and grab it. I have a little time before I have to pick up the boys. We can have a late lunch. Who's it from?"

"A law firm in New York. Mathers and Mathers."

"Really? Never heard of them. Will you open it?"

She hears the slitting of an envelope, papers spilling out, little flips and he sorts through them.

"All right. There's a cover page that says 'In case of my death, please deliver to Kira Newport Hutchinson.' There's a newspaper clipping about a murder. And a letter from the firm."

"God, okay. Read it."

Her father's warm baritone is tense. "'Dear Ms. Hutchinson, this letter is to inform you that the last will and testament of Columbia Jones was recently filed for probate with the Manhattan Surrogate's Court of New York. Because of the private nature of this endeavor, there will be an in-person reading of the will on May fifteenth, one p.m. ET at my office. All beneficiaries are required to attend. If you have any questions about the will or the probate process, please do not hesitate to contact me. With my condolences, I remain, sincerely, Preston J. Mathers, Esquire. Senior Partner, Mathers and Mathers.'"

"Wait. You must have read that wrong. They're saying *I* am a beneficiary in Columbia Jones's will. *The* Columbia Jones. The author?"

"It's a pretty unique name. Apparently so."

She rolls her eyes. "Daddy, that is preposterous. You can stop playing now. Did Luke put you up to this?"

"I would love to say 'April Fools,' honey, but this letter is real. Very real." He pauses, and when he speaks again, there's a new note in his voice that makes the hair on the back of her neck stand on end. "You should come over, Kira."

"I'll be right there."

She hangs up and calls out to Alex, "I'm wrapped. Don't forget we need three dozen GF lemon cupcakes for Mrs. Wilson's garden party. She requested we do the almond-flour blend, not the rice. She'll be by to get them at three."

"Got it." Alex peeks out of the kitchen door. "Sorry I was late. Everything okay? That guy was a cop, yeah? Was it about the author who died in Denver?"

She nods, keys already in her hand. "Yes. Don't worry. I'm sure it's all fine."

The bakery's café is full, as always, the staff humping it, slinging pastries and coffees to Boulder's loyal patrons. She waves at a few familiar faces as she crosses the room but doesn't stop to chat. The bell dings on the door as she exits her simple life. She jumps into her white Jeep, which is parallel parked on the street a block down from the store and needs a bath; she can't help but think something is dreadfully wrong with this situation.

CHAPTER THIRTY-TWO
RILEY

Nate rouses Riley by setting cups of tea sweetened with stevia and bowls of peanut M&M's on the side table, nothing that will pull her from the zone. When she looks up, hours later, she's written a solid three thousand words and her hands are cramping. Nate is sitting in the chair opposite with an ankle resting on his knee, a laptop balanced in the space between.

"You got it?"

She stretches, neck popping. "A draft. It's usable. But I feel like there's too much I don't know." She flips through the pages of her notes, which are now wrinkled and worn. "We talked so much about the book, her previous titles, and her writing process, about Darian and New York and what it meant to her to share her stories with the masses. What we didn't get into, what she always shied away from, was her upbringing in England. All she shared was her family lost everything, and she had to start over in the States. So I haven't been able to confirm anyone from her childhood yet, and I did a brief visa search, but it hasn't shown anything. I was actually hoping you'd send me to England so I could interview in person. Obviously, we don't have time now. I suppose I could talk to Darian—if she'll answer my call. The last time we were face to face, it didn't go so well. She doesn't care for me. But if anyone knows the details of the early days, surely it's her."

She realizes Nate doesn't seem to be paying attention to anything she's saying, though he's staring contemplatively at her. "Why do you look like the cat who's gotten into the cream?"

"Knox Shepherd."

She wrenches her mind from Columbia's phantom early days in England to the name from the *Crossville Chronicle* article in the package Columbia sent her. "The murderer from that case in Tennessee?"

"Yes. The murderer from the case in Tennessee."

"I take it you've found something about him?"

"You could say that. Want me to show you?"

She pats the sofa, then glances at her hand. Sticky with chocolate, like a child. "Oops. Maybe stay where you are."

He goes to the bathroom and returns with a damp washcloth. Runs it gently across her fingers. Riley tries, and fails, to look away. She's seen Nate in a number of roles; tender protector is a new one. He gives her that crooked smile and swipes the clean side of the washcloth against the sofa cushion, then tosses it toward the bathroom door and sits next to her, setting his laptop on the table. There are multiple tabs open, and he clicks the first on the left. It's an online version of the newspaper clipping. The next tab opens, and there's a booking photo of a handsome young man with a square jaw and curly hair. He feels very familiar, and she knows why. "That's the guy from the theater in Denver." She looks at Nate. "Columbia knew him, right? Is that why she gave me his name?"

Tab three opens. This, too, is a booking photo, of a young woman. It takes Riley a second before she realizes what she's seeing.

Herself.

Nate has pulled her own arrest record.

Oh, shit.

Riley's heart begins to pound, adrenaline rushing her like a thief in a dark alley. She feels dizzy, feels her worlds colliding at light speed.

Before, and after. She's been so careful not to let anyone in her shiny New York life know the truth about her past. No one knows. Not Nate. Not Oliver. And now it's staring her in the face.

"I—I—why?" She whispers the last word, tears choking her voice, memories she's forced away rushing back, leaving her breathless. Tears make her voice tremble. She should have known better. She should have known it would all come out someday. But why now? Why now, when she's already vulnerable, already on the police radar for the murder of her subject? Sutcliffe would have pulled this eventually, probably, if he looked closely. A cop, yes. But Nate? God, why did it have to be Nate? It doesn't matter that she's seen him at his worst, and he's nursed her through a few scrapes, too. The one person who now has her future, her livelihood, her life in his hands is about to blow her wide open.

And then he's going to fire her. She knows it. It's all over. Everything she's built, screeching to a halt. But she has to try. Beg, plead, whatever it takes.

She's debating exactly how to proceed when Nate reaches for her hand. "Hey. Hey. It's okay. What's wrong?"

She sniffs. How much to tell? "Please, before you make any judgments, let me explain. It was so long ago, and they ended up not charging me when they found out what really happened. I—it's not technically public record. I was a juvenile. How did you even find it?"

Nate's face is getting more and more confused. He gives her a little laugh. "Riley, I'm missing something."

"It's not funny, Nate."

She's up and across the living room in three strides, shaking. The persistent flashing strobe lights of New York worm their way through the curtains. Sirens bleed through the air, echoing the past. It's true what they say, the city never sleeps. And pasts never stay hidden. She was stupid for even trying. It's just been so long since anyone looked at her with pity and derision. Since that night, since her mother . . .

Nate still looks baffled. He points to the laptop. "Riley, this is the arrest record and mug shot for Devon Mears. She was tried for manslaughter in Crossville, Tennessee, in 1995, a few months after Knox Shepherd's conviction. It's all public record. I just pulled this off the paper's archives."

"What?"

He's looking at her with new eyes, head slightly cocked. He frowns, looks at the laptop, then back at her. Frowns again. Then sighs and pats the sofa seat. "Wanna sit down and tell me what the hell that freak-out was about?"

"Not yet," she manages. "Who is Devon Mears?"

"Knox Shepherd's lover. According to the court transcripts, theirs is a story as old as time. Devon and Knox met and fell in love. Unfortunately, there was a Mr. Mears. They got him out of the picture but were caught. It follows the plot of the short story. But in real life, Shepherd did fifteen years of a twenty-year sentence for second-degree murder, was released in 2010. Mears did three years of a ten-year sentence. Interestingly, she drops out of the public record after that point."

He's staring again, looking at her, then the computer. "I'll admit, there is a resemblance. Around the eyes, especially. It's not as marked as you think, but it's there. Want to tell me why you thought that was you?"

A reprieve. He didn't know. And of course, she'd panicked. Fuck. Fuck! Now she will have to give him a bone, a sliver, or he will worry her forever.

"Not really." She's amazed at his calmness. Nate has always been in perpetual motion, but right now he might as well be a snake sunning himself on a rock. He's at peace, blending into the background, but ready to strike in a heartbeat.

With a huge sigh, she flops back onto the sofa.

"Can I see it again?"

CHAPTER THIRTY-THREE

Nate pops a finger against the track pad, and the screen lights up with the booking photo. He hits Command-Plus a few times, enlarging it. Riley looks closely. He's right—this isn't her. But the resemblance . . . She does some math in her head. It's conceivable. But no. That's silly. Isn't it?

"Riley?" Nate prompts.

"Okay. I don't know that we have time for the whole story, so I'll give you the highlights. There was an accident. When I was in high school. My sister was driving me home from a party. We hit a tree and were both thrown from the car. I was banged up, but okay. She broke her neck, her back, and had a traumatic brain injury. The cops who came assumed I was driving because I was incoherently drunk and took me into custody. I was too screwed up to explain that Maisie was driving until the next morning. No one believed me at first, which is why they arrested me. By then, she was in a vegetative state. The doctors told my mom she would never wake up. But my mom is not a quitter." She swallows. "Maisie's still alive. She's in a facility in New Jersey. My mom has been in court for years, keeping her tethered to the machines. The doctors wanted to take her off life support that first weekend."

"Jesus."

"Yeah. My mother . . . well, she loved Maisie, loves Maisie, and blamed me from the get-go. She said some pretty hideous things that first week. But it all boiled down to the fact that I was adopted. That I killed her *real* child."

"You didn't know you were adopted?"

"Not until that day after the accident, no. When the dust cleared, when she could see reason again, when the cops proved to her I was riding, not driving, Faith apologized several times, said that wasn't how she wanted me to find out, that she'd vowed never to tell me, that she loved me just the same as she did Maisie, but it was clear none of that was true. What was done was done. My sister was in a coma, and I was no longer myself. I was a stranger in my own life. And now you know why I didn't say anything. It's tragic, and sad, and all my fault."

Nate's voice is soft. "Oh, Riley girl. Why in the world would you hide this? No one would care. No one would judge you. I certainly don't."

"I care! I killed my sister, but she's not dead. My mother has lost her mind and kept a dead girl alive with court orders and injunctions, moving Maisie from facility to facility, draining all our resources, all our money. Every dime I make goes to help pay the bills, and God knows where she gets the rest, because my salary doesn't cover everything, and she hasn't worked in years. It killed my dad, he couldn't handle it. No one could. It's so unfair to poor Maisie. She's grown up in a hospital bed. She's not there. Anyone with half a brain can see it's a torturous existence. She's skin and bones, bent and twisted, brain dead. But Faith has *faith*." The bitterness in her tone is palpable. "She's convinced Maisie is in there somewhere and doesn't want to let go. Who knows, maybe she is. That's a question for the ethicists and God. Not me. Certainly not my mother." She blows out a breath. "My adopted mother."

"Do you know who your birth parents are? Was it an open adoption?"

"No. Totally closed. I've never tried to find them. I mean, what's the point? They didn't want me then. Why should they get the benefit of the doubt now?"

"Oh, honey."

"I'm not your honey," she snaps, and immediately regrets it. "I'm sorry, Nate. I am on my last nerve here."

"Understandable," Nate says, but his tone has cooled. The spell is broken. He gets up and moves to the chair opposite. She tries not to be hurt by his absence. She's used to people walking away from her. Has put so many layers of protection around her heart, she can tell herself it's okay, that she doesn't feel the sword slice through her.

"I should extend Faith a little more grace," she says with a sigh. "She lost both her daughters that night."

Nate shakes his head. "Don't do that. Don't deflect. She hurt you, she lied to you, and she took revenge on you. She doesn't deserve your grace."

"You sound like my therapist." She winds her hair around her fist. "You don't think I'm related to this Devon Mears woman, do you?"

"That's a really good question, Riley. I don't know."

"Where is she? Did she get out of jail?"

"Yes. There's an obituary for her about a year after she was released, but it doesn't say how she died. That's all I've found."

"And her husband? The one that was killed?"

"Benjamin Mears." He shows her a photo of Mears.

"Gosh, he looks young."

"They were nineteen. Married out of high school. She got pregnant their senior year."

Riley sits with all this information. Does some math in her head. "Well, that can't be me. The timing doesn't work. It's off a year. He died in '95. I was born in '96." She pushes away the thought that her birth mother could be a murderer who killed her biological father—*Holy shit,* that *would be a story!*—and refocuses. "I feel like we should go to Tennessee and dig into this. And we still need to figure out what's going on in England. Columbia's article isn't going to be complete without these facts. There's something huge here. We need to find out what it is. What weird tie Knox Shepherd and Devon Mears have to Columbia, and why she chose me to write this piece."

He holds up a hand. "And why she was killed. Also, I've been thinking about the will reading. The stipulation didn't say that the whole article has to be published, right? We can break this into parts. What you've written works as part one. Part two can be the investigation into her death. Part three will be the conclusions, the revelations, what the connections are to this murder in Tennessee. How does that sound?"

She nods, thinking about the structure of what she has, how it can be broken apart into discrete stories. It will take an hour or so to unwind a few threads, but it's doable. "Okay. I can live with that. Don't know if the estate lawyers will play along, and no idea if Columbia's people will go beyond the original payment structure nor fight us about being a multipart story instead of one huge piece, but at this point, I'm not sure I care. I know there's something important in her will that we're going to need to finish the story. It's bad enough that I'm in possession—by her hand—of an unpublished story. The lawyers are going to have a field day. When Tony cracks into this flash drive? Who knows what we're going to find."

"Excellent question," Nate replies.

"We should reach out to the detective in Denver. Give him this information. That we know who the man in the theater was. And give him the connection to Devon and Benjamin Mears. He might have more details about how she died."

"You're right. Of course we should reach out. But what if he tells you to stop investigating? What if he says you're in danger?"

"You're here, and I am not going to stop. This is too important. Do you agree?"

The smile on his face is all the answer she needs. "I do."

"Good. How do we reach out? Text? Email?"

"Call. Here's another burner," he says, reaching into the bag at his feet.

"How many of those do you have in there?" she teases, trying to return them to some sort of equanimity.

"Another three." He looks at her, almost through her. He does that when he's thinking. "Who do you think stole your bag, wrote in your notebook? Who is trying to watch out for you?"

"You can't be suggesting it's this Knox Shepherd man. I have no idea who he is."

"But he's tied to Devon Mears. And you bear an uncanny resemblance to her. It's worth a shot, don't you think? We can call the number, ask him his name, see what he says. Maybe he'll give you a clue about your past."

"Maybe we should reach out to the detective first."

"Maybe."

It's clear to her, though, that Nate is on the side of calling the stranger first.

"All right. What do we have to lose?" She pulls out the number, and Nate reads it and dials. It rings five times, ten.

No one answers.

"He said tomorrow, same time. Maybe he's not near this number, maybe it's not a phone he carries with him."

"Possible."

"Then I think it's time to call the detective. We need professional help here, as much as I hate to say it."

"How much do we share?" he asks.

"All of it. Let's let him deal with Knox Shepherd and the Tennessee connections. We can stay on why I can't find any record of Columbia Jones in Bromley."

"Fair enough. But I gotta tell you, before we call? My stomach is growling. I'm famished. Can you eat? Now that the draft is done?"

She nods.

"Thank God. I need fuel. What about Love and Dough? You can eat their pizza still, yes?"

The Brooklyn pizza joint is one of her all-time favorites, popular among the city's food-allergy crowd for its incredibly tasty gluten-free corn-flour crusts. "Yes. We're not going to be very undercover there, though."

"Security will deliver. What's your pleasure? Sausage and mushrooms still, no oregano?"

"How do you remember all these things? It's been years since you ordered me a pizza."

"You're pretty memorable, Riley girl," he says lightly, standing and moving to the door.

When the door shuts and she's alone, Riley takes a few deep breaths, does some yoga stretches, and gives herself a pep talk.

Okay, think this through. Analyze. Don't use your heart, use your head. Facts, only. You know what you know. Add in this component.

Riley is in Columbia's will. Columbia chose Riley to come on tour, to write the piece. She'd been unfailingly kind, indulgent, even, considering Riley was a reporter.

Was it more than getting good press?

She's been in the business long enough to know that there are no coincidences. Columbia has a murky past. Of course, if she hadn't died, Riley wouldn't be thinking that. She'd still be thinking Columbia just hadn't gotten to her childhood yet and would be pressing for those details. The perception of the woman—the author—was curated. The reality is starting to look totally different.

Riley sits at Nate's computer again with the blown-up photo of Devon Mears. Now that the panic of her history coming out is gone, she can look at this familiar stranger with more dispassion.

And what she sees confuses her. Nate has more than one tab open with photos of Devon Mears. In each, she looks slightly different. Riley clicks, and clicks again, and that opens a file of a hospital photo. Devon's face is nearly beyond recognition, black and blue with bruises, cuts, stitches; her nose and her lips are swollen to almost comical proportions. Her eye sockets are both fiery red, and the sclera of her eyeballs themselves are filled with pooling blood. She'd been severely beaten. But she's still recognizable as Devon Mears.

And Riley really does look like her. But someone else does, too.

Darian.

This is bananas. Totally impossible.

And just weird enough to possibly be true.

That blonde hair spilling over the pillow, soaked in blood, was so familiar. So like Darian's.

So like Riley's.

Could Devon Mears and Columbia Jones be the same person? And if that's the case . . .

Riley runs to the bathroom, peers into the mirror. Runs back out into the living room and grabs her battered copy of *Ivory Lady*, takes it back to the bathroom and holds it up in the mirror. The photo on the back is recent, done for this jacket, and Riley tries her damnedest to envision the woman staring out of the photograph with the jet-black bob with blonde hair. It doesn't work. She picks up a hank of her own hair and drapes it over the edge of the photo, covering half of Columbia's face.

Something about the mouth, and the nose. Maybe the brows?

Is she losing her mind? Columbia Jones isn't her mother.

Is she?

The job offer. The intimacies. The will.

Riley and Darian had been mistaken for one another multiple times during the tour. Had been asked countless times if they were sisters. Even Columbia had remarked on it a couple of times.

Because she knew. She knew you and Darian were sisters.

Legacy Draft— Chapter Five

I didn't speak to David that night. Nor the next. I didn't know how to tell him I was leaving, because I knew in my heart he would never let me go. Not really. I had long ago stopped being his partner, his lover, his wife. I was simply his possession. But my fear was no longer for me. It was for Saria. While David might be willing to see reason eventually when it came to our thwarted love story, his daughter was an entirely different matter. With Saria, his love was untainted. She was a beauty, rosebud lips and ivory cheeks, with his eyes and just the beginnings of strawberry in her curls. She looked much more like him than me; the resemblance was clear from the moment of her birth. I think that's why he never blamed her for his circumstances. It would have been too much like blaming himself.

His magnanimous nature had reasserted itself in fatherhood. If he hadn't been so cruel to me, if she hadn't been born in blood the way she was, I might even have gone along with it. He was sweet to her, kind to me, a dream husband and father. He hadn't had a drink in two weeks, so far as I knew.

He was so besotted that I was able to leave her with him to run errands on the weekends.

Those errands had a single goal.

Patrick.

He wasn't content to wait for me to leave David to have me, and I wasn't willing to wait any longer, either. I had never felt desire like this before. Oh, I thought I had, a child's anticipation of the fumblings in the back seat of David's car the night we made Saria had me tingly for weeks beforehand. But the second I found out I was pregnant, I stopped wanting. David. School. A future. And when you stop wanting, you stop living. Saria was my death sentence, long before she was the death of me.

The first time we made love hurt, but I didn't care. I wanted to hold Patrick inside of me. I wanted to feel him fill me. I held myself back from clawing at him, anything, anything to get him closer. After, in his soft sheets, the ceiling fan twirling above us, cooling the sweat from our bodies, he marveled at me. I'd already lost most of the weight I'd gained with my girl, though my stomach felt doughy and unnatural. Patrick didn't care. He was much more upset that I had to take a shower and hurry home before David got suspicious. Grocery shopping only takes so long.

We managed to be together only a few times before Patrick insisted once and for all I tell David I was leaving. He wasn't content to sneak around, and honestly, after getting a taste of what his love was really like, I wasn't either. I was starved for more. I was the desert, and he was my mirage, only he was real.

I agreed, and this time, also agreed that Patrick could come to the house in order to make sure I got away safely. He'd wait outside, only come in if there was trouble, and honestly, knowing he would be standing guard, that I had a home to go to, safety, love, gave me the courage to go through with it.

I dressed carefully. Did my hair. Fed Saria and put her down. Then went to the kitchen to prepare a meal for my soon-to-be ex-husband.

I chose his favorite—lasagna. I don't know if he likes the way it tastes or likes how labor-intensive it is, but I got to work, and had it in the oven, the table set, a nice bottle of red wine open and breathing, before he came in the door.

I'd debated the alcohol, but to be honest, I needed a little liquid courage myself. I just didn't know how he was going to react.

The answer was not a surprise.

Not well.

It was as bad as the night Saria was born, only worse. David wouldn't let me go without a fight, that I expected. The need to put his stamp on me, to cow me into submission the only way he knew how, with fists and words, that I expected. But the need to possess me? To hold me down, rip off my clothes, and force himself inside me? To ignore my cries of pain, of fear? To hurt me, over and over, until he crowed with his climax, filling me with his seed with a howl of triumph, and collapsed on top of me, inside me, dripping and panting and laughing? The bastard laughed. And then he raised up, ungluing himself from my body, and kneeling over me, punched me, square in the nose. I felt it break, felt the blood gush.

"You aren't going anywhere, you stupid bitch. Now clean yourself up."

Those were David's last words. The baseball bat caught him on the side of his head, and he flew off me to the left, crashing hard against the door to the kitchen.

That's all I remember. When I woke, the blood was dry, the body was cold, and the house was full of the mournful cries of a baby who needed her mother.

Legacy Draft—
Chapter Six

When the baby is finished eating, you will call the police.

As I feed Saria, I test what I am going to say again, out loud this time, so my voice doesn't waver at the wrong moment and give me away.

"My husband is dead."

"My husband has been murdered."

"Please hurry, I think he's dead."

"I woke to find him this way."

"I don't remember what happened."

When the baby is satiated, washed and changed and happy again, I put her in the counter cradle, pick up the phone, then put it down again. I haven't checked the mirror. I don't know what truths and lies my very body will tell.

I stumble past the living room. The smell is overwhelming, and sorrow fills me. It didn't have to be like this.

In the tiny powder room, I flick on the light with my elbow. I'm afraid to look but do anyway. The vision before me is terrifying. I am a mass of purple bruises and covered in cast-off blood. I am in pain but numb. I don't care if it hurts. I do not clean myself. I can be only an observer of my injuries.

It was supposed to be simple. A fall, a broken neck. Me, returning home to find him collapsed at the base of the stairs, already gone.

Nothing ever goes the way you think it will.

I force myself to go past his body again. The baseball bat is covered in blood and muck. He was so strong. Too strong.

I can't wait any longer. I have to call the police. I blow out a breath and squeeze my arm hard, pinching the tender flesh until fresh tears come. I call the sheriff's office, the sobs in my throat as real as the horror I feel when a woman I know answers the phone, and the entire script flees from my head.

"Sally? There's been a break-in. I think David is dead."

Sirens sound different when they're coming for you. Normally when I hear one, I say a small prayer for whomever they're rushing to help. These are viciously loud, their wail breaking the calm air. Lights and sirens, the firetrucks, the police, the ambulance, they come screaming into the driveway. My call rattled them.

I glance at David's body. I can see his legs from this angle, splayed out. I joggle the baby to comfort her, then clutch her to my breast and close my eyes, knowing these are the last moments I will have to myself for a very long time. I wait for the sirens shrieking to a halt before opening the door and spilling out, screaming.

The EMTs take one look at me and cart me off to the hospital. They dab at my cuts, put ice on my bruises, ask again and again, "What happened? Can you tell us who hurt you?" But I stay mute. What can I say? He is dead because of me. There's nothing that will change that fact.

When we arrive and they take me to an exam room, a nurse tries to take the baby from me. Then I speak up, vociferously, insist on keeping her with me. They agree, placating me with gentle hands and soft voices "—Of course, of course, she can stay here for now—" which sounds ominous. I haven't thought this through. I need more practice. I never was any good at acting.

CHAPTER THIRTY-FOUR
DETECTIVE SUTCLIFFE

Sutcliffe isn't about to clue in Darian Jones on his suspicions about Shepherd, not until he gets a lot more information. But he now has three independent verifications, plus his own visual, that Knox Shepherd was at the event in Denver.

Shepherd is involved in this. Up to his neck. He knows it.

He looks up a number, dials it. It's been years since they talked, but with luck, she still has the same number. The phone clicks, and a woman's voice comes on the line.

"A and A Investigations, how can I help you?"

"Can I speak with Skye Abbott, please? This is Detective Byron Sutcliffe, Denver Police. She'll know who I am."

"Hold for a moment, Detective."

A song comes through the speaker, the Muzak version of a tune he is more than familiar with. Sutcliffe grins. God, it's been a long time since he was roaming the Nashville clubs late at night, crushing hard on Schuyler Abbott, doing anything to see her onstage wailing away in her black skinny jeans and her bleached-white hair. The Deathwish Bunnies, that was the name of her band, and they were the hottest local punk rock band in the region when he was coming up.

Some form of ironic punishment, or a very silly inside joke, putting those antiestablishment anthems into canned elevator music to play to callers of Abbott and Associates Investigations.

A voice made sweet and smoky by years of screaming into microphones bursts onto the phone. Like Amy Winehouse and Shirley Manson had a love child—punk rock all the way.

"Sutcliffe? The hell? It's been a decade since you called me."

She's still loud, he'll give her that.

"Skye," he replies, a stupid grin spreading across his face. "You sound exactly the same. Like too many cigarettes and the back of a tour bus."

"Oh, God, you do remember. I so hoped that years of Jack and Coke wiped your memory."

"It would take an act of God to make me forget."

They laugh, two old friends with plenty of memories to tide them over. Her laugh is raspy, and she coughs, clearing her throat.

"Couldn't get them fixed, I take it?"

"Not entirely. The nodules have never truly healed. But it doesn't hurt. I don't sing much professionally anymore. Just serenading my shampoo bottle."

"That's a shame."

"It is. I miss the stage. But Aunt Joy keeps me busy. Anyway, don't tell me you're calling to accept that job offer, all these years later. You're still with Denver Police? Married, I hope. Passel of rug rats running around?"

"Yes to Denver Police, no to the rest. And no, don't need a job. Do need to run a name by you, though. Knox Shepherd."

All the joviality is gone from her ravaged voice. "Yes?"

"I have a murdered author, and Shepherd was at the event from the same night."

A hiss of breath. "You're working Columbia Jones?"

"Yeah. And it's a weird one. Got a minute?"

He tells her what he's discovered so far—the stalking, the cameras being jammed, the lack of a cause of death, the possible poisoning. "I've got three people, plus a video confirmation I've made, that Shepherd was there at the event. The question is, Did he then go to the hotel and kill her?"

"The question is, What's a felon from Tennessee doing at an author event in Denver? What in the world tie could he have to her? Jones was in Nashville, they had to do the event at the Ryman to get everyone in. My aunt Joy went. She loves her. Loved. He could have killed her closer to home, you know?"

"He might have been at the Nashville event, too, I don't know. But if you need to kill someone, maybe you don't do it in your backyard, especially if you've been on the straight and narrow for fifteen years."

"True. What do you need from me?" she asked.

"Direct as always. I'm feeling like this is a bit too coincidental for my liking. Thought I might take a run down to Nashville. Maybe the two of us could go have a chat with Mr. Shepherd."

"Oh."

"Address on file is on the edge of Franklin."

Her voice softens. "I haven't thought about that case in years. On purpose."

"I don't blame you. It was a fucked-up time. I will grant you papal dispensation if you don't want to get involved."

"What, you're Catholic now?" She blows out a breath, and a few moments later, says, "All right. Let me give you my private number. Call me when you land. Our offices are downtown, it will take me as long to get to the airport as it will take you to walk out to the curb. I'll pick you up and we can go visit Mr. Shepherd. In the meantime, I will do a little background, just to see what he's been up to all this time."

"You're the best. I'll see you tomorrow."

"You need a place to stay?"

"You offering?"

"Hell no. My place isn't fit for visitors. But I can get you a room, Aunt Joy has an in at the Hermitage. We stash folks there sometimes."

"Swanky. I'll take it."

"Consider it done. Tomorrow, then."

She hangs up, and Sutcliffe heads to his lieutenant's office to fill him in.

Chances are he'll have to pay for this trip himself; he has no probable cause to get a warrant for Knox Shepherd's arrest, only a gut instinct that something big is at play here. He doesn't believe in coincidences.

He's halfway down the hall when his cell rings. It's an unfamiliar number, but that means nothing these days. The bane of existence for a cop—caller ID can be too easily spoofed.

"Sutcliffe," he answers, taking the stairs up.

"Detective, this is Riley Carrington. I'm with my editor, Nate Walsh. We've uncovered something I think you should be aware of. I know who was at the theater. I know who made Columbia faint."

"Do share," he says, stopping on the glass-walled landing and looking toward the mountains. Ever watchful, they stand sentry, a buffer against ill tidings.

"His name is Knox Shepherd. And he's a former convict who went to jail for murder. He killed someone named Benjamin Mears."

Bingo.

"Want to tell me how you found out that name?"

Her voice shifts. "You aren't surprised. You already know?"

"Yes. I already know."

"Are you going to do anything about it? I mean, odds are slim he isn't involved, especially since she left me the article about his conviction."

Sutcliffe laughed shortly. "I'm investigating, Miss Carrington. Not much more I can do than that. Columbia Jones left you something with Shepherd's name on it?"

"An article from the *Crossville Chronicle*, the day he was found guilty."

Sutcliffe's mind races to fit this information into the matrix he is cooking up. "What else did she leave you?"

"Just that, and some papers, an early short story about a woman and a man who get together and murder her husband. And the letter from the lawyers that I'm in the will. And a flash drive, but it's password protected."

"Oh. Just that? Can you at least send me a copy of the story?"

"I can try."

"Thank you. Is everything okay with your apartment? Have the NYPD given you any information?"

He hears a little intake of breath. "I don't know. I'm not in it. I'm trying to get the article done so the will can be read, and I can find out what Columbia Jones wanted with me. Nate is keeping me safe until we can take the next step. Some creeper followed me yesterday, so this seemed like the smartest thing to do."

"Creeper? How old was he? Could it have been the man you saw at the theater?"

"Hmm . . . No, I don't think so. This guy was younger. My age, a little older maybe. Different build, too. I don't think it was the same guy."

"All right. Feel free to keep in touch. Is this your new number?"

"No. I'm not using any of my devices right now. We found a tracker in my bag. We're assuming that whoever took it in Denver put it in."

"Well, hell. Okay. Good to know."

"There's more. So you know how my bag was stolen, but nothing was missing? Inside my notebook was a note and a phone number. It said my devices were compromised, and to get in touch with more info. Nate and I called the number from a burner, and a man answered. He says he's trying to keep me safe. I . . . believed him. There's something about his voice that seems familiar, but I can't place it."

"And he didn't identify himself?"

"No. And when we tried to call again, just before we called you, he didn't answer."

"Will you share the number with me?"

Riley rattles it off. Sutcliffe writes this down in his notebook. "Great, thank you. How can I reach you if I need to talk? And I want you to be able to get to me, too."

Nate Walsh chimes in. "You can call the main number at *East Fifth Magazine*, ask for Tony Grann. He can relay a message and we'll call you right away."

He reels off the number. Sutcliffe adds this info to the notebook, then stashes it in his back pocket. "If you trust someone at your office, Mr. Walsh, I guarantee you can trust me. I have access to a lot more support than your IT guy."

"You will be able to get to us within minutes. Tony is solid."

"Okay, Miss Carrington, Mr. Walsh. I'm sure I don't have to impress upon you the danger you could be in. Be careful. Watch your backs. Stay in touch."

They hang up, and he feels anxious, but also excited. This is the right path. Shepherd is the key to Columbia's murder. He's involved in this up to his eyeballs. He spent enough time in prison that it wouldn't be hard to find someone to terrorize the Carrington girl. The world is a big and scary place, full of thugs who will do most anything for a buck.

He needs to hurry; he has to book a flight as soon as possible. His boss is in her office, typing on her computer in a frenzy, and he knocks on the doorframe. "Yo. Got a minute?"

Lieutenant Rebecca Foley looks up in a slight daze, then sees him and focuses. "Yeah. Hey, Sutcliffe, what's up?"

"I gotta go to Nashville. A suspect has emerged in the Columbia Jones case, and as it happens, I'm familiar with the man from an early case of mine there."

He fills her in. Foley is a good egg, always fair, someone he enjoys working for. She wastes no time, recognizes the opportunity.

"Go. Keep your receipts, we'll sort out the finances later. I'll get in touch with Metro Nashville and warn them you're coming. See if they can't scare up a warrant. Extradition is a whole different matter."

"Cross that bridge if we have to. Better call Williamson County, too. That's where he lives. But . . . maybe we hold off bringing in the cavalry until I talk to him? I've been in touch with my old partner— she's a PI there now—and we've got a plan. We were the two who arrested him way back when. There's always been something off about his story, and right now . . . I don't have any probable cause for a warrant. We go in guns ablazin', he'll clam up. He's stoic like that."

Foley has wheat-blonde hair that stays in a neat ponytail at all times. She fiddles with the end of it when she's thinking.

"Okay, play it your way. I'd be more comfortable if the locals knew what you were up to."

"That's fine. I'd just like a chance to talk to him first. Something about this feels off, and I'd like to get a handle on it. If he bolts, they won't be caught off guard by an urgent call."

"Do you know anyone there still?"

"Yeah, talk to Detective Mike Cooper. He's solid, won't get in our way, but will pull things together fast if needed. And if you could put a trace on this number? Just in case he runs. It's probably a burner, but I think it belongs to Shepherd. I think he called Riley Carrington and told her to watch her back."

"So he's threatening the players?"

"Not threatening. She said she felt like he was trying to keep her safe. I don't know what to think yet."

"Got it. Will do. Happy hunting."

"Thanks, LT. I'll keep in touch."

His next call is to Duran. He gets to his truck and dials her number. She answers on the first ring.

"Brodifacoum!"

"Excuse me?"

"Columbia Jones. The results are back. My instinct was spot on. She was poisoned with a hefty dose of brodifacoum. I'd say things are leaning toward her being murdered. Whether it was intentional or not, you'll still need to determine."

"What swayed you?"

"The CBD oil tested positive. It was a brand-new bottle, almost full. And there's a big fat partial thumbprint on the cap, like someone dropped it on the floor and picked it up. It doesn't match any of the exclusionary prints we took from the scene. The rest of the bottle was clean. Only Jones's fingerprints were on it. But this one, we're running it. Nothing's popped yet, but we'll find it."

"It could belong to a dealer, too. Someone from the outside who tainted the bottle. It could be a fluke. You could have fifty bottles of rat-poisoned CBD floating around."

"It could, absolutely. Or a maid in the hotel who knocked it over, or any one of the people who were at the scene. But we haven't had any other cases reported. I have a gut feeling on this."

"Okay then. I have a name for you to try and match that thumbprint to, from Tennessee. Knox Shepherd. He'll be in the federal database."

"Excellent, thank you. You know how fast this system works, but it's only as good as what it's been given. I'll run him."

"Are you going to release the cause of death?"

"The wolves have been baying for blood. Yes. I think we need to."

"Gotcha. I'll let the LT know. Thanks for rushing all of this."

"Now you have to do your magic. I know you'll find out who did this. What's next for you?"

"I'm heading to Tennessee. I need to talk to Knox Shepherd in person."

CHAPTER THIRTY-FIVE
KIRA

Kira stops at her parents' place to pick up this crazy letter. The drive from the bakery to their house on the ranch property takes twenty-five minutes, and she spends every one of them worrying, while reminding herself stress isn't good for the baby.

Heroes being murdered aren't good for anyone, though.

The Taernan Ranch, home for all her life, is situated between Boulder and Eldorado Springs on one thousand acres. There's the main house, where her parents live, and three other houses, one of which belongs to her and Luke and the boys. There is a large horse barn, meadows, grazing pastures, a decent-size creek, a greenhouse for her mother's winter garden, and plenty of hiking trails and elegant red rock formations. It's a slice of heaven, a place she's never wanted to leave, even after she and Luke got married. He's running the ranch for her dad now.

Her father, a Marlboro Man if there ever was one, so similar in nature and emotion to Luke, a protector, a genius, kind and present, greets her in the foyer, offering hugs and kisses. He's tall and broad, heavily muscled through the chest and arms, salt-and-pepper hair leaning more to salt these days, and he's wearing his omnipresent khakis and golf shirt. This one is pink with darker red triangles, one she bought for him a few Christmases ago.

"How are you, sweetheart?"

"Good. Confused. But good. Is Mom here?"

"She's making tea, she just finished up a spin class. That Peloton was a great pandemic buy, and now she's so invested with the instructors and her network that she's thinking about killing her gym membership."

Kira's mother is a former Miss Colorado who got into triathlons in her twenties. Her knees are shot now, so the running is out, but the biking and swimming are her favorite activities. Her dad golfs, and they both still ride. The horses are another thing her dad and Luke have in common. Luke was a ranch hand here during the summers, making money for school. Kira was entranced by the handsome boy who was so polite, whom her father clearly respected. They got married the weekend after graduation. Of course, the babies came fast and furious, and now they have the life she's always wanted—owning the bakery, tending to Luke and the boys, riding horses and hiking the gorgeous wilderness around them. They are a close-knit unit. On the other side, Luke's parents are not a daily part of their lives. They live in Chicago and only visit on holidays.

She's so grateful that her folks live close by, that they are able to be hands-on grandparents to the kids—not to mention being there for Kira and Luke. They retired young, selling the advertising agency they started in their twenties for more than enough to live on for the next forty years and then some. They wanted to enjoy their lives after working their tails off for so long. Kira admires them and wants to emulate them, as well. But she has a good twenty years of work ahead before that's possible. There are her little people to consider—college tuition to save for, and now, their latest addition . . . Yeah, Kira's going to be in the trenches for a while.

Her mother joins them in the kitchen, her ivory skin tinged pink with healthy exertion, carrying a mug with a mint tea bag in it. She is physically Kira's opposite, tall and lithe, almost rangy. Kira is lush in all the right places; three pregnancies, breastfeeding, and the bakery have made sure of that. Of course, she doesn't exercise with the frequency of her mom, either.

"You look lovely today, sweetheart. Did you change your hair?"

Kira stabs a finger toward her bangs—not her finest decision, but not a recent cut. They're actually growing out; she should make an appointment. "No. It's . . . well . . ." She touches her belly and rolls her eyes.

Her mother utters a *meep* of joy and grabs her into a hug. Her father's eyes are shining, and they are both grinning like loons.

"When?" her mother asks. "Oh my gosh, I am over the moon!"

"Would you believe Christmas? We weren't trying, so the timing is a little more out of our hands than the rest of the boys. I went to the doctor yesterday and my levels all look great. It's early for me to be sharing, so please don't tell anyone."

Her mother zips her lips and throws away the key, and Kira giggles. Her mom is fun, always has been. She's been a friend as much as a mother all these years. Her dad, too.

"Who would have thought we'd get so blessed to have four grandbabies," her father says. "It's almost too good to be true. Come here, sit down. You're probably tired."

"I am tired," Kira admits. "But I'd like to see this letter. I'm sure it's a mistake, they must have delivered to the wrong place or something. Wrong person, same name."

Her dad looks immediately guilty and hands over a manila envelope with a printed label on the outside. Kira's name, care of her parents' address. All the happiness is gone now.

"I'm sure it's just a miscommunication," she says, pulling out the letter. She reads it with incredulity, then hands it to her mom. "It's a mistake, right? I mean, she's a world-famous writer, and I'm . . . me."

Her mom takes the letter but doesn't read it. She glances at Kira's father, a look of marital shorthand that makes Kira go on alert immediately.

"What is going on?" she demands, using her best you-boys-are-gonna-get-it mother-disciplinarian voice. "Tell me right now."

"Let's sit down, sweetheart," her mother says gently. Her dad steers her through the living room toward the kitchen, and the round table—the place all major conversations take place. Since her childhood, this thick round slab of oak has been the site of every report card, grounding, decision, conversation, celebration. Now, a grown woman with a family of her own, she is thrust back to those years. The memories parade in, and Kira marks this moment, the way the sun is moving through the room, the blue jays on the feeder, the wood beams and the stone fireplace, the distant whickering of the horses in their paddock, all of it, because something tells her nothing is going to be the same again.

She sits. They place themselves opposite, a wall of love, united, as always. Her parents are very close. They finish each other's sentences and can speak without talking. For the moment, they seem at a loss, then her mother takes a deep sip of tea and starts.

"You remember I had a hysterectomy when you were sixteen?"

"Yes. You have endometriosis, that's why I don't have any siblings. I'm the miracle child."

"The miracle child." Her mom's smile is warm and soft. Her father touches her hand, then grabs it tightly in his. Oh, God.

"Tell me you don't have cancer. Mom, tell me you're okay!"

"Oh, honey, I am fine. I'm not sick, that's not what this is about. No, we tried, for so long, to have a baby. It wouldn't work, no matter what. We tried everything, but my insides were simply not workable."

"But then you had me."

"Then we had you," she echoes. "But I didn't give birth to you."

The silence is deafening. Kira shuts her eyes and opens them again. "I don't think I heard you correctly," she says.

"You did." Her father finally speaks. "Sweetheart, we adopted you. You were an infant, only days old. We were incredibly blessed. You were a dream come true for us. We loved you from the second we saw you, and that will never, ever change."

Kira realizes her mouth is gaping open and closes it so hard her teeth snap. "Let me get this straight. I'm adopted, and I'm a beneficiary of Columbia Jones's will. You people are crazy."

Her mother laughs, but there is a sob, deep in her throat. "Probably. Oh, my sweetheart, I know this is confusing. We decided not to tell you when you were little, and as you've grown into a woman, a mother, a leader in this community, we selfishly kept this to ourselves. You might as well have come from inside me. I love you more than words can say, and your dad does, too."

"That's right, peanut." The old nickname pushes her over the edge, and Kira collapses into tears. They hold her, and shed their own, over the life they once had, and the truth that now will define their future.

When Kira's sobs slow to hiccups, her mother gets her a cool wash-cloth, and her father pours her a fresh cup of tea. "There's more," he says. "Are you ready, or would you rather wait?"

"More?"

He nods. He looks so stricken, so lost. His hair has more gray in it than she remembers, and his face is lined more heavily. It's the first time his mortality seems close, and it makes her want to scream.

"I'm honestly at a loss for words, so you might as well keep talking."

"I appreciate you being willing to listen to what we have to say. I know this is a shock and the last thing you thought you'd be talking about today. We never wanted to hurt you. We love you too much."

"Then why didn't you tell me?" The words are tinged with anger; she can't help herself. "It's not just about me. I mean, the kids, we need their medical history, all of it."

Her mother sits back down. "We have that information. We received it with the adoption papers. Don't worry, there's nothing alarming, nothing unusual. Your biological mother was healthy."

"Do you know why she gave me up?"

"We do. I assure you, it wasn't because she didn't love you."

"Let me guess, she was a teenager, and her parents forced her."

"Definitely not that." Her mother—God, she will never not think of this woman as her mother, no matter who birthed her, and that gives Kira a measure of peace, enough so that she squeezes her mom's hand.

"Just tell me."

"There's no good way to say this. Your birth mother had you in prison."

Kira drops her mom's hand and raises her own. "Stop right there. Wait. *What?*"

"This isn't entirely unusual. Sometimes they defer sentences, and sometimes they don't. The children go into the foster system if there aren't family members to take them in. We were just getting established in the foster system when you were born, and when we heard about you, a newborn infant, we immediately asked to get involved. We adopted you two months later."

"Is she . . . Is she still in jail?"

"We don't know where she is, love. It was a closed adoption, and there was no way for her to contact you. We moved from Tennessee to Colorado the moment the courts said we could. We wanted to have a new life, with you at its center. Now that you know, though, we can talk with the lawyers and see what can be done about opening the records."

"And what the hell does this have to do with me being in Columbia Jones's will?"

Her dad shakes his head. "We aren't sure. I mean . . . the woman who gave birth to you is certainly not Columbia Jones, she's from rural Tennessee, and Columbia wasn't even in the States then, right?"

"I don't know exactly when she came over, it was in the nineties sometime, I think. I'd have to go check her bio."

Her dad nods. "She knew her, somehow. They could have been friends. Or Columbia was doing research for a book, and they met, and somehow after that you got on Columbia's radar. We honestly don't know."

"We're going to have to be patient, sweetheart," her mother says. "Wait for the reading of the will and find out the rest then."

"The fifteenth, that's next week, right? I'm supposed to fly to New York, and wait until then to find out the truth? God, this is insane."

Kira gets to her feet. Movement is the only solution.

"We will talk about this more. I love you, and I want to understand all your feelings, and motivations for keeping this from me. But I'm hurt, and a little freaked out. I have to go, I have to talk to Luke. I need to tell him what's happening."

Her parents don't try to stop her, just nod sadly as she leaves the kitchen. It is a place of betrayal now, not comfort. The place where life as she knew it has now ended.

In the car, she rips open the envelope and reads the letter inside.

My darling daughter,
    I'm not going to hide this from you anymore.
Many, many years ago, I did a very bad thing.

Kira reads the letter, becoming more and more confused, until she reaches the very end.

"I love you very much. Mother."

The word sounds profane on her tongue. *Mother* is the woman sitting at the round oak kitchen table right now, face in her slim hands, shoulders shaking as she cries. Not some stranger who did a very bad thing. What the heck does that even mean?

There's no other way to put it together. Columbia Jones actually knew her birth mother. She's held this letter for her, all these years, and now, in her last act, is giving Kira this incredible shock.

Was that why she was so kind at the VIP meet and greet? Why she lingered in conversation with Kira, long past when she should have moved on to other readers? How could she know Kira was this woman's daughter? Unless she kept tabs on her all these years?

She has to do some research, figure out whether her birth mother is still alive, why she would entrust Columbia Jones to share this news.

And the best person to help her do that is Luke.

CHAPTER THIRTY-SIX
DARIAN

When Vic shows up on her doorstep, Darian is only mildly embarrassed to have to call down for him to hold on while she gets her clothes on. She's fallen asleep in Mason's arms again. She doesn't know why she's so tired, unless the grief is pulling at her, tearing her down. He shifts but doesn't wake, and she rolls to her side, and swipes open her phone, fighting back a yawn.

"Hey, Vic. Be there in a sec."

She pulls on her pants and a top, yanks her hair into a knot, and hurries from the bedroom. Mason still doesn't move. The stress is getting to them both.

Down the stairs, flight after flight. She opens the door, noting it is a beautiful sunny day. Maybe they can take a walk later. Stroll around Central Park. She's feeling claustrophobic in the house.

Vic enters the foyer and gives her a huge bear hug. He's wearing chinos and a blue polo, Top-Siders without socks, and a sweater tied around his neck. He looks every inch of his sixty-five years, with a shock of white hair and deep creases on his tanned face, a sailor happily aging into retirement. She doesn't know what she'll do without him, one of these days. Her mother's death has brought everyone's mortality to the forefront.

"Did I take you away from the boat?"

"I'll get out there later. Bess has already gone to the island for the summer, she's setting up the house. It was early, but she's been itching for peace and quiet. I'm doing long weekends until Memorial Day, then I'll join her full time and work from there a few days a week. It's nice to have a place to go." He smiles softly, and she knows what he's thinking about. Bess is a sweetheart who lifted him from a deep depression when his first wife died of breast cancer, and the summer house comes from her side of the family.

"Montauk is so peaceful this time of year. I'm jealous. Come on in. Have you heard about the online crap?"

"Yes. I'm so sorry, Darian. This isn't how her exit from this life should be."

"I agree."

He follows her into the foyer and up the curved staircase to the living room. When he's seated on the powder blue sofa, he nods. "I found something on Riley Carrington. You're not going to like it. She has a sealed juvenile record, and I can't get into it."

"Seriously? For what? What did she do?"

"That's the issue, I don't know. But that's not all. I talked to Preston Mathers again. The will is legit. Your mother went in herself and set it up. I will say they're very willing to move forward. That's why the date was set for the fifteenth. But your mom has a verbal stipulation that the article Riley Carrington is writing must be published first."

"Why? Why would she do that?"

Darian realizes Mason is lurking on the stairs. She waves him into the room. Vic eyes him, then coughs. He was a smoker for years, and Darian cringes at the wet hacks. Despite quitting, despite the nicotine gum he chews instead, he doesn't sound well, and that depresses her.

"I don't know, dear. Who's this?"

"Victor Guul, Mason Bader. He was part of my mom's security detail. Mason was a combat medic with the Navy SEALs. Then a corpsman on the USS *George H. W. Bush*. He joined Celestron Security when he got home and has been detailed to Mom's team for the past two years."

"That's all very impressive. Went into the private sector, did you? Celestron has a good reputation, we recommended your company to clients often. Suggested them to Columbia, too. But I'm not sure this is information we need to be discussing outside of the family, Darian."

She wants to laugh at Vic's disapproving tone but decides to take a chance. "Yeah, um . . . he's my boyfriend." She is almost afraid to say it, but Mason's face splits into a wide, happy grin. He puts out his hand respectfully.

"Mr. Guul, I assure you, nothing said here will leave this room. I have Darian's best interest at heart. I'm here to protect her. I failed to protect her mother, and I have to live with that mistake for the rest of my life."

"Were you on duty?"

Mason shakes his head. "No, sir, but that doesn't matter. I feel very responsible. We know Columbia was being stalked, and with her death, I am more intent than ever on keeping Darian safe, too."

"I'll hold you to that. Call me Vic. Looks like you have something to add?"

"Maybe she just wants to be sure Riley is paid. Could a contract exist between them, or at least between Columbia and *East Fifth Magazine*, regarding the parameters of the article?"

"Hmm," Darian says. "There's not a contract between them, per se, but there was a collaboration statement that said Riley wasn't paid until the article was published. You might be right. It could just be altruistic."

"Your mother was such a wonderful woman," Vic says, voice thick, tears sparkling in his eyes. "I just can't believe this. I can't believe someone would murder her, and then to hack her online profiles and create such filth . . . She was beloved. She deserves better."

Darian puts a hand on his knee. "I know. It's a nightmare. I keep hoping I'll wake up and everything will be back the way it was."

She sneaks a quick glance at Mason. Maybe not everything.

"Mr. Guul—Vic—is there anything we can do to get the will prior to the reading? Isn't Darian, as a beneficiary, entitled to that?"

"Unfortunately, it's not my call. That's up to Mathers, and he's not budging."

"Then we need Riley to publish the story, stat," Darian says. "I'm going to call her."

Riley's phone goes immediately to voicemail. "Riley, it's Darian Jones. Please call me as soon as possible." She clicks off. "So much for that. Hopefully we won't have to wait long, she's usually pretty responsive. Vic, there's something else. I called my grandmother to tell her about Mom, and the woman who answered . . . Well, she said if Columbia was dead, so was my nana, and demanded money from the will. Has my mother ever mentioned a woman named Vonda West?"

"Vonda West. Vonda West." Vic shuts his eyes, concentrating. Like many lawyers, he has a photographic memory for names and statutes. "No, dear, I can't say I recall that name. And I'm confused. Your grandmother isn't your grandmother?"

"Apparently not. There isn't anyone named Yvonne Maxwell-Dodd on the record in England. And the woman I spoke with, her voice—accent—shifted back and forth between the woman I thought I knew and this nasty, money-grubbing witch. Liam looked it up, and her phone number and address go to this Vonda West person." She pauses, thinking. "Vic, do you by chance know any of the other people Mom was familiar with back then? Old friends, people she worked with? You've known her the longest."

Vic coughs. "Darian, you need to understand your mom was very private. Always. It was part of how she managed when she was getting started as a writer. When she wrote—" He stops, shaking his head a little, as if there is something important that he can't—won't—say, and Darian goes on alert.

"When she wrote *what*?"

Vic shakes his head. "It's nothing."

Mason squeezes her hand. "Attorney-client privilege—" he starts, and she cuts him off.

"Doesn't hold after death. Not with her daughter. Tell me what you were going to say, Vic."

"Darian, please. Let me do this the right way, the way she wanted."

"Tell. Me. Now."

Vic coughs again, an extended set of hacks. Darian, worried, fetches a glass of water. When he takes a few sips, he sighs heavily. "Do you know how your mom and I met?"

"It was on her first book contract, right?"

"Right. But the first contract wasn't with Mary."

"That's not right," Darian says. "She's been with Mary from the beginning."

"No, she hasn't. She had a deal before that. For several years, she wrote category romance under a pen name. She hired me to negotiate the contract. She met the editor at a conference, pitched her a story idea, which she accepted on the spot. She'd already written two of the books. She turned them in, and not surprisingly, they did well. Well enough that the house bought the rest of the series."

The manuscripts on the hard drive.

"What are these books? What was the pen name?"

"D.E. Shepherd. We kept it very, very quiet. When she wrote *Bright Candy*, it was such a new direction, and I convinced her to go with her own name. Obviously, you know the rest. The book was a critical and commercial juggernaut. A shift in the literary landscape, a new kind of story, a genre all to its own. And Columbia Jones became a household name."

"Holy shit." Darian can't wrap her head around this.

"But D.E. Shepherd has more than six books," Mason says. He has his phone out and has opened Amazon. He turns the phone around and scrolls. "There are at least twenty titles here."

Vic sighs again.

"No. She couldn't have." Darian tries to do the calculations. Her mother always was a fast writer, but writing the massive stand-alone titles that she did, with all the research it took, couldn't have left time for other projects. *Bright Candy* took her two years; that was typical of her novels. Even when Darian started to help, that only cut out a few months. The Shepherd novels must be a series, or much shorter than the stand-alones, to pull off that much writing so fast. "Vic, there's a bunch of files on Mom's computer, and a crazy letter. Maybe these are the files from those books."

"Very possibly. She gave it up after you got into school. It was a labor of love for her, Darian. She learned a lot, made some money, and it helped springboard her into the life she wanted for you. It was always for you, my dear. Everything she did was for you."

Darian sucks in a breath. *Do not cry. Do not fall apart.*

And then it hits her. "D.E. Shepherd. Vic, there's a suspect in Mom's murder—well, it seems like a suspect. His name is Knox Shepherd. Does *that* name ring a bell?"

"I can't say it does," Vic replies. He smooths his hands over his chinos, then stands. "I'm sorry, but I have to go. I have another appointment. We'll get to the bottom of all of this, my dear. You hang in there."

"Wait. Why aren't these titles mentioned in the literary estate papers? I don't recall seeing them at all. She went over everything with me. Why would she want to hide this from me? It makes no sense."

Vic scratches his nose. "Because I have a separate literary estate set up for the pen name. I think she was just so busy being Columbia Jones, hon, that she wanted to let the past be the past."

"It's still pulling royalties?"

He won't meet her eyes, but replies, "Yes."

There's more, she can feel it in her bones. Vic isn't telling her the whole truth, and now she's on alert. "And when were you going to tell me this?"

"When you were ready to go through everything after the funeral." He taps the paperwork from Mathers and Mathers. "Turns out she was keeping secrets from us both, my dear."

CHAPTER THIRTY-SEVEN

Darian walks Vic to the door and closes it behind him, feeling utterly betrayed. How could they have kept this from her? Her mother dies, and her whole world turns upside down. She is unmoored, and more grateful than ever for the tall ginger in the living room. She tries Riley's number again, then, fed up with waiting, calls *East Fifth Magazine* directly.

She is rerouted a few times and ends up talking with a man named Tony, who promises to get word to Riley that Darian needs to speak to her.

She returns to the space to find Mason holding his phone in one hand and the remote in the other. He looks stricken, face pale, and holds out a hand to her as if he knows she's going to need bolstering.

"What is it? More online nonsense?"

"No. They've finally declared your mom's death a murder."

He turns up the volume.

The news anchor is appropriately grave with that undercurrent of restrained excitement that comes from delivering bad news. Mason has timed it perfectly; they are coming back from a break and the screen is suddenly filled with her mom's angled black bob and a red-lipped smile. Darian's heart clenches.

"Returning to our top news story, the Denver Police have released the cause of death for famed author Columbia Jones, who was murdered in Denver last Friday at the end of her book tour. The police say the author ingested a large dose of brodifacoum, which is a common rodent poison, though they have not released the delivery mechanism. Let's go to our panel for more."

The screen bifurcates to four talking heads Zooming into the station. The first words out of the first mouth fill her with horror.

"As you know, poison is a woman's method of killing. I hope they're looking closely at her—"

Mason snaps off the television before the words lodge in her brain, but she hears that unspoken moniker.

Daughter. I hope they're looking closely at her *daughter.*

The sense of triumph that coursed through her moments earlier— *Of course she was murdered, I've known this all along*—is followed by a tsunami of sorrow, so intense she has to take a seat on the sofa and put her head back. The room is swimming, she feels nauseated. Was this how her mother felt in her last hours, like she was coming unmoored from the earth?

Mason has dropped to his knees and is feeling her pulse. She opens her eyes to see him frowning.

"I'm okay. Just lightheaded. It's very real all of a sudden, you know?"

"You can't listen to what they're saying. You can't let this get to you. Liam will fix things. He's really good at his job. And no one will think you were behind this, Darian."

So he heard it, too.

"We've known I've been an unspoken suspect this whole time."

"Let them talk. You're innocent. I know you are, and I'm all that matters, right?"

"Well, it matters that Detective Sutcliffe believes that, too. But how do you know, Mason? We've only been together a few weeks. Maybe I hated my mother so much I brought her a glass of water dosed with rat poison. Maybe I held her head as she drank it, and I watched her eyes bug out and laughed as she grabbed her throat, and all that blood poured out of her. That's what they're going to say, that I stood to gain everything if she died. And I do. Or I did, before this phantom will appeared."

He rocks back on his heels, still holding her wrist. "Darian Jones, there are many things I still need to learn about you. But one thing I know in my bones. There's no way you would purposefully hurt your mother. As difficult as your relationship was, you adored her. And she adored you."

"Maybe. But that doesn't mean the world won't jump to believe the most salacious accusations lobbed at me. I'm surprised her feed didn't just say *Darian Murdered Me*."

He rubs her wrist, seemingly at a loss for words for once.

"I need to look at these files again. There has to be answers in there."

"I'll help."

"No, that's okay. I'm sure you have other things to do besides babysit me."

"If you think I'm leaving your side right now, you're nuts. I wasn't kidding with Vic. I feel responsible."

"I don't want you here because you feel responsible. You didn't do this. You didn't make the world a terrible place, and you didn't make my mother hide things from me. You have a life. You have a career. I'm quicksand, and we both know it."

Mason nods sadly. "If you don't want to be with me, Darian, just say it."

"I wouldn't have told Vic you're my boyfriend if I didn't. I just can't ask you to stand by me as my world shatters."

He moves closer, pulling her to his chest and burying his face in her hair.

"I want to keep your world from shattering, Darian Jones. And if I can't, then I want to be here to help you pick up the pieces. I love you. Don't you realize that?"

Before it totally sinks in what's just happened, what he's said, what it means, her phone rings. She forces herself to take a deep breath and step away from Mason but smiles up at him. "To be continued, okay? I should get this. It's probably Liam."

It's not. It's a reporter.

"Darian Jones? I'm Daniel Donnelly, WICK News in Denver. I need to speak with you about your mother's murder, and the legacy she leaves behind. Specifically, I believe I've just spoken to your sister."

"I don't have a sister, and I don't want to speak with any media right now." She starts to hang up but hears one last squeak from the reporter before her finger mashes the End button.

"Wait! Her name is Kira Hutchinson, and—"

CHAPTER THIRTY-EIGHT
KIRA

Kira sleepwalks the car home, completely shell shocked. Their place is a ten-minute winding drive from the main ranch house, closer to the barns, which makes Luke's morning commute easier.

She has to tell Luke in person. This isn't the kind of news you tell someone over the phone.

Their nanny, Ella, who is in love with the kids and has been rooting for Kira to have ten more for her to help with, is alone in the kitchen, eating a cup of yogurt and reading Kira's signed copy of *Ivory Lady*.

"Hey," Kira says, dropping her bag and shoes in the mudroom, quashing down the urge to yank the book away in case something spills on it or a page gets bent. She intends to buy a separate reading copy of the book. It's even more precious now. "Have you seen Luke?"

"He's down in the barns. Something about bonding with the new foal? What are you doing here? I didn't expect you home for a couple of hours at least. The kids are at school, everyone's okay as far as I know."

"It's not the kids. I got some weird news. Wanted to tell Luke in person. How's the book?"

"Incredible. I promise I'm being super careful with it—now that she's gone, this is sacred, I know."

"I know you are. But I'll buy you—and me—a regular copy when I go back out, okay? You're right, it is special. More special than the others."

Kira has all of Columbia's books, all signed, but this one, personalized, a token of meeting her hero in person? A hero who is now dead, and might have answers about her past?

"Sure. Of course." Ella closes the book and pushes it toward Kira. "Laundry is all done, kids' rooms are straight. I'll go pick them up after school and take them to soccer so you can *talk* to Luke." She winks lasciviously.

Kira steals the book from the counter with a smile. "Thank you, Ella. And thanks for understanding. I'll have a new copy for you in a couple of hours."

"No worries. Go talk to that handsome stud out there."

Kira blows her a kiss and grabs two bottles of water. The barns are hot this time of day; Luke won't say no to a cool drink.

She takes the golf cart, zigzags down the gravel trail. He's not in the office, but his truck is parked outside, so he's here somewhere. She waves to a few of the hands who help manage the horses, and they point her down the stone walkway.

She finds Luke in a stall with the new foal, rubbing him down, an adorable black beauty with a perfect white star on his forehead. Doing it himself instead of letting one of the men they've hired for these things, of course, because that's the kind of man he is. The future of the ranch isn't something he'll let just anyone handle.

"Hey," she says. "What's his name?"

Luke looks up and grins when he realizes who it is. He accepts the bottle of water, takes a deep drink, and spills the rest over the baby's nose. The foal loves it, jumps and kicks in happiness.

"Oh, that life was so simple," Kira says.

"I think we should call him Orion, for that big ole star on his forehead."

"That's adorable. I agree. Hello, Orion. How are you, baby?"

"Hungry, watch your hand. I'm going to bring him to his mama. Need to talk?" He looks at her fully then. "You've been crying. Is every-thing . . . okay?"

"Bakery is in good hands, Alex is making the cupcakes for the gar-den party." She touches her stomach with what she hopes is a reassuring smile. "Everything is fine with us, but . . . um, I just came from my parents. They got a letter I wanted you to see."

Luke leads the colt from the stall, goes down three doors, and puts him in with his mother, who nickers in relief. He pats her on the nose. "Good girl. Feed Orion, I'll be back to check on you in a minute."

The happy sounds of sucking and grunting fill the stone room, and Luke locks the gate and comes back to his wife.

"What was this letter?" he says, stealing a sip of water from her bottle. She waves him off when he tries to give it back.

"It was from a law firm in New York. Apparently, I'm a beneficiary of Columbia Jones. I'm in her will."

"What?" She's heartened by the incredulity in his voice. This upside-down world they've just found is not something she can navigate alone.

"There's more. So much more. Let's sit down."

Kira finishes telling him the story and reads him the letter. She clears the tears from her throat.

"I think she must have known my birth mother. Maybe she was doing research on the jail system—there is a book she did called *Nobody Forgets* that is partially set in a small-town prison in Appalachia. The woman is a heroin addict who is wrongly accused of a murder, finds books in prison, and ends up being a lawyer, but when she's freed, is ostracized by the community anyway and has to start over in Philadelphia. Huge hit. Lots of research, I mean, to get the jail scenes so incredibly accurate she had to do a ton of interviews with incarcerated prisoners. She must have met my mother and struck up a friendship. Maybe promised her something. She'll probably reveal her name to me at the reading. And she entrusted this letter to her to make sure I would pay attention and take it seriously."

Luke is genuinely flabbergasted, and for a man like him, for whom nothing is a mystery, that's saying something. Kira watches him pace for a few minutes, then put his hands on his hips. He's stirred up the dust motes, and they dance around him joyously, showing off in the sunlight. Finally, he says, "I don't understand how your favorite author has you in her will if you're not a direct relation, hon."

"I admit this is all very weird, but there's no way, Luke. We know her life's story. She's never been in jail. And I hardly think my parents"—her voice catches slightly on the word—"would lie to me about this now."

"That you know. Maybe she based that book on her own life, and everything you think you know about her is BS."

"Luke. That's impossible. We live in the information age. Columbia Jones is a public figure. Her background is out there for the world to see."

"Maybe," he says lightly. "Still, I think—"

"Excuse me. Is that Kira Hutchinson?"

They both whirl around to see a young man with a microphone in his hand and a photojournalist standing behind him.

"Who the hell are you?" Luke growls, lunging forward as he pushes Kira behind him. The man—he has to be a reporter—takes a step back but doesn't bolt. Kira gives him a point for courage; Luke looks about ready to murder someone.

"Daniel Donnelly. I'm a reporter with WICK News. I wanted to talk to Mrs. Hutchinson about Columbia Jones. How she feels to be the daughter of a legend, and if she talked to her mother before she was murdered."

"What are you talking about?" Kira says, stepping out from behind Luke. "I'm not related to Ms. Jones."

"Not what I've heard." Donnelly waves a stack of paper. "We got a tip, a copy of a letter that you're a beneficiary in the will. Just wanted to verify—"

Luke has the reporter by the collar a heartbeat later and is marching him out of the barns. Kira follows, moving fast. Luke doesn't take kindly to unannounced strangers, and one who has dropped by and lobbed a bomb at them, quoting a private legal document? This isn't good.

But as they approach the house, Kira can see that Donnelly isn't the only reporter; he's just the one who was brave enough—stupid enough—to breach their yard. There are ten or so people milling about the drive, a couple of local news trucks, and Ella wringing her hands on the front steps.

How the hell they've gotten onto the ranchland is beyond her; her parents must have left and the gate must be open, because they would have called the sheriff immediately.

Her name is called, and the scrum begins, a mass of paparazzi with cameras flashing, reporters with boom mics, all swinging her way like the hundreds of swallows that gather in the dusk and loop through the pale-orange sky, synchronous, moving as one creature.

"Kira! What do you have to say about your inheritance?"

"Kira, how long have you known?"

"Kira, come this way, we're doing a story . . ."

"Luke," she calls. "Let him go. We need to get inside."

Luke listens and gives Donnelly a little push as he releases him. "Get off our land. Do not come back, do you understand?"

Donnelly waves a hand. "Doesn't matter if you kick us out. Your wife's big news, sir. She's Columbia Jones's long-lost daughter."

CHAPTER THIRTY-NINE
RILEY

Riley wakes with the sunlight streaming into her room—she didn't get the curtains closed all the way and the sun is pouring in joyously. The suite is quiet; Nate is probably asleep, too. When he came back with the food, he told her Columbia Jones was being dragged through the public square by her hair, rocks being thrown at her body.

She didn't need to see the horrors online. She'd seen too many people taken apart, their lives dissected, their worlds torn asunder, because of an ill-timed tweet or an unpopular opinion. She felt the violation without even seeing the posts. And she felt for Darian, who she knew would be trying to mitigate the disaster.

She was having a nightmare when she woke, her heart is pounding still. She closes her eyes and reaches for the fragments—a dark cave, a crone bent over a cauldron, like a Disney witch, warning her that something awful is about to happen, and to be prepared.

Great.

She stretches, realizes she's starving. She finds the last banana and eats it, then jumps in the shower. Refreshed, she goes into the shared living space to see Nate asleep in the chair, head lolling at a dangerous angle, papers still clutched in his hand.

It's the article. He printed it out and marked it up, and she eases the papers from his hand but wakes him as she does. He catches her hand.

"You okay?"

"Yeah. I slept some. Did you sleep out here?"

"Yeah." He wipes his free hand over his face and blinks hard, then sits up. "It's really good. Make the changes I marked, and I'll get us some food." He glances at his watch. "We should be wrapped by two and can go live by three."

"There's leftover pizza, or I can go down—"

He grins. "Nope. No way. Eggs? Bacon? A little brunch for the sleepyhead?"

"Fruit, and I'll take some bacon if you can make sure they cook it separately. If there's a hard-boiled egg?"

"There will be if I have to cook it myself."

He's still holding her hand. Silence spreads between them, then Nate sighs and jumps to his feet. "I'm off."

He knocks three times, to alert security he's coming out, then cracks open the door.

The hallway feels empty. The carpets are mostly dark, with a cream stripe in them, and across that cream stripe is a long streak of red. A trail of blood leading away from their room. She can see it from the couch. She hurries to the door just as Nate is swinging it closed. The guard's body is slumped against the wall, and there's a note on his chest anchored in place by what looks like a large nail.

"Shit," Nate says, slamming the door closed and whipping out a phone. He dials his security guard, and Riley hears the phone ringing, ringing, ringing. She opens the door just enough to look out, toward the noise, only to see the phone itself lying against the baseboard, vibrating. The guard's eyes are empty. He does not look like he's asleep, but instead very, very dead. She thinks the nail is actually a syringe.

"Get away, shut the door, lock it."

She does what he says. "I didn't hear a thing. And no one's in the hall. It must have just happened. He's here, Nate. He's come for us."

Nate is frantically calling other numbers, and she hears the eerie echo of how this nightmare started: "Sir, what is your emergency?"

"This is Nathanial Walsh, editor of *East Fifth Magazine*. I'm on the fortieth floor of the Sheraton Times Square, and my security officer Robert Chartson is down. I need backup, right now."

The operator asks him a million questions, and Nate hands Riley another phone, with a number preprogrammed. "Call it. Tell them."

She takes a few deep breaths to calm her skittering heart as she does. It's Tony from the IT office. She's surprised at how calm her voice sounds.

"Security is down, he was killed in the hallway. Nate wanted me to call you." She's not sure what a twenty-three-year-old hacker is going to be able to do, but she's astounded when Tony says, "Got it. I have a call in to the supervisor on duty. Hold on. A team will be there in five, tell Nate, yes?"

She does and he nods, face tight. Her own pulse has spiked. What the hell is going on? How were they tracked? And by whom?

"Put Nate on."

She hands the phone to Nate, who listens, nodding. She gets half the conversation. "Yeah . . . yeah . . . good . . . You're kidding? . . . Once the team gets here, yeah. Good job."

He hangs up, and in the moment of silence she hears the clanking and shouts as the rest of his security team arrive. She blows out a breath. "Nate, what's happening?"

"I think it's safe to say we've been spotted. How, I don't know. Apparently the video to the building's been jammed, they were able to get in without a trace."

Riley chides her heart, which has leaped to life and is galloping so hard she can barely focus. "That's a trick we've seen before. The blood— the guard. Is he dead?"

"I think he is—" Before Nate can tell her more, heavy fists slam against the door. Riley utters a little scream of surprise.

"Mr. Walsh? Open up!"

303

Nate goes to the door, standing sideways by the frame, as if he can avoid being shot if the bullets come through, and Riley is again surprised. The security guys have trained him, she sees that. He's always thought he was the target, though. Not her. And yet he hasn't even blinked.

She's put him in danger, and Oliver, too. And for what? Why, if Columbia Jones was murdered, would Riley be a target, too?

You know the answer already.

Obviously, she's uncovered something in Columbia's past. But what, exactly, still eludes her. She has to get boots on the ground, there's nothing more she can do scouring the online world. And right now, they have no proof of anything. No proof that Columbia was another person, long ago. No proof that Riley is her daughter, the child in the story. Which means it has to be the flash drive. There's something on it worth killing for.

Oliver said they would figure out the password together. How did he know it was password protected unless he'd tried to open it himself?

She thinks back to what he said. She was so angry she barely heard him. Something about Cabo and helping her research the drug cartels. She did a piece on the cartels a few years ago, but Oliver didn't help her with it. He certainly didn't go to Cabo with her. On the contrary, he warned her to stay away from it because he was worried they'd retaliate. Oliver was always worried that her work was going to get her in trouble. And Riley always explained to him she was honor bound as a journalist to dig into the stories and find the truth, no matter where that led her.

Why would he say he was in Cabo with her?

The room is full of security moments later, and Riley breathes out a little sigh of relief. Despite her recent run-in, she is still of the generation that was taught the police equal safety, and these men are as good as. She knows how privileged that makes her, knows too many others don't have that feeling. She sits on the sofa quietly while Nate explains what's happening, trying to quell her fear that one of these men will suddenly seize her, cuff her. Like what happened in Denver.

Unbidden, the moment the security guard tackled her after she found Columbia's body plays like a video in her brain, the conversation.

"What have you done? Why did you kill her?"

He was frantic. And that growly voice . . .

"Not. Me. Found. Her."

"Bullshit. You're a bloody mess."

"So is she. Ow! Be careful, you idiot."

"Why'd you kill her?"

"I told you, I didn't. I had no reason to hurt her. I came to do my last day of interviewing and found her like this."

The stranger called for the hotel manager then and disappeared.

She puts her hands over her ears, blocking out the conversation between Nate and security—he's relaying the night, what they've done, the pizza delivery—and replays it again.

The voice. It was the same as the man they'd called, she is sure of it. And his face. Tired. Sad—devastated, really. Older.

She flips open Nate's laptop. Looks at Knox Shepherd's booking photo. Really looks.

"Nate."

He is by her side in a heartbeat. "What? What's wrong?"

"It was Knox Shepherd. He was at the hotel in Denver. And he is who we called. I'm one hundred percent sure of it."

CHAPTER FORTY

Nate makes long eye contact, assessing, then nods. "Okay. I think it's more important than ever that we get somewhere safe. The team is going to escort us out of here. Another security team will meet up with us in the lobby. There's going to be a lot of people with guns, okay, so don't freak out. They're going to move you quickly to the car, and we're out of here."

"Where are we going?"

"My place."

"That's hardly circumspect, Nate."

"Well, they found us here, and at least in my house I have the means to keep us safe. Safer, that is."

"But the Upper East Side—"

"Not that house, Riley."

Oh. Nate's family has a camp on an island off the coast of Maine that they escape to in the summers. She has to admit it will be safer: the only way to get there is by sea or air, so they can control ingress and egress, see if anyone's coming for them.

And that tiny voice rears its head. *"You can't trust anyone. Not even Walsh."*

Is it a good idea to flee the city with Nate and his security team as her only companions? She feels a spike of fury at the stranger for putting such doubt in her mind. If Nate wanted to hurt her, he had every opportunity while she slept last night. Still . . .

"We can't leave the city, Nate. Oliver will lose his mind."

"What Oliver doesn't know won't hurt him. We have to find out what Columbia was hiding, and we have to figure out how Knox Shepherd is tied into all of this. I can keep you safe at the camp. Plus, Tony will come. He's cracked the password on the flash drive. Says there's a lot on it."

Riley's never been to the camp, but she's seen it in photos. *Architectural Digest* did an article on it five years ago. *Camp* is of course a misnomer; though a ubiquitous term for anything on the water in the Maine wilderness, this is more of a presidential hunting lodge. It was built by the same architect as Camp David. Nate's great-grandfather was college chums with him, they worked in the WPA together.

"I don't want to run."

"Riley—"

"If I'm in danger, and Columbia's dead, who else do you think might be a target? Oliver. Darian. Anyone who's been a part of this the past few days could be in danger, too."

"I don't care. *You* are my only responsibility." Nate's eyes are flashing; she recognizes his danger signs. They are excellent at fighting, and she knows just what buttons to push. She doesn't want to fight now, though. This is too important.

"I care. I can't just leave them."

"That woman accused you of murdering her mother. She got you arrested. Now you want to help her?"

"That woman might be my sister. If it's not safe for me here, it's not safe for her. We need to at least warn her, if not take her with us."

"You realize there's a solid chance she's involved, right? By fingering you, she's deflecting attention from herself."

"That's a very good point. But let's be real. She'd just found her mother dead. She was going to lash out at the closest thing, regardless. She doesn't really think I'd hurt Columbia. Seriously, we need to warn her. I need her to at least be on the lookout for the guy I saw at MoMA."

"Sir, we're ready to move you. We've handled the body until the police are involved." The security officer is hardly interested in their argument. He's just under orders.

"You have to let me take care of you, Riley. Please. Let's go."

Riley's hands are on her hips, and she plants herself in the middle of the room. "Nate. This is why I'm pissed at Oliver. Don't be high handed with me. We're going to warn Darian, and Oliver. Period."

Nate's eyes narrow, and he growls a little under his breath. "Fine." To the guard, he says, "Hold on a second, okay? We need to make a couple of calls."

The guard frowns but steps away, and Nate hands Riley a burner. "Make it quick. Call Darian now, and then we are leaving, and we'll call Oliver from the road. I tried him a couple of times last night, but he didn't answer. He was pretty pissed when we hung up."

"Thank you, Nate." She dials the number from memory and is surprised when Darian answers before the first ring goes through.

"Hello?"

"Darian, it's Riley. I need to talk to you."

"Well, finally! Took you long enough to call me back. I don't recognize this number."

Nate shakes his head in warning.

"I'm sorry, I lost my phone. You were trying to reach me?"

"Yes. I need to know what my mother told you about her past. About her early days as a writer. I have a couple of names to run by you, too."

"I assume you don't think I murdered her anymore?"

Darian's voice is tight. "No, I don't. And I apologize for reacting the way I did."

"That's good, because I need to tell you that I think you're in danger. Someone's been tracking me, and I assume it's because of what your mom left me."

"Left you?"

"I'm a beneficiary in her will."

The shriek is enough to make the cops waiting for them jump. Riley looks at Nate, makes a snap decision. "Listen, we're getting out of town, and I think you should come with us. There's too much to talk about by phone. Pack a bag, and we'll be by to get you shortly."

Nate's jaw drops. She can tell he's furious, but she doesn't care.

Darian demurs. "I can't go somewhere with you. I have to go to Denver for my mom's cremation."

"Listen to me. We need to speak in person, Darian. It's important. I know things that you probably don't about your mother's past. And there's someone after me. At least give me a day, then you can go deal with Columbia."

She hears quiet words, then Darian comes back on the line.

"Mason has to come."

"Mason . . . the security guard?"

"Yeah. We're . . . together. He's helping me sort through this mess."

Nate is holding his head in his hands, moaning dramatically at this additional inclusion. She ignores him.

"Fine. We're on our way. Warn him there's a lot of security, okay? I know he's former military, don't want him to be surprised." She hangs up and raises a brow.

"Nate, you've always taught me to trust my instincts. My instincts say she's in danger."

"*You're* in danger. *I'm* in danger. That's what I care about."

"You have a huge team around us now, and we're not going to argue about this. Either she comes, or we park it there at her house while we talk. Honestly, I think getting out of New York is the right thing to do. I also think we should file the piece before we leave, see if we can't buy some time while we figure out the rest. Darian obviously knows something, too. If we put our heads together, we'll solve this."

"Are you sure you don't want Oliver to come, too? Maybe his dad? The whole team at Mathers and Mathers? What about Columbia's people at her publisher?" At her scathing look, he holds up both hands in apology. "I'm just saying, if one's in danger, all are."

"Fair enough. But none of them are beneficiaries, and that's where I think this is all headed. The reading of the will. Will you please try Oliver again? He said something when we talked that's just registered with me, something weird about Cabo."

"Yeah, that he was helping you do research there. I didn't think he went with you on that trip."

"He didn't. That's why I'm worried."

Nate huffs out a breath through his nose.

"Can we at least just stop by the flat so I can grab a change of clothes? Maybe talk to him, see what he was trying to say? He must have known you were listening."

The closest guard says, "Sir, we're getting word that there's been a development in the Jones case." He goes to the television set, flips it on the first twenty-four-hour news channel he finds. Sure enough, the spinning chyron is flashing a news alert. Riley feels the breath leave her. Confirmation of what they've all known, deep in their hearts: Columbia Jones Murdered

CHAPTER FORTY-ONE
COLUMBIA

One Day Before the End

"This is the last of them. You're a trooper, Columbia, really you are."

She signs her name with a flourish and drops the Sharpie on the table. "Phew. How many does this make?"

"Seven hundred. In an hour. I am impressed. And at the end of your tour, too! Your wrist must be screaming!"

Columbia's wrist *is* sore, but she doesn't say a word of complaint to Ruby, who has spent hours making sure this event flows smoothly. Considering Columbia added this stop to the tour, and all the machinations that have gone into it, she has no room to complain.

"Do you want a snack before the meet and greet?" Ruby asks.

"No, actually, I think I'd like to get started. Are they here yet?"

"Several are, yes."

"Excellent. There's one in particular who I'd like to start with, if that's all right with you. Kira Hutchinson? Assuming she's here?"

"Oh, yes." Ruby grins. "She and her handsome hunk of a husband. Goodness, they are quite the pair. You won't be able to miss them."

"Maybe you could bring them here first. It will give me a little breather, and then I can gear up to meet everyone at once."

"Sure. Hang tight, I'll go get them."

If Ruby suspects this is unusual, she says nothing, just disappears out of the room, then comes back with the couple in tow before Columbia takes a full breath to prepare herself.

She's seen Kira before, of course. But they've never spoken. When the girl's radiant smile blinds her, Columbia is, for a moment, speechless. She isn't as tall as Columbia, but her vibrancy makes up for the lack of height. She fills the room, resonating with health, and excitement, and an inner glow that makes Columbia wonder if there's not another little Hutchinson on the way. The thought makes her smile, and the girl takes this as an opening.

"Oh my God, I can't believe I'm meeting you. You are my absolute hero. When Luke told me I was going to get to meet you, I thought he was lying. Hi, I'm Kira. Can I give you a hug?"

Before she says "Yes, absolutely," the girl's arms are around her and Columbia's struck dumb, tears forming. She squeezes Kira back. "You're a good hugger," Columbia manages. And she is. The girl's arms are full of love, and empathy, and Columbia can only imagine her in her tidy kitchen at the ranch, kneeling down, arms widespread, waiting for her boys to run into them.

"Let the woman breathe, hon." A rumbling bass laughs, and Columbia is bereft when Kira releases her.

"Oh, wow, I am so sorry, I just can't help myself."

Get it together, Columbia tells herself. "Do not apologize. That's why we have these moments, to celebrate together. I'm honored to meet you. You, too, Luke."

"Ma'am," he drawls, the perfect laconic cowboy.

"You run a bakery, I understand?"

Kira's face lights up more, if that's even possible. "You know about the bakery? Wow. Yes, I do." She gestures to her lush figure. "Obviously, I like to bake."

"You are perfect," Columbia says, and sees Luke, out of the corner of her eye, smile. He thinks so, too; that's certain. "And your boys? Tell me about them."

Kira is taken aback for a moment, then does, gushing as only the mother of three sons can: pride, ruefulness, and humor all tied into knots.

Columbia listens, smiling, repeating the boys' names over and over in her head.

Caleb. Hudson. Asher.

They would all be great lead character names. She'll have to add them into her repertoire.

Ruby comes in and signals—the meet and greets are only supposed to be a few minutes long, enough for a picture and a handshake, and this has stretched into several. Kira sees and says, "Oh, we should probably let you go."

"No, no, it's fine. Luke, could you let Ruby know Kira and I are going to visit a little longer?"

He nods and moves off, sending his adorable wife a soft smile of encouragement. Kira can't help but watch him stride away.

"He's a doll," Columbia says. "Seems like a nice guy."

"Oh my God, he is the nicest. We've been together since we were teenagers. I took one look at him and fell, hard. He runs our ranch, and is a really great guy. A great dad. I'll keep him."

Columbia laughs, and Kira, emboldened, keeps on. "So I saw Riley Carrington out there earlier. She's doing a piece on you for *East Fifth*? That's amazing. I'm a fan of hers, too. You two are a match made in heaven."

"You know Riley?"

"No, no, we've never met. I know of her. Read her work religiously. You're lucky, she's smart and fair."

"I am lucky," Columbia says, then leans in. "Between you and me, I'm going to have her write my memoir. Don't tell anyone yet, okay?"

"Oh, that is so cool!" Kira's delighted smile shoots to Luke, who is chatting with Ruby. "Can I tell Luke?"

"Nope. It's our little secret."

"Okay then." Kira smiles. "Does Riley know this?"

"I may have hinted, here or there. You should meet Riley. You'd like her."

"I will try, for sure. I have a feeling it's going to be a wild night. I know you need to go, but can I just say, your work, your words . . . it's like you can see into my soul. My mom gave me your first book as a birthday present, and I have read all of them at least three times. You really are my favorite."

Columbia clears her throat, swallowing past the lump that's formed. "Tell your mother she has excellent taste."

"Columbia, dear, the time," Ruby calls, and with a reluctant smile, she turns to Kira once more. "You take care of those boys. And yourself. Okay?"

Kira nods, and Columbia hugs her again, memorizing the feel of her arms and the smell of her skin, then releases her and salutes Luke. "Good to meet you both. Thank you for coming, and for being such great fans. All right, Ruby. Onward."

CHAPTER FORTY-TWO
KIRA

Now

Inside the house, her sanctuary now disturbed, Kira realizes her hands are shaking. She calls her mother while Luke paces, locking doors and windows, yanking closed the curtains in the living room. The crowd of press mills in the drive, restless as sharks. They know that a simple wall holds her from them, but they can't get in without breaking the law, so she is safe, at least for the moment.

"Mom, I need you to make sure Ella brings the boys to you, and take them somewhere that isn't tied to us. We have reporters crawling all over the property. If you don't see any at your place and you can get out, please go now."

"Reporters? Why? Is this because of the letter?"

"Yes. Apparently so. Someone sent WICK a copy as well. They know more than we do at this point."

"Oh my gosh. Okay, I'll get them. We'll go to the bookstore. I'm sure they'd love a few new comics."

"Thank you. Maybe the movies, too? It might take us a while to sort this out, and I don't want the reporters scaring them."

"Absolutely. I'll call before we come back. Honey, I know you're upset with us. Just know that we love you, very much, and always will."

"I love you, too, Mom. Thanks for taking care of the boys."

Luke has his phone in his hand. "I'm going to call Jack, have him come get these yahoos off the property." Jack Towers is the local sheriff. He and Luke are best friends; he will certainly help.

"That's a good idea. Though Donnelly's technically the only one who violated the property. See if Jack will arrest him for trespassing."

Luke's face is grim as he dials the sheriff's private line and hits the speaker. Jack comes on with a hearty hello, but Luke interrupts him. "We have a bunch of reporters here, and we need your help."

"Reporters? Why? Did Kira burn the muffins? Baker blows it, news at eleven."

Kira laughs despite herself. Jack is a good guy. "If only it were that simple. Apparently I'm Columbia Jones's long-lost daughter. They want a comment on the story."

Jack whistles. "Hold on." They can hear him talking in the background. "Okay, dispatch is sending two of my boys, who are already in the neighborhood. We'll get things under control. Columbia Jones, that's the writer who was murdered?"

"Was she murdered? We hadn't heard."

"Yeah, it's all over the news. She was poisoned with brodifacoum."

"Rodent poison?" Luke asks. "Pretty common stuff. We have some in the barn."

Jack's tenor shifts. "Buddy, do me a favor, and do not say that aloud to anyone else, all right? Go secure it, right now, and let me get over there with an evidence bag."

Kira looks at Luke in alarm. "Jack, we were there the night she died. We were at the hotel. There was a VIP experience, and we stayed over. We met her. Talked to her."

Jack curses. "I'm on my way. Seriously, do not tell any of the reporters that."

"We won't, we're locked inside," Kira says. "I sent my mom to get the boys before they waylaid my parents, too. Jack, what the hell is going on?"

"I don't know, but let me find out. I know Luke surprised you with tickets to the event, I remember him telling me about it. You stayed at the Brown Palace?"

Luke is clenching and unclenching his fists, something he does when under extreme stress. "Yes. There's a detective from Denver Police working the case, Detective Sutcliffe. He has a suspect, I think. He showed Kira a six-pack, and she picked out a guy who was there."

Kira hears the car start. Jack is on the move. "I'll get in touch with him once we have a chance to chat. These hotels have cameras everywhere. I'm sure you'd already be sitting in the police station if Sutcliffe thought you'd done anything wrong."

"Maybe he leaked your name," Luke says.

"How would he get the lawyer's paperwork, though?" Kira asks.

"How did the reporter? *Someone* leaked it. Y'all hang tight, I'm ten away. Do not talk to anyone. Not even Sutcliffe, if he calls. You hear me?"

Kira feels her stomach turn and puts up a finger, bolting from the room. She hears Luke call "You okay, honey?" just as she makes it to the bathroom. She prays morning sickness isn't giving way to all-day sickness, but she had mild cases of hyperemesis gravidarum with all her previous pregnancies, so the odds are not in her favor.

Purged, she leans on the counter with both hands, staring in the mirror. Her life has shifted so dramatically in the last forty-eight hours that she hasn't had time to actually think it through. She's operating on nerve at this point, knowing if she allows herself to sink into the reality of the situation—*We adopted you. I love you, Mother*—she will be lost.

This is exactly what she has never wanted for her life. She craves calm, comfort, a sense of belonging, a sense of place. She is a homebody, through and through; home is the heart—and the hearth—of her life. Her boys, her husband, her parents, her business, itself a comfort to herself and others, their quiet and beautiful lives in one of the most gorgeous settings imaginable: this is what she's fought for. It's almost as if the universe warned her there is chaos on the other side of this door, and she agreed never to open it.

And now the door has been splintered, and there's nothing she can do to stop it.

Luke knocks.

"Kira? Are you all right? Jack's pulling in."

"Yeah. I'll be out in a second."

She washes her face, rinses her mouth, twists her hair back into its clip. A stranger watches her from the mirror, and with a tiny shake of her head to admonish this new woman, Kira joins Luke to face the disaster head on.

CHAPTER FORTY-THREE
RILEY

Nate finally caves, agreeing to go to Riley's apartment to grab some things and leave word for Oliver, but only if she's escorted by him and his phalanx of security. She's fine with that; relieved, actually. The edges of her world are fraying, and she feels the need to trim them, tidy everything, because she can feel in her very bones that everything is about to change.

Traffic is terrible, and Nate is annoyed with her and preoccupied with making arrangements, so Riley has plenty of time to think. About her past, and Nate's immediate acceptance of her confession. About her mother, Faith, and her sister, Maisie, how her entire world was upended when she found out she was not Faith's daughter, not Maisie's sister, but an interloper in their lives. About Columbia, and Darian. About the crazy short story.

About mothers. And what they are willing to do. Some give up their children, whether willingly or with great sorrow. Some go to the ends of the earth to keep them. Yin. Yang.

Riley thinks she turned out okay. Maybe she's not in a rush to be a mother herself, but once she stopped acting out, stopped trying to punish Faith for the revelations about her past, got the alcohol and sex under control, found worth in her abilities instead of her body, things have been solid. She wasn't lying to Nate, she never did try to find her birth mother, mostly because she didn't know what it would gain her. The woman clearly wasn't interested in ever knowing her; the adoption had been closed, sealed entirely. Yes, she can put her DNA in the system and hope someone pops up, but to what end? Maybe she will one day, if she has kids and she wants a medical history or something.

But her resemblance to a woman who went to jail for murder is undeniable. Yes, the timing is off by a year, but it shouldn't be too hard to do a records search on Devon Mears in the prison system and see if she had a baby in jail. A baby she gave up for adoption, not because she didn't want the child, but because she couldn't raise her. And then she died, only a year after she got out of jail, according to the obituary, so it's not like she would be upset by the revelation of a grown daughter.

But what if she hadn't died after all? What if she changed her name and created a new life for herself?

But why leave her child behind? None of this adds up.

The window is cracked in the black Suburban, the streets of New York fresh from a downpour, a drizzle still dampening the concrete. She hadn't realized it was raining, cooped up in the hotel room finishing the piece. The city is reborn in these moments, even brighter and shinier than usual.

Nate is on the phone, arranging for the camp to be opened to accommodate five souls and a wad of security. She'll be safe enough there, and she and Darian can figure out what they need to about the crazy situation they find themselves in. Tony will show them what's on the flash drive, and all will become clear.

Hopefully, Oliver will forgive her. She just wants to talk for a minute, assure him that she's working but she can't text or email, to be on the lookout. It must be in person. She's written him a note, and hopes he'll read it dispassionately, not in fury. She doesn't like how they left things. Even though she senses things are too damaged between them, she doesn't want it to end like this—in words of anger and hurt feelings.

Her finger taps the edge of the glass. The rain picks up speed again; the gray afternoon is going to turn into a wet night. The tires of the cab slosh along the pavement at every turn.

Tap. Tap. Tap.

Columbia Jones wrote a story about giving away a baby.

Tap. Tap. Tap.

A story she sent to Riley. Not Darian. Riley.

Tap. Tap. Tap.

And she was murdered, poisoned.

The car finally pulls up to her building, and she leaps out with barely a thank-you. She hurries to the elevator, shaking her head, thinking. Was she killed because she was about to tell the truth about her past? Is that why Knox Shepherd stood up, to warn her off?

Nate presses the up button. "You've been lost in thought. Everything okay?"

"Yeah. I'm just doing the math. Say there's a story to be told about a woman who had her lover murder her husband, got caught, went to jail, and lost her kid in the process."

"Sad. But compelling. Human Interest 101."

"Right. Okay. Now look at our society as a whole. We are fed information in a constant stream. There's almost too much to process. So we start taking that data at face value. We take exactly what we're given and believe it, because our brains don't have room for anything else. We don't investigate any further. Even the media, these young journalists who don't bother sourcing properly, just run with stories based on innuendo and rumor, don't do the kind of due diligence we used to insist upon."

"A travesty that's ruining journalism."

"Agreed." The elevator dings. They're almost to her floor. "A writer's bio is the definitive introduction to the reader, right? It's on every book, every website, in every article. Why wouldn't we believe it? Why would an author lie? What do they have to gain? They're almost always found out. It ends careers. And with the data we have access to, it's incredibly easy for a layperson to dig into someone's past and find out if they're fabricating the truth."

"Where are you going with this?"

"There's no record of Columbia Jones in England. It was one of the questions I had for her in our last interview. I hadn't wanted to go there until we were almost wrapped, because I wanted her to trust me, and if I led with 'Hey, I can't verify one of the cornerstones of your life,' she might have gotten spooked."

Nate runs a finger over his lip. "You think she's lying?"

The elevator gets to her floor. The door slides open.

"I'm almost sure of it. I think she built an amazing house of cards, and now somebody has decided that they want to take it apart. I think Columbia Jones isn't her real name. I think her real name is Devon Mears. And I think she's my mother. And I have to let Darian Jones know that. And figure out why someone killed Columbia to stop her from telling me."

Nate is right beside her, hovering as she starts to unlock the door. "That's . . . more than compelling. That's Pulitzer."

"It's conjecture. We have no proof."

The dead bolt isn't on, only the push lock. That's strange. They're always so careful not to leave the doors unlocked. After a break-in? She's surprised Oliver hasn't already changed the locks and added more, truth be told. "I wonder if the break-in damaged the dead bolt," she says, but Nate has moved her to the side and nodded to one of the security with them.

"Go careful," he says, and the guard draws a weapon and eases open the door.

She knows immediately something is wrong, even before the guard says "Keep her back, keep her back" and talks into his comms unit, saying words that freeze her heart. "We have a civilian down."

"What? Who is it?" she shouts, ripping herself from Nate's arms and shoving past the guard, who reaches for her but misses.

"Riley, no, don't—" Nate starts, but she ignores him.

She enters the flat and can't make sense of what she's seeing.

A leg, twisted.

An arm, limp.

A head, angled oddly.

Glasses, broken in two.

Blood.

So much blood.

Her screams echo through the room, ending in a wail. She kneels at his side, pressing a hand to the stain of blood on his chest, the seeping flow cold and hardened.

"Oliver! Oliver! Oliver! Noooooo!"

CHAPTER FORTY-FOUR

Riley can't think. She can't process. Oliver is dead. Dead.

She is up and running a heartbeat later. She ignores the shouts, ignores Nate's arms reaching for her, breaks through the security guards, bolts to the elevator. She slaps the button to the elevator three times, turning in circles to ensure no one approaches her. The doors slide open, and she jumps inside, for the moment, blessedly alone. She hits the Lobby button. They have a doorman and a front reception desk. She will be safe there until the police come.

"You can't trust anyone. Not even Walsh."

Nate's been with her the whole time, though. There's no way he could have killed Oliver. Right? No, he's gotten food a couple of times. She slept for several hours; he could easily have left and returned. He could have had someone do it.

He could kill you next.

Her heart thunders, and she fights the adrenaline rush. Think. Think. What is going on here? First Columbia. Then Nate's bodyguard. Now Oliver. God, the blood, it's on her hands. She's covered in blood again. It's all over the elevator buttons.

The elevator hits the ground floor, and she tears toward the front desk, skidding to a stop in front of the wooden counter. Rami is on duty again today.

"Hello, Miss Carring—oh my, are you okay?"

"Rami, it's Oliver . . . Oliver's been shot. Call the police. Call them now."

He stares at her in shock for a moment, then picks up the phone, calls it in. With a delicacy she will remember forever, he hands her a Clorox wipe. The building still follows the COVID protocols they'd started during the pandemic, and hand sanitizer and wipes are readily available in all the public spaces.

She wipes her hands clean, then starts to pace, fearing if she stops moving, she will be overwhelmed by the tidal wave of grief coming her way. She can't control it, though. Tears pour down her face, blinding her, until she finally stops by the worn velvet sofa, drops into it, and gives in to the sobs.

Then Nate's there, shushing her, and she lets him, because it is unfathomable to think that he could have anything to do with this. His security mills about the lobby, talking into their earwigs, and that's where the police find them all, shell shocked, Nate holding her, inconsolable, in his arms. Rami leads them to the mail room, so she doesn't have to see all the crime scene techs pouring into the building.

Nate doesn't let go of her, as if his touch will keep her from shattering. They sit at a table she assumes must be where the doormen eat their meals, a thick rectangular chunk of wood with letters carved into it and take-out packets of condiments scattered on the side that touches the wall. Chopsticks in paper sleeves stand in a foam to-go cup from the sushi takeout down the street. It's messy, but a comfortable messy.

The police officer who's babysitting them is gentle and calm. She asks smart questions and doesn't flinch when Riley collapses into tears again and again, just nods her understanding. Finally, the tears dry up, and Riley is able to tell them what happened.

She gives them almost everything. Everything that matters. Everything that can help solve the case. Her own suppositions are just that: conjecture. Hearsay. Inadmissible in any true legal sense. Instinct and rumors don't count.

She answers their questions, trying, and failing, not to see the state of Oliver's body in her mind's eye. The way his arms spread wide as if, in the end, he'd decided to take Savasana and relax into death. The tilt of his head toward the door, as if he'd watched his killer depart. The way the blood pooled beneath his body, tacky and hard in the overly air-conditioned room. She doesn't tell them all she knows.

She doesn't dare.

The police officer runs her through it again, then a third time. Riley repeats the words almost verbatim.

"We fought. We had a fight. He was moving out for a few days because he's a lawyer and I'm a beneficiary on a will he's working on, and my subject was killed in Denver, and I've been staying at a hotel working and I think I'm in danger. I know I'm in danger. But why would they kill Oliver? Why not me?"

"They couldn't find you," Nate says with a finality that reverberates to her soul. His voice is thick, too.

"Who is 'they,' ma'am?"

"I don't know I don't know I don't know. There was this man in a red ball cap who followed me yesterday, but I don't know who he is."

She's a waste. She needs to get it together. She just can't shake the images of the past few days, of the angry twist of Oliver's mouth as she bolted out the door, the meaty scent of his blood on her hands, the twist of his neck above where the bullet entered . . .

"Oh, God. I have to call his dad. I have to call Mr. Mathers."

"We are going to take care of that, ma'am. We have some more questions, if you don't mind? The detectives want to speak to you, and I know you don't want to go back upstairs."

"No. No, I don't." She clutches her bag closer to her body and shakes her head, rocking with the motion.

So for the second time in a week, she is hauled to a police station, though they are gentle with her this time, as if she might break into a thousand pieces if they touch her the wrong way. She's been to this precinct before, working a story about an actor who overdosed, so the wooden desk and stairs are familiar, at least.

They separate her from Nate, put her in a room with glaring bright white lights, and bring her a cup of coffee laced with cream and sugar. She sips it, not caring if the cream is free of natural flavors and carrageenan and all the crap the companies add to the most basic foods to make it last longer and taste better that tears her up inside because the immediate comfort of something warm outstrips her worry that she'll be sick in an hour. Who cares if she gets sick? She deserves to. Oliver is dead.

When the door finally opens, what feels like hours later, and a female detective with a sympathetic smile steps through, a single moment of clarity penetrates her panic.

They are going to think you did it.

She can almost hear Detective Sutcliffe.

"First Columbia. Then your boyfriend. Is there something you need to tell me, Miss Carrington?"

And then, an even more terrifying thought.

Who's next?

Riley resolves then and there to be very careful with what she says. She can grieve Oliver later. Right now, her own life could be on the line.

Riley listens more than she talks. That's why she is a good reporter. She knows what questions to ask to get her subject going. She reads body language; smiles, nods, clicks her tongue in sympathy or horror at the appropriate moments. She is a professional interrogator.

So when she realizes the detective—who introduced herself as Detective Shanda Ingles—is using all her own reporter tricks, but with an edge to them, like a bird on a warm summer morning watching for a worm to sneak up to the dewy surface, as if she thinks Riley's answers aren't quite truthful, she sits back with a shuddery breath and changes tack.

"How many murders do you see in our area every year?"

Ingles looks surprised but plays along. "Lower Fifth? In a building like yours? None so far. This is the first."

"There are cameras all over our building. All you need to do is pull up the feed and see who walks in the door that doesn't belong. You don't need to be asking me all these questions. I've told you everything I know."

Ingles sits back in her chair as if she, too, is done with this line of questioning. "Have you, though? I find that it's such a shock, finding a loved one like this. It's so easy to overlook something little that could solve the whole case."

"I've told you everything. For some reason, Columbia Jones hired my boyfriend's firm to handle her estate, and I'm a beneficiary in the will. I've been writing a piece on her for *East Fifth Magazine*. That's as far as this goes on my end. Clearly someone wanted to stop Oliver from sharing this news with me."

"Miss Carrington, you've had a terrible shock. I don't think it's safe for us to assume anything at this point. The home invasion that resulted in your boyfriend's death is going to take some time to sort out. But because of the circumstances, I'd like to put you in protective custody." Ingles is so sympathetic, and Riley tries not to give in to this woman who seems to actually want to help. She can't fall apart. She can't succumb.

"I don't know that I want to do that."

"I can keep you safe until we figure out this mess."

"We don't know that I was the target. Whoever did this was looking for something. Oliver might have gotten in the way. Or they came after Oliver."

"You're a smart girl. You don't really believe that."

Riley sits back in the chair, too. Of course she doesn't. And she knows this is a logical move. The two people she's had the closest relationships with for the past month are dead, and she's been left material that she hasn't had time to fully examine. She has to be able to search through everything. If she's stuck in protective custody, who knows what they'll do with the contents of the envelope. She will be safe with Nate in Maine. Safer. She can stay on her guard, but she needs to be away from New York now.

She straightens her spine and wipes her face. "I don't want to hide. I have a job to finish. So if it's just the same to you, I prefer to go."

"That's your right, though I really don't recommend it. Where will you be?"

She hears Nate's voice as clearly as if he's sitting next to her, and the stranger's, too.

Don't tell anyone. Don't trust anyone.

"At work. *East Fifth Magazine.* You can contact me there if you need me again."

Ingles stares at her for a few moments, then shrugs. "Suit yourself. But watch your back. And Miss Carrington? A bit of friendly advice. You might consider a lawyer, just in case."

They release her, and Nate is waiting, looking decidedly pissed off.

"We need to go to Maine," she says, and he nods, mouth a thin seam. "Can we get Darian, we—"

"I've already sent a team to get them. They'll meet us at Teterboro."

"Are you mad at me?"

He shakes his head briefly. "I'm mad at this." He sweeps a hand toward the front doors of the station, and Riley sees the flashbulbs starting through the thick glass.

"Media?"

"Yeah. Someone leaked the story."

CHAPTER FORTY-FIVE
DETECTIVE SUTCLIFFE

Sutcliffe exits the Nashville airport, shocked at the humidity. He's gotten used to Denver's crisp air and longer cool seasons. He stops to roll up his sleeves, then sees a pristinely rebuilt open-air CJ-7 Jeep waiting at the curb. It is burnt orange, with large tires. The lanky driver is leaning against the passenger side door, arms and ankles crossed, a pair of Ray-Ban aviators perched on her face. She has short white hair in a pixie cut, black brows, and bright-red lips. She's wearing a sleeveless jean jacket, and her arms look like she enjoys a workout. A sleeve of intricate white tattoos snakes up her left arm. Nope, Skye Abbott hasn't changed a bit. Except there is a Belgian Malinois in the passenger seat, tongue lolling in a happy greeting.

"There she is, the private eye to end all private eyes!"

"Give me a hug, you crazy beast."

There's much backslapping and joy in their greeting, which makes all this worthwhile, even if he hits a dead end. It's been too long.

"And who's this beauty?" Sutcliffe asks, throwing his bag into the back and ruffling the dog's ears.

"Her name is Kat, with a *K*, short for Katerina. Her people are on their honeymoon, and I agreed to puppy sit while they were gone. But that's not why you can't stay with me—I'm renovating. The place is a disaster."

"You're always renovating," Sutcliffe says. "Damn good to see you, Abbott."

A sly smile crosses her face. "Good to see you, too, Sutcliffe. Kat, c'mere, girl." The dog immediately moves to the back seat, where her harness is attached to the lower end of the Jeep's roll bar. Skye secures the lead with the seat belt so the dog can ride safely. "She loves the fresh air."

"She's gorgeous. Good thing it's not going to rain." They get into the vehicle, and Skye turns over the engine.

"Shoulder months in Nashville. It's eighty degrees one day, forty the next. Thought I'd take advantage of this lovely day to drop the top."

"I can't believe you still have this bucket of bolts." He taps a loving hand on the dash of the Jeep.

"Hey! I'll have you know Big Orange still purrs like a kitten full of her mama's milk." She taps the accelerator, and the Jeep's engine roars smoothly. "See? Perfection."

"Hush and drive. This kitten's starving."

"Your wish is my command."

Sutcliffe really likes that they've fallen back into the rhythm so quickly. Good friends are like that. They can go years without laying eyes on each other yet fall back into the same pattern without blinking. Abbott and Sutcliffe used to haze each other pretty hard when they worked together. Abbott was totally one of the guys while still being a feminist powerhouse on the force.

Out on the highway, Sutcliffe looks at the approaching city with shock. It used to sport two skyscrapers; now it rivals Atlanta: multiple buildings stretching to the sky, cranes everywhere, traffic, too. "Good God. What town is this?"

Skye's laugh is humorless. "Nashville's changed. In more ways than one. The skyline is the least of it. The people still rock, though."

She takes the Fourth Street exit and expertly winds them through a downtown he doesn't even recognize. Restaurants and hotels crowd each block, groups of bridesmaids in cowboy boots and tiaras, women in sky-high heels precariously perched on scooters darting across the street against the lights, the skunk scent of marijuana drifting through the air. The music, already rollicking, pouring out of every doorway.

"Damn. The river's the only thing that hasn't changed. Even the bridges are different."

"Pretty much. Do you want to check into the hotel, or eat, or what?"

"Food first. Tell me there's still decent barbecue."

In answer, she whips the Jeep around the corner and pulls up in front of Martin's Bar-B-Que. "Jack's is still here, and still good, but I don't feel like battling the masses. Plus, Kat prefers Martin's. Don't you, girl?"

The dog woofs happily and jumps from the Jeep when prompted.

"She's really well trained."

"She is. She was supposed to be a military K-9 but flunked out for being too personable. Her dad—his name is Zack—and her new mommy, Juliet, split time between here and Colorado. You'd like them. Good people. You know the skier Mindy Wright? Zack's her dad, Juliet's her aunt."

"Holy shit, seriously? That means her mom—"

"Yeah. We don't talk about that much. Crazy case. Anyway, we're up. Wanna beer?"

"Yeah. I think I'm going to need one." They order and, in minutes, take the food to a table. Kat gets her own plate with a beautiful meaty bone, which she promptly starts to lick.

They chitchat for a few, talking about Skye's life and family (large, boisterous, and always into some sort of trouble, no one romantically on the radar right now, loves the PI world) and Sutcliffe's (only child, always wanted siblings, not married, loves working for Denver PD, the upcoming Ironman), until they circle back to the reason he's in Nashville.

"So," Skye says, dredging a fry in some ketchup. "Knox Shepherd, huh."

Sutcliffe takes a sip of the icy cold beer. "Yeah."

"What are the odds you were the cop who caught the case? I mean, it's quite a coincidence."

"Too much of one. There's a reason. Maybe he was trying to send a message. I was requested for the case—the hotel manager asked for me specifically. I was getting ready to hit a trail when my LT called."

"Creepy." She watches the dog, a small frown on her face. "This sounds intentional. You've been pulled in purposely."

"I don't disagree. Which is why I want to talk to Shepherd and find out why." He takes a pull on his beer. "You know, I never did think he was guilty of killing Benjamin Mears."

"Me either, obviously. And being told to hunt him down and arrest him no matter what didn't sit right with me. It was the last straw, you know?"

"I do."

They'd both quit soon after the Shepherd case. Skye had joined her aunt's private investigation firm, and Sutcliffe, an Army brat who'd landed in Clarksville, Tennessee, for his last year of high school and had no deep ties to Nashville, had moved to Colorado, jumped into the lifestyle there, and never looked back.

"You know how these small-town cases can get political. The captain was cousins with the sheriff in Crossville. And Mears was definitely murdered, no matter who did it. When Shepherd copped to it, there wasn't much that could be done after that."

"True." The large men's watch Skye wears slides up her wrist as she drinks from the sweating bottle. "It's a big thing to cop to, murder. Never understood why he did it, unless he was trying to protect Devon Mears. Anyway, now he's a suspect again."

"He is the best lead I've got. He was at the theater the night she died, and a witness places him at the hotel, and possibly even in her room, too. Gotta have a chat, find out why. The daughter said someone was stalking her mother online. Maybe I can rule him in or out for that, too."

"Speaking of online . . . this Columbia Jones thing is out of hand."

"How so?"

"You still don't have social media, do you?"

"God no."

She scoffs a laugh. "Oh, the luxury of being a cop and having a department do that work for you. As a PI, I can't *not* have access. You'd be amazed how many people I can bust just by acting like a friend online. Anyway, long story short, her feed got hacked and started sending out some pretty disgusting deepfake videos with her face on a chick's body. Porny stuff. The accounts have been deleted, but the sickos took tons of screenshots and downloads so it's all still available. Then some folks decided to start calling her a fraud, then a murderer, and the whole thing blew up. It has its own hashtag—#Legacy. It's everywhere. Once these things catch fire, it's hard to put out the flames."

"Back up. Someone accused Columbia Jones of murder?"

"Yup."

"Did they say who she supposedly murdered?"

"Well, that's where it's gotten interesting. Speaking of Devon Mears . . . name ring a bell?"

"Stop teasing me, you know it does. Someone online is accusing Columbia Jones of killing Devon Mears? Shut up."

Kat finishes making sweet mouth love to her bone and sits up straight with a tiny woof.

"I'll get you some water, sweetie," Skye croons, and Sutcliffe raises a brow.

"You speak dog?"

"No, Kat speaks human. Like I said, she is very well trained. I'll be right back."

Sutcliffe finishes his beer in a long gulp. This case has gone from weird to weirder.

The dog's needs met, Skye sits back down and takes a huge bite of her pulled pork. "I did some background while you were flying. Obviously you know Knox Shepherd got out early for good behavior. He's been down there in Franklin minding his p's and q's ever since. Got into construction—that's one of the easiest paths to success for a felon who's gone straight. He learned the trade in the joint, and while he can't get a contractor's license, he took all the courses and, from what I hear, is a damn good carpenter. Also builds furniture and does other woodworking. Sells it on Etsy. He's pretty successful at it."

"He struck me as a smart guy. Can't get through med school if you're not. I'm not surprised he landed on his feet. So no brushes with the law since he got out?"

"Clean as a whistle. Even has a little family."

"And Devon Mears?"

Another fry drowns. "Dead. Died a year after she got out of prison. Obituary doesn't say how, it was pretty bare bones."

"I suppose her family had cut her off completely by then."

"Seems like it. You know how it is. She got herself pregnant in high school, then married at eighteen, then in jail as an accomplice to murder. The scandal alone can drive a wedge, but in a small town like that? Benjamin Mears was the local football hero. She was a pariah."

"They still around, her folks?"

"Yeah. Old and gray and crotchety as hell. Her mom called me some choice names and hung up on me when I called to ask about Devon's passing. Told me to leave her alone."

"So tell me how a world-famous British author murders a kid from Crossville, Tennessee, and gets away with it." He laughs. "I love the internet sometimes. The conspiracy theories write themselves."

"Not so fast."

"Shit, if there's more, I need another beer."

"Grab me one while you're at it."

He goes to the counter, gets two more beers, plonks them onto the table. Tosses Kat a fry, which she licks politely.

"I'm powered up. Talk to me."

"Devon Mears goes off the radar after she gets out of prison, right? She doesn't get a job. She doesn't go back to Crossville. She picks up her kid from foster care, and then she totally disappears."

"The kid. That's right. I forgot about the kid. Man, she was a little thing. Newborn, basically."

"Yeah. Four, five weeks, something like that. She went into DCS, was a couple of years old when Mears got out."

"So when Mears died, what happened to the kid?"

"See? This is why I always liked you as a partner, Sutcliffe. You have a brain. I wondered the same thing. Kids have to go to school, they have Social Security cards, all that jazz. So I start looking. And looking. And I don't find anything. And that seems really weird. The only trace of Devon Mears and her kid is that obituary."

"But?"

"I did come across a sealed record. And I maybe had a chat with a friend of mine who's maybe an advocate and maybe she took a quick peek for me in the system, and guess what?"

Sutcliffe is catching on. It all is starting to make sense.

"Devon Mears did die," he says. "And was reborn as someone else. A phoenix from the ashes."

Skye taps her nose. "And a pretty-pony prize if you can name that tune in two notes."

"I can name it in one. Devon Mears reinvented herself entirely as a British woman named Columbia Jones."

"Ding ding ding."

He sips the beer, processing. It's genius, really. "So a formal petition for a new identity, in court, the whole works?"

"Yep."

"Tell me how? I thought felons couldn't do legal name changes."

"Depends on the state. Here in Tennessee, they can if they make a case for their own safety or the safety of their immediate family. This hypothetical file says there were threats made by the victim's family to Devon Mears. Easily verifiable, many of those were in public. The newspapers carried that story, remember? When Benjamin Mears's father swore he'd hunt down Devon and take her child. That he refused to have his grandchild raised by a murderer. He was going to fight for custody, the whole thing, though he backed off. Who knows why. Anyway, a sympathetic judge recognized that, sometimes, a small town can get pretty insular and that, sometimes, certain men have outsized amounts of power, and felt a new identity was warranted."

"I mean . . . you can't make this shit up."

"Nope."

"She must have had a high-powered lawyer to pull this off. Where does an ex-con get that kind of juice?"

"Also an excellent question. I went back through my copy of the original files, and in one of her early interviews, when everyone thought she'd been raped and all that, she told the cop at the hospital to get in touch with a woman named Jamie Cline. There's a marriage certificate a few years later for a James Evelyn Cline to a man named Victor Richard Guul. Cline did die for real, of breast cancer, several years ago. Guul is licensed in New York, Massachusetts, and New Jersey. He's remarried, and he still practices."

"And the obituary?"

"Good question. She had to have something to close the chapter, right? What better way to make sure no one came looking than to have that little gem online."

Sutcliffe worries a napkin, shredding off little pieces. "Everything about Columbia Jones is verifiable—I've run her top to bottom. Her IDs check out, she pays her taxes, she owns property. How the hell did she pull this off? And why adopt an accent? It's distinct. And how does no one recognize her from her past life?"

"Elocution lessons don't cost a lot. Anyone can be trained into a new accent, actors do it all the time. After enough time, she could easily subsume it, and matched with a long tenure in New York, if a few Americanized phrases and tones show up, no one will think a thing about it."

She puts down Devon Mears's booking photo, and a current photo of Columbia Jones from her website. Her author photo. A life ended; a life begun.

The two look nothing alike, not really. Maybe an echo, more than a likeness.

"She had to have surgery, right?" Sutcliffe asks. "After the murder? She was beaten pretty badly."

"Yeah. Her face was battered to hell. We can probably pull those documents, too, but I think she probably had more work done over the years, the usual bumps and plumps, but also some reshaping of her jaw and cheekbones. But her eyes . . . Sutcliffe, that's her. For sure." She taps Columbia's author photo. "That's Devon Mears."

"This is insane. I can't believe you got all this done so fast."

Skye smiles, a flash of pearly whites. "Come to the dark side. I'll teach you a few tricks. We don't have the same constraints that you do. And I don't need this to hold up in court, so I can look at a broader canvas. But I had some help. Remember Taylor Jackson? She left Metro and is working with me now. She's a hound dog for these kinds of details. She dug up a bunch of good stuff."

"I remember her. Cool chick. So the daughter, Darian, she's all legit, too?"

"Yes. They changed her last name to Jones, it was just a piece of paper. She's findable in the school systems in New York, went to Dartmouth, works for Columbia Jones, LLC."

Sutcliffe rubs his eyebrows. He's got a headache forming, the beer catching up to him.

"This is incredible."

"It really is. So how does Knox Shepherd fit into all of this?"

"He knows. He has to. Either she told him at some point, or he figured it out. It would make sense that he figured it out, got some tickets to some tour dates to confirm it, and then was trying to reach out and talk to her. He loved the woman enough to go to jail for her. How would you feel if your life was wrecked, and you're stuck doing construction while your former lover is on *Forbes*'s richest-people list?"

"I'd be pretty pissed."

"Pissed enough to kill her?"

Skye's eyes go still and flat, and she puts both hands on the table. "Absolutely."

CHAPTER FORTY-SIX
KNOX SHEPHERD

"Daddy? Hey, Daddy? You in here?"

Knox has his foot on the pedal of the lathe and his hands wrapped around a piece of cedar. So soft, this wood. It takes a delicate touch, and if he stops now, he'll lose the shape of the bowl he is making.

"In here, honey. I can't stop or I'll—" And that little bit of distraction is all it takes. The bit drills right through the bottom of the bowl. "Shit." He sits up, staring ruefully at the ruined bowl.

Tamsin appears on the other side of the lathe. "Sorry, Daddy. I didn't mean to wreck it. That's pretty."

"You didn't wreck it, sweetheart. It was crap wood, soft and knotted. It was more for practice than anything else, I was going to try a new wax on it. No biggie, I'll make some planks for the coat closet instead. What's up?"

"Mom wants you to come in for dinner. This is your fifteen-minute warning."

"Of course she does." He runs a hand down each arm, sawdust falling in thick sheafs to the floor.

Tamsin, eight going on forty-five, a blonde, curly-headed sprite that makes his heart squeeze with joy every time he looks at her, lingers, picking up items and examining them. Knox turned a few bowls this morning before he got to the chunk of cedar, works that are worth taking to the small shop where he sells his goods. The rest, that was just practice.

"Yeees?" he asks, dragging out the word.

Tamsin looks over her shoulder, then whispers, "How was your trip? Did you talk to her?"

Knox shakes his head. How does he explain the past week to his precious daughter? The chaos, the grief. The fact that he will never have closure.

"Saw her. Chickened out."

"You went all that way, and you chickened out? What kind of bad-ass dad are you?" Tamsin grins.

"The kind who has a soft heart." He stands, brushing the remaining sawdust from his work pants. "I better change before dinner."

"You have time for a shower, too." She wrinkles her adorable nose.

"I smell?"

She uses two fingers to pinch her nostrils closed. "Like sawdust and cedar and *sweat*."

"Okay. A shower it is." Great. More time to stand alone and grieve. "Tell Mommy I'll be there in a second."

She skips off, and he shuts down the lathe and cleans up the shop, sweeping the dust and wood shavings into a corner, putting up his tools.

He isn't about to tell Tamsin the truth, that despite trying twice, he didn't get a chance to speak to Devon, that she is gone, that he'd seen the delicate white hand trailing off the bed and the blood and heard the cries of her daughter . . . No. She is too young, too impressionable. A mature child, but a sensitive one, too sensitive to hear the whole truth. All she knows is he went to see an old friend, and that's all she ever needs to hear about this.

He enters the saltbox cottage through the mudroom, tosses his work clothes into the washing machine, and steps into the small shower he built to handle his messes and the dog's muddy shenanigans. Soaps up and rinses off and towels dry. He has a terrible gnawing sensation in his chest, has since he tackled the reporter in the hallway of the hotel.

It chased him home, has set up shop in his body. After all he's been through, he recognizes it for the corrosive beast it is.

Fear.

Emily is just pulling a lasagna from the oven when he enters the kitchen. Tamsin bum-rushes him, head down like a little bull, directly into his stomach. He *oofs* and grabs her and flips her upside down, and she shrieks with mad joy.

Emily shakes her head indulgently. "You're going to make her sick."

"Baaaarf," Tamsin shouts, and Knox flips her right side up and tucks her underneath his arm, carries her to the table, and deposits her in the chair.

"Can't have that," he says. "Smells good, babe."

Emily smiles, plops down a plate of garlic bread. Pours them each a glass of red, milk for the kid.

It's all so normal. So typical. They've done this a hundred times, a thousand.

But nothing is the same.

He knows it, deep in his soul. He's just waiting for the other shoe to drop—again.

For someone to show up on his doorstep, to drag him into a small room with fluorescent lights beating down on his skull, to push and prod and form conclusions without basis. They're coming. He knows they're coming. He was dumb enough to get involved; they'll trace his face or the phone soon enough. And here he sits, pretending everything is all good, with his beautiful wife sipping her wine and his adorable daughter shoveling lasagna in her mouth as fast as she can. They don't know how tenuous life is. Oh, Emily thinks she does, but she can't ever truly understand the knife's edge Knox walks, day in, and day out. And now . . . it's just a matter of time.

Knox lost so much time, lost so much of his life. His freedom. His calling. And all for what? Love? Lust? He was an idiot. An honorable idiot, who sacrificed everything for someone who wasn't worth it. But there's no undoing the past. He must live with his choices, and the consequences. And honestly, every step he's taken, every decision, has led him to this moment, sitting down at the kitchen table he made with his own hands, with the woman he adores and the baby they made. He can't be mad for long about his lot in life, looking at their identical smiles, expectantly waiting for him to dig into his own dinner.

He spent years learning how to heal people, and when that was taken away, he spent years learning how to build things. Despite his record, despite being a felon, he's managed to carve out a small business with the locals who don't hold his past against him, especially when they see the gentle curves of his furniture, the elemental gift with which he carves wood, turns bowls. He learned it all inside. By one heaven-sent fluke of luck, he was paired with a carpenter in jail for forty years for running over his wife in a fit of drunken anger, and the man had taken pity on Knox from the jump, had offered protection and, eventually, taught him the trade, chipping away at the depression, the sadness, the embarrassment Knox suffered from. They bonded over their shared love of the wrong women. When Sammy had a heart attack, two weeks prior to Knox's release, Knox eulogized him, then counted the days until he got sprung himself. There were only two ways out of their prison, and Sammy had another twenty to go, so Knox honestly felt he'd been blessed. Another minute in that place and he might have lost his mind himself.

The outside world had changed—no big surprise there. The medical board had suspended his license; he didn't even try to get reinstated, knowing the odds were against him. Instead, he started looking for work with construction companies. There was always a contractor willing to cut a guy straight out of prison a break, especially if they wanted to be paid cash and didn't need paperwork outside of a parole check here or there.

It took months of hard work, but he scrabbled together enough money to rent the house, put a down payment on a truck, and slowly, painfully, build out his tools.

He was one of the lucky ones. The oblivion of drugs and alcohol didn't appeal. He hadn't found religion; he hadn't joined a gang. He kept his head down, did his assigned work, and tried to salvage what he could of his dignity. How he did his time was how he lived his afterlife—with as much honor as he could.

He met Emily at the library, of all places. She was working the desk, newly transferred, and he was looking for a book he'd heard of, by Spike Carlsen, *A Splintered History of Wood.*

Emily thought the title hysterical. She found the book, insisted on reading it as soon as he was done, and gently flirted her way into his life from there.

He never stopped being amazed that the adorable brainiac librarian down the street wanted him, of all people.

He told her everything the night he proposed. Everything. There was no room in their world for secrets, not with his past.

She said yes anyway. God bless her, she did.

Tamsin was their miracle child, born after two previous failed pregnancies.

They made a life together. It wasn't flashy. It wasn't gaudy. They certainly weren't rich. But they were happy. So happy.

Until she dragged him to a book signing at the Ryman, and his world shattered.

"Babe?" Emily asks, holding out another piece of garlic bread. He realizes he's been staring into space, jaw clenched, forces himself to relax. He takes the fragrant chunk, nibbles the edge, crusty with baked parmesan cheese.

"Thank you. This is yummy. Nom nom nom nom nom." He plays a rabbit for Tamsin, who glows with excitement.

"Yummy!" Tamsin shouts.

"Weirdo!" Knox yells back at her, making her double over in gales of laughter. Emily laughs, too; they all do. How has he gotten so lucky? Tamsin is possibly the best thing that ever happened to him. She is perfect. Emily, too. For a guy who's gotten a second chance at life, he's hit it out of the park.

So why does he feel like it's all about to come crashing down?

"Oh! You have a letter," Emily says, jumping up from the table, wiping her hands on a dish towel. "I totally forgot. I put it in my bag as I was leaving for work and totally spaced it. Sorry."

She hands him the envelope—manila, with a New York address. His stomach flips. New York lawyers writing him?

"When did this come?" he asks, casual, slitting the top open with his knife, getting sauce on the corners. *No big deal, play it cool, man.*

"While you were at Home Depot. A messenger—I had to sign for it. What is it? It looks important."

He has the letter out now, reads it quickly.

> Dear Mr. Shepherd,
> This letter is to inform you that the last will and testament of Columbia Jones was recently filed for probate with the Manhattan Surrogate's Court of New York. Because of the private nature of this endeavor, there will be an in-person reading of the will on May 15, 1 p.m. ET. at my office. All beneficiaries are required to attend.
>
> If you have any questions about the will or the probate process, please do not hesitate to contact me.
> With my condolences, I remain, sincerely,
>
> *Preston J. Mathers, Esq.*
> Preston J. Mathers, Esquire.
> Senior Partner, Mathers and Mathers

"Motherf . . . trucker!"

CHAPTER FORTY-SEVEN

Columbia Jones. Even the name is farcical. Knox has no idea who she stole it from, or how she hasn't been outed. All this time, parading around as someone else. She doesn't look like the woman he knew; he will admit that. Part of it was out of necessity. She'd had surgery after Mears's murder—the bastard had done a number on her face before Knox got there to stop him—but there's been more since her trial, to make sure she didn't look like the girl he once knew. She got out of jail, reinvented herself, moved to New York, lived a glamorous life. Left him far, far behind. She never even wrote to him, never came to visit while she was free, and certainly didn't come after he got out. He ruined his life for that bitch, and what does she do—leave him a token in her will? He'll have to scrape together the money to get to New York anyway. He should just skip it. He doesn't want to reopen this chapter any more than he has.

"Tams, want some screen time?" Emily says, and Tamsin, shocked by this surprise allowance, is no dummy—she runs immediately to the living room and boots up the Apple TV.

"We're going to be singing tunes from *Frozen* for weeks, you know," he says, struggling for control, for normalcy. He hates these thoughts, the anger that slides into his brain.

"Oh, she's moved on. She's decided she needs to watch *How to Train Your Dragon* so she can find one in the garden to ride." A roar of attack comes from the living room, and Emily puts her hand on his.

"What is it?"

He thrusts the paper into her hands. "Her will is being read. I've been summoned." His voice cracks, bitter with recriminations.

Emily reads, brows furrowed. "Why would they require the beneficiaries to attend? That's strange."

"Who knows. More manipulation. She can even make people dance from beyond the grave." He stands, the chair screeching back. "I've gotta get out of here. I need a walk."

"Go," Emily says, nodding. "I'll clean up."

He doesn't argue. If he doesn't move, he might explode.

He takes the dog, creatively named Shep by Tamsin (Shep Shepherd the German shepherd), who is happily gnawing on a bone in their fenced-in backyard but even happier to go for an unscheduled early-evening walk. The air outside is soft, humid, readying itself for a sunset rainstorm. He can't breathe properly. He keeps seeing that pale hand, trailing, smelling the meaty scent of her death. It takes him back to the night he wishes never happened, the night when it all went wrong.

Control yourself, man. You're having a fucking panic attack in the middle of the street.

Emily is a freaking saint to let him wallow like this. He knows it, and he's not going to waste a moment of her indulgence. He has a family to support, a woman he loves, a daughter he thinks might be an angel incarnate. He's got more than he deserves, and he can't—won't—fuck it up.

But there are moments when the past overwhelms him. The frustration, the memories, the horror he's been through find their way to the surface and try to drown him.

He starts to run and snaps the lead. Shep speeds up with him, thrilled at the pace. He ignores the wave of a neighbor, the orange Jeep that does a rolling stop at the red light, and turns at the corner, heading for the park. Shep knows this route and bays once, excited to be loose and free.

They reach the park, and Knox slows to a jog so the people who might recognize him don't think he's insane, running full speed through the park. He takes Shep to the dog run, puts him inside. There are two other dogs, a big black goldendoodle named Jak Jak that Shep adores, and a greyhound Knox doesn't recognize. Their owners are chatting together on the other side of the pickets, and they wave. He waves back, watching carefully to make sure Shep doesn't do anything stupid. There's plenty of yipping and sniffing, then in moments, he's heartened to see the greyhound fall into line with Shep leading the way. The three dogs prance and play, and Knox drops to a seat on the bench, defeated.

"Shit," he mutters.

It was a mistake to accept the ticket to see Devon on tour, to try to talk. Forgive. He knows better than to indulge his emotions. Running away isn't going to solve anything. But damn it, seeing her alive brought back all the worst memories. Seeing her dead made it ten times worse.

"Having a bad week, friend?"

Knox sits straighter, stares up at a bald man with ice-blue eyes. *I know you. But from where?*

"Just fine, thanks."

"Hmm. I'd think after seeing her dead like that, you'd be pretty torn up. Sure looks like that's the case."

Knox tenses. What the hell is this? And then it hits him. Sutcliffe. Shit. He had hair the last time he saw him, wasn't as fit. You'd think he wouldn't forget the face of the man who put him in jail, but he has. *You brought this on yourself, telling the hotel's manager to ask for him.*

"Detective Sutcliffe, Denver Police. Remember me? May I sit?"

"Yeah. And it's a free country." Knox stands, heart in his throat, starting toward the gate of the dog park, but Sutcliffe catches his arm.

"Stay. We need to talk, and I'd much prefer having a chat here than dragging your ass back to Denver and doing it there."

"You're pretty far out of your jurisdiction, Detective. There's no reason for you to take me to Denver, and we both know it."

A woman approaches with a gorgeous Malinois on a lead; she's been standing to his right in the setting sunlight. Her hair is white, her lips red, her eyebrows black as coal. She's not in uniform, wears jeans, worn Dr. Martens, a sleeveless jean jacket. He recognizes her immediately, though he hasn't seen her in many years. She's aged well, he'll give her that. Better than Sutcliffe.

"Ms. Abbott." He acknowledges her with a small ironic salute. "Not sure what your title is now."

"Good to see you, Mr. Shepherd."

God, her husky voice is the same, makes a shiver curdle through him. The first time they met, she was busy slapping handcuffs on him and shoving his sorry ass into the back of her cruiser. The dog is on alert at her side. The message is clear: don't even think about running.

Stay cool, man. You've done nothing wrong.

"To what do I owe the pleasure?"

"Sutcliffe here gave me a shout about the death of a woman in Denver named Columbia Jones. Ring a bell?"

"I've heard the name," he says warily. They know. They know he was there. He's about to say the magic word—*lawyer*—but decides to hold off. Just in case. He doesn't want to look guilty.

"I appreciate that you've come all this way, but I don't know anything about this situation."

"Don't lie to us," Sutcliffe says. "That's just going to make me want to put you in handcuffs."

Knox doesn't move. He thinks about sweet Tamsin and Emily and Shep and sends a plea to the universe: *Don't let this be it. Don't let my life with them be over.*

The cop keeps talking. "Listen, we know Devon Mears reinvented herself as Columbia Jones. We know you were at the theater the night she died. Stands to reason you found out and went to see for yourself. There's no crime there."

Just wait until you hear I'm a beneficiary. Now I have real motive.

"And?"

"We also think there's something hinky about her murder. Since you were there, we thought maybe you could shed some light on the situation."

A fishing expedition. This is both good news, and bad.

"You still a cop?" he asks Abbott.

"PI. I left the force not long after you went to jail."

"Well, you both know I didn't kill her. And that's all I have to say without a lawyer."

"Ah, man, don't do that," Abbott says. "Seriously, we're just trying to find some answers."

Sutcliffe nods. "You start acting like a suspect, I'll have to treat you as one. I just want to know why you were there. Someone was stalking her. And here's the most important figure from her past, sitting front and center the night she's murdered. You been a bad boy, Mr. Shepherd? You find out your former flame got rich and wanted a cut, and she said no? You show up in her room with a knife and—"

"She was stabbed? Someone stabbed her? Oh, God." *Fuck, stop talking.* But that news makes him want to be sick. He hates her, but he loved her, once. He's seen people stabbed before. It's not a pretty death. Explains all the blood he saw.

Sutcliffe is watching him carefully, waiting for another excited utterance, but Knox clenches his jaw tight, crosses his arms on his chest and stares them down. Seconds tick by. No one moves. No one talks. They're deciding what to do, he knows. Whether to cuff him and go back to the house and tear it apart looking for the knife that killed her.

"If there's nothing else, I have someplace to be." He stalks off, half waiting to hear the ratchet of cuffs, to be tackled from behind, the dog's jaws clamped on his arm, but they do nothing, and he gets Shep without trouble from the enclosure and heads back toward the house, trying to look cool, not sprinting away, his heart thundering.

They don't stop him. Which means they don't have any proof that he killed Devon. Which means he might—might—have some room to breathe if he plays his cards right.

Back at the house, their sweet saltbox that he's worked on for years to make their own, Emily is sitting on the porch. She sees him coming and stands, knowing instinctually something is wrong. He hurries to the gate, lets Shep in, and locks it behind him, walks to the workshop. Emily meets him at the door, and they enter the small woodsy space.

"What's wrong?" she asks sharply.

"Cops," he replies, aghast to hear his voice crack on the word. Emily immediately grabs him in a hug.

"It's okay. It's okay."

"They're here about Devon. Waylaid me in the park. Said she was stabbed."

"Well, you're here with me, so they didn't arrest you. What did they want?"

"To talk. They're the same ones who arrested me originally. One's from Denver, the other, the chick, is a PI now, apparently."

"So what's a Denver cop doing with a Nashville PI?"

"They were partners when everything happened. I don't know what they're up to now. I said the magic L-word and got out of there. I've been waiting for them to grab me. They might, still." He fights the panic. He needs to be strong, but he wants to run, run fast and hard and far. "They know. They know I was in Denver the night she died."

"But you didn't have anything to do with her murder."

She doesn't leave any inflection at the end of the sentence; it is a declarative statement, not a question. A vehement statement at that.

"No, I didn't. She was dead when I got there. But I was there, and now that it's out that she was stabbed—"

"Rat poison."

"Huh?"

"She wasn't stabbed. There was rat poison in her sleeping pills. Or CBD, whatever. Someone poisoned her. I looked online when you left. The news has been feverish in their attentions today. The story is everywhere."

"That's a horrible way to go. Why would they tell me she was stabbed?"

"Maybe to see if you contradicted them or had anything else to add. Maybe they were trying to trick you. Honey, what do you want to do? Do you want to get a lawyer and talk with them again? Tell them she sent you a ticket, that she asked you to come? Do you want to leave?"

He grabs her, holds her to his chest, still fighting the sobs that want to tear from his throat. He wants to run. God, he wants to. But he will not. He's done nothing wrong, and this time, he's not about to throw himself as a sacrifice on the pyre.

"The letter says the will reading will be in New York on the fifteenth. Should you maybe head up there?"

He stares into her gorgeous eyes. "You're serious. You think I should run?"

"That's not running. That's taking a trip."

"But—"

"You didn't do this. I know it. You know it. But they are going to try and railroad you, because that's what the police do when they don't have answers, they look to the closest scapegoat and lay it all at his feet."

He cups her chin. "I can't run. The last time cost me almost everything. If I'd stood my ground, if I'd been truthful—"

"I might never have met you," Emily says softly. "Knox, everything happens for a reason. I don't discount the pain you've been put through. But look at Tamsin. Look at us. Look at you. You're an honorable man. If you want to stay and fight, I'll do it with you. But I can't lose you."

"You won't. I've done nothing wrong. And this time, I can prove it."

CHAPTER FORTY-EIGHT
DETECTIVE SUTCLIFFE

Sutcliffe watches Knox Shepherd walk away as if he's waiting to be shivved in the prison courtyard, shoulders tense, fists balled, the dog silent at his side as if he knows this is no time to play.

"That went well," he says to Skye.

"Spooked the shit out of him."

"Considering, yeah. What do you think?"

"He reacted pretty intensely when you said she was stabbed."

"Shocked, I'd say. I just wanted to see what he'd do, and that reaction was genuine." He runs a hand over his bald pate. "This is ridiculous. He's easily the prime suspect here. Means, motive, access. There's absolutely zero good explanation about why he was at the hotel."

"I agree. What do you want to do next? Go to his house and detain him?"

"I'd have to get with the locals for that. But I do want to talk to him some more. I think he knows more than he's saying."

"No kidding."

He shoots her an amused look. "Sarcasm always helps me think."

"He's going to lawyer up. He looked scared to death."

"False accusations coming back to haunt him, you think? Or did he do it? Did he find a way to poison her CBD, get into the hotel room, plant it, then wait for the show to start? And when it didn't go quickly enough, inject her with the same poison?"

"It's a reasonable theory. Revenge always is. He figured out who she was, got pissed, and decided to make her suffer."

Sutcliffe taps his fingers on his lips. "But to risk everything once he's finally back on his feet . . ."

"Then who else had direct access to her? The daughter?"

"Yeah. Her reaction was so intense. She blamed the reporter immediately. Was she trying to throw us off? Give me a second. I want to check on something." He pulls out his phone and calls Duran.

"Hey. How's Nashville?" she asks.

"I just made contact with my suspect. I'm having doubts. Did that thumbprint ever pop anything?"

"I just sent you an email. It wasn't a match to Knox Shepherd. It was a match to Darian Jones. We missed it the first time."

"The plot thickens," he says. "Thanks, Doc." He hangs up, shaking his head. "I don't see any way around it. My only other lead to Shepherd just fizzled. There was a thumbprint on the cap of the bottle of CBD, but it belongs to the daughter. It's reasonable to expect her prints to be on anything in that bathroom, and plenty of ways it could have gotten there that don't involve poisoning her mother. They did have a fight that night, so I can't rule her out entirely, but her boyfriend alibied her before I even talked to her. She was with him in his room the night her mom died."

"She still seems as good a suspect as Shepherd."

"Maybe. Might be a greed thing. She wants the money and wants her mom out of the way. Occam's razor, though. The ex with the legitimate axe to grind or the frustrated daughter who is ready to benefit from the family business."

"Poison is a woman's method."

"Used to be. There are plenty of crazy dudes out there putting Drano in their wives' orange juice now."

"All right. Back to the CBD oil. If the daughter's thumbprint is on the new bottle, can we assume she gave it to her mom before she went to sleep? You could pop her for the semantics of killing her mother, see if she'll crack and admit to injecting her, too."

"Or we can arrest the most logical suspect. The one with the most to gain, not the most to lose."

"You've decided then?"

He nods. "Yeah. I wanna take Shepherd in for questioning. Even if he lawyers up, I'd like to rattle his cage a little, see if anything shakes loose. He's a proud guy, but if he's guilty, we have history with him copping to it."

"And the daughter?"

"Let's see how she reacts when I tell her we have a suspect in custody. Meanwhile, let's go talk to the locals and do some paperwork. Try to pinch him before he runs."

CHAPTER FORTY-NINE
KIRA

The sheriff's arrival on the scene is enough to make the reporters pay attention.

Kira watches from the window as Jack clears them off their land, grateful they were distracted enough to let her mom slip out to get the kids. She called when she picked up the boys, so Kira can relax and focus on the situation at hand.

What doesn't help is the second sheriff's vehicle with the crime scene techs inside. There was no way to get them into the ranch without going past the reporters now lining the entrance. She knows that's going to do nothing but feed the flames.

She's honestly too nauseated to worry about it. She manages to hold down a spoonful of peanut butter and a Sprite long enough to take half a Unisom, which will make her sleepy but works best for this kind of lingering malaise. She was hopeful this pregnancy would be easy, and honestly, there's no telling what's going to happen for at least a few weeks. Right now she just has to gut it out.

She waits for her churning stomach to calm, then takes the golf cart to the barns, where she knows she'll find Luke and Jack.

She recognizes one of the crime scene techs as a guy they went to high school with.

"Hey, Terrell, how are you?"

"Kira! Hey. I was just telling Luke it's been ages since we saw you. Oops, no, don't hug me, I'll get dust all over you. Sorry about all this." He waves toward the scene. His team is crawling over the barn. They have Luke's spare tack room open and are moving in and out with the efficiency of an army of ants. "We're printing the contents, all the options, just in case. Luke says he hasn't had this room open for at least a month, but there are some scratches on the lock, so if someone got their hands on your stuff, we might be able to pull some prints."

Alarm fills her. "You mean someone might have broken into our tack room and taken rodent poison?"

"That's what Jack's having us look at, yeah. I better get back to it. Good to see you."

Now she really feels sick. She sits in the cart's shade and waits for Luke and Jack to emerge. They do about ten minutes later, and Luke sees her immediately and comes over.

"Hey, babe. Why don't we head up to the house? Jack and I need to check something, and you're looking peaked."

She doesn't argue, lets Luke take the wheel. Jack sits on the back, his crisp tan uniform spotless. "Hey, girl. Sorry about all this."

"Why does everyone keep apologizing? It's Luke's mess to clean up." She smiles, and the guys laugh and, for a second, all feels normal. Luke whips the cart around and heads up the path.

"What do you have to look at?" she asks.

"Security system. Cameras. Someone's been in the spare tack room, the lock was broken. Set back on its hasp with a little glue of some sort, just for looks. The minute I touched it, it broke off."

"How could someone get in there without us noticing?"

"Excellent question," Jack says. "Luke tells me the barns aren't wired into your house security system, but there's a trail camera, so there's a chance we might capture a shot of who got in."

"It's mounted on the blue spruce over there, gives a perfect shot through the branches into the doors. I put it in when the bear was sniffing around last year, remember, babe? We wanted to see if she moved on or if I needed to help her migrate. Normally all I use it for is to see when the hands are bringing out the horses so I know when to head down in the morning, and I haven't been looking at our overnight guests recently. The feed will be on my laptop."

Luke's office is on the second floor, near the boys' rooms. They have a bunkhouse of their own, an open space with a foosball table, a swing, and a sitting area where they can play video games. It's the perfect setup for rough-and-tumble little boys close in age. And there's a free bunk, just waiting for their next sibling.

Of course, a girl would have her own space. A girl. Kira laughs at the idea. She is destined to be the only one with estrogen in this family, outside of the mares.

They climb the stairs, and Luke boots up his computer. It takes him a minute of futzing to get the SD card uploaded and the camera feed up and running.

"Angle is about a hundred and twenty degrees, so if someone actually opens the barn doors, I can see it. It activates when animals move into the frame." He scrolls through the feed, seeking anything out of place. "Look, babe, the foxes are back."

"Focus, Luke. People, not foxes." But she leans over his shoulder and smiles at the small hunters, a mated pair, who trail past the barns in search of field mice for their impending brood of kits. They come around every spring. She's named them Kitsune and Reynard.

"Shit," Luke breathes a moment later. "Jack. Look. Stranger danger."

The call of their childhood. Stranger danger. Someone who doesn't belong is near. It's how Jack ended up in law enforcement and eventually running for sheriff in the first place; the kind sheriff who came to warn them about strangers in the area ended up capturing his interest, and the man was a good soul who saw an opportunity to win over a young fan. The day left an impression on them all.

"That's a damn good camera, Luke. Gotta get me one of those."

They both peer over Luke's shoulder at the screen. The high-quality infrared video illuminates the shadow of a man entering the barns, wearing black clothes and a baseball cap pulled low. The date and time stamp show three weeks earlier, at 3:47 a.m. The dark of night.

The stranger eases out of the doors fifteen minutes later. His hands are empty, but that means nothing; it doesn't take a lot of the brodifacoum to kill.

"Bait pellets in that bucket. No idea how many to start," Luke says. His voice is shaking, whether from fear or fury, Kira can't tell exactly. "He slips off to the north and is gone. Son of a bitch." He whirls around and buries his face in Kira's stomach. "I'm so sorry, babe. I'm going to pull the house security system into the barns tomorrow."

"The tack rooms are always locked?" Jack asks.

"Yeah. But the barn is open in case there's a fire. We don't want to waste any time getting the horses out, and we're sitting here in the middle of a thousand acres, so prowlers aren't generally a concern. I feel like an idiot. God, your dad's gonna kill me—"

Kira shushes him. "Let's just figure out who this is first, okay? Don't blame yourself, hon. He won't. I don't. Someone's playing a very sick game, and now Jack will have something to use to catch him. Won't you?" she says to their old friend, in a tone that brooks no argument.

Jack cocks his head to the side.

"You're lucky there's something suspicious on these cameras. I would have hated like hell to have to arrest you."

WEDNESDAY

CHAPTER FIFTY
RILEY

Nate's family "camp" sleeps twenty-six comfortably and has overflow buildings for even larger parties. Built on a small island off the coast of Portland, it is quintessential Maine luxury—cedar shakes and wrap-around porches and brick chimneys, private beaches, docks for fishing, romantic paths for walking. It's nestled in the trees but the views of the water, sunrises, and sunsets are unimpaired by the strategically groomed grounds. It has sunrooms and living rooms and dining rooms and a high-end chef's kitchen that is more suited for a small wedding party than their motley crew. It is bright and sunny and classically homey in the way of New England wealth that makes you want to sink into a sofa and read a yachting magazine. For all she knows, there is a yacht parked out back, the boat that brought them over being more appropriate to the crossing of Casco Bay than puttering up and down the coast with champagne corks popping indiscriminately.

"Nice place," Riley says mildly.

"There was talk of making it a retreat space for private rental for a while," Nate says, dropping Riley's bags in her room, across the hall from his own. He's wearing a faded pair of chinos and a creamy sweater that's seen many a summer clambake and looks as disreputable as a pirate on vacation. "But my folks decided they wanted to keep it for the family. They have dreams of grandkids running amok."

"I can see why they wouldn't want to let it go," she replies. "It's pretty incredible, Nate."

"It's safe, which is all that matters right now. We can at least control who gets onto the island. In case . . ." Pain skitters across his face.

"You can say it. In case whoever killed Oliver comes to kill me, too."

He looks at her closely. His voice is gentle, and he takes her hand in his warm one. "Are you okay? I know finding him like that was horrifying."

Is she okay? No. She will never be okay again. Oliver's death is all her fault. If she'd not been so anxious to make her mark, not leaped at the chance of money and prestige, and stuck to the basics, none of this would have happened. Reaching for the stars has a price.

She shakes her head, suddenly not trusting her voice. Every time she blinks, she sees Oliver's lifeless body; sees the security guard—she didn't even know the man's name, but he died for her, protecting her; sees Columbia's pale skin, blood everywhere. These scars will never heal properly, she already knows this.

"I will do anything, everything, I can, to help find who killed him, Riley. I swear it. We've already posted a reward for information. We're working with NYPD on finding who got into the building, how the cameras were disabled, all of it. Tony thinks it's a hack with a jammer, but who the hell knows. What will help you the most right now? Do you want me to leave you alone? Do you want to work? Do you want to go for a walk, or a swim? No, probably not a swim, the water will be too chilly until tomorrow, when the heaters have kicked in all the way on the pool. The bay is too cold, period, it's only May. A drink? A sandwich? There are lobster rolls downstairs, we've brought in the lobster fresh, and they've hand-made everything gluten-free in a separate, uncontaminated kitchen for you, so you don't have to worry. You name it, it's yours."

He's chattering in his nervousness, and that spikes her deep in the heart. She didn't say more than yes or no when they left the police station. The flash of the cameras, the shouts from the reporters, all of it, it was too much. Nate just talked, soothing and persistent, until they arrived here. Now that she's admitted her deepest fear—that Oliver will not be the last victim of her ambition—there doesn't seem to be anything of relevance left to say.

What she wants is oblivion. To sink away into nothingness and forget all the horrors of the past several days. But she can't give in to this feeling. Not yet. She heaves in a breath, what feels like her first since they arrived: salt and wind, the sweet and spicy clove scent of the early rhododendrons and azaleas that surround the grounds, Nate's subtle cologne and—fuck, blood. She smells blood. She smells Oliver's blood. Her hand goes to her sloppy bun, she'd thrown it up at the station because it was getting in her eyes, and she feels something crusty.

With a cry, she runs to the bathroom and turns on the shower, stripping off her jeans and turtleneck—they're fresh, Nate had brought them to the police station and she'd changed there before they left, but the scent is coming from somewhere—and steps into the hot spray, scrubbing herself hard, washing her hair—*his blood is in my hair, oh, God!*—lathering it again and again with something leafy-green and clean until it clouds the meaty smell; then she collapses on the marble floor with her arms around her knees.

She thought she was all cried out, but the shock seems to be wearing off, and she sobs in the hot water until she realizes there are arms around her, and a fluffy towel protects her nakedness, that the water has been turned off, that she is leaning into the strong chest of this man she loves and it is wrong—wrong!—to be glad of his support because it is her betrayal that killed the other man she loved. She wants to push Nate away, but she can't let go. And he holds her while she battles with herself, saying nothing, letting the war play out, the blades of her heart crossing in the sunlight, clanging and clattering as they come together again and again, both sides drawing blood, until she starts to shiver.

"Riley," Nate starts, but she puts a finger over his lips. Follows with her own mouth; kisses him softly, chastely. Appreciates that he holds back, though she can sense his restraint is fading, about to slip, that with one more touch of pillowy softness, he will lose all control and take her here in the shower, and that she wants him to, wants that oblivion, wants to satiate her body's needs and to hell with what her mind says, but that can't happen. Not now. Forgetting is for later.

She then pulls herself together. This is not over. She has to find out what happened, and why. And there's only one way. She stands, wrapping the towel tightly around her body.

"Just want to fast-forward to the fifteenth. You know?"

He looks at her thoughtfully. "Maybe I can do something about that."

"What?"

He already has his phone out. "Roger? It's Nate. We have a situation I'm wondering if you could help resolve. You know Riley Carrington, on my staff? She's the beneficiary in a will that's doing a formal reading on the fifteenth, the firm is Mathers and Mathers. Unfortunately, Preston Mathers's son, Oliver Mathers, has been murdered, and we've moved everyone involved to the camp for safety. There's a lot more to this story, but for now, I'm wondering if you could talk to Mathers and Mathers and suggest the reading be done here, as soon as possible. As I understand it, there could be more beneficiaries. I will happily fly them here and guarantee their safety to the best of my abilities."

Roger Novak, the Walsh family lawyer, comes back with an affirmative. "I'm so sorry to hear that. Oliver was a good kid. Let me see what I can do. You take care of yourself, Nate. I don't like the sound of this situation."

"Yeah, me either. Thanks, Roger. Get back to me as soon as you hear."

He smiles at Riley. "One step forward, yeah?"

"It's a good idea. I wonder who the other beneficiaries are? Do you think Darian knows?"

"There's only one way to find out. She's downstairs with Mason and Tony. Tony has some news to share, too, stuff he's found on the flash drive."

"Then we need to get downstairs, don't we?" She realizes she is still in her towel, hair dripping wet, and Nate is watching her, smile rueful. His eyes telegraph all she needs to know. He understands her struggle. He will wait for her. He has been waiting for her all this time.

Riley runs a finger across the crisp white comforter. She is so tired. She will take a nap after she blows up Darian's perfect little life. She towels her hair to reduce the moisture, and Nate points her back to the bathroom where a comb and brush, mousse, gel, all the items from her bathroom are neatly laid out on the counter on white washcloths, waiting for her.

When did he do that? How did he know what she needed?

"Thank you," she manages.

"There's something else." He looks nervous to tell her, and she tenses in anticipation of the worst. "A reporter in Denver claims he's found Columbia's long-lost daughter. Someone sent him a copy of the beneficiary letter that she received, and a copy of a handwritten letter addressed to her signed by her mother. Kira Hutchinson is her name. Tony's been doing background on her, but he hasn't dredged up enough to tell if it's legit or not. She owns a bakery and has three young sons. I thought you'd want to know."

"So it's not me, after all," she says at last, the reality of this sinking in.

"I don't think so, kid."

She rubs her eyebrows. This is both good and weirdly disappointing news.

"So the beneficiary, why I'm in the will, it's for the book, I bet."

"Probably so. And maybe we can find out sooner rather than later, if Roger can work his magic. Meanwhile, we'll stay snug as bugs here at camp. We'll be able to figure out the rest of the story, the British connection, the ties to the case in Tennessee, all of it. We have more brains to work on this now, and more material from the flash drive. Apparently it really is a treasure trove."

Riley is amazed to feel disappointment. She'd been wrapping her head around the idea of being the daughter of a famed author. The book-trope fantasy of an adoptee: that the birth parent was a princess or a queen, and the child was stashed away for their own safety and now must be retrieved to rule the kingdom. It was a silly pipe dream, and she resolves then and there to put her DNA into the databases and see if she can find her real family. It's time.

The thought sparks a moment of grief for Maisie, the sister who never was, and the life cut short because of Riley's juvenile foibles. It would be easier to mourn her if she was truly gone. She vows to go visit as soon as she can, to be more generous with her time. To try to forgive Faith, and maybe, maybe, start to forgive herself, too.

"You're disappointed that you're not her kid, aren't you?" Nate says.

"It's not that. It's just the timing of all this is so weird. She just hired me a couple of months ago. Now I'm in her will. She's dead. Oliver's dead. The bodyguard who was supposed to be protecting me is dead. Someone is circling me, killing people, and I don't know why. I'm just some reporter doing a story . . . Either I uncovered something major that I just don't know, or there's a nutjob who's set his sights on me. None of this makes sense."

"I agree, it's all very strange. But let's see what Tony has found. Maybe there will be answers."

She finishes dressing and grabs her bag with the files inside.

"The answers are in this story. I know it."

Tony is set up in the large dining room with an array of computer screens, typing furiously on a wireless keyboard. He waves with one hand without looking at them.

"You gotta see this. Did you know she wrote under a pseudonym? D.E. Shepherd. All the files are on here, there's gotta be twenty-odd books here. Plus, Riley, you're going to lose your mind when you see it. She has files labeled for you. Your name is on the folder, and there's a slew of documents in it. Looks like she was pulling things together to work on a memoir. I've read a few pieces of it and it's absolutely . . . Well, sorry, you should see this yourself."

He swings one of the screens her way, and Riley plops down in a seat and starts to read aloud.

"'The trick to telling a good story is limiting yourself to a specific time frame so you can find the proper beginning, middle, and end. The natural inclination when telling the story of a life is to start at birth and end at death, but that's a guarantee for failure. No, you're better off finding a moment of true crisis, keeping in medias res, then explaining how you came to be in such a sad situation, and how the crisis was resolved—that tension and limitation keep the story engaging. So I've chosen a time frame for you.

"'I'm starting with the lie. My name is not my name. My life is not my life. It is time for you—for the world—to know the truth.'"

She looks up, confused. "It ends there. But there's more, isn't there?"

Tony reminds her of a bobblehead doll on a dashboard, talking and nodding, excitement emanating from him. He could light up a room if they plugged him into a socket.

"The files aren't in a clear order, it's like she was telling the story as it came to her, not in any sort of chronological way. It's incomplete, but I think you're going to get the idea. I pieced them together as best I could and have them all open, you can just move from left to right. And there's another version of that short story, too. In case you want to read it again."

Nate says, "I'll get you some tea."

"Thanks. I'll be right here, reading."

Legacy Draft— Chapter Seven

A police officer eventually comes to my room. She explains she has driven up from Nashville, that she specializes in these types of assaults and will work with the local sheriff. I want to tell her not to, but I can't. It will give everything away. She is kind and solicitous. She has white-blond hair that can't be natural at her age, given the depth of her black eyebrows. She wears red lipstick, the color of blood. An ironic choice.

Is this what shock is like? A focus on matters irrelevant?

She insists the baby go with the nurses, just for a little check-up. I don't see any way to prevent this; the baby is fine. It is me who is broken.

The cop asks me questions. So many questions.

Talking is painful. My jaw aches. Every inhalation through my nose feels like a knife's blade to my face. But cooperation is vital. The story must be told.

After what feels like hours of interrogation, I gesture to my body, helpless to go on. Her eyes flash with compassion, and something else, a dark gleam that sets my teeth on edge. She believes me, and yet, she doesn't.

"I know you're hurting. We need to catch who did this to you, and I swear, I will. Only a few more questions, then we'll let the nurses get you cleaned up. Let's go back to the man who broke into your house. Run me through it again. Did you know him? Or was he a stranger?"

My mouth forms the word before I can stop it. "Like I said. Stranger."

"Can you describe him?"

I manage to shake my head, a jarring sensation I feel through my entire being.

"Mask," I manage. "Tall. Broad shoulders. I think he had blond hair."

"Okay, these are great details. Do you remember his clothing?"

"No. It was dark."

"And you're absolutely sure he was a stranger? It wasn't someone from the neighborhood, someone who you might see on the street, at the market?"

I swallow. Even that small act hurts. Screaming. I'd been screaming.

Don't don't don't don't don't.

"Where is my daughter?"

The officer glances over her shoulder. "The nurses have her. Just a quick change and feeding while we finish up. She's a sweet girl."

I want to shout bring her to me right now! but I don't. She has her father's eyes. I can't imagine that I will ever be able to look into their navy depths again. I have failed her, as I failed myself. Will she blame me?

"Based on your injuries, we need to do a sexual assault kit," the officer says now, softly. "Are you okay with me sending in the nurse? She's a very sweet woman who specializes in this, and I promise she will make it as painless as possible."

Panic fills me. "No, no! I don't want to. I just want to take a shower. I want to get his . . . this blood off of me. Can't I just shower?"

"Collecting samples will help us catch this monster, ma'am. I know it's hard, but it will help. So much. As soon as you're finished, you'll be able to shower. The doctor will set your nose and you'll be free to take your daughter and go home."

The panic rises again, loosening my tongue. "I can't go back there. Can someone get the dog?"

She nods knowingly and lays a hand on my shoulder. "Yes, I'll take care of that. Do you have someone we can call?"

I try to think, my brain is sludgy. I have no one. But I tell her another lie. "My friend Alex will come for me. You can take the dog to David's parents."

"Excellent," the officer says. "All right. You're doing great, ma'am. I'm so sorry for your loss. I promise we'll figure out who did this to you and your husband."

My heart thumps once, hard, showering me with some blessed adrenaline that clears my head at last. I meet her eyes. This is perfect.

"Good."

The nurse is gentle, but the indignity reverberates. She scrapes under my nails, clips them, has me lie on my back and scooch down to the end of the table while she takes the samples from between my legs. I try not to think about what she's doing, though she's talking the whole time, telling me exactly what is happening so I won't be surprised. Her touch is gentle, and I find myself relieved that she has a soft voice and quick hands. Then it is over, and she takes me to a shower room and hands me a towel and a kit with some shampoo and soap that has no scent at all. For this I am grateful. I am making sensory memories, I know this, can feel them happening. The way the water hits me, the sweet relief I feel at being clean, the horror at the bruises, the sting of the water on my cut, bruised face.

I will never forget these things, even though doing a rape kit will be pointless in the end—he was my husband, after all. Husbands can't rape their wives in this town.

When I emerge, she has a set of scrubs for me to wear. She helps dry my hair. Tells me that a surgeon will come by shortly to assess the facial fractures and she knows he'll make me my pretty self again. I am struck again by the kindness, but feel the pity, too.

I don't deserve it.

Legacy Draft— Chapter Eight

The kind officer from the hospital comes back with a detective right after David's funeral. The whole town showed up. His family was popular. They were kind to me and the baby. I hadn't cooked a meal, there were plenty of people to sit while I recovered. My bruises were fading, but my left eye still had a red spot from the broken vessels, and my nose was still casted.

"Mrs. Simpson," the detective says, "we know who killed your husband. We have a DNA match to an open paternity case. A man named Patrick Connolly. He works at the hospital. Do you know him? Do you recognize the name?"

Heart in my throat, I shook my head.

But she knew. The sweet, kind, lovely police officer knew I was lying, and she'd told the detective everything.

I didn't know about DNA. I didn't know they could find him on me, on the bat, on David.

I should have known better, should have known there was no way they'd have a DNA match that quickly. And Patrick didn't have children. They were fishing. The police are good at lying, too.

The detective sensed he was close to breaking me, so he asked again and again, what happened? And I swore to him, again and again, that I didn't know.

"We were having dinner. We had an argument. He . . . hurt me. He punched me, and I blacked out. When I woke, he was dead."

I said it so many times, even I started to believe it.

But we hadn't been as careful as we thought. People had seen us together around town, and one of the shitty, nosy neighbors told the police that Patrick had been hanging around the house. So they'd gone to talk to Patrick himself, who had a shift starting in an hour. He wasn't there. His supervisor shared that Patrick hadn't come to work in days.

And of course, he wasn't at home.

They caught him south of Nashville, making plans to escape the country to Mexico. He was mere hours from freedom.

Me, they held in the county jail. I had pillows and three meals a day; he was ragged, had lost weight, stealing food and hitching rides. They tried to get me to testify against him. They tried to get him to testify against me.

In the end, we stuck with the story I'd concocted the night we killed David.

"I told David I was leaving. He beat me. Patrick came to get me and the baby and walked in on a melee. He was just trying to get David to stop hurting me. It was an accident. It wasn't planned. Patrick grabbed the first thing he saw and hit David to get him off me because he thought I was going to be killed. It was self-defense. He panicked. I panicked. We didn't want to end up right where we are, today, on trial for David's murder, so I said it was a stranger who broke in.

"Love makes people do awful things.

"We are so very sorry."

CHAPTER FIFTY-ONE
DARIAN

Darian stands in the lovely sunny room in a stranger's house, ignoring the spectacular view of Casco Bay in favor of staring at the television, which is muted. She's watching a replay of the media shouting questions at Riley Carrington as she exits the Seventeenth Precinct station on East Fifty-First. A handsome man has his arm around her shoulders, the infamous Nate Walsh, who has just whisked them away to this island in Maine on a private plane.

Darian is actually happy about this—not only because apparently they're all targets of some madman who has now murdered three people that they know of, and staying in the town house waiting for something to happen a moment longer will make her scream, but also because she knows the media scrum will come for her next. She's shocked they weren't camped on the doorstep already. The reporter who called from Colorado has tried a few more times, but she is not about to talk to him until she can figure out what's going on, and that means the reading of this damnable will. In the meantime, her mother is dead, and Riley's boyfriend is dead, and they are all hiding from the world on a coastal island, and she doesn't know which foot to put in front of the other next.

She is hungry, and frustrated, and confused. Nothing in her world makes sense anymore, especially the fact that Riley Carrington somehow holds the key. The only thing that's remotely sane is Mason.

She starts to flip off the television but sees the scene has shifted to a single reporter standing outside what looks like the entrance to a ranch. He wears black glasses and a white button-down and looks excited, like a little boy at the top of the stairs Christmas morning. She turns up the audio just in time to hear the reporter say "Columbia Jones's long-lost daughter has refused to comment. There's more to come on this story. Reporting live from Boulder, Colorado, this is Daniel Donnelly, WICK News."

"Her name is Kira Hutchinson," the reporter had said before she cut him off. She hadn't had time to even search for the woman before Walsh's security guards arrived at her door.

Darian goes to the window, looks out onto the water. She is momentarily surprised to see it placid and gently lapping the banks below her, sunlight dappling its edges; it should be roaring, twisting, screaming in its fury, splashing foam onto the rocks. Everything should be in turmoil, the way she is inside right now. She takes in the tall and gentle giant sitting in the chair on the deck, a breeze ruffling his collar. He, too, stares at the water, and she's struck once again by how lucky she is. Another, lesser man would have run screaming for the hills when faced with all the drama she's had this week. Instead, he seems to get more and more settled, kinder, gentler.

"Mason, I need to—" She is cut off by her phone ringing. It is the detective; she recognizes the 303 area code. "Wait a sec. It's Detective Sutcliffe," she says, and answers. Mason comes in from the deck, and she puts it on speaker.

"Miss Jones. I have some news."

"You found out who killed her?"

"There's a suspect, yes."

She feels the spike of relief all the way to her spine. "Who is it? Is it the Knox Shepherd character? Why did he kill her? What has he told you?"

"I'd like to talk to you about this in person. I can be in New York this evening."

"Oh. Oh. Um . . . I can't do that."

"Why not?"

She can hear the tone sharpen; his interest is piqued.

"Detective, I don't know how much you've seen about the past couple of days, but someone killed Riley Carrington's boyfriend, Oliver Mathers. We've all gone someplace safe until this madman is caught."

"What? When was Mathers killed?"

"I don't know exactly. Monday night, maybe? Regardless, whoever killed my mom followed us back to New York. We think he was trying to get at Riley."

"How? What was the cause of death?"

"As I understand it, he was shot."

The detective grows quiet. "I need to know where you are, Miss Jones. This is an official police investigation. People are dying. You can't run off somewhere and think that you're safe. Let me take you into protective custody until we find the person responsible."

"No. No way. Trust me, I am totally safe here. Nate Walsh has a full-blown SWAT security team on us."

"Nate Walsh? So Riley Carrington is there, too?"

Mason cuts a hand across his throat.

"I need to go. Please let me know when you've formally arrested the killer, and then we'll feel comfortable revealing our location."

"You know I can just trace this call, right?"

"Trust me, Detective. We're safer here than you could possibly make us."

She hangs up the phone. "Can he really trace the call?"

Mason nods. "Of course. It will take him a day or so to get a warrant for the records. By then, this will all be over."

"What do you mean?"

He tucks a stray piece of hair behind her ear. "He has a suspect. He'll get a confession. And then we'll all be able to sleep at night."

"I hope you're right. We need to talk to Riley. And I need to see what Liam has dug up."

"Give him a call. Just don't say where you are. No sense taking chances."

"Liam wouldn't hurt a fly."

"We can't trust anyone right now, Jonesy."

She drops the phone to her lap and stares at him. "How did you know that was my nickname?"

"Jonesy? I didn't. I just made it up. It suits you."

"No one's called me that since college. Just surprised me, that's all."

"Would you rather I find something else? Babe? Honey pie? My darling sweetheart? Snookums? No, that's probably what Nate's dad calls his mother." He adopts a Thurston Howell III affectation. "Snookums, are there fresh towels in the sauna? The gentlemen have been free balling again, and I simply can't have those vulgar views."

She bursts into giggles and throws a pillow at him. How he can make her laugh when the wheels are coming off the bus . . . "I love you," she blurts, and is rewarded with a huge smile. He pulls her to her feet and into his arms.

"My Jonesy," he whispers. "I'm glad to hear it. Because I am mad for you."

"Same here. But I need answers. I need to know who killed my mom, and who this Kira Hutchinson person is, and why Mom didn't trust me. Maybe if I can figure that out, I can figure out why we're really here instead of being in Denver where I'm supposed to be. It's so freaking frustrating."

"I know. I mean, I can't know, not entirely, but I feel for you, Jonesy. This is a lot to handle. Wasn't Liam digging into the Vonda West situation for you? Maybe he can fill in some blanks on Knox Shepherd as well."

"Yeah. Good call. Let me reach out and see if he's made any progress."

She dials his number, but he doesn't answer. She sends him a text.

Can you update me? Sutcliffe has a suspect and I'd like to know more. Knox Shepherd is his name. And please run this Kira Hutchinson person for me. The press is saying she's related to my mother somehow.

While she waits for Liam to answer, she pulls on a pair of running shoes and grabs a sweater.

"We going for a walk?" Mason asks.

"I want to talk to Riley. Maybe she knows more about this Knox Shepherd guy."

He shakes his head and sighs. "Poor Riley. She's pretty messed up right now. Her boyfriend . . ."

"Yeah, I know. But at some point, we all have to talk. Let's just see if she's willing, okay? God, where's Liam? It never takes him this long to get back to me."

She sends another text to Liam.

You okay?

Nothing.

"Okay, now I'm starting to get worried. He always answers."

"I'll keep trying him if you want."

"No, I want you by my side while I enter the lion's den. Let's go down."

Mason shuts the doors to the deck, locks them, and takes her hand. They wind their way down the stairs and through the house until they find Riley.

The reporter stands in the living room, her bouncy blonde hair in a perfectly pert ponytail, her trademark turtleneck tucked into her well-tailored jeans. She's like an undercover movie star.

And she makes Darian squirm. Riley is everything Darian is not. She's making her way in the world. She's commanding the respect of the industry with her insightful essays. She's leggy and blonde and curvaceous in a way Darian could only dream of if she stuffed her bra and got a Brazilian butt lift.

Riley reminds Darian of Columbia, actually. Larger than life.

She forces back the image of Riley standing over her mother, reminding herself that Riley, too, has lost someone dear to her, and steps into the room.

Riley turns at the noise, and Darian can see the ravages of the past few days streaked across her face. She feels even worse for her nasty thoughts.

"Hey. I'm so sorry, Riley."

"Thank you," Riley says. She seems to be vibrating, whether scared or excited, Darian doesn't know. She can't read her mother's choice of amanuensis. Yes, they spent a month together on the road, but it wasn't like they were having pajama parties and braiding each other's hair. They each had a job to do, and they did it. They were moons to Columbia's planet. Not to mention Darian had filled a lot of her downtime in Mason's bed. She hadn't been paying close enough attention, and it got her mother killed.

"You want to tell us what's going on? Why we're here?"

Riley's beautiful face turns hard. "Have you gone through your mother's hard drive yet? Her laptop?"

"Jesus, Riley. She's only been dead for a week. But yes, I have scoured my mother's hard drive. It was my first priority."

"Good." Riley is digging in her bag now. "Then I assume this won't come as a shock. My boyfriend had this for me when I got home. To be given to me upon Columbia's death."

"What? What is it?"

"A story. Clearly an early one, it's pretty rough. But it's a message, too."

"Let me see that," Darian snaps, just stopping herself from lunging at Riley. This is utterly absurd. Her mother left a story for a stranger?

Riley hands over the stapled pages. "I'll be in the kitchen while you read. It's not long." A pause, her eyes searching Darian's face. "Do you want a cup of tea?"

Darian swallows a retort and nods. Riley gestures to Mason. "You, too?"

"Sure. Thanks."

She disappears into the wide kitchen, and Darian can hear her clinking around.

She looks at the pages Riley thrust into her hand.

"What is this?" she says, almost to herself. She flips to the cover page—*LEGACY*—in old typewriter font, the pages themselves thin, worn, as if they've been read and reread for decades, and starts to read.

When I wake, the body is cold.

Legacy Draft—Chapter Nine

When I began throwing up a few weeks after David's death, after Patrick's arrest, I knew immediately what was happening. That night, that horrible night, had left more than one scar on the world. David was having the last laugh, after all.

I didn't want it. But she was mine, too. Saria would have a sister, and we would be a family.

The trial coincided with the baby's birth. I was able to watch on television from the hospital while she nursed at my breast. She came so quickly, and with such little fanfare, just a few pushes and she was out.

But Patrick was not.

It was our word against a dead man. The baby and the dog were the only witnesses. The DA called it second-degree, the judge agreed. Ten for me, twenty for him. Patrick sacrificed himself for me. He took the blame.

And I let him.

My heart went to jail for murdering my husband. It didn't matter that David deserved it. It didn't matter that it was in defense of the woman Patrick loved. A jury of his peers found him guilty, and he was sentenced to life.

He disappeared into a different world.

I never saw him again.

In the end, I couldn't keep on pretending that every time I looked at Krista, I didn't see the dried blood. Didn't feel the stiff pliability of the cold, dead flesh of her father next to me. There were parts of that night that were foggy for me, but the moment of her conception was burned as bright and searing as the noonday sun.

She was better off without me. Without us. She needed a life untainted by the horrors that brought her into being. She deserved a mother who could love her fully, unconditionally, like I did Saria.

And so I gave her away. And then I ran. I left my legacy behind, and I created a new life. A new world.

The End

CHAPTER FIFTY-TWO
DARIAN

Ten minutes later, Darian turns the final page and looks up at Riley, who is sitting quiet as a church mouse, an array of teacups in front of her, waiting for her reaction.

"Well. It's raw, but who knew she had thriller chops?" She sets the pages down on the table carefully.

"I agree," Riley says. "It's lacking the panache and style she clearly learned from writing story after story, being edited, the works. But it's visceral, and so clearly her voice. It's more than a short story, though. I think it's a message."

Riley's face is so earnest Darian pauses. "A message about what? It's insane enough that it was given to you—it belongs to the literary estate. Why would she want you to have one of her early stories?"

Riley's face is shuttered. "Because it's a confession. It's about her. It's autobiographical."

Darian scoffs. "Riley. No offense, but I think the stress has gone to your head."

"Listen to me. I'm adopted."

"Okay. That means nothing. A lot of people are adopted."

She gives a frustrated huff. "I'm starting in the wrong place. Maybe this will get your attention. Your mother's real name isn't Columbia. Your last name isn't really Jones."

Darian's face shutters. "You're insane. I have her birth certificate and her Social Security number. My birth certificate, too."

"She changed her name. She changed *your* name."

"You're absolutely bonkers. How did you even dream that one up?"

"I'm not making this up."

"So what is her real name?"

"Devon Elder Mears."

Darian is stupefied. A little voice reminds her of the pen name. D.E. Shepherd. The suspect in the murder from Tennessee is named Shepherd. Devon Elder . . . Shepherd? Her head is spinning, she feels ill.

"This is impossible. How did you even stumble onto this?"

"Research. It's what I do when I'm doing a piece. I'm a natural skeptic, and I like to know everything I can about my subjects. That's my job, to ferret out the truth that sometimes stays hidden. But many people never look past what they're fed. Most just run with the bio that they're given. And Columbia's been a part of this world for many, many years. She had a reputation; she has a history. She's been publishing for over twenty years, there's plenty of verifiable things about her in public."

Darian rolls her eyes, though inside she's feeling as skittish as a fawn. "You're saying my mother's bio is a lie? I mean, come on, Riley. I wrote the damn thing. I think I'd know."

"If you're working with the whole truth, yes. It says she's from Bromley, England, right? I wanted to include the hospital she was born in in the piece, just as a frame. The local-girl-makes-good-in-New-York-City angle. But there were no Columbias born in Bromley in the years before or after her birthday. She's not from England. She's from Tennessee. She changed her name after she got out of jail."

Again, that voice. *Vonda West posed as your grandmother. Is this why? Did Mom create a person to back up her story? No. No, this isn't possible.*

"This is a joke, right?" Though Darian can see that Riley isn't kidding. She is composed and serious. The fractures are building, Darian can feel it, like a glass shield about to burst under pressure.

"There's more. After I got the pages, and article, I did some digging. The court case, in Tennessee, from 1995? The defendant is Devon Mears. She was tried for being an accomplice to the murder of her husband."

"Come on. You're reaching," Darian says.

"Hear me out. The defendant's name is Knox Shepherd. He's accused of murdering a man named Benjamin Mears, who was Devon's husband. Shepherd went to jail for fifteen years and got out on parole in 2010. The woman who was tried, Mears's wife? There is a wedding certificate on file in a little town called Crossville. The woman's name is Devon Elder. I'm pretty sure that's your mom's maiden name. She was young, only nineteen."

Darian slumps in the chair. "This is ridiculous. You actually think the short story is her life's story?"

"A version that she was exploring, yes. There's a birth certificate on file in Crossville, too. A little girl named Darian Rebecca Mears. Born November 15, 1993."

Darian is getting mad now. This is too much. Who the hell is Riley damn Carrington to be shoving this insanity in her face, with a wild story supposedly written by her mother to give all the textual clues? Yes, her mother told her something about her dad being killed in a home invasion the night he died, but this is bullshit, all the way through.

"And you were going to confront her? And dump all of this into your stupid essay? It's libel!"

"No it's not. And of course I wouldn't just run with this without having actual backup. Which this is. Don't you see? Columbia wrote her own story. She wrote what actually happened. She wrote about your father, and the man who murdered him."

"My father was a good guy. He never hit her. He—"

That's it. Darian collapses into tears. This is just so unfair. She lost her dad so long ago, her mother only a week ago. And now this reporter is trying to twist her life into a huge piece of fiction. Just like Columbia herself would have done.

And then Riley deals the death blow. She touches Darian on the shoulder, featherlight, in case it's an unwanted gesture.

"I think you're the baby who was born in the closet, Darian. I thought I was your sister for the longest time. It still might be me, but it's definitely Kira Hutchinson. She lives in Colorado. She was there the night your mother died. You met her at the VIP event."

"You're bonkers."

"I'm not. I swear I'm not. She had twins in jail."

Darian is about to lose it because this is all just so incredibly stupid and impossible. She feels her heart breaking in two distinct pieces—the life she knew, the life she's facing. Her mother couldn't have lied to her this whole time about who she was. Who they were. She couldn't have given away another child—much less two of them. The Columbia Jones Darian knew might not have been the most nurturing woman on the planet, but she loved Darian fiercely. Darian never once felt otherwise. Yes, they butted heads, yes, her mother was often cold and aloof, but that was just the creative spirit in her. Sometimes she turned inward to investigate the people in her brain instead of being present with the people in front of her. That's what art does to families.

If this is true . . . she lied to you for years, Darian. She didn't tell you anything about her pen name. She and Vic created a whole world and cut you out of it entirely. Why couldn't this be true, too?

There's only one way to find the truth, and that's in her mother's will. Wouldn't that be the place to have your confession, should you be living a massive lie?

Riley is still touching her shoulder, trying, failing, to comfort.

"There's some good that can come of this, right? This is why I think you need to check her computer and see if there's anything else, some-thing she's left for you to read, or—"

"I don't need your advice on what to do here, Riley." Darian sounds stronger than she feels.

Riley pauses as if she might argue, then nods. "There's more. She left me a flash drive, and it has a confession on it."

"What?"

Riley pulls the small flash drive from her pocket and sets it on the table between them.

"She wanted me to write her memoir. And she's left me some information that I think you should see."

Darian's phone rings. Liam, finally, calling her back.

"I have to take this," she says, and stalks to the balcony. She can hear Mason and Riley talking.

"Liam, where have you been?"

"Darian, I'm so sorry it's taken me so long to get back to you. Long story. But I did a quick run on this Kira Hutchinson person. It's impossible to know if the media reports are true, but she was sent a letter from your mom, it came from the law office that's doing her will. There's a chance she's for real. That she's your sister. Hey, where are you? I stopped by your place, and no one answered. Did you go to Colorado to get your mom's ashes?"

"No. I'm . . . well, I can't tell you where I am."

"Cool, no worries. So the Shepherd guy? He lives in Franklin, Tennessee, married to Emily, daughter Tamsin. That's all I've found so far, other than his police record. He was in jail for murder, you know that, right?"

"I do."

"And he was at the event in Denver the night your mom died? Man, that's a headfuck. At least the police have him as a suspect now. They'll nail him. You'll be safe."

"I hope so. Thanks for your help, Liam. I'll be in touch when I get home."

"Sure thing, Darian. You take good care, okay? I'd hate it if something happened to you. Oh, hey, the article in *East Fifth Magazine* is out. Want me to send you a copy? It's pretty benign, but it hints that there's a lot to come. Part one of three, they say."

"Sure. Send it to me. And thanks, Liam. I'll talk to you soon."

She hangs up, and her email dings. The article. The reason this all started, finally manifesting itself.

Before she can read it, Nate Walsh joins them in the living room.

"Hey, so I just heard from our family lawyer, and Mathers and Mathers have agreed to do the reading of Columbia's will here, at the camp. Tomorrow, assuming we can get everyone here in time."

Darian's curiosity outweighs the incredulity that Nate Walsh is now making decisions for her. "Everyone? Do you know who the other beneficiaries are?"

"I do. The primaries are you, Riley, Knox Shepherd, and Kira Hutchinson. Kira is in Colorado, and Shepherd is in Tennessee. They've both been notified and have agreed to come here. Vic Guul has also been asked to come. He's your lawyer, correct?"

"He is." Darian sighs heavily. "I just don't know which end is up, you know?"

Mason takes the seat Riley vacated and puts his arm around her.

"It's a lot, Darian. To have your mother murdered, to find out she wasn't being truthful with you. But everyone here has nothing but the best intentions. We all want you to be okay. Me especially."

She swallows back the tears and nods. "I still need proof. I guess this means we have time to comb through the rest of these files, see if we can find it."

She looks at Riley, standing nearby, nervously playing with her hair, watching Darian's reaction. If what they're saying is true, this means the girl she accused of murdering her mother is actually her younger sister. And Columbia knew it when she invited Riley into their lives.

It's flabbergasting. Why didn't she just share the truth with Darian? Why she hid this, lied about it, is beyond her ken. And until she knows for sure, until there are DNA tests done that prove things without a shadow of a doubt, she isn't going to open her heart to this stranger.

But Darian is not her mother. And she is in control of whether any good comes of her mother's murder.

She crosses to Riley's side. "Look at me," she says softly.

Riley complies. Darian searches the brows, her eyes, her cheekbones, her lips for traces of the mother they might share. And the more she looks, the more obvious the resemblance is. Why she never saw it before, she doesn't know. But strip twenty years off her mother, back to the woman Darian remembers picking her up from the public school down the street and making SpaghettiOs when they couldn't afford both the New York rent and dinner, before she started the "maintenance" that reshaped her face and lips, and damn if she doesn't look like Riley. Not exactly, but wow. She really does.

Riley bites her lip, and Darian feels her heart melt. She touches the girl's cheek, shaking her head.

Sister. This is her little sister. And there's another out there.

She's not alone in the world after all.

"What are you thinking?" Riley asks.

Darian sniffs, and smiles. "I'm thinking we should figure out what was worth killing for in these files. I want to know who killed our mother."

CHAPTER FIFTY-THREE
DETECTIVE SUTCLIFFE

Nothing is ever as easy as it should be. Sutcliffe has run up against all manner of frustrations when it comes to getting arrest warrants, but being denied one in Williamson County on the grounds of insufficient evidence to extradite Shepherd has him grinding his teeth. And now the news that Oliver Mathers was killed in New York while Shepherd was on the road back from Colorado makes him even antsier. He's on the right trail. There's a bigger picture, a puppet master. He's sure of it.

They've set up shop in Skye's conference room, files spread before them, her three laptops running like mad. The dog naps in the corner on a sheepskin bed, chasing rabbits in her dreams.

"Let's keep putting the pieces together. You're only working with half the box right now."

"Only working with half my brain, too," he grumbles. Sutcliffe hadn't slept well, the air conditioner came on at odd times, and once, the hallway was filled with drunken guests hooting and hollering. He got in a short run, but he's cranky.

His phone dings with a text from Duran, and all his complaints disappear.

CODIS popped a DNA match for you off that hair in Columbia Jones's hotel suite. William Carl Reeves, 30, no last known. No idea if he's part of the hospital staff, hotel staff, what. Just wanted to give you the name so you could start looking.

You are the best, lady. Thank you.

Keep being careful.

He looks at Skye. "Bingo. We have a DNA match. Wanna run a name for me?"

"We'll run him in a second. The files from New York are in. Mathers's autopsy." She turns around the computer; she has the files pulled up. "Ballistics match a 9-millimeter that was used in another open shooting a few months ago, a bodega robbery in Manhattan. That's interesting."

"So you think this was a robbery gone wrong?"

"Honestly? No. That would be quite a coincidence."

"But at least we know they're dealing with a repeat offender."

"No way to know that. Suspect could have bought the gun off the street."

"We should change your name to Sherlock."

She grins. "Don't be bitchy with me."

"Yes, ma'am." He flips through his notes. Something is nagging at the back of his mind. "Can you run Reeves's record? I still need to check out the tech guys who work for Columbia. The company is called 49 Spiders. I've done a cursory look but haven't run any of the people yet."

Her head shoots up. "A hacking group?"

"Naw, they do social media for Columbia. Website management, techie stuff."

"No, seriously, 49 Spiders is a hacking group. Or used to be, at least. They might have gone legit, or they have a legit front, most of these guys do. But I've heard of them. Currently white hats, do penetration testing, mostly DDoS attacks, sending in a false email that crawls through the company's network and crashes their servers. One click and they're in. They hold the server for ransom. You'd be surprised at how much money they can make. Companies hire hackers—excuse me, penetration specialists—to test their systems, see how secure they really are. We have one or two on staff here. They're some of the best hackers in the business, they've just chosen to do it for the right reasons instead of nefarious ones. Of course, anyone can turn their coat at any time, you know?"

He checks his notes. "Okay, this is weird. The IT guy's name is Liam Reeves. DNA belonged to a William Reeves. Could they be related?"

She smiles. "Liam is a nickname for William, you know."

His heart gives one spectacularly huge thud. "And . . . please pull up the site?"

She does, and an intricate spiderweb on a black background that pulses and shifts dances on the screen. An animated spider wearing a red baseball cap rushes across the web strands. She clicks to the About page.

"'49 Spiders is a social media management company that helps businesses grow their online platform' . . . yada yada. Nothing remark-able. They certainly don't share that they're doing nefarious work. But by having access to all their clients' social media, ad platforms, all of it, they have a window into the whole net. With that sort of access . . . heck, they can create a person out of whole cloth. It's pretty freaking creepy, actually."

"Look here, the client list has a ton of brand-name authors. Columbia Jones is right at the top. How in the world would she— would any of these people—get hooked up with a hacker?"

"I would assume she didn't know. I mean, it's not like they advertise this to the world, it would ruin their rep in the business, you know? The social media business is a legit cover. A front for the real work of crawl-ing for data, and when they find an opportunity to exploit, they do."

"Why do both? That makes no sense to me."

"You'll have to take that up with them. For now . . ." She types in the name, and a few more pages pop up in rapid succession. "'Meet the Team.' Liam Reeves. Brought up in Memphis. The bio says he's a former Army information tech—that makes him sound legitimate and trustworthy—and he started the business to help grow the platforms of his favorite authors. There are quite a few military-thriller writers on his client list. It's easy enough to check, let me pop his name into the system and see what I can find."

She types away, and a few minutes later, sits back in the chair. "I stand corrected. William Carl Reeves from Memphis, Tennessee, *did* serve in the Army, MOS 25B—that's an information services expert, he worked on military computer systems. You have to have a security clearance for that, which means a serious background check. I have his record, here's his enlistment photo. Familiar?"

The kid in the picture is fresh faced, some faded acne scars on his forehead, brown hair cut high and tight, and serious dark eyes.

"No. Doesn't look familiar at all. I'll send it to Darian and see if she can confirm, I'm sure she's met him."

Skye continues reading. "He got out on a medical waiver. Rollover car crash, non-combat-related, spent a few months in the hospital. Burns."

"That's awful. Anything else?"

"He's got a record, prior to his military career. Assault with a deadly weapon, a few other things. He was in juvie—holy shit, Sutcliffe. He was in Wilder. The youth development center in Somerville. Outside of Memphis."

"So he was a bad boy, went to juvie, got rehabilitated, joined the military, and because he was good with computers, gets into IS. Has an accident, leaves, starts working for 49 Spiders. Has a nice front doing publisher marketing and PR, while behind the scenes is probably stealing wads of information for ransom, real or fake."

"All of that, and he was in your victim's hotel room the night she died."

Sutcliffe forces himself to take a breath and think this through. "Okay. That just leaves the million-dollar question. What possible reason would he have to want Columbia Jones dead? Was he after something and she wouldn't give it to him? Or was he involved in her reinvention? Wait, no, that doesn't fly. He's only thirty, he was just a kid when Devon Mears became Columbia Jones."

"Maybe he discovered the truth about her, though, and was threatening to expose her. Maybe things got out of hand?"

"That's as good a theory as any. If he's a hacker in his spare time, it's very possible he found out she was actually Devon Mears and was blackmailing her. The financials aren't back yet, forensic accounting takes a minute, but if we could tie them together . . . Roll with me for a moment," Sutcliffe says. "The hotel in Denver, the cameras went offline—"

"They went out at Mathers's crime scene, too." She clicks a few times, then reads from the NYPD report. "'The building's security system malfunctioned, and the cameras were not operational at the time of Mathers's murder.' And there's more. Part of the statement that Carrington gave is relevant. I'll be damned. 'Riley Carrington states she was approached at the Museum of Modern Art by a man in a red baseball cap and had to flee after he made lewd comments. The security tapes at the museum were overwritten, so there was no way to see when the man entered the building, nor whether this statement can be corroborated.' That tone . . . they clearly think she's involved, don't they?"

"She is involved," Sutcliffe says, "but she's as much a victim as the rest. She didn't do this. I don't think she did, at least. And now we have three different incidents of the cameras going offline. Gotta be the same person. Could that be done with a jammer of some sort? Or a hack?"

"Sure."

Sutcliffe taps his forefinger on the table, thinking. "Why didn't the theater cameras go offline?"

"He wasn't there?"

"Or he wanted to make sure we had a suspect to look at. Knox Shepherd."

"You're assuming Knox Shepherd and our camera jockey aren't the same person."

He sits back. "I am. Why am I assuming that?"

She raises an inky brow. "Because if Shepherd were responsible, he would have jammed the cameras at the theater that night to cover that he was there."

"Yes. That flies. Darian Jones told me there was a stalker who was leaving notes on her mother's social media—just a few words, over and over again: *Do You Remember?* The person was impossible to stop. She said that every time 'Liam, her computer guy,' filed a complaint and blocked a profile, another popped up in its place. She also said that the night Columbia died, the stalker's IP address registered in another state. She was totally dependent on the computer guy's word, right? She trusts him. Implicitly. And"—he's on his feet now, pacing—"the online barrage of hateful porn and accusations originated in Columbia Jones's social media feeds. There were deepfake videos, accusations that she murdered someone, that she was a fraud . . . and it all came from within her account to start."

Skye is nodding along. "It's time to pick up this Liam Reeves character. The DNA is enough to hold him for now. All of this online work is well within the power of a decent hacker. The physical part, too. It's sophisticated, but not rocket science."

"But proximity to her murder isn't enough to prove he did it. He's her IT guy, his hair could have fallen in her suitcase in New York and got disturbed. No, I need to prove he was actually there. I need to expand the coverage of the cameras at all of these scenes. Unless he managed to jam up the entire block, I bet he's on a traffic cam somewhere, either in Denver, or in New York. Having a shot of him would be really helpful. What's the range of jamming devices?"

"Depends on how sophisticated they are. If it's a small EMP, he could take the whole grid offline, but with the right equipment, a simple wireless jammer could easily block the camera signals on an entire Wi-Fi network. For it to be an extended period, he probably just left it in place."

"All right. I'll ask my folks in Denver to look for it. We were operating under the assumption it was a mistake, or that because a celebrity was in the hotel, they did it for privacy, but not if cameras at both MoMA and the Mathers crime scene were offline, too."

"The bigger question is, Where is Liam Reeves now? And more importantly, Where are Riley Carrington and Darian Jones?"

"Somewhere safe, supposedly, according to Darian. Nate Walsh has personal security, and he's whisked them off somewhere. But there's not a chance in hell they're safe from someone like this. I need to get some paper on Darian's phone and trace it. Then I'm going to take that flight to New York, and talk to the NYPD, see what we can't pull together from the two scenes in New York. What are you doing?"

Skye was typing furiously. "Looking for property records. Someone like Walsh will probably have their real estate through a trust or . . . That was easy. Thank you, *Architectural Digest*."

She turns the computer around, and Sutcliffe sees a high-end photograph of a cedar-shake mansion. "A six-page spread on their 'camp' near Portland, Maine. It's a private island. Ten bucks that's where they are. Someone like Walsh would have the false sense of security that an island full of guards would be enough of a deterrent."

"It's not?"

"Not if the girls are targets, too." A text dings, and she looks at her phone, then grabs the TV remote in the center of the table and turns on a twenty-four-hour cable news network. A reporter stands in front of the tie-crossing branding of a ranch.

"Columbia Jones's long-lost daughter has refused to comment. There's more to come on this story. Reporting live from Boulder, Colorado, this is Daniel Donnelly, WICK News."

Sutcliffe knocks on the table, thinking. "Kira Hutchinson. I interviewed her. She was at the hotel the night Columbia died. There was a VIP meet and greet, too. She's her long-lost daughter? What the hell am I missing?"

"Shhh. I'm thinking."

"Think faster."

"We need the prison records."

"Are they online? Digitized?"

Skye types furiously, then picks up the phone. "Hi, Ceena, it's Skye Abbott. Could you pull a prisoner record for me? Devon Mears, probably early 1996. Can you see if she had any medical interventions? Yes, I'll wait." To Sutcliffe: "Ceena's a genius at records. If there's anything to find, she'll find it. While we wait, what are your thoughts on Shepherd?"

"I don't have enough to tie him to *this*, for sure. Does he have the computer skills to pull off something this sophisticated? It doesn't feel right. And there's one other thing bugging me. Someone left Riley a note in her notebook that she was in danger. She talked to him, and he warned her to be careful. She feels it was the same person who spoke to her at the hotel when Columbia died. But she swears he's trying to protect her."

"Doesn't sound like the same person to me. I never have felt that Shepherd did it. But he's certainly been served up on a little platter, hasn't he?"

"He has. And with that cute kid and pretty wife, I don't know if he's going to make a break for it. He might. But he's a beneficiary in the will, too. The reading is May fifteenth, it's only a few days from now. Maybe see if he shows up."

"I can keep an eye out here for you, too, just in case."

"I'd appreciate that."

Her phone rings. "Ceena," she says and puts it to her ear. "Hi, whatcha got? Hold on, hold on. Seriously? Okay. That helps. Thanks." She hangs up, shaking her head slowly.

"Don't keep me in suspense."

"Devon Mears was pregnant when she was sentenced. And on March eleventh, 1996, she gave birth in the prison hospital."

"Let me guess. To a little girl named Kira."

"Even better. *Two* little girls. Twins. They went into DCS and were adopted out."

All the pieces of the puzzle lock together. "That explains it, then."

"Do tell," Skye says.

"Columbia Jones is Riley Carrington's mother. And Kira Hutchinson. And Darian Jones. They are all hers."

"And who's the father?"

"Benjamin Mears sired Darian, for sure. But I'll bet you Knox Shepherd is the father of the twins. The question is, Does he know?"

CHAPTER FIFTY-FOUR

Sutcliffe's phone rings with an unfamiliar Colorado number.

"Hold that thought," he says, and answers.

"This is Sheriff Jack Towers, Boulder County. I understand you're working the Columbia Jones case?"

"I am. What can I do for you?"

"I have some friends who've gotten into a bit of a jam. Name's Hutchinson."

"Kira Hutchinson?" Sutcliffe asks.

"And her husband, Luke. I understand you spoke with Mrs. Hutchinson about the murder?"

"I did. Don't tell me she's come to you complaining."

"Quite the opposite. She said good things. I wanted to touch base directly because we have a bit of a situation. Long story short, I just took a pail of rodent bait into evidence from a tack room on the Hutchinsons' ranch."

Sutcliffe puts the call on speaker. "Sheriff, I'm in Nashville with a colleague pursuing a lead. I'm looping her in. Meet Skye Abbott, my former partner and now a private investigator."

"Ma'am," the sheriff says, politely laconic. "So I've known Kira and Luke Hutchinson since we were kids. They called me when some reporters trespassed on their property, and the news had just leaked about the manner of death for Ms. Jones. Luke—Mr. Hutchinson—told me in an utterance how common that brodifacoum is, that there was rodent poison on their property. In light of the fact that Mrs. Hutchinson was interrogated in this murder investigation, I exercised caution and instructed him to freeze all operations until I could arrive with an evidence team. I was just being cautious, but we quickly found their spare tack room had been broken into, the lock was damaged. That's where he keeps the poison. We were able to take a pail into evidence, dusted for prints, the works. Nothing popped. But the good news is a trail camera near the barns caught a stranger entering their complex three weeks ago. I can send you that video if you give me a good address."

"I would appreciate that." Sutcliffe reels off his work email. "Any chance the Hutchinsons can ID this stranger?"

"No. But it sure feels weird to me, that Kira—Mrs. Hutchinson—is closely tied to a murder victim, and there's a break-in at their place, and there's a tie to the same poison that killed your victim. Is it true that Mrs. Hutchinson is the daughter of Ms. Jones? The media here have been having a ball."

"We don't know for sure, only DNA will tell, but we've uncovered evidence that Columbia Jones was a pseudonym for a woman named Devon Mears, who we've discovered had twins in jail who were given up for adoption. We think Kira is one of those twins. So yes, it's possible that what the media is saying is true."

"Are you gonna tell her that, or should I? 'Cause she's already pretty wigged out, and confirmation of this is gonna make things worse."

"I'll leave it to you, since you're friends."

"Let me ask you this. Where is all this coming from? How does the media have hold of the beneficiary-will letter? Your office been planting info out there to scare up a suspect?"

"Good question. If there's a leak, I don't think it's coming from my office, nor the OME. Not intentionally, anyway. We have a line on a suspect who's involved with a hacking group. It's possible he's gotten into our system, but we've held back a secondary COD, just because there's so much floating around. But we didn't have anything specific to Columbia Jones's will. That's coming from outside." Sutcliffe's email dings. "Hang on, I want to look at this video."

He pulls it up and hits play. He sees the shadow enter the barns, and then exit. When he does, his hat is pulled, but there's an angled view of the man's jaw and nose, more a profile than anything else, in shadow.

"You got a shot of his face."

"Sort of. Think there's enough to send to the FBI, see if they will put it in their NGI facial recognition database? I know this is a local matter, but I'm feeling pretty antsy that someone might be trying to frame the Hutchinsons. I will personally vouch for them, there's no way in hell they're involved in this woman's death."

"I understand. I will send this to my LT, she can get it into their system. This is really helpful, Sheriff. I'll be in touch when I get back to Colorado, or if there's a match, whichever happens first."

"Well, there's one more thing you should know. A lawyer just reached out to Kira. The reading of Columbia Jones's will is taking place tomorrow, in Maine."

"Maine?"

Skye puts out her finger and thumb in the shape of a gun. "Pow," she whispers.

"Yes. On a private island belonging to the Walsh family. They own—"

"*East Fifth Magazine.* Among other things. I appreciate the info. Is Mrs. Hutchinson going to Maine alone?"

"No, her husband will be traveling with her. She was told other beneficiaries are being flown in, as well. That's the other reason I wanted to give you the heads-up. I know how you city folk get when your suspects start moving about the country."

"Ha ha. She's not a suspect yet. But she is involved in this murder investigation, and you're right, I do appreciate the heads-up. Keep in touch, okay? I gotta go chase this down."

They hang up, and Skye is grinning. "Dude, this is getting good. That's confirmation on Walsh's island. Bet you ten bucks that's where Darian and Riley are, too."

"I am not taking that bet. But I need to get up there. I want to talk to Shepherd again before I go."

"Agreed." Skye plays with a piece of hair. "So Darian Jones has sisters. I have to say it . . . if she found out she wasn't the only one inheriting, that gives her one hell of a motive. And she's the only one who we know one hundred percent had access to Columbia Jones the night she was killed. She handled the CBD, her thumbprint is on the bottle."

"I know. You're not wrong. She's the one who stands to gain the most by her mother's death. Do we know for sure who's the father of the twins? Was it the husband, Benjamin Mears?"

"It's gotta be Shepherd. That's where the DNA match came from that let us pop him, remember? An open paternity case. Matched her "rapist" that night to Shepherd, which was when their whole story unraveled. Mears admitted she was lying about it being a stranger who killed her husband, and that she and Shepherd were having relations. It's part of her plea agreement, remember?"

"Vaguely. That's why Shepherd went to jail, right?" He scrambles through the paperwork and pulls the trial transcript. "Okay, I remember now. He said he heard screaming and entered the house to find Benjamin Mears beating his wife. He acted out of defense, hit Mears upside the head with a baseball bat. He then admitted he was having an affair with Devon Mears. They couldn't make the first-degree charge, so they dropped it to second."

"Correct. And you thought he was lying. You thought he was covering for her."

"I did. I still do. I think Shepherd got all noble and went to jail for his lover. And now I know why."

"Because she was pregnant. And her sentence was shortened, which meant she could get out and take care of the kids. They must be his. At least, he must think they are."

"So she wasn't raped that night at all?"

"Depends on how you define rape. Her husband forced her, so that qualifies in my book. And there were two DNA strains found, Shepherd and Mears. I don't know that she ever did a paternity test."

"So Devon has a couple of kids, who go into the system. Where is the tie to Liam Reeves? Why would he be going after her as Columbia?"

"Good question." They both go quiet, thinking. Sutcliffe closes his eyes, and can't help but see the 49 Spiders website: the twisting, swirling web of white on black pulsing, the spider skittering across the screen. And it hits him. All the pieces fall into place, and it all finally, finally makes sense. "'Oh, what a tangled web we weave, when first we practice to deceive.'"

"What?"

"The open paternity case. I'm going to go out on a limb here, but tell me if this doesn't make total sense. Liam Reeves is Knox Shepherd's son."

Skye's brows shoot to her hairline. "That's one hell of a leap."

"But admit it, it makes sense. And if he's Shepherd's son, that means he's related to both the twin daughters. He's related to Kira Hutchinson."

"You have the DNA from the crime scene—does it match Shepherd?"

"Again, time reveals all. I'll ask Duran to start looking."

"If he was there, then you have a shot at proving this wild theory."

"Yeah. Damn. It's going to take me weeks to sort through all of this, Skye. I have to prove Reeves was in Denver, and in that hotel room. If the stranger on the Hutchinsons' camera turns out to be Reeves, that's a big help. A DNA match to Shepherd would help tie this up nicely." He thinks for a few. "I'm going to try to get Darian to talk to me again before I do anything else. I want to send her a shot of Reeves. Make sure we're talking about the same person." He's already dialing her number, but the phone just rings and rings. He gets her voicemail.

"Miss Jones, this is Detective Sutcliffe. I have something important to discuss. Please call me as soon as you get this." He hangs up. "I want to warn her properly, but I have to assume that Reeves has access to her voicemail, too. I don't want to chase him off."

"Smart. Listen, I have a friend who could maybe take a quick look at the phone record and see where she was when she answered. We can confirm they're in Maine. Want me to look? It's going to cost. Favors, not money."

"Do it. I have a terrible feeling all of a sudden."

Skye excuses herself and leaves him staring at the figure of a spider in a red ball cap.

"Liam Reeves. Who the heck are *you*, buddy?"

His next call is back to his lieutenant. He fills her in, and ends with "Can we run the traffic and sidewalk cams in a four-block radius around the Brown Palace? I have a photo for facial recognition, we can get into the NGA database and see if he appears. If we can make a match, I think I have the killer."

His LT is very excited. "I will get right on it. When will you be back? The media is baying for blood, they cornered the Hutchinson girl and we had to work with the sheriff to get them off her property."

"I just spoke with him. That's where I've gotten the video to send you to go into the NGI database. There was an intruder on the Hutchinsons' property a few weeks ago, and he had access to pellets containing brodifacoum."

"So it's not Knox Shepherd?"

"It's not him on the video. I'm going to Maine. Columbia Jones's will is being read tomorrow, and they're flying in the beneficiaries. Shepherd is one of them. Kira Hutchinson is another. I have a trace starting on Darian Jones's phone, but I bet it pings to Walsh's estate. All the players are going to be in one place, and I'm concerned everyone involved is a target. I'll let you know what I find, you let me know if there's an ID on this intruder."

"Okay. But after the will reading, I need you back. You have cases here, too, Sutcliffe. Don't forget that."

"I won't, I promise. This is about to break. Trust me."

And as he says it, prophetically, his phone rings. He answers it, antsy for a run, to move, to clear his head. To think all the revelations through.

"Detective Sutcliffe? It's Knox Shepherd. I need to speak to you. I've just been summoned to a private home in Maine for the reading of Columbia Jones's will."

CHAPTER FIFTY-FIVE
KNOX

The last person Knox Shepherd wants to be sitting next to is the cop from Colorado.

But he's used to sacrifices; this is simply another in a long line of them.

No, the cop is one thing. But it's the girl and her husband that are making him shift uncomfortably in his seat. *Girl* isn't a fair assessment; she is a woman, certainly, and pregnant—that was shared when they got on board, and she bolted to the head before they took off. They've already been on the plane for two hours, flying in from Colorado to Nashville.

Her husband didn't need to explain what was happening; she has that look, glowing, inward. He recognizes it from Emily's three pregnancies. He thinks of his wife, and his daughter, and wonders why, exactly, he is on a plane flying into his past. What good will it do? Curiosity is never a friend to him. He is always better off keeping his head down, staying focused on his work, his family, his life. Walking out the door this morning, leaving the happy world he's created, was the hardest thing he's ever done, because he knows, knows in his very soul, that nothing will be the same again.

And yet here he is, with the cop and the girl and her glowering husband, and he can't help thinking of Devon.

He has spent years putting memories of her in a lockbox, never to be examined. But today, he must.

She was so young. He had no right to pursue her. That simple act set their course in motion. He ruined her life in so many ways. That's why, in the end, he didn't begrudge taking the sentence. He'd earned that for his mistake.

The heart wants what the heart wants. She was so broken when he found her. Her life had been inextricably altered by a simple mistake, thinking she loved a boy who, in the end, only wanted to hurt her, to blame her, instead of taking responsibility for his actions. Oh, yes, he'd done the "right thing" and married her when he learned of the pregnancy, but the carefree love of two teens can rarely sustain the need to grow up so quickly. To be a husband and father at eighteen, to give up dreams, to live in a small town and go from being a local hero to the one being gossiped about, is impossible.

So he took it out on the one person he could. The one he blamed for his downfall. The one who stared across the table with hopeful eyes, only to have that hope dashed again and again until it became desperation instead.

And Knox decided to play the hero, and look where it got them.

The echoes of these choices resound. He doesn't know what he's flying into. The cop is clacking away on his keyboard, headphones on, doing God knows what. He seems decent enough, as far as cops go; not a lot has altered over the years in the man's demeanor. He at least has kept an open mind, though he hasn't shared his thinking. When Knox called, Sutcliffe leaped on the opportunity to "informally escort" him to the reading, which is why he's on this plane and not in jail.

Knox showed him the letter he received with the ticket to Columbia's event in Denver, a simple *Forgive me, and come meet your daughter* typed on a sheet of paper. Sutcliffe was interested in that, for sure. It helped his credibility, that he hadn't sought her out, but had been invited. Then he asked if he'd ever done a paternity test, but the answer was no. He had girlfriends before Devon, of course he did, the most serious of which was a nurse at the hospital he worked at the year before he moved to Crossville, a year before he met Devon, but she certainly hadn't been pregnant. That, he would have known.

He'd taken one look at Riley Carrington and known immediately she was his. His protective instincts kicked in, and he knew he needed to warn her. Keep her safe. Someone had just murdered her mother, and he couldn't lose her, too, not when he'd just found her.

Sutcliffe understood that, too.

The girl—Kira—lies prone on the small sofa, a cool washcloth on her forehead. She reminds him of a young Devon, beautiful, fragile, and that makes him sick to his stomach, because there are things he now suspects, but doesn't know. And he certainly isn't ready to ask. Instead, he turns to the husband.

"Is there anything I can do? My wife swore by ginger tea when she had morning sickness."

Luke Hutchinson shakes his head. He is rugged and handsome, with tanned skin and a webbing of laugh lines extending from the corners of his eyes that makes him look older than his years. "Yeah, she gets like this. Motion always makes it worse. She'll be better when we land."

"You work horses?"

"I do. We have a ranch—well, Kira's parents own the ranch, but I do the day-to-day. Just had our foaling, haven't gotten a lot of sleep. What do you do for work?"

Knox looks at his hands, broad, capable, calloused from holding tools. "Construction, woodworking. Build some furniture. Tables, mostly. Turn some bowls."

They're off, discussing the best planing tools and cuts of wood, and the rest of the flight passes quickly, two men who work with their hands building the mutual respect that engenders. Luke certainly knows Knox is an ex-felon, there's no way the cop didn't mention it, but he doesn't bring it up, and Knox is grateful. His past always simmers beneath the surface, waiting to explode at just the wrong moment and burn everyone involved. It's always Emily who puts out the flames, and he misses her terribly right now.

They land in Portland, and a car is waiting for them. There is security, men not hiding their weapons, which makes him terribly nervous. He doesn't like guns. He doesn't like people who carry guns. He especially doesn't like being wedged inside a speeding vehicle with strangers bristling with weapons.

But the ride is short, and they are soon on a small boat, heading across the bay to the island. The sun has started to sink, and the sky is turning glorious oranges and pinks. A lipstick sunset, as the John Hiatt song goes. Kira gracefully vomits over the railing a couple of times, Luke holding back her hair, and Sutcliffe looks into the distance toward the heavily forested island approaching. He hasn't said much, and that makes Knox wonder what the hell is going on in his head.

He is at the mercy of this man, and he'd really like to know what's going to happen.

But he bites his tongue, hands over a bottle of cool water to the girl, who collapses in a damp heap next to her husband, groaning a little, and takes a seat himself, waiting. It's something he's learned how to do, and he excels at it. Prison teaches patience. The air smells of salt and fish and fog, and he shuts his eyes, saying a prayer to a God he no longer believes in to give him strength for whatever is ahead.

They arrive at the dock, and Kira and Luke are escorted off first. Knox follows, with the cop striding by his side, a backpack thrown over his shoulder.

"Nice place," Sutcliffe says, whistling when the camp shows itself between the trees.

Rich people, that's all Knox can think. The people he makes furniture for. He's not meant to socialize with them, nor stay in their houses. Yet here he is. This is the world Devon moved in. The people who surrounded "Columbia Jones" were ones so unlike her past, so unlike him. He would have never fit in and is almost relieved she never tried to make him.

"Yeah. Nice place," he says, and Sutcliffe casts a glance his way.

"You okay?"

"Sure. Peachy. Uncertainty is great for me."

The cop narrows his eyes, then seems to make up his mind about something and shows Knox a photo on his phone. The screen shows an unfamiliar young Army recruit in uniform.

"Watch out for this guy, okay? I just sent out an official BOLO. He's a suspect in Devon's murder, we have facial recognition from both the Hutchinsons' ranch and from a traffic cam near the Brown Palace Hotel. Name's William Reeves, goes by Liam. Computer hacker, former Army, washed out early after a noncombat accident here in the States. This photo is a decade old. He has ties to Darian and Columbia Jones, he was working their IT. In case you see him, let me know."

Knox memorizes the face, forcing down the spike of anger. Though Sutcliffe hasn't said it, he knows in his gut this is the man who killed Devon. This stranger, who was supposed to be a hero, turned bad somewhere along the way. He'd seen plenty like this one in prison. One wrong decision can send a life spiraling into chaos. Some relished it, some were spooked by it. But in the end, they all ended up the same. Twisted.

"You got it."

Then another stranger comes to the path to greet them, and Knox shuts up and watches. It's what he does best.

He notices a tall blonde fleeing into the woods, down toward the beach—*Riley. God. She is a stunner, like Devon could have been if she wasn't cowed by Mears*—then lets his mind refocus on the man standing in front of him.

"I'm Nate Walsh. Welcome to my home."

CHAPTER FIFTY-SIX
RILEY

Our mother.

When Darian touches Riley's cheek, searching her face, her eyes, looking for traces of Columbia, Riley freezes, realizing that what she's wanted since that horrible night her world was torn apart is coming true.

Family. A real family.

She doesn't want to scare Darian off, and she doesn't know how to approach all the emotions coursing through her. The joy and the guilt and the sorrow and the possibility. The confusion, the assumptions—let's not pretend they aren't all making a massive leap of faith here—turning suppositions into facts. But in the gentleness of that touch, the acceptance, Riley sees at last the shell Darian has around her, as intense as a force field, falling away, and the vulnerability in her eyes is too much.

She can't be in the house with Darian a moment longer. She knows she's leaping to conclusions, something that's been trained out of her: get the facts, then make the call, that's what Nate has always said. But like it or not, it's becoming quite clear she is related to Darian Jones, and that somewhere out there, another sister lurks, waiting to be unearthed. It makes her frantic to find out the whole truth, and she knows that's why Columbia wanted them all together. There's going to be something she's left with the lawyers that will blow this story wide open, some sort of explanation.

The sun is setting, and she just wants to go stand by the water and watch it slip behind the trees and feel the soft air caress her skin. And she wants to do it alone.

"I need a minute," she says, and Darian nods.

"I do, too, actually. We can tackle the files in a bit. Let's take a break." She darts a glance toward Mason, who immediately moves to her side, and Riley almost bursts out laughing. The two of them are heat-seeking missiles, magnets. Where one moves, the other has an equal, opposite movement. They bump together, then apart, a hand brush here, a look there, and it makes her sad and happy at once, and the longing for Oliver creeps into her being. She's been doing a good job compartmentalizing, but seeing the two of them so obviously in love is not helping.

"Thank you," Riley says. She waves off Nate as he starts to follow her outside. "I'm just taking a walk. I'll be back. We came here to be safe, yeah?"

His brows furrow in concern but he nods. She's grateful as hell for the protection he's provided, the leeway to figure out what's happening, but she's also a very independent woman and has been under lock, key, and perpetual scrutiny for the past few days, and that combined with all the emotions she's feeling is too much. It's getting to her.

"Don't be long, okay? I see the boat's here with the rest of our guests."

More people. Great. "Back in a few," she assures him.

She heads out the living room doors that open onto the back deck. Down the stairs, breathing in the salty air. It rained while they were talking, and the sandy path has little puddles she has to skirt. She sees the group of people—three men and a woman—coming up from the dock and veers down the other path. She just can't do all this right now. She needs to be by the water. She just needs time to process.

She glances over her shoulder. The woman who scurries up the path, pale and slightly green, is the third of their triad. The man next to her must be her husband; he looks worried, seems to be holding up his wife with his left arm alone. There is Sutcliffe, marching along, and a third man, dark curly hair. Knox Shepherd. He is the man from the hotel. He is the man from the theater.

He is probably her father.

She stops, watching him, and he turns to look at her. Their eyes meet, and a small smile lights on his face. Wistful. Hopeful.

She turns away and dives down the path.

The hope is almost too much.

The shells crunch under her feet, and Riley finds an Adirondack chair by the water and sinks into it. The beach is rocky, the sand probably brought in, but it is quiet, and she shuts her eyes, listening to the water lap the shore. A metronome of waves, little wet crashes, the squawk of sailing birds, a long warning horn in the distance. She breathes. Calming, centering. She hasn't had time to exercise, meditate, exist outside of reacting for what seems like days, and this moment of quiet feels so good. She thinks.

Of mothers.

Of fathers.

Of sisters.

The air turns cool, and she opens her eyes to see a fog bank rolling in, fast. She watches, fascinated, as it grows and thickens, the clouds building, creeping ever closer, until she can no longer see the mainland, nor the dock, nor the boat that's brought the strangers to her life. Just as quickly, it sweeps on land, and she is enveloped. The mist cools her skin and makes her shiver, droplets forming. She doesn't have a sweater, and now it is dark, cold. She must go back to the house.

She stands reluctantly, puts on her shoes, and starts back, only to realize she has no idea where she is. The fog has enveloped her entirely, and she can't see the path back to the house.

"Shit."

She takes a step, then another. Another. Should she wait it out? Surely they aren't going to be socked in all night. She shivers again; no, she's chilled to the bone and must get inside.

She hears something, off to her right, in the brush. It sets off her heart, and she lurches forward, hands stretched out in front of her. She hits a tree, and a small nervous laugh escapes her lips. She'll just keep ping-ponging her way back; the path is lined with pines and spruce.

She moves forward again, hits another tree, then another, and then, a hand grasps hers.

"There you are. I was starting to get worried. Did you enjoy your lobster roll? I made them especially for you."

That voice.

A man's face appears from the gloom. He has shiny skin and is wearing a red ball cap.

It is him. The one from the museum.

"No!" she says in horror, trying to rip her hand away, but he laughs.

"Oh, Riley. Stop. I don't want to hurt you. It's not time for that yet."

"Who are you?" she spits, teeth gritted, then screams, full and loud. "Nate! Nate!"

The man slaps a hand over her mouth, and she claws at him, biting, and he grunts with anger. "Don't make me hurt you. Stop it, right now."

"You killed Oliver," she tries to say but he has his hand so firmly over her mouth her lips are cutting into her teeth.

She panics. What is he going to do to her? Is he going to kill her, too?

"Riley!" She hears her name being called. The voice is so far away. She has gotten turned around in the fog and moved away from the house instead of toward it.

"Riley!" Another voice calls, this one a bit closer.

"They're coming for you, sweetheart," the man says. He kisses the side of her head and releases her, shoving her to the ground, and then she is alone. She hears his retreat through the gravelly sand.

She cries out, "Nate, Nate I'm here." And then the curly-haired man she saw on the dock appears.

"Hey. Hey, I got you. I'm Knox. You okay?"

Is she? No. She is not. But she lies, so relieved to have been released.

"Yeah. I think so. Who was that man?"

"I've got her. I found her," he calls, voice strong through the mist. And then Nate is there, and he yanks her body to his, holding her in his arms.

"What happened? You got lost in the fog?"

"No. He's here! The man from the museum, the man who killed Oliver. He's here. Knox scared him off."

"How could he be . . . We've had everything on lockdown."

"I don't know but he is. Please, can we get inside?"

Nate and Knox walk her back up the path, and she feels like a complete idiot. It was right there the whole time.

"People get disoriented in the fog," Nate says. "It rolls in so quickly sometimes we don't have time to get everyone inside."

"You're okay?" Knox asks.

"I'm fine," she says, though she feels shaky and scared. "Thank you for finding me."

"Sure," he says gruffly, then they're on the porch and inside the house. Nate shuts the sliding doors behind her. "I'm going to let security know what just happened," he says grimly. "They need to organize a search, figure out how he got onto the island. Damn it."

"He said something about making the lobster rolls, maybe he was with the caterers."

Nate looks even more alarmed. "Jesus. No one eat anything. I'll let them know."

Riley sees the whole room of people staring at her, strangers and the familiar, all distorted now by her fear. The blonde woman and her handsome cowboy husband, Darian and Mason, Knox, Detective Sutcliffe.

It's a trap. It's been a trap all along. He's herded them like cattle to the slaughter.

"We're not safe here," she says. "He's come for us. He knows too much, he knew we would be here. He was waiting."

And as the words leave her mouth, the lights go out in the house.

CHAPTER FIFTY-SEVEN
KIRA

Lightning strikes, the storm following the fog as sudden as the switching off of the lights. The beautiful sunset only an hour earlier was a lie.

Nate Walsh calls to the room. "Hold tight. There's a generator, it will kick in momentarily. The lightning can trigger the breaker. Happens all the time in storms."

The room is filling with people; Kira can sense them. Luke squeezes her hand. Then the lights come back on with a snap. Everyone murmurs in relief. Nate has returned with a couple of his security guards. A young man someone calls Tony is with them, eyes wide.

Riley Carrington is pale as a ghost but moves to his side immediately. "You okay?" Nate asks her.

"Yeah."

"What the heck is going on?" Kira asks quietly. "Are we truly not safe?"

Riley's eyes are huge. Kira feels an odd zing—she's seen that look on the boys' faces when they have a nightmare. "There's a man who's been stalking me, and he's here, on the island. He grabbed me out in the fog."

The detective steps toward Riley. "Is this the man?"

She looks at his phone. "I don't know. Maybe? He's got shiny skin, like he has a skin graft or something. He was wearing a red baseball cap, both tonight and the last time I saw him."

Darian steps forward. "Let me see."

The cop shows her his phone, and she stares at it. "That's not possible."

"You know this man?"

"Yes. I mean, he's much younger in this photo, but it's Liam Reeves. He's our computer IT expert. Why do you have a picture of him?"

"Because I believe he killed your mother."

"But it's . . . Liam," Darian says, disbelief in her voice. The tall red-headed man next to her, he'd been introduced as her boyfriend Mason, shakes his head.

"Have you done any sort of age progression? Do you have a more current photo?"

The cop shakes his head. "No. We're working on it."

"I could probably help with that," Tony says. "I have an AI program with a filter that ages you. Let me see what I can do."

Sutcliffe tries to text the kid the photo, only to realize it won't go through. "I don't have any service. Mr. Walsh, how long will the generator hold?"

"Nate, please. A few hours. We have time. But yeah, the internet is down. I don't know why, it doesn't usually go out when we have storms."

"Can we get off the island?" the detective asks.

"In this?" Another crash of lightning, and the heavens open, rain coming down hard and fast. "Not advisable to get on a boat until it calms down. Y'all just made it here. I wish you hadn't, I wish the storm had kept you from the crossing. I feel responsible for this disaster."

"There's safety in numbers. I'd want to talk to the head of your security and get a plan in place for how we're going to keep everyone safe. Figure out how this guy got on the island in the first place."

"I'll take you to him," Nate says, leading Sutcliffe from the room. Knox follows them, leaving Luke and Mason to watch over them.

"This is crazy," Kira says to Luke. "I have to lie down, I'm feeling ill again."

Luke makes a nest for her on the sofa, both Darian and Riley watching her as if she is a bomb that could go off at any moment. When she's settled, she gestures to them.

"Come talk to me."

They approach warily. Riley sits on the floor, Darian on the sofa. They look at her, and she at them.

"Is it true? Am I Columbia's daughter?"

Darian nods once. "I think so. Riley, too. We won't know until there's DNA done, obviously, but my mother left some notes for Riley that certainly seem to confirm it."

Kira shuts her eyes for a moment, then stares at Riley. "I had no idea. Did you?"

Riley is staring at her, too. Kira can see the resemblance between them.

Riley smiles. "No. But I'm really glad to meet you."

"I am, too. I am having trouble wrapping my head around this. Columbia Jones has always been a hero of mine. To go from meeting her in person to a few days later finding out I'm related to her? It's mind blowing."

Riley nods. "Completely mind blowing."

Before they can go further, there is shouting outside the house, and the sharp retort of a gunshot. Its muffled echo gets lost in the storm. There is a second shot, echoing, louder, then a spray of bullets and screams, then silence.

Moments later, Knox appears in the doorway, eyes wild, and beside him, a man in a red ball cap, who has a large weapon pointed at the older man.

"Over to the wall, all of you. Line up." He shoves Knox toward the group, and Kira sees the weapon he's holding is a submachine gun of some sort. Plenty of ammunition to eliminate all of them in a few seconds.

"Babe, get behind me," Luke whispers. She senses nothing but anger in his voice, puts a hand on his arm so he doesn't try to play the hero. He's grown up around guns—they own a ranch in the wilderness; knowing how to use them is unavoidable—and is the type of man who would consider it noble to sacrifice himself to save people. She can't let him do anything like that.

Darian looks flabbergasted. "Liam? What are you doing?"

"Shut up," he snarls, pointing the weapon at her, and she retreats, alarmed.

But Riley steps forward. "Where's Nate?" she spits out.

The man in the ball cap moves, his mouth stretching across his cheeks in a creepy approximation of a smile. "He won't be bothering us. Nor will his security team, or that stupid cop. God, they are a mess. Wandering around outside in the fog, thinking they've protected all the entrances. It took all of five minutes to set a fire and draw them into the boathouse. Those doors lock from the outside. They're going to be like me, soon enough."

He points to his cheek. Kira realizes she can smell smoke, and horror fills her.

Mason has Darian behind him, just like Luke has with Kira. They're making themselves targets on purpose. Knox, though, stands with Riley, shoulder to shoulder. He tried to step in front of her, but she shoved him off.

"What do you want?" she demands, becoming their spokesperson. She is going to fight for them, and Kira is suffused with emotion. Her sister. This is her *sister*.

Dear God, please don't let us die before we can get to know each other.

"Hmm. Excellent question," Liam Reeves answers at last. He swings the weapon from one side to the other casually. It is strapped to his chest; he won't be easily unarmed. "All the usuals, I suppose. Money.

Love. Happiness. You know how it is. You of all people know how life can take a sudden turn, don't you, Riley? Poor Oliver."

"Money? So this is a robbery? You've followed us out here to steal from us?" The disdain in Riley's voice makes Kira stand up a little straighter. This woman is fierce.

"Steal from you. Yeah. I guess you could call it that. You're inheriting *millions*." He enunciates the syllables, biting at them. "A few falling off the cart into my pocket won't hurt you a bit. Say five, six mil, and we'll call it even?"

Darian chimes in, fury in her voice. "Why didn't you just ask for the money? Why kill my mother? She would have given it to you if you'd told her you needed it, no questions asked."

"Your mother? *Their* mother, too." He uses the weapon to point to Kira and Riley. "All three of you, sweet little sisters who had no idea the other existed until I came along. I've done you a favor, don't you realize that? And trust me, I tried. I asked nicely. Columbia would barely give me a raise, much less a cut. I asked gently at first, made it clear there would be repercussions if she didn't help me out. She just wouldn't see sense.

"But you . . . you're smart, Darian. You'll make a deal for the lives of your sisters, and I will ride off into the sunset with enough cash to last me three lifetimes. Won't you?"

"Sure," Darian says. "You can have whatever you want. As soon as you explain why you killed my—our—mother. Is it really just about money? Or is there something else you want to tell us?"

He taps the side of his nose. "Money, yes. But this is about the truth." He's pacing now, enunciating the words. The stage is cleared for the main character to give his soliloquy, and it's almost as if he's planned it, rehearsed it. Kira feels Luke squeeze her hand, squeezes back in response, understanding what he's telegraphing. The more Liam talks, the better chance someone can make a move on him. He shifts her a bit to the right, and Darian grabs her other hand. The connection centers her.

"Your mother was living such a huge lie. You went along with it, too, helping her write the books that made her famous. Pretending to be this perfect little daughter, managing her mommy's career, helping her get more famous, more rich. And here she was, masquerading as a saint, when in fact she was a cold-blooded murderer."

"Where are you even getting this from?"

"Oh, you haven't seen the video yet, have you?" He laughs. "Took you long enough to crack that flash drive. Boy, you're going to be surprised. Columbia Jones was a total fraud. She murdered a man, and she let *him* take the fall for it, and then she reinvented herself and got stinking rich." He points the barrel of the gun at Knox. "And *you* let her, you complete idiot. You took the blame. She had some magical snatch on her, I guess."

"Don't you speak of her like that," Knox snaps.

"Yeah, whatever. How much did you get in the end, huh? Did she even reach out and give you a teensy little bit of help? No, she let you twist. She let you go to jail for her. You're gonna get some blood money now, but does it matter? She ruined your life."

"Why do you care?" Riley challenges. "Why do you care what she did to strangers?"

"Because Knox Shepherd is my father!" he screams. "And that makes me your brother."

"That's not true," Knox says. "You're out of your mind."

"You are such a fool, Dad."

Kira can't even wrap her head around what's being said. "I'm going to be sick," she mutters to Luke.

"You have to let me take her to the bathroom," Luke says to Reeves, who laughs meanly.

"Puke all over Walsh's pretty little sofa. I don't care. You'll be dead and I'll be gone."

The smell of smoke is getting stronger and stronger, and there's a tang to it, a strange chemical spice, and she can't hold back anymore. She turns away from the group and gags, and at that moment, Knox Shepherd launches himself toward Liam with a roar of fury.

CHAPTER FIFTY-EIGHT
DETECTIVE SUTCLIFFE

Sutcliffe comes to, realizes there is smoke forming all around him. The flames are getting nearer, warming his legs, and he scrambles away in the dark out of pure instinct. He uses the meager light from the fire to locate Walsh and the rest of the security team. He doesn't want to underestimate Reeves anymore; the man's managed to subvert a six-man security team with some sort of knockdown gas, and now there's a fire encroaching. He takes a breath and wishes he hadn't: the chemical tang makes him cough. He can feel it curling in his lungs, poisoning his blood. God knows what this is, some sort of homemade gas—but it's not fatal. At least, not yet.

He crawls away from the fire and smells fresh air. He takes a sip of the cool breeze and then another. The open window is dissipating the gas; it's probably the only thing that's saved them. There's a thick curtain blocking the air. He manages to yank on it, and it comes down. Air whooshes in, but that helps the fire get purchase.

He digs his phone from his pocket. The service is down, but the flashlight still works.

Walsh is in the far corner, pale as a ghost, blood leaking from his side. That's not good. The rest of the security team are in various positions, either dead or knocked out from the gas, he doesn't know which.

The fire crackles, and he stops wondering and gets his feet under him. He is oddly off balance. He stumbles to the door and isn't surprised to find it locked. The window is the only way out.

It takes an interminable time to drag each man across the planks to the window and shove them out. His lungs are burning, and by the time he gets to Walsh, he fears it's too late for them both. The fire is spreading faster now, flames licking at Walsh's leg. Sutcliffe is feeling unbelievably weak, but he manages to drag Walsh a few feet, then a few more, and finally gets him to the window. He shoves him up and through but has to rest before he can follow. He is nauseated from the gas, and his head is swimming. He is covered in blood; a few of the guards have been shot as well—a submachine gun, his mind helpfully provides, maybe an HK MP5 or MP7, he couldn't tell exactly in the dark, though it sounds right—but the night air, foggy still, lets him breathe fully at last.

When his head clears a bit, he crawls to Walsh. Being pushed out the window has made the wound in Walsh's side bleed heavily, and his pulse is thready. Not good. They need a medical evac, right away. He triages the others: three dead, two wounded, one woozy and starting to come to. Maybe there's a phone that works, a landline that's not dependent on the wireless signal.

But that means getting into the house.

Sutcliffe totters to his feet again and fights his way to the path. The flames are rising, and he's hopeful that someone on the mainland might see them and call for help. He double-checks the wounded aren't in the range of the flames, then staggers toward the house. He falls twice; he's lightheaded and his ears are ringing, but the chuckling fire behind him drives him forward. He manages to get to the porch that leads to the living room and crawls up the stairs to see a row of people standing against the wall, like lambs to the slaughter. He stands with a shout just as Knox Shepherd bursts from the group and charges across the room.

A volley of bullets, and the glass shatters, the huge floor-to-ceiling window collapsing into pieces on the porch. Sutcliffe has his hand on his weapon and is through the glass, adrenaline kicking out the rest of the muzziness from the gas, to see Shepherd wrestling with Liam Reeves. There is cacophony as Riley, Darian, Kira, and Luke realize the window has been blown out and start scrabbling out onto the deck, shouting, and Sutcliffe gets in past them just in time to see Mason Bader step to the scrum of Shepherd and Reeves, call out something, then shoot Reeves in the head.

Reeves goes limp, light dying in his eyes, the red ball cap falling to his side the same shade as the blood leaking from the hole in his forehead.

Shepherd rolls to the side onto his back, chest heaving.

Sutcliffe draws down on Mason. "Put down the weapon, put it down, put it down. Police, police!" he shouts, coughing and staggering closer, and the big man complies.

"He's down, he's down," Mason says, and Sutcliffe can see that but feels for a pulse anyway, kicking the MP7 away, realizing it's a miracle they aren't all dead after Reeves sprayed the group with bullets outside.

"It's over," Mason says, his face full of shock. "Oh my God, what happened to you?"

Sutcliffe looks down, knowing he is covered in blood. "Not mine."

"Yeah, it is," Mason says. "Dude, your head!"

"Walsh needs help," Sutcliffe manages, before the darkness takes him and he pitches headfirst to the carpet.

CHAPTER FIFTY-NINE
COLUMBIA

A Moment Before the End

It is deeply dark when Columbia, frustrated by a restless few hours, climbs from her warm nest of a bed and pads out to the hotel's living room. There is no light from the hallway where Darian's room lies. At least someone's getting some sleep. Of course, she might be off with Mason. They think they're being subtle, but anyone with half a brain can tell they're sleeping together. Half a brain, or a mother's instinct. She hopes they're being careful; Darian is a grown woman but a young one. That is Columbia's fault. She's not given her a chance to go out into the world, to stumble and fall on her own. She subsumed her into the business as soon as she graduated because it was the best way she knew to protect her. Of course, she can't tell her that. Darian would lose her mind if she thought Columbia was worried about her.

No, this little dalliance with Mason has been good for her. She's blooming.

Columbia hates it when they fight. She and Darian have always had an edge to their relationship, but the older Darian gets, the more it rears its head. She will apologize in the morning. Calling Darian names was childish, and Columbia is not proud that she lost her temper. She's just feeling off, has been this whole tour. No wonder, with everything happening: she's never known when a stranger will pop out of the crowd and ruin her life. Worry, fear, stress, all of it collided in a perfect storm tonight. Onstage!

She is mortified. It's her worst nightmare, getting ill before an event, not being able to put on a good show.

Well, you put on a show tonight, all right.

She replays the ER doctor's warning that she needs rest. Real rest. And a full workup from her doctor when she gets home. Apparently, the hospital's tests tonight showed her blood isn't clotting properly. He suggested she might have some sort of vitamin deficiency. The way she's feeling, she wouldn't be surprised. Run down. Nauseated. Frustrated. Scared.

She sits at the hotel room's dining table and opens her computer, silently berating herself for her inability to sleep. It's something that's happened more and more lately, these diurnal disruptions. It's her age, she's been told by her doctor. She's starting the change, and it's going to be a rough few years. She knows it's that, but more; it's the low-level anxiety humming through her, keeping her on constant alert, waiting for her world to disintegrate. But she is not willing to concede, fights every night. They've offered prescriptions, but she hates drugs. Darian brought along a bottle of CBD oil that she got at the dispensary near their home in New York. It doesn't really work, makes her nauseated enough that she hasn't wanted to use it, but she will try it again later, if only to appease her daughter's frustrated nagging. Everything is starting to suffer from her insomnia. Passing out onstage, for God's sake. The lights were bright, she hadn't eaten, and yes, maybe she needs a physical, but still. How embarrassing.

Admit it. You just don't want to think about him.

But she must. She knows what this means.

It was one thing seeing Kira tonight. She needs to thank Liam again for making sure she received the tickets. But to also see the ghost of her past rise from the loge box—she panicked. The threats have been relentless, and clearly, he's determined to ruin her.

She can't even form his name on her tongue. Just the thought of him brings such a sharp pain to her heart that she gets lightheaded and breathless again. The doctors at the hospital have no idea. She is unwell for too many reasons, and can't share any of them. Everything—her entire world—is about to unravel, and she is helpless to stop it. She's been on a speeding train toward a wall for months now.

She's taken all the precautions she can. She's indulged her curiosity. She's seen and talked to all the parties involved.

Now she waits. It won't be long. She can feel him there, lurking, ready to drop a nuke into her world. The only one who knows everything. She doesn't blame him for hating her, not anymore.

She opens the laptop. Opens the browser, goes to the webmail server. The email sits there, waiting, as she knew it would. The message as cruel and heartless as all the others.

It's over. Go public. Tell the world the truth. Or I will.

And one more that comes as she's watching, as if he's been waiting for her to open the computer. It's the one she's known was coming.

Time's up.

This little byplay has gone on for months now, and as soon as she sees the email, or direct message, it disappears. She's had Liam looking into it, and he's trying to break the connection, but her stranger has skills. And she can't tell Liam the truth. To do so would be to expose herself. So she's suffered in silence and let this little game go on unremarked. Publicly, they post innocuously unidentifiable comments: *Do You Remember?* Privately, they tear her heart from her chest, over and over again.

Now that the tour is finished, now that she's gambled with everyone's lives and won, now that her ghost has been dragged back into her life, she must put an end to it. She has to involve the authorities. She has to tell Darian the truth and pray for her forgiveness. Has to gamble, one last time, on the world not hating her too much when they find out the whole story.

At least she's got everything in order. No matter what happens now, all her people are taken care of.

She closes the computer and goes to the bathroom. She almost doesn't recognize herself without the wigs and makeup anymore. She will never recognize the woman in the mirror, regardless. The one who started with a little dream, who saw her world shattered into a million pieces, who sacrificed and suffered, who rose to take over the literary world, and who now is being undone by an anonymous troll . . . After what she's been through, this, this is nothing.

A bit of fire returns to her eyes.

Tomorrow, as soon as she finishes with Riley, she will sit Darian down, and she will tell her the truth. They will face this together, if Darian stands by her side. Maybe she will tell Riley the truth of her involvement, too, if all goes well. And then she'll move to Kira, and the rest of her beloveds. Her beautiful, stunning grandchildren.

But right now, her heart thick with sorrow, she can't stand being awake a moment longer. She wants to find the blissful oblivion that sleep brings, just once more.

She pulls the cap off the bottle of CBD drops and drips ten of them under her tongue, then ten more, for good measure, shuts off the light and returns to her bed.

She hears the door to the suite squeak. Darian, coming back from her evening's dalliance. Footsteps pad closer to her door, pause, and she starts to call out "Good night," but before she can, her heart starts to hammer in her chest, her mouth is filled with bitterness, and darkness overtakes her.

She doesn't hear the door to her room open. Doesn't sense the quiet steps, the body next to her, the hatred, the seething hatred, raining down upon her being. Doesn't feel the needle.

Doesn't know anything, anymore.

FRIDAY

CHAPTER SIXTY
RILEY

Now

Riley finds herself in another hospital, on the other side of the country, this time visiting multiple people. The Maine Medical Center was the only Level I trauma hospital nearby, and the mass casualty event that was their night at Nate's place is all over the news. Mason saved both Nate's and Sutcliffe's lives; without him there, his medical acumen, they both would have died. Sutcliffe had taken a shot to the head that penetrated his skull but didn't make it through to his brain, a completely lucky circumstance. And while Nate made it through surgery, the doctors had to remove his spleen, and he was touch and go for hours. He's now resting in the ICU, and she's just given him a kiss goodbye to go touch base with Sutcliffe before she leaves. It is time to put an end to this chaos.

Because of the catastrophe, they moved the reading of the will back to New York, and the beneficiaries—all still alive, all still well—herself, Darian, Kira, and Knox, accompanied by Luke and Mason, of course, will be heading to New York in an hour.

The threat has been neutralized. Liam Reeves's apartment has been torn apart by the feds, NYPD, and the Denver Police, who sent another representative the moment they heard Sutcliffe was injured. A baggie of rodent-poison pellets was found, along with so much explosive matériel that when the bomb squad showed up to secure the area, people were evacuated for a three-block radius. Liam Reeves was planning on killing more than just Columbia Jones. The knockdown gas he developed had been sickening people in his apartment building for weeks, though no one knew where their symptoms were coming from. His computers were seized, and there were experts trying to get into them to no avail—but the hacker was going to be hacked properly, sooner or later.

Riley knocks on the door of Sutcliffe's room and enters. His head is wrapped in a large white bandage, his blue eyes as vibrant as the sky against his pale skin.

"Hey," she says. "You feeling okay?"

"Sure, ready to run a marathon." His voice cracks: the damage from the gas is going to take a while to get all the way out of his system. It's burned his vocal cords.

"I just wanted to say thank you. You saved us."

"I think Mr. Shepherd did that. I just stood there and screamed."

"That's not how I remember it. You both took him down. Mason, too."

"Thank God for Mason." She knows he means it. Nate had shown him where security had stashed a weapon in a drawer on the sofa table, just in case, and he'd had the presence of mind to grab it when the chaos began.

"We're heading to New York, they're going to read Columbia's will at the law offices instead of here. Though I hardly think there's anything left to learn."

"You never know. Be careful, okay?"

"Liam's dead."

"Guys like that don't always work alone. He might have friends out there."

"Ugh. Okay, I'll be on alert forever. Thanks." She laughs a little. "Is there anyone I can call for you?"

"Naw, I'm good. My people have all been in touch. Just do me a favor?"

"Anything."

"Let me know what the end result is, okay? I have to admit, I am curious if there's more to what Reeves discovered."

"Will do. Take care, Detective."

They assemble in the Mathers and Mathers law offices. Riley is dreading seeing Oliver's dad, but when he comes in, a carbon copy of his son down to the glasses, and comes to her side, sweeping her into a huge hug, she is relieved after all.

"I'm so sorry," she says, tearing up. "I am so sorry."

"I am, too, Riley," he says. "I hope, when all of this is done, you won't forget about us."

"Of course I won't. I thought you'd rather me not be around. Since it's my fault he was killed."

"It is not your fault. Never think that. It was Liam Reeves who killed Oliver. Not you." His voice cracks with emotion, and she squeezes him tight. This decent man might have been her family, eventually. It is strange to be here, knowing her life has taken a jagged turn, that the future she'd expected will not materialize.

"Let's get started, shall we?" Preston says, releasing her and gesturing to the table.

Luke and Mason, not being beneficiaries, are asked to wait outside, while Riley, Kira, Darian, and Knox enter the conference room and take seats at the table. Another man is there, and Darian introduces him as Victor Guul, Columbia's lawyer. There is a bowl of fruit, and cookies on a plate, and water, tea, and coffee. No one takes anything. They all just want this done.

Preston Mathers clears his throat. "As you know, Columbia Jones approached me last year to update her will. She did so of sound mind, and not under duress, at least not that I was aware of, though as we've learned, there was more to the story. She brought me a video that she asked to be shown before the formal reading of the will. I will now play that video."

Riley glances at Darian and Kira, giving them both a reassuring smile. Finally, they are going to get an explanation for why there has been so much destruction, so much death, including Columbia's own.

They are not disappointed.

Columbia's face fills the screen in front of them. Her natural hair is down and curled, and all three girls suck in a breath. They do resemble their mother; they've seen more photos of Devon Mears and can pick out their features easily now.

"Hello. My name is Columbia Jones. I don't know if you know me as Columbia, or Mother, or Devon, but regardless, I owe you an apology. I haven't been honest with you. None of you. And I hope it's not too late to make amends."

CHAPTER SIXTY-ONE
DEVON

"You've read the story by now. It mimics the truth, as well as such a thing can. I don't want to blame my tender age or my ridiculous circumstances on what happened. I found Knox intoxicating. I couldn't get enough of him. He was kind. Handsome. Electrifying. He made me realize how horrible Benjamin was. That we could never sustain a marriage, that he would have killed me eventually.

"But it was all my fault. I was the one who pursued Knox. Yes, he flirted, but I wanted him.

"I was the one who started taking walks in the park by the hospital, and he started taking breaks to get some fresh air at the same time. We'd wander, and we'd talk, and soon enough, we fell in love. He was so gentle with me. So kind.

"The affair was a mistake. I think we both knew it. I was never dishonest in my feelings. I loved my husband. Truly, I did. And I didn't want a divorce. I was just so bored, with everything. So claustrophobic. And Benjamin was unpredictable, becoming more volatile than kind.

"When Knox and I met, and he started to flirt, I flirted back because it felt good to be appreciated. To be seen.

"What he saw in me I will never understand, cliché that I was— the idiot high schooler who managed to get herself pregnant on prom night, who did the remainder of her senior year full of baby. Benjamin had to give up his scholarship to UT and get a job in his dad's law office. When we got married, I had just turned eighteen and was showing. It was quite the scandal.

"Knox didn't care about any of that. He saw me, only me. He wanted to take me and the baby away from everything.

"We knew Benjamin wouldn't let that happen. We knew there must be another path.

"He must have known we were up to something, though. When I came home, instead of finding Benjamin at the base of the stairs with a broken neck, he and Knox were locked in battle. I panicked.

"'Knox,' I said. 'Don't.'

"Oh, the betrayal on their faces. Both of them. The horror from Benjamin when he realized what was happening, that it wasn't a stranger invading his home. The anger from Knox at me trying to stop him.

"Benjamin lunged at me. Knox grabbed for him, but missed.

"His fist connected first with my nose, then my cheek, then my abdomen, still shrinking from Darian's birth. Then Knox pulled him off, and I was able to scramble away.

"Benjamin kept the bat from his last game propped against the wall in the foyer. It was for protection, he said, but I knew it was more to remind me of all the ways I'd ruined his life, taken his dreams from him. Football, baseball, he could have been on either—both—teams at the university.

"It was large in my hands. I gripped it tightly, whirled in a circle, and swung.

"I hit the side of Benjamin's head as he lunged toward me. Oh, it was a sickening crunch. He went down, blood leaking everywhere. Finality.

"Then Knox had me in his arms, cradling my broken face, crying 'I'm sorry, I'm sorry' over and over. The baby was screaming in fright. The dog was barking from his crate. Chaos.

"Until that moment, we could have tried another route. Until that moment, we had choices. When Benjamin hit the floor, we had nothing. I did the only thing I could. I concocted a lie.

"And lies hurt."

Columbia shifts in her chair, tears slipping down her face. She wipes her eyes and sips from a clear glass of water. When she looks at the camera again, the tears are gone, and she smiles.

"And then there were the babies. You beautiful, lovely girls.

"In the horror and the craziness, the lies and the cover-ups and the truth finally exposed—what truth we allowed them, that is—I was able to ignore all the signs. But when I fainted during my trial, and they asked me at the hospital if I could be pregnant, I couldn't say no. A test confirmed it. And the markers were off the charts. They were both thrilled and aghast when they told me I was pregnant with twins.

"So we had, at last, a small drop of goodness from a terrible situation.

"The problem was, I had no idea who you belonged to. Benjamin made use of my body regularly up to the end, even the day he died. And I gave myself freely to Knox in the days before that night, the night we killed Benjamin, before the bruises and the blood, a frantic, terrified coupling.

"Either of them.

"My lawyers argued my sentence should be deferred. I should be on house arrest until the babies were born. But this was a small county with, sadly, plenty of experience with maternal prisoners. Darian went into the system, and I—pregnant with her siblings—did, too."

She sighs heavily.

"Prison was difficult, but I deserved the punishment, so I bore it. What did or did not happen there is of no consequence. What's important is what happened after the babies were born, and after I got out.

"You three girls were the only thing that mattered to me anymore. I'd ruined my life, ruined Knox's life, and ruined yours, too. Benjamin's family didn't want anything to do with me, and that included their grandchildren. Horrible people, but who can blame them? I ruined their lives by taking away the one thing they truly loved.

"All of you were in foster care. I didn't have a choice, they wouldn't let you stay with me. It broke me to let you go. Three years is a very long time knowing pieces of your heart are living outside your body.

"When I was released, I went first to you, Darian, because my lawyer told me legally you still belonged to me. The family fostering you was worried about letting you go with me at first, because you'd adjusted well and were happy with them, but oh, how you cried when you saw me. They had been so diligent about bringing you to visit on holidays, showing you photos of me, telling you I'd come for you, that you knew me immediately. You threw yourself in my arms and screamed 'Mama, Mama,' and we both cried with joy. There was no question you were coming to live with me—I was staying with Jamie, and she had room for us both.

"The twins, though. You girls were another matter.

"I was supposed to be in jail for a decade, my darlings. And though you were born in blood, born from a terrible event, I loved you with all my heart. Giving you up was the hardest thing I've ever done. I asked that you be placed together, but that did not happen. You were split apart, adopted by families who loved you so very much. When I got out, I went to see you both. I stood on the street and watched you live your new lives. You were both so happy. So adjusted. You'd known no other parents, no other mothers than the ones who held your hands. You certainly didn't know the truth about where you came from. The adoption was closed because I thought that was best for you. All I could give you were your names. Riley and Kira.

"Will I regret leaving you with your new lives for the rest of my days? Yes. Always. But the future for me at that time was so uncertain. I had no job. No place of my own to live. No skills. Only a sword of Damocles hanging over my throat and a three-year-old who barely knew me.

"Jamie gave us succor, let us stay with her, nursed me back into the world. She was the one who suggested I try to write my way out of the depression I'd slid into. She remembered my little stories in school, silly things full of fairies and romance, and thought I could try telling them as an adult.

"Little did she know her attempts to pull me out of myself would become my forever path.

"Riley, I've left you that first story, if you want to include it. It was such a clumsy attempt to disguise what had happened to me, to you and Kira and Darian. Much of it is conflated with the truth. A truth you should find in the files I've left for you, as well. But I found such peace in the storytelling. I wrote another, and another. The words poured out of me, and I was shriven by their existence.

"Jamie was in law school then, and that's where she met and married a good, kind man who I hope you've had a chance to meet. Of course I'm speaking of Victor Guul. Hopefully he's here today.

"Without Vic, none of it would have been possible. He and Jamie encouraged me to attend a writers' conference in Nashville, and I met an editor who liked the idea of my little romances. Vic negotiated a deal, and because I couldn't write under my own name, we concocted a pseudonym: D.E. Shepherd. A name I dreamed of taking one day until I messed it all up so badly.

"The books did well. So incredibly well that I was able to start setting aside some money, and got us a little place. Darian, I don't know if you remember it, you were so young. Just a small cottage on the outskirts of town, but it was all ours.

"Then I had the idea for a new story. A bigger story. Something I knew was going to put me in the spotlight. I wanted to submit it fresh, clean, as a debut. I didn't want to be tied to the romances directly. We searched and searched until just the right combination of names appeared.

"Columbia Jones. The book was accepted, as you know. And did rather well.

"Vic and Jamie suggested I change my name legally, so I could step out of the shadows I was living in and take my place in the world. The specter of my life before was too much to surpass. I needed to become someone totally new. My face was different from all the reconstructive surgery, so it wouldn't be as easy to identify me. But I felt I needed a complete makeover, top to bottom, to exist as a totally new person in order to eradicate the past.

"While Vic handled the legal aspects, getting a judge to make an exception to the rules because of the danger I was in from Benjamin's family, Jamie and I handled the realities of how I would live day to day. I was always good with accents, but British was my best, so I became British. I grew up in a small council estate near Bromley. I was a widow—that much was true—who came to the States looking for a new life. I was a rags-to-riches story—so few can prove the rags, and who cares about that, really. All they want is the success.

"And I wanted you to have a chance at a normal life, Darian. So we found someone who could play that part when necessary. Vonda West was a client of Vic's firm; she'd been visiting the US and got sideways with immigration, overstaying her visa. Vic got her out of trouble, and the only payment needed was playing the role of grandmother. It was just the one time, and a few prearranged phone calls. She was paid handsomely, though I have left her a little bit more for the trouble she went to. I hope her life is good from here on out.

"Because money was the only thing I could give. No dollar amount would ever undo my actions, but I could smooth the paths. Riley, Faith was provided with all the funds for your schooling, and when poor Maisie was hurt in that accident and Faith made her decisions, I made sure she was taken care of properly. All the money you've put into her care has been saved and is being returned to you. Faith was under strict instructions to let you help. I hate that you had to grow up so fast, my darling, but you are a better person for the struggle.

"Kira, your parents received money for your schooling as well, and a little boost here and there to help get their business off the ground.

They're smart, they didn't need me, but it made me happy to see them succeed.

"But of course, all good things must come to an end.

"Someone found out and decided to blackmail me. I was honestly surprised it took as long as it did—in this internet age, nothing stays secret for long. I played along for a bit, but things have gotten untenable. He is threatening to expose me if I don't do it myself, and I can't risk that. I've become this woman. Devon Elder Mears no longer exists. I don't want the fans, the publishing house, to know I am a fraud. My pride's gotten in the way, my ego, I suppose. I am going to try and talk sense into him, but if that doesn't work, I thought it prudent to make this video and make sure you're all taken care of.

"Riley, your access to Mathers and Mathers made them an easy choice for a backup will, which supersedes any I've made with you, Vic. You have been my dearest friend for years, and holding this secret has cost you. I owe you so much more than I can possibly give. I hope you'll forgive me for exposing your role in the charade. When we lost Jamie, I didn't think you'd ever recover; I am so glad you've found love again. I dedicated *Ivory Lady* to her in your honor.

"And that brings me to you, Knox.

"The girls might understand my choices, and they might not. I hope they forgive me.

"But you. You captured my heart from the moment I met you. You saved me, even if it was only for a few months. You took the blame for Benjamin's murder. You suffered most of all, and there is nothing I can do to fix it. There is not enough money in the world that will give you back the life you lost. No apology big enough to fix my lies. I am a horrible person, letting you take the blame. I was young, I was scared, yes. But I shouldn't have let you be damaged in the wake.

"You will want for nothing going forward. Your family will be well taken care of. And this confession will be made public so your name will at last be cleared. In the process, I've come to realize the truth is the only path forward.

"I've left my journals with Mr. Mathers, and it is my greatest wish that Riley write my biography. I'd hoped it would be a memoir that we'd work on together, darling girl, and that Kira and Darian could be a part of it, but that sadly was not meant to be.

"Release the next part of the video to the press as soon as you see fit. I love you all, very much."

She shifts in her seat again, sitting up straighter, and looks dead into the camera.

"You know me as Columbia Jones, but my real name is Devon Elder Mears. I murdered my husband, Benjamin Mears, when I was nineteen years old. And I let Knox Shepherd take the blame. He is innocent, and always has been. It is my last wish that you give this man grace and let him be a father to his twin daughters now, the way he should have been all along.

"I should never have allowed him to go to jail for my sins. Let my final words clear his name.

"And let it vilify mine. The truth doesn't matter to the dead."

CHAPTER SIXTY-TWO
DARIAN

Eight Months After the End

The boat rocks in the water, the waves heavier than any of them were expecting.

Darian holds the urn, and as morbid as it seems, Mason takes a picture of her with Riley and Kira on either side, their hands touching the container that holds their mother's ashes.

None of them are smiling, but they are together, and this last step is vital to their healing.

Columbia's will specified her wish that her ashes be spread off the coast of Manhattan, and the girls have complied. They are currently three nautical miles offshore, and the echo of the skyline of Columbia's beloved adopted hometown is brought into bas-relief by the setting sun.

"Should we say something?" Riley asks.

"What is there to say except we forgive you, Mom?" Kira asks. Her stomach nearly touches the railing; her twin girls are due at any moment. Girls she's planning to name Columbia and Devon, after their grandmother.

"Do we?" Darian asks. "Do we really forgive her?"

Kira squeezes Darian's arm. "We do. Because she brought us together. In the end, she brought us together. And she cleared our father's name. She had a hand in all of our lives from the beginning, she took care of us, and she gave me you. So yes, I forgive her."

"I forgive her, too," Riley says. "She tried to protect us all by keeping the secret. If I'd known she was paying the bills of Faith and Maisie, that alone would let me forgive her. But she took care of you, too, Kira. She made sure your parents had enough money to start their advertising business. And she wrote all those books and had the royalties set aside for us. We're all set for life because of her. Yes, I forgive her."

Darian swallows hard. "I don't. I can't."

"You will eventually, honey," Kira says. "You'll see."

But Darian doesn't know if she ever will. The truth about her mother's life—the truth she shared in the video—is too much for her to take in. Columbia—Devon—murdered a man. She murdered Darian's father. He was hurting her: that she can understand, empathize with, maybe even applaud. But she murdered a man and let another take the fall for her. That is what Darian is struggling with. Knox Shepherd is a decent guy. An honorable man who got caught in a terrible situation and, instead of handing over the truth, went to prison for her. And all she did was leave him a few million dollars. For a man like Knox, that wasn't enough.

"It's time," Riley says, wrenching Darian from her thoughts. She opens the urn, and they take turns dipping in their hands and shaking the contents loose over the water. Darian is weeping; the twins are, too, all of them saying goodbye in their own strange way.

Tonight, they will stand in the bookstore while Riley reads from the biography she's written about Columbia Jones that releases tomorrow. Mary is publishing it, of course; they crashed it through the system to capitalize on the momentum of the media surrounding their story. The *Ivory Lady* movie benefited from the death of its author; likewise, this new story has already been optioned and is making waves. The girls are going to see their lives played out on the big screen, and Darian really doesn't know how that makes her feel.

But tonight, it is just for them. Riley will wear the green dress that Darian helped her pick out that shows off her eyes, and they will have another kind of goodbye, one that is private, not public for all the world to see. An intimate evening before the dogs are set loose. Columbia Jones has died, and in so doing, she has created an unbelievable scandal, and the world will viscerally celebrate it, and then mourn with them.

Darian has read the book. She helped write parts of it, places Riley couldn't find the words, or the context, or the story. Her life has changed so dramatically, and she revisits the months that have passed as the last vestiges of her mother's corporeal being disappear into the water. She has been careful to only use her right hand; her left glitters with a diamond, an oval set on a thin gold band encrusted with diamonds that sparkle like fairy dust. She doesn't want her future contaminated by her past.

Riley puts her arm around Darian's waist and smiles at her big sister. "You good?"

"Yes."

She is lying. She will never be good. She will try, but she doesn't know if she can ever be right with this situation. Especially since Detective Sutcliffe let her know that the DNA on the hair found at her mother's crime scene was not a biological match to Riley and Kira, nor to the open paternity case in Crossville. Liam Reeves lied when he said he was Knox Shepherd's son.

Sutcliffe assured her he was still looking, but even he has better things to do. Liam Reeves was a madman who murdered her mother after a monthslong campaign of terror, murdered Oliver Mathers and several of Nate Walsh's security team, and almost killed Sutcliffe himself. Since these cases are solved, what remains doesn't matter, not really. As her mother famously said, the truth doesn't matter to the dead.

But it is an open thread that makes her uncomfortable. She likes all the bows to be tied, all the loose strands to be resolved. It's the writer in her, the true gift her mother left her.

We can't always get what we want.

She looks to the women to whom she is now joined, and nods.

"Let's go home."

EPILOGUE

Mason is grateful Darian wanted a more casual wedding, because he sucks at bow ties, and if he were up here alone trying to get into a tux, he might just scream. She chose morning suits instead, which meant a nice gray tie, which he is happy to wear. The wedding is white, the bridesmaids—Kira and Riley—in the same shade as their big sister, their little sister, Tamsin, holding a basket of white rose petals. It is a nod to their mother's false-flag past in England: the morning suits, the all-white, everything done with a British style. Mason thinks this is deliciously devious of Darian and has applauded her all the way.

He can hear the girls getting ready next door, giggling and playing. They've found such joy in one another. Kira's family is here—all three boys and the newborn girls—and Riley's invited her adopted mother, whom she's speaking to again, after her sweet, innocent sister has finally been allowed to pass. Columbia's death brought these girls together, made them softer, gentler people. This is a good thing, he thinks. These women are good for each other.

Knox Shepherd is downstairs as well, and Mason hopes he has a chance to chat with him later. The twins' father is a decent man, and Mason has a vested interest in him. Shepherd is going to walk Darian down the aisle, and he thinks that is more fitting than they know. Her first choice, Victor Guul, sadly passed away last month. The cancer finally ate him up inside.

The detective is here, too. Darian insisted on inviting him. Sutcliffe is a good cop. But thankfully, he's not quite good enough.

Mason checks his email again, and vows to deal with the situation as soon as he gets back from Crete. Fucking Liam, and his fucking noisy brain, still creating havoc from the dead.

Yes, there is another email.

There's been one every day for the past year. The subject line, again and again and again, with that emphasis shifted—*Do* You *Remember?*

Liam must have written it before he went to the house in Maine, knowing there was a good chance his madness was making him reckless. One job, that's all he had. One job. That's it. And instead, he went around the bend and started killing people, stalking people, and very nearly exposed everything. And in the end, it was Mason who'd had to finish things. Liam was too sloppy, dosing the CBD, thinking a drop here or there was enough to kill her. The injection was the only way to make sure Columbia didn't wake up.

It's good that Liam's taken the fall. It wasn't as clean as Mason would have liked, but he's spent the last several months trimming the frayed edges. There's just this one left to deal with.

The email has been forwarded from a closed account that's on a repeater—a little trick Mason hasn't figured out yet. He will once he has the mental space to really dig into the issue.

> Surprise, dickhead! If you're reading this, then I'm either dead or in jail. I wanted you to think you were in the clear, that your little plan worked. But it didn't, did it? You're reading this, so you're screwed now, too.
>
> I did everything you wanted, and it wasn't enough, was it? It's never enough for you. From the day we met in the hospital, when you showed me kindness and made me loyal to you, to the day you asked me to make her life a living hell, to punish her for what she

did to you, what she took from you, what she did to your dad, I did everything your way. All willingly, but if you're reading this, you threw me under the bus.

The DNA doesn't lie, friend. One of these days, Riley and Kira will figure out they're related to you, and I hope they skewer you when they do. They'll realize why their mother really died, for you to take your petty revenge. Guul will no doubt figure it out, he's been searching our pasts hard. He'll out you to Darian, but in case he doesn't, I've documented everything, and you will never know when it might appear. You're going to be looking over your shoulder for the rest of your life. I will haunt you forever, you fuck.

Liam

Tamping down the spike of rage, of fury, Mason deletes the email, goes into the server and erases it there, too. He's done this every day, and soon he's going to have to figure out a better solution. It's not perfect, but it will have to do for now. That little bastard knew that once it got into the email ecosystem, it existed to be discovered under the proper circumstances. Forwarding it means it lives in his old system, too, which Mason will have to penetrate.

Haunting him forever, indeed.

But you're dead, you scum. And I enjoyed seeing the light die in your eyes.

He slips his phone into the breast pocket of his jacket and brushes his rusty hair back from his face. Composes himself with several deep breaths.

He won't let this rattle him. He has a big day ahead, and he is excellent at compartmentalization.

His bride awaits, and he is going to make her the happiest woman on the planet in about thirty minutes. He is going to stare longingly into her eyes, pledge to love, and honor, and cherish, in sickness and in health. He is going to slip the diamond-encrusted band on her finger to match the one he put there already and raise it to his lips in a silent pledge of his own.

That he is finally going to live the life he was meant to live, with the trappings of wealth he was meant to have. The life her mother stole from him when she accused his father of murdering her husband; the father he never got to meet, rotting in jail; the mother who died of a broken heart when the father of her child discarded her like a whore in favor of the young woman he fell in love with. None of that is going to matter anymore.

He is about to marry the beneficiary of one-fourth of Columbia Jones's vast estate, and her daughter didn't make him sign a prenuptial agreement. She trusts him implicitly. Why wouldn't she? He's given her everything. Protected her from harm, slain the dragons, ridden off with her into the sunset.

He is hers, and now, she will be his.

It's going to be an interesting honeymoon.

AUTHOR'S NOTE

I don't like killing people.

That's a terrible admission for a thriller author to make, but it's very accurate. The driving question of this story—Who killed Columbia Jones?—caused me many sleepless nights. I didn't want to kill Columbia. From her conception, I'd fallen in love with the very idea of her—as a character, as a woman, as a friend, as a mother, and, especially, as an artist.

Coming off *It's One of Us*, a story so deeply personal that I boomeranged the opposite direction for its follow-up, this squeamishness wasn't helpful to the writing process.

And two rather terrifying things happened while I was drafting this novel that both hindered its growth and helped it in many ways.

First, Sir Salman Rushdie was attacked—stabbed onstage at a literary festival—a voice violently, though not permanently, thank God, silenced. Our worst nightmare realized: something dreadful happening while we're on tour. It was a Twitter conversation with a friend about my past doing presidential advance work and the security risks of authors on tour that launched the idea for this book in the first place, many months before this awful incident. To have it play out when I was halfway through the writing felt prophetic, in not-good ways.

Second, Eliza Fletcher was kidnapped and murdered in Memphis, Tennessee. The hashtag frenzy that unfolded over the several days she was missing was exactly what I'd envisioned when I first conceived #Legacy. The rumors, the craziness, the false flags, the trolls; the groups popping up on FB and Twitter and Reddit, chock full of conspiracies; strangers from all over the world utterly convinced they knew exactly what was happening; bots who started pushing the women-shouldn't-run-in-the-dark narrative and the creeps who insisted they had insider details (and shared them); the race-baiters and the ghouls, making raw and reprehensible claims that would make anyone close to the case weep. The truth was abandoned in favor of these salacious details and only came out in teensy slices. Even when the facts were presented—incontrovertible facts from professional sources, facts that were, of course, far worse than the sordid imaginations of those glued to their computers—the debates raged on.

It was exactly what I'd planned in my synopsis.

But to have two major elements of my story so brutally realized gave me pause. Should I keep going? Is this too real, too on the nose? Do I want to tell this particular story, in this particular way, at this particular time?

These twin events gave me a terrible case of writer's block. I stumbled for a few months, unable to reconcile fiction with reality.

And then, I lost my cat.

One of my twin-sister kitties, Jameson, who battled valiantly for a year after a torsion last summer, was too sick to continue on. I won't pretend it didn't break me. It did. But when her ashes came home, something in me unfurled. I finally understood Darian's grief in a way I hadn't before. Riley's grief. Columbia's grief. And something clicked. Before I knew it, the book was finished.

I extend my deepest sympathies to the Fletcher family, who lost a daughter, a wife, and a mother, much too soon. And to Mr. Rushdie, who is inspiring to a fault. He was not conquered by the attack; on the contrary, it has made him stronger than ever. And I give forever gratitude to the little cat whose ashes are on my desk, still helping me get through each day, and her sister, Jordan, who misses her as much as we do.

J.T. Ellison

Nashville, 2023

ACKNOWLEDGMENTS

We writers are never alone on our journey to finishing a book, and I am no exception. To the following, I give my deepest, most heartfelt thanks:

Liz Pearsons, my editor extraordinaire, for helping me shape Columbia's origin story into something magnificent, and watering my very dry garden;

Gracie Doyle, for the lunch that changed my life;

Danielle Marshall, for that coffee all those years ago, and everything since. I'm sorry about that awful red sauce!;

The amazing editorial and production and art teams at Amazon Publishing, who have blown me away with their dedication to helping me look my best on the page;

Laura Blake Peterson, agent, friend, coconspirator, for too many reasons to count, but weeks of calls and love and support and ideas;

Holly Frederick, for planting the seeds of season two;

Barbara Peters and Miranda Indrigo, whose offhand comments about Agatha Christie's house and advance work for presidential travel respectively sparked the cornerstones of this story;

Barbara, again, for the friendship, the support, and the best book-store in the country;

Jayne Ann Krentz, partner in crime, who worked through the middle with me, and helped me see the path;

Sherrie Saint, for years of research assistance, but especially the skull key and the pot laced with brodifacoum;

Meg Gardiner, for advice on the lawyerly bits;

Laura Benedict, beloved sounding board and first reader, who encouraged me to take the knife out of Columbia's chest and be more subtle . . . boy did that work!;

Ariel Lawhon, for the trip of a lifetime that shifted it all, the friendship, the reality checks, the queso, and the Wordles;

More of my favorite people: Traci Keel, Lisa Patton, Patti Callahan Henry, Paige Crutcher, Helen Ellis, Abby Belbeck, and Marybeth Whalen, whose love, laughter, support, and feeding of mind, body, and spirit make me a better person and a better writer;

Cal Newport, who continues to inspire and educate me in the ways of focus, deep work, and the value of slow productivity;

Joan Huston, for catching all the commas;

Holly Pratt, for making the most spectacular Reels;

Paige Jenkins, who wrangles all the news so well;

David at the ticket desk of the Museum of Modern Art, for letting us in free at 4:45 p.m. to do one last running pass through Gallery 403 so I could capture Riley's sense of panic properly;

Olivia Barry, screenwriter and friend, for helping me with the New York walks;

My friends in the online world, from my Literati Facebook group to Instagram to BookTok to Substack, who keep me humble, engaged, and otherwise dedicated to not being a hermit;

The incredible librarians and booksellers who get these books into your hands and have faced too many challenges these past few years—we couldn't do it without you!;

My WNPT colleagues, who make me a better writer by allowing me to interview the most amazing authors in the world;

My fabulous family, including, of course, my mom and dad, who are such huge supporters of my work and such a source of joy, and my awesome brothers, who also put up with constant recitations of the day's word counts (a girl must present her finished homework at dinner), and my in-laws, who shake their heads with joyful bemusement for every imaginary person who dies on the page;

And for my darling Randy. This one was quite the journey. I don't know how I would ever write these books without you by my side, the shining example of all that is good in this world. You are in every hero, every good word, every deep emotion that pours onto these pages. And the way you held me up and patched me together when we lost the little gray cat will never be forgotten. Thank you for taking me to see Hemingway and changing everything. I love you forever, baby.

About the Author

Photo © 2023 Kidtee Hello Photography

J.T. Ellison is the *New York Times* and *USA Today* bestselling author of more than thirty novels and the Emmy Award–winning cohost of the literary TV show *A Word on Words*. She also writes urban fantasy under the pen name Joss Walker.

With millions of books in print, her work has won critical acclaim and prestigious awards. Her titles have been optioned for television and published in twenty-eight countries.

J.T. lives with her husband and twin kittens, one of whom is a ghost, in Nashville, where she is hard at work on her next novel.